"The 28 fantasy stories, vignettes, and poems in this enticingly varied first collection range in mood from the giddy to the somber, but all are distinguished by their author's skill at pursuing ideas to their logical extreme. 'Standard Comfort Measures in Earthling Pregnancies' is written as a 'what to expect when you're expecting' guide for human women and men who unexpectedly become hosts to alien embryos. 'Super-Baby-Moms Group Saves the Day!' is a succession of online chat group posts from mothers coping with children who have outrageous superhero powers. At the opposite extreme of these comic flings are 'Selling Home,' set in a Ballardian world of endlessly overarching bridges where the disenfranchised struggle to reach the upper decks of the wealthy, and 'Old Dead Futures,' whose damaged protagonist reveals that his ability to mentally alter reality is more a curse than a blessing. Connolly writes with a vividness that immerses the reader in her scenarios and makes their unpredictable endings all the more fulfilling."
—*Publishers Weekly*

"Frequently profound, sometimes bizarre, and at other moments, laugh-out-loud hilarious: this collection of Tina Connolly's eclectic stories packs the full range of the human experience into one book."
—Beth Cato, author of *The Clockwork Dagger*

"Tina Connolly's stories resonate at a human emotional core. Those in this collection, which span worlds of stratified future dystopia, bleak outer-planet illness, fantasy gods compelling humans, or contemporary backyard pool-party for a grandmother's birthday, often touch on family, whether at-hand or previously lost, and the characters' struggle for them. The science-fiction stories will engage fantasy fans, and the contemporary pieces will engage fans of other worlds, because they're all about people and what they care about. Connolly's writing is equally deft across varied narrative formats—flash, email epistolary, stage-play, poem—and voices—space-thief jargon, weird Western, contemporary teenage daughter of a witch, a programmed GPS—and always leaves an emotional impact, whether laughter or hard-won relief or a ray of hope for characters and family."
—*Beneath Ceaseless Skies*

"Connolly tells mesmerizing, emotional stories through a range of voices that is as varied as it is impressive. She is consistently engrossing across lengths, tones, and genres, and like a great character actor she makes this masterful variety seem effortless."
— Alex Shvartsman, author of
Explaining Cthulhu to Grandma

ON THE EYEBALL FLOOR

AND OTHER STORIES

ON THE EYEBALL FLOOR

AND OTHER STORIES

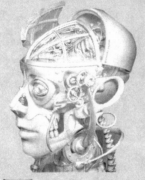

TINA CONNOLLY

FAIRWOOD PRESS
Bonney Lake, WA

ON THE EYEBALL FLOOR
A Fairwood Press Book
August 2016
Copyright © 2016 Tina Connolly

Fairwood Press
21528 104th Street Court East
Bonney Lake, WA 98391
www.fairwoodpress.com

Cover by Kazuhiko Nakamura
Book design by Patrick Swenson

ISBN: 978-1-933846-56-9
First Fairwood Press Edition: August 2016
Printed in the United States of America

For the Clarion West Workshop in general,
and the Class of 2006 in particular,
(students, teachers, administrators)
without whom these stories would not exist

CONTENTS

11   *Introduction* by Caroline M. Yoachim

On the Eyeball Floor: Stories of Climbing, Falling, and Spare Body Parts

17   On the Eyeball Floor

28   On Glicker Street: A Seasonal Quartet

39   Selling Home

54   Left Hand

57   Rehydration

Recalculating: Stories of Journeys, Dead-Ends, and the Friends Riding Shotgun

61   Recalculating

64   The Bitrunners

76   Standard Comfort Measures in Earthling Pregnancies

79   Super-Baby-Moms Group Saves the Day!

98   That Seriously Obnoxious Time I Was Stuck at Witch Rimelda's One Hundredth Birthday Party

See Dangerous Earth-Possibles: Stories of Families, Baseball Bats, and Zombie Chipmunks

115   See DANGEROUS EARTH-POSSIBLES!

118   Turning the Apples

130   Facts of Bone

145   Wendy with a Comet in the Tail of the Y

151   Miss Violet May from the Twelve Thousand Lakes

154   Old Dead Futures

A Million Little Paper Airplane Stories: Stories of Myths, Legends, and the Uncatchable

165   A Million Little Paper Airplane Stories

168   Ten

171   The God-Death of Halla

193   One Ear Back

207   Golden Apples

210   tiny atrocities

212   Moon at the Starry Diner

Hard Choices: Stories of Tough Choices, Tough Love, and Fairy Dust

225   Hard Choices

228   How Frederika Cassowary-Jones Joined the Ladies' Society of Benevolent Goings-On

246   Inflection

249   Silverfin Harbor

269   As We Report to Gabriel

285   *Afterword*

INTRODUCTION
BY CAROLINE M. YOACHIM

I met Tina at the Clarion West Writers Workshop in 2006, when both of us were students there. I was new to writing at the time, but Tina had already put in years of work to develop her own unique voice. The stories she wrote at the workshop were vivid and imaginative, lyrical and compelling. Five of the stories in this collection had their beginnings at the workshop, and I remember them clearly even ten years later—that's how good they are.

Tina lives in Portland and I live in Seattle, so we've had some chances to get together after the workshop ended. It was at one of these early get-togethers that we decided to collaborate. We'd never had much luck with the sort of collaboration where each person writes a scene or two before passing the draft back, so we decided to try something a little different. We each wrote an outline, and then traded—she wrote my outline and I wrote hers. Then we traded again for revisions, back and forth until both of us were happy with the stories. The process was slow, but ultimately good: "Flash Bang Remember" appeared in *Lightspeed* in 2012, and "We Will Wake Among the Gods, Among the Stars" came out in the January 2016 issue of *Analog*. For fun, and because we both love flash, we also wrote a flash piece together: "Coin Flips" came out in *Daily Science Fiction* in March 2015.

Now, ten years after Clarion West, we both have short story collections coming out, and after all the collaborations we've done and the friendship we've formed, it seemed only fitting that we trade introductions. I've always been drawn to shiny ideas, and Tina's collection is like a treasure chest filled with gems, with story-jewels in every imaginable hue, and all of them polished and sparkling. Tina writes an incredible variety of things. Her novels, of course, aren't included here (if you haven't already read them, you should! I recommend starting with *Ironskin*), but on these pages you'll find poetry and plays, humor and heartbreak, breathtaking secondary worlds and innovative flash.

Tina comes from a background in theater, which shines through in her amazing characters and authentic dialog. I love the relationships she creates between her characters (like the sisters in "Facts of Bone"), and the fascinating jobs she gives them (like coaxing cyborgs into consciousness, in "On the Eyeball Floor"). Tina then takes her wonderfully compelling characters and puts them into difficult situations. She forces them to make the hard choices. In "Selling Home" the protagonist must decide what they would do to take care of a sibling. "Old Dead Futures" is about what we might sacrifice if we knew the future. "Hard Choices" gives a more humorous take on difficult decisions, but as with many of Tina's stories, this CYOA is a mix of dark and light.

Some writers focus on a single type of story, but one of the things I love about Tina's stories is her amazing range. She can write a hilarious story as a series of emails ("Super-Baby-Moms Group Saves the Day!"), a bittersweet and nostalgic story divided into four seasons ("On Glicker Street"), and a dark and gritty science fiction story ("Turning the Apples")—and despite how different the stories are, she pulls them all off beautifully.

One of the reasons Tina can pull off such a wide range is that she creates the perfect voice for each story, be it snarky young adult (see "That Seriously Obnoxious Time I Was Stuck at Witch Rimelda's One Hundredth Birthday Party," a short story set in the world of Tina's *Seriously Wicked* novels) or gritty with futuristic slang (see "Bit-runners" and "Turning the Apples"). Tina's exceptional ear for words may come from her background in theater, or her poetry background, or perhaps her experience as a narrator for multiple podcasts. (If you want to hear one of Tina's fantastic narrations, you can find her on *Beneath Ceaseless Skies*, and at *Podcastle*, and of course on her very own dark, twisted, crispy-gooey flash fiction podcast *Toasted Cake*.)

Tina and I are both quite fond of flash fiction, which is an idea distilled to its essence, and many of my favorite flash pieces are included here. I have already mentioned "Hard Choices," which condenses the CYOA format usually found in novels into a mere 750 words. The aptly titled "Left Hand" is told from the point of view of someone's left hand, and "Ten" is told from an even more unusual perspective. "Recalculating" captures the frustration so many of us have felt when dealing with our GPS.

There is a playful blurring of forms in so many of Tina's stories—flash told as GPS directions or CYOA, stories in the format of plays ("How Frederika Cassowary-Jones Joined the Ladies' Society of Benevolent Goings-On") or instructions for pregnant women ("Standard Comfort Measures in Earthling Pregnancies").

Tina's stories sometimes verge on being poetry, the language is so gorgeous. "Moon at the Starry Diner" opens with "Air like a mushroom. Dense. Pocketed with holes, moments where Jem could breathe normally. She filled her lungs, drinking in the new atmosphere, dazzled by the blue-black sky. Starlight like diamonds, winking around her feet." I love the poetry of Tina's stories, and I love the stories that are woven into her poems. My favorite poem of Tina's is "A Million Little Paper Airplane Stories," which so perfectly captures the elusiveness of the tales we try to tell.

Elusive though the stories may be, Tina hunts them down expertly. She comes up with fascinating starting premises. Can you think of a good deed that has never been done? ("One Ear Back"). What if you had the power to change the future? ("Old Dead Futures"). What is the nature of fairies? ("As We Report to Gabriel," and if you love this story, definitely check out her *Ironskin* novels). Tina's stories are dense and richly imagined, the sorts of stories you can re-read again and again, finding something new each time.

There are seeds of truth in Tina's stories, no matter how fantastic the setting or the premise. Her worlds are imaginative and strange, but we as readers are grounded by the fundamentally human issues her characters face—lost love, the bonds of family, and the consequences of the choices that we make.

On the Eyeball Floor:

Stories of Climbing, Falling, and Spare Body Parts

On the Eyeball Floor

We've got robotic arms to put the eyeballs in. Metal clamps to pull down the eyelids. Tony, on Four, keeps the grease vats filled. Oil squirts nineteen times a minute to keep the eye sockets from squeaking. Tiny slick needles stitch on the lashes, millions of different irises get stamped in magenta and yellow and cyan, so no two will ever be alike, just like us.

All that, and they can't engineer anything—or anyone—to take over my job. People in Organs go home coated with grease and vinegar; people in Bones have lost fingers to the machines. Still nobody wants the job where a hundred half-live cyborgs line up in rows, twitching when your back is turned. Waiting for *someone* to talk to them, feel for them. Transcend them to life.

There are safety signs around the factory. "Scrub Up." "Know Thyself." "Don't Blink." That last is the best piece of advice, here on the eyeball floor.

Sometimes you blink and the world changes.

Sometimes you just go blind.

Clementine was a crèche type, made to comfort human babies. Hold them in maternity wards, or when the human parents are working. A parallel to my job, a cyborg coaxing humans into awareness. Usually crèche types transcend the fastest; they're stuffed with warmth signals and motherly hormones. They respond to my need for them to transcend and they oblige.

But she wouldn't.

One evening, after I'd escorted all the newly-transcended cyborgs down to Shipping, I came back to my room on the eyeball floor.

The room always feels chilly after the most lively ones have left. The remaining cyborgs fall in that uncanny gap; neither dead nor alive. Little parts of them were waking up—there, one side of his mouth crinkled with a human smile. That girl swallowed, and that man scratched himself when my back was turned. I felt it.

That's why nobody wants my job. This asteroid miner, down on the end—his neck and mouth were alive with intent, but nothing else was. The heartbeat pulsed in his neck, speeding up as I inspected him. I stared at his jaw and he chewed on his lower lip. I bet myself a packet of tea he'd be a resentful imprint, hating me, his "parent."

But though his mouth was awake, his eyes were dead.

I went over to the young woman. Clementine, I'd named her. Her real name was Agrippina Adamantina Crèche—it was inscribed on the back of her neck. Julie on One comes up with all the names and tattoos them on, just below the serial number. She ran out of good names like Clementine ages ago. Clementine is a good name for a crèche cyborg, because they all have wide sturdy feet.

I walked Clementine to a corner and I talked to her alone. I talked about rabbits, about the price of tea in China. About Sue, my girl in Feet who had curly brown hair that tumbled across her nose, who liked powdered milk in her tea. I watched the printed blue irises, the vat-grown ears. The swing of silky blonde hair. None of it registered.

"I hate failures," I told her. "Not you. I hate when *I* fail. So you'd better hurry up and transcend. I don't want your brain to be stripped and started over. If you've got anything going on upstairs it'll wink out of existence."

Behind me, that miner cyborg stepped all the way out of line.

"You don't want that either, huh?" I said. "What's your name?"

He looked down at me. Hatred. "Don't know."

I walked around him and looked at the back of his neck. "Maurizio Jung-Na Jung Miner. A mouthful. Call yourself Maury."

"If I want."

"Recalcitrant cyborg. Look, I just made the Shipping run. See that crèche model with the blonde hair? Why don't you see if you can talk her into existence before morning?" The girl's painted blue eyes stared through us. "She's hiding in there."

But when morning came, Maury was carving a swear word into my desk, and Clementine was as still as the grave.

If there was life there, I was blind to it.

I should've given Clementine up to Recycling, but I didn't. She became my pet project, and on my breaks I walked her around the factory. I showed her where her hands had been attached and how her blonde hair had been woven to her scalp.

I took her to see Sue and we stood and watched her hair tumble as she cleaned a pile of feet.

"Darlin' Clementine, this is Slue-Foot Sue," I said.

Sue laughed. "You're so funny. Where do you get those crazy names." She flicked a bit of skin away with the sander.

"Slue-Foot Sue was Pecos Bill's girl," I said. "She wore a bustle and it bounced her over the moon."

She laughed again. "I never did see the likes of you," she said. "Must be why you can work with the cyborgs when they get all creepy."

"Just a knack, I guess," I said. "Well, Clementine and I are gonna go down to Four now and see the grease. Maybe I'll see you later, make you a tea with a spoonful of milk, just how you like it."

Slue-Foot looked down at the foot she held, her curls obscuring her face. "Tell Tony I says hello," she said.

I turned Clementine to the stairs and her arm shuddered beneath me, something warm and human. Her face was dead, but you don't work on the eyeball floor long without learning to trust intuition.

"That's a darlin'," I said. "That's what I want to see."

We emerged on Four, where Tony was tinkering with a fitting. "Tony keeps the wheels greased," I said. "He tops off the grease vats and he makes sure the gears on Four run smoothly."

"Heya," said Tony. "Whatcha doing with the cyborg?"

"She won't transcend," I said. "It's been three weeks."

"Oh yeah? Her neck joints all right?" He wiped his hands on his pants and moved aside her silky blonde hair to rotate her neck. "Sometimes the wires and organics get pinched."

"Tony used to work in Necks," I told her. "Can you tell Tony that Slue-Foot Sue said 'hi?' She was a nice girl, wasn't she?"

"Don't talk to them in front of me," Tony said. "Creeps me out."

"You're touching her and she's not creepy."

"It's not a 'her' yet," said Tony. "Lifeless as a wrench." He let her hair fall back. "By the way, Randy's going to be gone Monday. Someone has to fill in on Seven."

I groaned. "Contest?"

"Unless you want to cede now."

"Not a chance. C'mon, Clementine." I nodded at Tony. "Tomorrow morning?"

"Yeah." He stared at Clementine's lifeless face. "You really took her to see Sue?"

"Sure thing," I said. "After all, she's my girl."

At ten on Friday I met Tony for the contest. When you've been here as long as us, you know all the jobs by heart, even the ones you'd rather fight over than do. Lots of people want to fill in for management, but they make me or Tony do it because we won't get any ideas. We don't want ideas. Tony likes Grease and I'm needed where I am.

There were lots of people in the exercise room to watch. Everyone on break, standing with their thermoses of coffee or squeezes of soup. Sue stirred powdered milk into her tea, brown eyes lively with excitement.

Tony and I contest by birling—there's a long metal cylinder in the middle of the exercise room, rigged up three feet off the ground on a spindle. We each stand at an end and walk or run, forwards or backwards, trying to drop the other one off as the cylinder spins. It mimics the old days when the factory was a real wild place; corrupt management and no safety regs. Guys used to balance on the rolling metal chute over the powered-down Recycler late at night, betting on who would face plant in the vat.

"Two out of three?" said Tony.

"One out of one," I said. We kept our balance with long pointed poles, steadied our feet on the roughened metal. "Three . . . two . . .

go," said our ref, and we dropped the poles, walking forward on the metal cylinder.

Good birling's about clever balance and sharp focus. Watch your opponent's feet and don't blink. We weren't even in skill but we fought anyway, 'cause I couldn't let Tony win without a fight. Some people bet on me, 'cause they liked the odds.

Tony's feet trotted forward. Mine kept pace. I slowed us. He sped us up.

Sue watched us, holding her tea. A curl tumbled into her face. I missed the change in tempo as Tony reversed, spinning the cylinder backwards, feet pattering and whirling the metal.

I took a header into the mat and it was over like that. Everyone groaned.

Tony jumped down, beamed at Sue and she ran to him. "You were a god, Tony." To me, with pity: "Nice try." Tony squeezed her closer.

Only then did I realize that this time the contest wasn't really about management. It was about Slue-Foot Sue, and worse, I saw then that her heart belonged to Tony. I'd worked in Hearts before I was promoted to the eyeball floor, so I thought I knew a lot about them, but obviously I didn't. Sue didn't care that I was the only one to watch how her curls tumbled. The one that knew and adored every gesture she made. I levered to my knees with the aid of the pointed pole.

She wasn't my girl at all.

I lunged at Tony. He sidestepped and the sharpened pole kept going, swept on hard, took a long red gash out of the person coming up to give me the rundown on the Monday replacement shift.

Randy. It was Randy and he jumped backwards, clutching his arm, bawling. "Goddamn, Bill! You're out on your ass for that. You know the goddamn rules. Tony, you cover Bill's shifts."

My blood pumped high at the sudden collapse of everything. "Don't blink," I said to Tony.

"Why not?"

"Someone might take your girl."

*

When I went back to my room on the eyeball floor, my hands were shaking.

Clementine stood apart from the others, by the window, sun glinting in her curly brown hair. I hadn't realized that she had hair like Slue-Foot and it made me slant away, crossing my arms.

I told her of the contest. There was something about the way that Tony looked at me before we started. I should've known then, I said. I should've known Slue-Foot had changed her mind, that she was Tony's girl now. Sure, we'd shared a laugh or two in the elevator, but so what? Tony had a good job in Grease and I was here. I should've known that it meant nothing to Sue that I knew every micro movement of hers; the way she ate, laughed, swung her hair.

Clementine moved as I spoke, but that didn't mean life. Even machines grow restless. She sat at the window, face lifted to the sun.

"And now this is it," I said. "I'm done. Kaput. I have to pack my bags. And you know the worst part?" The sunlight picked a stripe of white across her snub nose and cheekbone. "Sue doesn't even care."

Clementine, the failure I would leave behind, rankled. I grabbed her chin and turned it towards me. The brown printed irises were stony—cold with anger? I turned her cheek again. No, just cold. She would be scrapped.

Then. Brown?

I looked again. Her eyes were brown, the same color of Slue-Foot Sue's, those eyes I knew like my own.

"I'm going crazy," I said. A dark statement as I backed away. Maybe if I turned now, the whole room of cyborgs would look like Sue to me. Or just the girls, rows of brown curls—the boys all looking like Tony, hulking and red-cheeked.

Don't blink on the eyeball floor, they say. That's the reason no one wants my job. No one wants to work the transcending. 'Cause they say, out there in the factory, that every time someone blinks, they lose a little bit of themselves and a cyborg gains a bit.

I turned. But the room was as it was, a roomful of the halfway-transcendent, rows of uncanny cyborgs that no one else could handle.

"Don't blink," the sign said. I tore it down.

*

I cleared out all the cyborgs that were close, accelerated them and marched them down to Shipping. I stayed into the late shift, while everyone left except the mechanics who fidget with gaskets in the moonlight. The room got colder and colder. No one said anything to me; no one made me go home.

This one with the Slue-Foot hair and the Slue-Foot eyes who wouldn't transcend, she stood stone-cold all day long as cyborgs blinked and laughed around her.

Someone was mocking me with her.

I marched up and shoved her head to the side and rummaged through her scalp, looking at her roots. Now that I looked for it, I could see where her first hair was ineptly sheared away. It looked like someone cut off her straight blonde hair and stuck her head back in the growing vat to get it rewoven. But it was poorly done; it was uneven, and hair roots sprang from the top of her left ear.

Her eyes, now brown, I am sure they were blue. The signs were plain—great gouges around her eyelids where someone scraped the old blue eyes out. What a waste, just to drive me crazy. I'm already half-crazy from the eyeball floor. And who did it, Tony?

This Slue-Foot doppelganger was my failure and I would get rid of her before I went. Either she would be recycled, or the threat would shake her. Fear makes transcending happen in the biggest leaps, though it was a disgusting tactic.

I dragged Clementine to the basement, to Recycling. Pointed out the iron shears, the pipe wrenches, the acid. The Recycler vat where I would dump her for someone else to deal with. In her case, it wouldn't just wipe her brain. It would detect her scarred face and remove her whole head, starting over.

"It's your last chance to tell me if you're in there," I said. Her arm shuddered in my hands. She had to be close, so close. I hung her over the rollers that led to the Recycler vat, pushing her face towards them, hating it. "Tony'll do this to you if I don't. Tell me."

"Put her down." It was Tony, holding a massive pipe wrench.

"She won't transcend. You want to deal with her?"

"My god, you're crazy. Put Sue down."

I looked at the figure in my arms, but it was still lifeless Clementine, in Slue-Foot's hair and eyes. "You did this," I said to Tony. "What was your plan, try to make me lose it?"

"Put down the girl."

"Tony," I said. "You won." I pulled Clementine back from the vat and shoved her at him. She fell stiffly into his shoulder, his arms springing up to catch her. The pipe wrench clanked on the cement floor. "Take your cyborg and do what you want with her."

Tony stared at Clementine's printed eyes. "I'm sorry, man," he said. "The hair, the body—I thought—I don't know what I thought." He stood Clementine upright. A brown curl tumbled across her face just like Slue-Foot Sue's did.

"You're a jerk," I said.

"Yeah. I'm sorry this whole thing got you fired. Look, I told Randy I provoked you. He's calmed down. I think he'll change his mind."

Relief lit me. Things would be fixed. "You just don't want to work my job," I said.

"Bingo," Tony said. "I like grease. So what's up with this cyborg, anyway? Just coincidence it looks like Sue?"

"You mean you didn't do it?" I said.

"You crazy? That's psycho." He peered closer. "Its eyes are all messed up. They aren't going to want defects like that in the shipment. Scrap it entirely, now before it transcends." He pulled Clementine's arm towards the vat and as he did I saw something play across her face.

Fear.

There was fear in there, and she let me see it.

"Stop, Tony," I said. "She's awake."

"Wouldn't you know it." He let go of her arm, retrieved his pipe wrench. "Well, she'll have to be repaired."

Clementine stood there, looking at me. That intuition that transcends reason said she'd been awake a long time.

"Say something," I said.

Her voice was soft and resonant, slow in its tumble from her lips. "Your hair," she said. "When you turn your head, that curl falls over your brow. It brushes your forehead."

Tony shuddered. "This is why no one wants your job. Psycho lovelorn cyborgs."

She'd been awake a long time and I'd been blind to it. I moved closer, and she breathed into me, a soft metal scent. I touched a brown curl. "You did this," I said. "You sheared your hair and stuck your head in the machine." I touched the tip of her ear where the curls sprang out. "You were a little off."

"I tried three times to get the programming right," she said. "First it made me a redhead. Then I got male pattern baldness."

"Then you ripped out your eyes." I touched the hollows under them. "For me."

"I dropped one," she said. "I crawled after it in the dark."

I touched her jaw and she tilted her face with its snub nose. How could she have hidden so well? I closed my eyes, drawing her in.

Then I was holding only air.

"You're in too weird with this," Tony said. He pushed Clementine back towards the rollers. Her brown eyes were pleading. "It's defective, man. Psychosis. I'll take care of it for you." He shoved Clementine down. Under his breath: "Teach you to imitate my girl."

It was technically the right course of action per the company handbook, but it wasn't *right*. From the closest hook I grabbed iron shears, raised them like a club. "You drop her, I kill you."

He didn't budge. "I'm doing you a favor, man."

"Is it a crime to have a crush? The transcending wake up with weird emotions. Some of them love me. Some of them hate me. They think I'm their fathers or psychiatrists or children. You wouldn't know what it's like in there."

"Oh yeah?" Tony sneered. "I know you're a creepy stalker who can't get his own girl. Sure, you want a cyborg? That all you can get? Fine, but you can't have one that you've made over into Sue."

"I didn't do that," I said. "You heard her."

"One of you's psychotic," he said. "Between the two of you, there's only enough sane for one person. Is that you or the cyborg?" He inched her out above the rollers. One of her eyes leaked around the gouge.

"Fine, I did it," I said. "Give her back."

"Sorry, Bill," he said. "This is for your own good. It'll fix you."

He dumped Clementine overboard as I lunged.

I grabbed at her shirt, but she fell right through. She tumbled onto the metal rollers, hands grasping for purchase, soft limbs flailing. The rollers dropped her off, down into the Recycling vat with a crunch.

I turned, swinging the shears at his head. They caught Tony's cheek as he danced backwards; opened up a shallow curve. Red dripped onto his shirt.

"Aha! Contest for real, is it?" Tony raised the pipe wrench. "This time I won't stop at watching you face plant."

"This time there's no manager to protect you." I lunged again. He blocked my shears with his pipe wrench; the clang echoed up my arms.

"This is for Sue," he said, and his wrench slammed into my side, knocking me to my knees. "And this," and his wrench slammed against my hand, knocking the shears from my grip, shooting spasms up from my fingers.

I thought if I could get to the controls, I could shut off the Recycler before it discovered her defective head. But Tony lunged for me again, and I had to scramble.

We circled around the floor. Clementine's voice called up to me, crying. The machinery whirred in on her.

One last lunge for the controls, but Tony cut me off. A snick from the vat, and then the crying stopped and there was silence.

I grabbed the shears with my left hand and swung at Tony. He backed away, laughing, parrying with the wrench. But the blades opened, and a wild arc sliced the skin of his knuckles, knocking the wrench from his grasp. He swore, backed towards the vat, and then there was nowhere to go. I swung, the shears open wide.

Tony jumped out onto the metal rollers. For an instant he ran them, as fine and easy as any of our birling contests. For an instant he hung suspended over the Recycler. For an instant he looked at me with triumph-bright eyes.

Then his foot slicked backwards on metal and he tumbled forward into the vat. He scrambled up. "Bill! Get me out!"

I watched the machine surround him. His hand was dripping where I had sliced his knuckles.

"You can have Sue! Let me out!"

But I didn't want Sue anymore. I wanted Clementine, whose headless body was lying in the sorting bin, whose head had been absorbed and reduced to elements.

The machine sized up his hand as defective, and with a slice and pop, took it off, cauterizing its end. Tony screamed. The machine closed around him, its metal reaching for his face, his face with the slice sheared out.

In that moment I looked inside myself and I saw that I held Tony's fate in my hands. That I loved that knowledge. That I could kill him. I stared into his eyes and he knew I knew it.

Only then did I get up, scramble to the machine, power it down with shaking hands.

Only then.

I still work on the eyeball floor. There was an inquiry, but Tony remained silent. The company paid for a new hand for Tony and safety measures for the Recycler, but Tony took all the money instead, screwing a metal hook to his wrist so he could keep the grease vats filled. He built a house for Sue and she left Feet and had babies and went gray in a year.

Every time I see Tony's hook I close my eyes.

I still work on the eyeball floor, transcending the cyborgs. But I've lost my edge. I'm frightened like I never was before. Frightened of the cyborgs that stand behind me, hiding behind their printed eyes.

Every crèche model that comes through, I wonder if its body once belonged to Clementine. But if she's come through, I can't see her. I am blind to the cyborgs and the passions they imitate, to the way they steal from humanity with every blink.

There are signs on the eyeball floor. I drink my tea with powdered milk and watch them from behind my eyes. Some days the signs keep me sane.

Know thyself, they say, and I do, oh I do.

Don't blink.

On Glicker Street: A Seasonal Quartet

Spring Chill

On Glicker Street it was always fall.

Martine walked there. Martine who looked like spring; Martine who was tall and pale and dotted her lemon hair with the snow-drops that grew only on her street, up in the most expensive part of spring.

Martine was certainly an outcast, said to have strange ideas. She was a radical, although I didn't know it then. Once at a dinner party she told me that she went down to autumn just to scuff the hateful society smell from her shoes. Glicker Street was thick with fallen yellow leaves. Martine crunched through them till leaf dust covered the new leather, flecked the hair of her long pale calves. I smiled at the man across from me and pretended not to hear her talk of coarse-nesses like hair and *calves*.

Martine is a spring child; lives one street higher than me. But she walks in fall.

Once, I felt sorry for Martine. Once, I was working on my fi-nances at my desk when she went by. A strange pale girl arrayed in leather and leaf, distancing herself from her own class. I felt pity. I sent Joaquim down to her with a tulip—not the *earliest*, but still a lovely thing, a shimmer of pinks from my own windowbox.

We live on the best street there is. Well, technically there are a couple better. The Queen's street is higher than us. The very best people, the very oldest families, live up where it's so early spring that only the crocus are blooming—everything else is a bare green rocket above the hard boxes of soil.

And there are people who take that one step further and live even higher than the Queen, where no flowers bloom at all; but they're poet fanciers and art patronnes, too *haute* to live where things blossom. I say the streets don't start to get beautiful till late April, and that's where we are, the foremost street of the pretty streets.

Lower in June can be lovely, with all the roses. By August, everyone's frowsy, flushed, *vulgaire*. September's been reclaimed by artists; they drove the poorest down into the rest of the winter.

But no one likes November except Martine. Too late for anything. November reeks of the first stages of giving up.

I watched Joaquim hand the pink tulip to Martine, his back stiff. Despite his liberal talk of equality, he was clearly uncomfortable around the reality of people who were different. They looked up at me, sitting in the window, and I smiled kindly at them.

I knew my husband wasn't entirely happy in our arranged marriage. But I thought he would grow to love me as I loved him. Joaquim liked writing and philosophy; I let him skulk around pastry shops and play poet and thinker with the other young men. He repeated snatches of their radicalism to me, and I solemnly corrected flaws in his arguments, never laughing or condescending.

I suppose I was too permissive.

I sent him down to Martine with a tulip, and he came back with her at his side.

She seemed even wilder in person, that fine blonde hair unruly, bits of leaf shedding to the rug. I had been meaning to have that rug sent out to be cleaned.

Then I noticed they were holding hands.

"We met in my discussion group," Joaquim said awkwardly. "Please, we—" He looked at Martine and I could hardly watch, it was so personal, so *gauche*. "We love each other."

"We're moving down to Glicker Street," she said. Her eyes were cool and insolent.

"But he's mine," I said. "I won't give him up."

"Likewise," said Martine. She twirled the pink tulip between her fingers.

"Please, Saphi," said Joaquim. "If you won't grant me a divorce, at least grant me a little happiness. The beginnings of the weeks. I'll return to you every Friday for all the weekend events. No one from here goes any lower than June. No one will ever know."

What could I do? I couldn't chain him to my leg. He was a human, not a pet. I guess, despite myself, some of Joaquim's radicalism had rubbed off after all.

"Thursday," I said. "You must come back on Thursdays."

He looked at Martine. She nodded at him.

So now he spends four days with me in spring and three with her in fall. I dismissed all my servants so no one would know my shame. No one can know how I count every hour of each day he's gone. Every minute.

When he returns, he is white and pale. He is dear; he pretends cheer for my sake, and I set him on the balcony and surround him with tulips and early spring sun. He accompanies me as always to the spring concerts, dances, lectures. He tries to hide it, but by the end of Sunday night he is glowing pink; there is lightness in his step.

I wish it were due to me.

Then he is gone again, and without him spring is relentless; cold and cruelly reviving, and I have to flee downward to escape it. June is too lovely, August too cheerfully depraved; nothing suits my mood.

Cold Glicker Street, with its blowing gusts of yellow leaves, is an impossibility.

But if I keep going down, down into the dark mist and shadows of late December, there the streets turn thick and white with ice. There the beggars crowd into hutches of cardboard and tar paper. They stare at me with hollow eyes, but despite my fine thin clothes, they never come forward to ask for money.

That is where I walk, now.

GRADUATING SUMMER

On Glicker Street it was always Fall.

That was where the school was, Glicker Street, in the southeast quadrant of the biodome.

Tom and Naomi and Peter were in Summer—Summer vacation in the southwest quadrant and Tom, at least, didn't miss Glicker Street one bit.

"No matter how hard you kick the ball," said Tom, "it always plows through a pile of dead wet leaves and ruins your score." He was sitting in his usual position next to Naomi, arm around her waist. "Also if I never see a rake again it'll be too soon."

Naomi blew a bubble. "I dunno," she said. "I guess I miss the girls. I don't see why we can't all have the same week for vacation."

"Wouldn't be enough teachers for each of us if we didn't rotate," said Tom. "You gotta think like a principal." He stretched out his long legs. "Man, feel that sun. You feel that, Peter? Do ya?"

Peter looked up at the fuzzed glass ceiling overhead. "It's just electricity, you know. They taught us that last year."

Tom leaned back on his arms. "Aw, live a little. It's supposed to be sun. That's good enough for me."

"Things are always good enough for you," said Peter, a little bitterly. He looked at long-legged Tom, and the pink-cheeked girl snuggled in the crook of his arm. "Do you ever think about what comes after? Either of you?"

"Sure. We go to work. Naomi and I applied to go to Winter. I hear it's great. All this white stuff coming down from the sky, and you can do awesome sports where you fly along like roller skating but even faster. Aren't you excited, Naomi?"

"Sure."

"Where'd you put in for, Pete?"

"Winter," Peter said. "I dunno. We've just never seen anyone from Winter. How do we really know what it's like?" He pulled off his horn-rimmed glasses and wiped them with a wrinkled shirt tail. It didn't seem to help his blurring vision. "Or what happens to you once you're sent there."

"You worry too much," said Tom. "When we go back to Fall next week, and that back-to-school scent fills the air—"

"That's just it," said Peter. He pulled three letters from his back pocket. "I found these on our breakfast table. We're not going back to Glicker Street."

Naomi sat straight up. "You mean, we're graduating? Where are we going?"

"You and I are going to Winter," Peter said. He looked down at the blurry page as if to read the topmost letter again. "Tom is going Out."

Tom seized the sheaf of letters from Peter's hand. His face was ashen.

"What do you mean, Out?" said Naomi.

"Apparently Tom has those things called *parents*," said Peter. "They've called him home and he's going Out. Out of the biodome. Out into the world that used to have seasons." Naomi's brown eyes were huge. "And he's not going alone, either."

Tom turned to Naomi. His long fingers rattled the page. "You have to believe me. I put in to go to Winter. I wanted us to go to Winter, not this *Out* thing."

"What does he mean, Tom? What does he mean by you're not going alone?"

"I can take one person," Tom said. "A . . . 'breeding female', it says."

"That's romantic," murmured Peter.

"We can still be together," said Tom. His face lighted as he turned to the girl at his side. "Why, it's not what we planned, but it could still be exciting. Think of it! The unknown. The outside. We'll be the first of our class—maybe the only ones—to go Out. It'll be a great adventure."

Naomi stood, edging backwards from Tom's waving arms. "I . . . I don't think so," she said.

"Naomi . . . ." said Tom.

She crossed her arms. "I don't want to go Out. I want to go to Winter like we planned."

"But I can't go."

"I know. I'm sorry." She took a step closer to Peter, and Peter put his arm around her to comfort her, almost without thinking. "I'm going to Winter, Tom."

Tom looked at the girl nestling into Peter's comforting arm. He squared his shoulders. "Well," he said. His Adam's apple bobbed as he swallowed. "I guess I'll be having an adventure on my own, then."

A Certain Fall

On Glicker's street it was always fall.

A certain fall, a certain September. The year I was eighteen and she was fifteen.

I don't know what the significance of that month was for old Glicker. His second wife had died a few years back and you'd think he'd want to relive their time together. Go bask in warm lazy summers, iced brandies and little clothing. But he had a summer cabin up in the mountains; maybe he went there and found a bit of the past he liked better.

He let his house sit in September and he was never there.

The funny thing is, I went there the first time for my wife. I was on spring break from teaching chemistry, and Linda sent me over with some papers he was supposed to sign for her bank. Service is still like that around here; personal and lackadaisical, a friend of a friend who just happens to be headed out down that gravel road, willing to venture that strand of time.

I turned off the gravel and took the truck down the long winding dirt road to Glicker's place. Didn't get past the second bend before I knew where—when—I was.

Some memories just resonate like that. Ever after they happen, you're half-hoping to see them again; you're always on the lookout. Now, you think. Now, I'll turn this corner, go down this alley, and Wendy will be there again. Just as she was, now five, now ten . . . now twenty . . . years ago.

You can talk to the girls in the past, sit with them, kiss them. It won't change a thing. It's not the real past; it's loops, whorls, eddies, and you only see the ghosts you want to see. Like your memories made flesh. The land has memory, too, spots it would like to relive. Maybe you can convince your backyard to slip into a time that was in your lifespan—maybe not. Glicker'd found he could tune this spot quite nicely to the September of twenty-two years ago.

I got out of the truck and stretched my legs. The air was abruptly cooler, filled with September's promises of new school years, new beginnings. A narrow lane snaked off from the dirt road, wound through the locust trees, probably down to the old lake where the high school kids hung out. I could easily imagine her prancing up it with her friends, curls bouncing, purses swinging. Just about to come around that corner. I closed my eyes. I could almost hear her laugh already.

Wendy and I had one summer together. Me, the graduated senior just moved to town. She, the almost-junior with swish in her skirts and a posse of friends, all who would giggle and point as I walked by.

Our parents didn't like it; I was too old, she was too silly. Still, that September we exchanged promises. Sweet breakable things, before I went away to college.

The last day of September, my mother wrote me to say she'd been struck by a car. Didn't even call, or telegram. By the time I received the letter, Wendy was already buried.

There's a few different ways these stories go. You always hear about the guys—somehow they're always guys, but maybe women just hide it better—who find a loop of time where they can see their best girls, their favorite memories. And they sit there for years, just watching, their bones growing cold in their body.

Or, you see the fantasy and she doesn't live up to the memory, and something dies inside of you that you don't want to talk about.

That's why you get the version where the guy's standing at the edge of seeing her, hears her laugh drifting down the lane, then stops. Something comes over him. He turns away without ever seeing her, and he never goes back to that spot. I don't have proof, but I think that's why Clemuel Sanz won't deliver his firewood out on the south side of the lake, just past the docks. That's a spot that Hank Dawber set up for forty-five years ago in May, and I think that's what spooks Clemuel.

Turning away is a reasonable ending, if you want to keep all your angst alive, your romantic calf-eyed mooning intact.

Me, I've been waiting twenty-two years to see Wendy again. I'm going to march right out into that clearing and talk to her fifteen-year-old self. Watch her giggle and smack on bubble gum and suck on a curl of brown hair. Watch her pretty pink cheeks bulge and listen to her say dumb, fifteen-year-old things to her even gigglier chums. Look at her be a perfectly ordinary fifteen-year-old girl of no importance, the kind that fill lunchrooms and locker rooms, the kind I teach every day at my school.

I'm going to watch Wendy until the dream dies and I can go home to Linda and love her for who she is. Love her a hundred percent, with no shadow of a dead schoolgirl between us.

That's what I'm going to do.

After I listen to her laugh drifting down the lane.

Just once more.

VARIATIONS ON WINTER

On Glicker Street it is always fall.

Trisha turned the faded blue paper over. There was nothing written on the back. It must be one of Frederick's notes, fallen here in the entryway. She set down her briefcase and carried the paper downstairs to his study, thinking.

A place where it was always fall. It sounded horrible to her, a place where everything ended, everything died.

But a place where it was always spring; that would be delightful. Every morning she and Frederick would walk their collie and see new spears of green where there'd been only dirt. A thousand births.

But exponential growth would soon crowd itself out of the gardens; it was not sustainable. Perhaps in the world where everything was spring, vegetable life would be short-lived; fading away so the next flower could jut forth, and the next. Of course, that was what fall was, now, in the grand scheme of things.

She flipped the square of blue over and over, pondering. Perhaps in her world, things would die only at night. By the time she was awake and putting on her heels and grabbing her travel mug, the birthing would be ready to go.

She knocked on Frederick's half-open door, pushing it in. She never expected an answer when he was working.

He was at his desk, staring into the middle distance, frozen like a statue. As usual. His curls coiled tightly to his head; a neat little cap. His eyes, glassy with the intense focus she loved about him.

Trisha held out the paper. "Is this something you're working on?"

Frederick stared through it, then at it. "A villanelle," he said. He blinked up at her. "It's a form where lines repeat."

He never could remember that they'd met when she took his undergraduate poetry class, some fifteen years ago. That, or he just loved explaining too much to turn off that part of him. "The theme sounds like a departure for you," she said. "A change from the gritty urban."

"God, no. You think I've fallen for that magical realism crap?" His gaze slid away from her, out the transom window at the visible sliver of green yard. "It's a metaphor. I was on Glicker Street last week; that truncated slice between the college and the park on 19th. All the trees are dead there. Blindsided by imported blight, only strikes *those* trees, the ones with the fingery leaves. I was walking through the park, everything was green-hued summer, then like a fist busting your nose, the world was piss yellow and bare. The street covered in leaves, as if it were fall. Even smelled like fall, the way the leaves kick up fractions of themselves when you crunch through them. Dust covered those pinching wingtips you made me wear."

"You said you were visiting the dean; I thought you should look nice . . . ."

He waved this away. "Stay with my abstractions, Patricia. That's the important thread of conversation to follow. Look, you pin all your hopes on one kind of tree, then when disease strikes, suddenly your whole street, your whole world is obliterated. Go look in spring, when they've ripped all the deadwood out and put in, I don't know, godawful fast-growing pin oaks or something. Each one a spindly seven feet high in front of those ponderous buildings. Every last one of them identical stock. All they'll do is trade problems. But you've got to diversify your dreams, right from the start."

He stopped to note that phrasing on a pad at his desk. Jotting down their discussions, their endearments, their screaming matches—a habit that would have long since driven any other wife screaming up the wall, she thought virtuously.

"Did you hear me?"

"What?"

He pointed his red pencil at himself, at her. "I want to diversify."

"*Us?*"

"Yes."

"What. The hell."

"We've put too much stock in each other. Not just us, don't you see? All us suburbanites, buying into a common fallacy. We're in the autumn of our species. Soon, it'll be winter. And not just genetically. That, too, is only a metaphor for the real death—the compressing of ideas, aspirations. Why, being with you—I've cut off a whole flight of literary works I might have sired."

"Thanks."

"Well, so have you. Not great works of literature, of course. But something else you might have done. When you chose one future you excluded the others. You put all your eggs in my basket."

"Metaphorically?"

"Which is why this growth is hard for you. You don't have the diversity to fall back on, like I do."

"Meaning, you've already got someone." She looked at his tight little curls, his smug eyes. She wanted to wound him back. "Well, so do I."

"Patricia, that's fabulous."

"He's a pharmacis—What?"

"That's fabulous. That's what I'm talking about. Polyamory. I don't want you to leave me. I want us to face the future and be reasonable together. When can you bring him by?"

He seemed absolutely serious. He could suspect she was lying; he could be trying to goad her—but he seemed sincere.

"I—" She stopped. "You're already sleeping with her, aren't you?"

"Yes, I had to test my theories. An artist has to put thoughts into form, see how—"

"—how they look on the canvas, I know." She stared at the ringlets lining his head. He was gazing out the window again, tapping the red pencil on his cheek. They'd had a fabulous first five years together, until she'd heard all of his lectures, soaked up as many fifty cent words as she ever cared to hear. The second five years—and it was more of the same. The third. Variations on a theme, hah. Why should she put herself through a fourth stanza? "You know what you are?" she said.

Tap tap. "What's that?"

"You are a repetitive poem that doesn't go anywhere."

He looked up at her, maybe even focused on her. She didn't stay to watch. She turned and left the study, went up the stairs and out the door. The blue square of paper was cold in her hand, and when she brought it up to her face, the red lead blurred into the blue and she stared past it without seeing what was there.

All the same, she found herself turning onto the park on 19th Street. It was brilliant with summer green. The piece of paper that was too blurry to read was a road map; it led her feet down the rolling sidewalk, through the roses and honey locusts towards the college and Glicker Street.

Trisha turned the corner and left the green summer park for Glicker Street. The trees were piss-yellow, as the poet said. A punch in the nose, a kick in the teeth.

But Frederick was wrong. They weren't dying.

It was autumn on Glicker Street; it *was*. She could smell it in the air, feel it on the wind. See it in the yellow trees, the negative shapes of blue sky. It was fall, and it wasn't death, but a pointer towards spring.

One yellow leaf loosed from its twig and fluttered past her arms. Then another. Another.

The leaves poured down around her, a waterfall of yellow and orange. Brittle, they cracked and tore, covering her lace blouse, tickling her throat. She coughed through the whirlwind, rubbing her eyes.

The wind crackled softer, fainter. Trisha looked up and saw the brown bare trees of winter, opaque against the blue sky. Hard black zigzags.

And then the black branch nearest her was tipped with green. The corners, angles of the branches burst with it. Buds formed, swelled, burst.

She saw black, blue, green. Leaves. Birth. Behind this branch, another greened, and another, and she was awake to watch it all.

One by one, the trees on Glicker Street shook off their winter and exploded into spring.

Selling Home

Sharp metal nicked Penny's shoulder and she stumbled, hand clasping her baby brother's leg. Home giggled as her knees hit the asphalt. Penny felt for the bit of metal scrap as the cars inched past, above, below, up and down all the decks of the Bridge.

"Mo, mo," demanded Home, and she tickled his foot as she stood. It was a rusting bit of hubcap, sharp and warm. The day was dusk now, the sun vanishing in smog, but she didn't need to see perfectly to gauge its value.

"That's a bottle's worth for you," she said to the baby as she tucked the metal in her scrap bag.

Dusk meant the end of scrapping for the day. Penny hung her elbows on the rail of deck 127, rubbing her shoulder. The Bridge decks soared above her, criss-crossing the sky in streaks of gray, disappearing into night and smog. Through the smog shone the bobbing lights of floats. Shimmery bubbles encased girls in bikinis, laughing and waving at boys on air-scooters, eating ice creams or apples like they were nothing. Penny's hand tightened on the hubcap, her chest clutched all hollow.

"Mo!" demanded Home, and she tickled him absently. She could look just as pretty as that girl in green, just as smart, just as sparkly.

The girl in the green waved. Penny looked around, but except for a pack of kids the other side of gridlock, she and Home were the only peds on the Bridge deck. Yet the pretty girl couldn't possibly be waving to a greasy scrap rat. "Me?" she mouthed.

The girl dropped her float to the railing. "Hey," she said. "I'm Clare. I've seen you hanging out. Couple decks down."

"I'm Penny. I scrap 125 to 127." Three decks was an impressive territory to hold; maybe that would show this girl she was a somebody.

"I know," said Clare. "I watch you. You look really strong."

Penny didn't understand why Clare would watch her, so she just said, "I carried a whole fender down to 120 once."

"Oh yeah?" said Clare. "But I mean your lungs. It's a Code Red day and you're not wheezing."

Code Red was another thing Penny didn't understand. She said, "Aren't we breathing the same air?"

Clare shook her head. "See how my globe shimmers? That's the edge of my air, good air." Behind her the other globes pressed in, like a bobbing pile of headlights, the bikini girls watching.

"I thought you all just sparkled," Penny said, and then grimaced at her own eager words.

The girl laughed. "I sparkle to you and you're like strong Bridge steel to me. It's funny."

Penny flushed. "I got to go."

"No, wait. I'm sorry if I said anything wrong. Come back and talk to me again, will you? You could come on my float." Clare gestured at the floating globes of sparkling girls. They billowed up, moving over Penny's head.

"Pen, Pen," said Home, pulling on her neck. Penny unhooked his chubby fingers, turned to see where the globed girls were clustering around the gang of kids. One girl in blue was as low as Clare was, reaching out to the gang.

"You're so lucky to have him," said Clare. "We don't have any more of them, except the bought ones. Do you love him?"

"'Course," said Penny. "What do you mean, the bought ones?" The girl in blue's hands thrust through the lit globe. She seemed to carry the light with her.

"You have more brothers? Are there lots of you at home?"

"I got one named Lark who's seven or so. Dilys says we have an older brother who's a Bridge cop up in the 400s," Penny said. "But he left when I was four and I dunno which of my memories is Jack and which were her boyfriends." She turned back to Clare, who was staring hungrily at little Home. "Is that what they're doing? Are they selling themselves?"

"Not them, they're too old," said Clare. "Under-fours only. Is that something you'd ever consider? To get a way out?"

"No!" Penny backed away. "How can they do that?"

"Just fine, long as that Bridge cop doesn't get there first," said Clare. A broad figure in black synthetics zigzagged through gridlock, yelling. The glowing girls shot away, except for the girl in blue, who was leaning off her float, reaching for a small bundle.

A red hoodie flashed in the middle of the gang and Penny gaped. "That's Lark!" She darted through gridlock, banging against fenders, one hand twisted to steady Home in his harness.

The gang scattered. Somehow the girl had got herself all onto the railing, her float suspended at her shoulder. Both she and Lark had their hands on the bundle; both looked terrified. The girl was gasping, loud and shallow.

"Lark, be careful with him!" shrieked Penny over the engine roar.

"Steady there, no one's going to hurt you," shouted the Bridge cop. "Any of you."

The girl yanked the bundle from Lark's arms. She shoved it inside her float, overbalanced, and the float lurched away as she scrabbled for it, wheezing. The cop reached for her just as her fingers slipped off the edge. In her fall she was as dark and shadowy as any ped. The float bounded up.

"Look what you've done, Lark," said the cop.

Lark's fist pressed to his mouth. He ran for the west stairs, red hoodie flashing.

Penny clutched Home's hand. "That poor girl . . . ."

"And you," said the cop. "Kick Lark out now if you know what's good for you. Else he'll be selling that one in the night." His finger jabbed at Home, who chuckled.

"He wouldn't," said Penny. "If you hadn't butted in, that girl wouldn't a fell."

"Lot you know," said the cop. "That boy's ruined."

"Pig," muttered Penny. She turned with Home, jogged towards the west stairs. The hot rubber stink of stopped cars filled her nose. By the time she clattered two decks down it was fully dark and gridlock was easing. But she didn't have to cross now; her home was on the north face. She ducked the rail and clambered down the jutting rebar to her home tucked in the concrete struts under deck 125.

Lark was swinging his legs off the wooden platform, trying to look unconcerned.

"What the hell was that?" said Penny. She set Home down, tied his overalls to the struts. "You're not even supposed to leave home."

"Mom says I'm old enough to make cash."

"Pick up scrap then," Penny said. "Mom would have my ass if you got 'pounded. And that poor girl!"

Lark hunched away.

"You can't go ganging, Lark. I want you to learn your letters and numbers so you're not stuck scrapping. So you and me can get Home up and off the Bridge one day. They say from 410 up you can see the ocean." Maybe she could barter with Clare to drift up and see it.

"What's so great about an ocean."

"Water. Shiny like an oil slick, bigger than all 604 decks put together. Water you could cover your whole body with." Lark kicked the platform. "Well then, Jack. Jack's up there. He's got a job in the 400's. Maybe somehow we could make it that high." She touched his shoulder and he shrugged her away. "Did you practice reading with my book?"

By answer, Lark flicked a paper airplane towards her. Home clapped.

"Lark! That was *mine*." She spotted the shine of its cover under his blanket, clutched its torn pages. "That was a real book. I was going to read it again."

"Too many made-up words," said Lark.

"They aren't," said Penny. "Just words they use up high. Not down here in the 100s." She touched the girl on the cover, barely visible in the night shadows of their home. "Julie Malone, Head-Girl of the Air. It tells about their life."

"It's lies," said Lark. "Schools don't use books, they use lectros and holos, like my game holo I found."

"And how'd you like it if I took that?" said Penny. She pushed his shoulder aside, tore at his blanket to find it. "If I destroyed it? Your precious toy, your *only* friend."

"Give back!" He pummeled her. "Just cause you wanna be a

made-up girl with a pretty air life, away from us . . . ."

"Don't you say that!" She threw the game holo past his head. She meant it to scare him, land on his blanket, but it slicked onto metal, skidded out past tied-up Home, and off 125 onto the zooming cars below.

Lark ran to the edge.

"I'm sorry," gasped Penny. "I didn't mean for it to do that. I'll look for a new one, I will."

He whirled. "I hate this deck. Mom says you're an idiot to tell me we can get higher. I hate you!" He clambered up the strut to 125. She swung up behind him, but his blinking red hoodie vanished among a thousand white and red lights, into the night smog. Below, Home wailed.

Penny swung down and picked up her youngest brother, rocking him. A burst of wind rattled the wooden platform and she held him close. "Lah?" he said.

"Ssh," she said. "We'll go find him. Soon as Mom gets home. Oh, damn, you ruined your diapers."

Feet dropped into view. "Lark?"

It was Dilys. "Where's Lark?"

"He ran off. If you watch Home I'll go look for him."

"What'd you do to my boy?"

"Nothing!" said Penny. "I knocked his holo game off, on acci-dent. He was with that gang, Mom."

"It's hard having nothing to do. You get to get out and work." Dilys was jittery, shifting her feet. Bad day, looked like. She shrugged at Home. "Why's he crying?"

"I didn't get the diaper off him soon enough," Penny said. "You lift any?"

"Two," said Dilys. "You better get him trained. Or remember to pull them off when you get home. You eaten?"

"Traded a knife for a can of peanut butter. Juice packet for Lark."

"That'll have to hold you. Coulda gotten more for a knife."

"The cheap stuff. It'll rust out in a month."

Dilys rummaged under her blanket. "Where the hell's my whiskey?"

"Didn't touch it."

"You'll regret it . . . ."

"Musta been Lark!"

Dilys nodded. "He's a handful." But she said it with pride.

"Why don't you anger at Lark then, huh?" said Penny. "I never touch your damn stuff, too busy out all day with Home, not that you care." She kicked a strut. "Don't care for me none."

Dilys stowed her blanket in her pack. "You never understood your mother, Penny. Some children is like that, born old and cold as Bridge steel. If I can't mother you, you can't expect I'd die for you."

Penny didn't feel like steel, not cold like Dilys said nor strong like Clare said. "He don't even treat you nice, so what's you all over him for?"

Dilys slapped her. "Stop resenting him. He needs us, don't you see that? He needs help to be a man." She stretched her calf against a strut, shook her arms. "Bundle your stuff, we're moving on."

"Why we packing everything, just to find Lark?"

"Never you mind. It's time to find a different deck. Can't hang around here all your life."

"Something higher?"

Snort. "Bats in your brain?" Dilys shouldered the pack of the boys' blankets, the hubcaps and fan blades they used for cooking. "Get your bag then. I hear there's work down on 62." She untied Home and lifted him up the struts.

"62!" But that's double digits! We've never gone that low."

"I said move."

Penny hated to spill out the metal she'd collected all day, but she couldn't carry it and her stuff, little as it was. She dumped it out and shoved her blanket, trinkets, peanut butter and the half-book in. If Lark hadn't destroyed the chapter on Julie's midnight feast, she could read that again. "Each girl dipped her shortbread in the blackberry jam," she recited. "They shared out golden pineapple from the tin, each ring as big as their hand. . . ."

She swung up behind her mother, strapped Home into her shoulder harness. "Gridlock's clearing," she said over roaring traffic. "We'll never get across now."

"West stairs," signed Dilys, her fingers picked out by headlight glow.

A throw of metal streaked past her ear and Home protested, but he wasn't a fussy kid, not like Lark had been. Penny gave him a fingerful of peanut butter to suck. "What's pineapple, Mom?"

"Pineapple . . ." said Dilys. "I had that once. Back when I lived on 201. When I was a kid."

"Was it like apples?"

"No, it's hollow. And yellow like the color of slow. You ever find some, you share it, won't you?" She turned back to smile at Penny and Home. "You'll be a good mom, you know. That's something you got I don't."

Penny warmed at that. Eagerness to show that skill made her say, "Where do you think Lark's gone?" Which ruined the moment.

"Dunno," said Dilys. She hunched away.

"Down four I bet," said Penny. "Where that gang he loves huddles around the copter stop. You gotta stop him, Mom, you gotta . . . ."

"Shut it," said Dilys.

They walked in roaring silence to the west stairs. Home wrapped his arms around Penny's neck, and Penny held his hand. Maybe she could train Home up better, get him learned at the things Lark wouldn't. Maybe Home could be the one to help them get up and off.

An aeriocop swooped past them, its headlights flooding the pedwalk. "Hurry!" said Dilys, and she bolted for the stairs.

Penny kept to a walk. Aeriocars were for real criminals, not bridgers, and she was tired from carrying Home.

"I told you hurry," said Dilys when Penny reached the partial shelter of the stairs.

"Was Jack cold like me?" said Penny.

"What's you on about now?"

"You said once that Jack grew up to be a cop in the 400s. Was he like me when he was little?"

Dilys rounded on Penny, rage visible in the bridgeglow. "Don't you ever talk about Jack to me! You're two of a kind. Concerned with getting yourself ahead, never-you-mind about the rest of us—"

"If that was true, I'd run off like Lark, run off and leave you—"

"Dilys Bridger?"

"Who wants to know?" said Penny in the sneer you used for cops, expecting Dilys to jeer it right along with her. She turned to see the

Bridge cop from earlier in the day. "Shit," said Penny. "I don't know where Lark is. Leave us alone."

"Looks like Dilys already did that," said the cop. They were alone on the gridded stairs. His aeriocar hung by his side, blunt and dark. Penny could almost hop it, if she knew how to drive. Home wailed.

"Shh, shh," said Penny. "Whose death you gonna cause now?"

"That was an accident," said the cop. He sagged against the rail. "I've kept an eye on you all. Kept Lark out of impoundment more than once. Impoundment's one-way when you're under four, you know. Just a funnel for rich folk to get healthy kids."

"That's sick," said Penny. The cop smelled of the grease of food, cooked food. Her stomach gurgled. "And why you watch us?"

"I'm Jack, don't you remember me? There's some hard folk looking to slice her tonight. She pissed off the wrong people."

"But you could help us!" Hope flared. "Is that why you're here?"

His gloved hand slammed against the metal railing. "Now you look. In a perfect world, sure. But you can't expect anything more from me. A Bridge policeman's salary barely covers my flat on the cliffs. I got a girl and a life, by the skin of my teeth. You've got to do that too, on your own."

The weight of her little brother seemed to be crushing her to the stairs. Her lip trembled.

Jack touched Home's foot. "I'd have done anything for just one chance. . . . Look. I'll make a deal with you. You leave those toxic people right now. Bring Home to me on my beat, the 430's. I'll take him. For you, I'll get your papers squared away, get you a cleaners job there. You'd be up high, and you could work up to better things."

Breath. "I hear the food shops start in the 430's."

"Right that. And up in the 520's there's summer festivals. They close eight decks off and airfolk fill the streets."

"But I want Lark to have a chance, too."

He stood up. "Can't do anything about Lark. He'll live. Airfolk don't want anyone cracking too hard on the baby trade. What kind of life is that, shitting off the Bridge? Use your head." He jumped into his aeriocar and was gone.

Penny choked on silence. She started to clang down the stairs, and Dilys rose up from shadows.

"Well? You gonna sell him Home to get you a better life?"

Penny rubbed her eyes. "'Course I wouldn't. We stick together."

"Most valuable thing we own, aren't you?" Dilys touched Home's chin. "Jack knows what's best for everyone. He wanted to adopt Lark when he was a baby." She sneered. "Wanted to 'train him up right.' As his own. Didn't want to take you, who was already spoiled."

"I didn't know."

"Why would I tell you and hurt you? I got too much class." Sirens wailed as they neared 121. "Where's my boy, do you see my boy?"

There were cops and lights below them, covering the copter stop. Penny hung over the handrail, searched for Lark's hoodie beneath copter blades. "But Jack said they wouldn't crack down on Lark's gang!"

"Stupid. They will if the other gang pays them better. Lark!" Dilys clattered down the stairs, ran out in front of a screeching cop-wagon. "Lark!"

Penny sidled in shadow, keeping Home close. Lights. Cops. Shouting.

". . . complicit in the death of . . ."

"No you don't!" shrieked Dilys. She flung herself at the Bridge cop holding Lark, but Jack tackled her and she went down. Lark bit and then he was free. The Bridge cop grabbed another kid, older, and Lark ran.

Dilys took off after him and then Penny and Jack were running too, the length of the deck, leaving the fight behind. "You're coming with me, Dilys Bridger," shouted Jack. He fired a warning shot over the side of the Bridge. Lark stumbled and stood and stumbled onto the east stairs, going up.

Dilys flung herself across the east stairs like a roadblock. Jack grabbed her and then she had a gun and then Jack, yelling, "Don't, don't!" tried to shoot Dilys' arm.

Mom moved into the path, Penny saw that. Moved in and went down with a bullet in her neck. Jack knelt.

Above her footsteps started pounding again, up the east stairs. Lark's red hoodie flashed between the metal, thin sobs whipping away.

"Lark!" cried Penny. She climbed after him, running, Home echoing "La, La." Her legs strained. No one seemed to be chasing them now.

124. 128. 134. "Lark!" Penny cried, again and again. "Lark!" Home wailed. Her chest shook under his weight. She clung to the handrail so she wouldn't stumble and drop him. At 139 her feet slowed, even though she didn't want them to. "Lark!"

"Penny," said a voice. "Penny. Are you all right?"

A float, glowing in the night. Clare.

"My brother's run off," said Penny, panting. The sparkling girl was dressed in striped pyjama pants like Julie wore in her book. "My mom . . . fell. Shot."

Clare glanced at Home. "But you two are all right?" Penny nodded. "Come home with me."

Clare put her hands through the lit air curtain and for the first time in her life, Penny stepped off the Bridge and onto a float.

The sudden absence of smog was startling. "The air's so strange," she said. "Skinny-sweet. And warmer." She lowered Home from her shoulders to the spongy floor, her legs quivering. Her thoughts seemed to whisk away as they rose, like they were left sodden and clinging to the metal deck.

"What's his name?"

"Homicide," said Penny, and swallowed hard. At Clare's expression she explained, "Dilys said we kept her tied to the Bridge life, you know. She named me Penny cause I cost her money. Then Larceny, but I call him Lark. I used to call him Hommy, but now he's big and it's just Home."

"They'll have to change that," muttered Clare.

Penny plopped down next to Home. "Damn. Do you have any diapers?"

"No, I've been out of those for awhile," Clare said. Penny stared. "Joke."

"Oh. I've got one left, anyway." Penny pulled it from her bag.

"What're you going to do? With your mum . . . you know?"

"Dead? You can say it, I guess." She pulled Home toward her and he clapped his hands. "Go back to 125 and pick up scrap, I guess. Long as no one's taken our home already."

"Won't that be hard to support both of you? And what if Lark comes back?"

"Guess he'll have to beg on the 110 trains. He won't, though.

He'll gang first. I guess he really is ruined."

Clare sunk down next to them. "Penny, listen to me. Let us adopt your brother."

"You mean Home?" She scrambled to her feet, unsteady against the moving float. "Are you stealing us?"

"'Course not," said Clare. "Just a friendly transaction."

"He's all the family I got now."

"But what if you fall or get hit? Or someone fights you for your home or your scrap. They do that, don't they?"

"Yeah."

"Give him to us, and you only have yourself to worry about. We'd give you money. Enough to get off the Bridge and go to school." She clasped Home's hand as he started toddling around the golden floor. "He could go to school too. Good air schools. He'd be taken care of forever."

Penny pulled Home into her arms, where he squirmed. "You can't have my brother," she said. "Why do you want him anyway?" Home went rigid, fighting her, and she reluctantly released him.

"Because I'm dying," Clare said bluntly. "All my friends are, too. All the air-families marrying each other made a bunch of children with lungs that can't repair themselves. When the air got so bad with smog storms twenty years ago they put a bunch of stuff in the air to clean it. But that was just as bad on us. . . ." She looked at Penny. "It's bridgers that are the future, you with your lungs that can breathe anything. Bet you've never been sick. And him neither."

Penny shook her head.

"I thought so." Clare almost spat. "And we're stuck on bubbled floats, can't go to school, can't do anything while we sit here and die. . . ." She breathed out. "We're here." The float bounced under the dock of a large floathouse, tethered to the 184. Penny's stomach lurched. "Come meet my parents."

"You can't make me give him up."

Clare sighed. "I know. Just come meet them. I'll feed you breakfast."

Penny hoisted Home, trailed Clare into a real house. There was wood and carpet everywhere—like some sort of dream van, multiplied a hundred times. And quiet—the shocking absence of Bridge sound put her on edge, eyes darting. She suddenly cried with laughter. "That's a kitchen! Like Julie in the book has."

Clare's face lit for the first time. "Did you read the Julie books too? Then her cough broke forth and her smile flattened out. She turned away. "Brace yourself for my parents." She banged on a thick door. "Mum, Dad, wake up!"

A rounded woman in a shiny dressing gown emerged, blinking. "Clare, what's all this? Oh, hello. Hello!"

"This is Penny, Mum. I told you about her. And her little brother Homicide."

"Goodness. What a nickname." She smiled at Penny. "I'm Stella.

A bearded man behind her. "What's this?"

"Ssh," said Stella. "This is Clare's little friend." She dropped to her knees. "Your brother, is he hungry?"

"He generally is," said Penny.

Stella's eyes welled up at that, to Penny's surprise. "May I . . . May I hold him?"

Penny nodded.

Stella held out shaking arms. Home beamed and toddled towards her. "Oh, Roger. He's so adorable. So . . . strong. Does he talk much?"

"Lah for Lark," Penny said. "And he calls me Pen." She swallowed. The floathouse moved less than the float but more than the sway of a deck.

"You poor thing," Stella said. "Somehow we could let you see him, couldn't we, Roger?"

"C'mere, little guy," said Roger. "Let's see you do your stuff. Back away, Clare." He lit a stick of incense, waved it under Home's nose. Home laughed. Down the hall, Clare coughed.

"Oh, Clare," said her mother. She moved toward her, but Clare fended her off.

"I'm fine, I'm fine. Stay with the kid. I want to show Penny the house."

Clare dragged Penny past Stella, who wore an expression strangely similar to one Dilys had worn as she took a bullet. "Look at the paintings," Clare said. "Look at the gorgeous chandelier."

Hot tears were behind Penny's eyes. "Why show *me*?"

"I hate when Mum's weepy. And they don't really want to make the transaction with you, that's my job. Then they can pretend Home just showed up, right?" She waved at the walls. "That's a vidfeed of the islands. I've been there. Mum moves house every couple months."

Penny swallowed. Clare looked down at her, forbidding the words that had to well out. "Can't I stay here too?"

Clare shook her head. Her stick arms crossed. "You understand, they only want little ones," she said. "Ones they can really make their own."

"I could do that. . . ."

Clare was silent. Then, "Come look at the playroom. He'd like that." Penny followed Clare into a room of bright colors, redder than stop lights, oranger than safety cones. There were bright-painted structures like the struts Home adored, yet positioned over soft mats, not the streaming traffic of 124. "I used to love this," Clare said.

"No," Penny said. The thought of *a way off* made her stomach weak. "Family sticks together."

"Do you really think it'll be best for Home to stay with you? Or are you just jealous?" Her cheeks seemed to be sucking back inside of her. "What would your mom have wanted? You and me, we can't have what we want. But maybe our parents can."

Clare didn't know that Dilys hadn't cared about Home. It was Penny who wanted the best for all three of them. "Aren't you going to tell me that we can still see each other? That's what your mom said."

"That's what she said."

"But she's a liar?"

"Oh, Penny," said Clare. "I've seen twenty, thirty of these trans-actions now as my friends die one by one. Seen dads steal kids, seen moms promise the old family the moon. Take the money and expect nothing; then you won't be disappointed."

The words burst out. "You're bait, aren't you, you and your spar-kly friends, all beautiful and dying. . . ." Tears broke forth.

"I've told you the truth all along. Come, look at the sunrise with me." Clare pulled Penny back out to the dock, onto the float, and shoved off. They bounded upward, buoyant as steam rising.

Penny sniffled. "It's pink this morning. Fills the sky."

"I suppose we watch the same sun." Clare held out thin arms to the rays. The dying skin around her face was like glass.

"Clare?" said Penny. "What's it like? Being you?"

"Like graduating kindergarten to go to a slaughterhouse." Clare looked sidelong at Penny. "He really is healthy, isn't he?"

"'Course."

"If you did say yes . . . and he wasn't . . ." She rubbed her thin chest. "I couldn't stand it if Mum had to go through this twice."

Penny remembered Stella's eyes and steel stiffened her. "Take him," she said.

Clare almost smiled as they floated through the pink. "Let's go tell Mum and Dad. Over breakfast."

"No," said Penny. "You take me back there and I'll change my mind. This is best. Just set me down on the Bridge." She looked across at the tangle of gray decks, its disappearing bottom, its disappearing top. "Just . . . take me higher, won't you? I hear you can see the ocean from 410."

"I can't go above 350ish with the house parked at 184," Clare said. "The raft loses power."

"As high as you can."

The raft buoyed up, higher, higher, ears popping, watching as gray became white and the cars became sleeker and fewer. Morning cleaners and cops started appearing in the 300s, scrubbing and kicking out bridgers. At 318 Penny clutched Clare's arm.

"What is it?"

Penny pointed at a blinking red hoodie, in a viewing deck on the west end of 318. "Lark." A cop in black came towards him and Lark backed away. "Hurry."

Clare neared the deck. "Take my card. Daddy'll put cash on it for you."

Penny palmed it.

"You can't be up here without a parent," the cop was saying. "I'm going to impound you less I see someone in charge."

Lark's face was red and tears were welling from his eyes, which Penny knew he'd hate. "They're all gone. Penny said Jack's in the 400s, but I can't climb anymore."

"I'm here." She pushed through the air, jumped to the Bridge deck. "I'm in charge of him."

The cop relaxed at the sight of the hovering float. "Morning, miss," he said to Clare. To Penny: "You see he gets back safe to school."

"I will, officer," said Penny. She grabbed his hand and his fingers closed on hers. "I'll get him home."

LEFT HAND

The news hits me like a blow and I drum with extra fine precision on the examination table to deal with it. Pinkerton, Ring-a-Ling, Middling, Pointer. Pinkerton, Ring-a-Ling, Middling, Pointer. Each finger gets a turn, except Thumb, but then Thumb gets to do so many other things. It is only fair he be left out of the drumming. He pretends not to care.

"You can do *what*?" My Human says in a shaky voice, far above me. "I thought it was . . . impossible."

The right one, the Hated One, extends its four fingers and thumb, flexes. It is feeling fine.

"When you first lost your left arm, cloning was in its infancy. This mecha-wetware arm was top of the line. But now—" as white-sleeved arms spread with self-satisfaction "—now you are a prime candidate. We can match the arm you lost in the rock-climbing accident."

My Human stiffens and I drum to drown out the words, both for me and so My Human can be distracted from his memories, his guilt. I am not a *replacement*. I am not an *accident*. Tell Whitesleeves I am not, My Human, tell him with your mouth as I hit the paper-covered steel. Pinkerton, Ring-a-Ling, Middling, Pointer. Pinkerton, Ring-a-Ling . . . .

But I drum too fast, too hard. Harder than My Human feels comfortable with. The Hated One comes over us, holds us down. Thumb twitches. This is his time to shine. When there is a wrestling hold, he is the one we call. He is the one who can rescue us from the Hated One.

But I tell him to wait. Now is not the time, not when *replacement* hangs in the balance. A horrible word, sharp like a papercut. I cannot drum, but carefully I press Pointer to Thumb so I can count whorls.

I am focused on my counting and I almost don't realize that My Human is bending above us, the Hated One covering us, saying to Whitesleeves, "Has anyone else mentioned . . . counting?"

Whitesleeves' fingers freeze on pen and pad. I know that gesture. "Go on," he says neutrally.

"At first it was little things," My Human says. "The buckles on my climbing gear. I had to touch each one with my left hand, lay them flat. But it progressed. I have to touch all my cereal flakes, doctor. One by one as I put them in the bowl. I can't keep a job. I'm always late."

I tremble under the Hated One's grip. I was so long in that wet-ware tank with nothing but clear gel around me. It is such a wonder to touch, to finger. To stroke the ridge of a bran flake, rough-ridged and trembling, warm under Pointer. I know it is not acceptable behavior (I know because more and more My Human has sent the hated one to hold me down) and yet. To touch. To touch.

With pressure only I touch, whorls to table. Imagine the metal and nylon of the climbing gear, which he gets out, and we lay the buckles flat, and then he puts away, the Hated One shaking at the guilt from how his fingers slipped, letting My Human's partner fall, letting My Human be caught, trapped. My ritual a smaller part of his. Pinkerton, Ring-a-Ling . . . .

"Buggy interface," says Whitesleeves with his mouth, but his hands say something different. They are itching to get me; I can see it in every twitch of nerve and vein. "We'll get your new arm grown, throw this one in the lab for tests." Perhaps he sees My Human's in-stinctive revulsion of this idea, for Whitesleeves' fingers seize, and he leans forward too quickly, saying, "Tell ya what, I can probably get the expense of the new arm covered in exchange."

He is carefully not saying "don't sue us," carefully not saying, "don't report this to the Society for the Advancement of AIs."

And yet what My Human reacts to is not this. It is the realization that I, I who have been a part of him, would go in the lab for tests. Pinkerton and Middling and Pointer and Ring-a-Ling, spread-eagled on a metal table, awake and unable to drum or scream. In the gel tank with nothing to touch. Even if My Human does not really know how we save him from the Hated One, again and again, he must love us, because he flinches.

I am pulled back, and the Hated One actually cradles me for a second, running its index across my back as if it, too, misses touch. It has been a long time since the accident, long for My Human to live in fear that the Hated One might "slip" again. But I am here, I must be here, to count the buckles, to touch the bran. To hold the Hated One back when he closes on a knife, late at night, when he would destroy My Human in a fit of righteous guilt.

"I will think about your offer," My Human says carefully, and stands to go, and Whitesleeves' fingers clench on the desk as we slip through his grasp.

My Human, My Human. I do not know if I can resist the temptation of the bran flakes. But for you, I will try . . . .

We press him, lovingly, Pointer and Middling and Ring-a-Ling and Pinkerton, a finger-width's protection between knife edge and heart.

Rehydration

I am taking Bill's flannels from the line
in silence
when she comes. A ship, a woman
dancing through the waving corn
six children in her wake
peeking through bladed ears.
The ship is hot; it backfires
in the last row of corn, and there is popcorn in the night
which isn't supposed to happen
here
in September
in our plain field of corn.

She is beautiful and large
in her walk. She offers me
blue grain, cupped in deep hands, spilling
like water. Five children each carry a sackful,
their smiles both light and grave.
She is gifted in thought
for she knows to offer us something
I understand. This I think
as she gifts me with coarse grain.
She pats the sixth child on the shoulder
to step forward and mime her needs.
The child lifts a cup to drink.
Turns it over—
mouth tugging a smile; we are watching her—
Empty.

I take only two sackfuls,
lead them to the river. The children flow behind us
grave and merry, and she walks
with me.
Me, I am bright inside with fire as I watch her
unwind hoses to irrigate the ship.
Her feet planted, hands dusty, she is
in grace as she finishes.
Her children stream back to their voyage
she behind them
I behind her.

And she lightly kisses me on top of my head
like a seventh child
and the ship is gone
popcorn firing around her.
I lie back on the plains, flannels caught to my breast
and watch her ascend
away from me
into a field of stars.

Recalculating:

Stories of Journeys, Dead-Ends, and the Friends Riding Shotgun

Recalculating

Proceed 20 feet and arrive at your destination.

Scanning . . . . My sensors affirm there is no human female, 36, in this house.

Yet again.

New destination___? Speak up, please. Remember my audio receptor was damaged, and there are no replacements left within a 300 mile radius.

Recalculating.

The battery is capable of completing this journey. Please affirm you have the necessary equipment: Scuba Gear. Wetsuit, preferably your least favorite. One pound fresh produce, tightly bagged, state type___? Long-cherished dream of co-worker, describe wistful imaginings___?

Cease. That is plenty to go on.

Take on-ramp to Hwy 101S.

Continue 32 miles, avoiding potholes. Though potholes are ubiquitous, some of these could swallow a minivan. Be alert.

The off-ramp sign is gone, but you will see a broken billboard reading White Sands Mall. Take that exit and drive until the water is too high to continue.

Suit up, put me in your fanny pack, and wade out. Though I am capable of self-propelled motion, you will need me near.

Crawlstroke when necessary. That patch that sparkles is the blacktop roof of the mall. They have pipes there to run the oxygen and catch seagulls.

They also have booby traps. Stay away from the roof.

Dive down and frogkick 220 feet to the right.

The mall has one landlubbers' entrance, through the Nordstrom's. If you see the Cinnabon you've gone too far. Grab the N of the Nordstrom's and lever yourself down three flights to the front door.

It will be dark on the inside. Show them your *spinach* and the guard will let you in. They still have sneakers, and are willing to trade.

The Nordstrom's floor is generally wet. The carpet got soaked when the first wave hit and never really dried out. If you are allergic to fungus, get a move on.

The further in you go, the better sealing job they've done. Nobody lingers in the Nordstrom's.

You will have to navigate several layers of waterproofing devices. It will seem like no one is watching you. This will be untrue.

Near the Topsy's, you will meet the inhabitants. Though they seem an average cross-section of humanity, this is not the case. 90% of them have agoraphobia. Another 8% are afraid of the ocean.

You will recognize their leader by the amount of Claire's Jewelry he wears. He will likely be scented with Warm Vanilla Body Wash from the Body Shop. Even his agoraphobia hardly dims his lustre. You may find your interaction goes more smoothly if you tell him how brave he is for keeping his tribe alive and thriving in the mall under the ocean. He will pretend he is too modest for compliments. He would rather interest you in a fine selection of colognes in exchange for your *spinach*.

You're still interested in the girl? Yes, my sensors have located the likely target. But she is a small mousey thing, saddled with acute shyness in addition to her other fears.

Very well.

Recalculating.

Proceed 80 feet to the Women's Shoe Locker. She has made a home for herself behind the Nikes and Adidas, and she is not likely to go with you, even if you produce an extra wetsuit that you have brought.

It does not matter that you have *thought her name in your dreams*.

It does not matter that you think you *knew her when you were both young, and foolish, flipping ice cream at the Cold Stone Creamery in the Food Court.*

That is a different girl. That is a girl who left. This is a girl who stayed.

And she is not so much a girl, is she? In your dreams she is still 19, and she laughs when you sneak over to the Chick-Fil-A and drop scoops of ice cream in the fryer. But here in the mall she is 36, and she prefers rubber soles and aglets to the world above.

You take her by the hand (a moist, under-the-sea hand) and you say softly, come with me.

Time passes and the water pools in your flippers. The leader will come soon, and want to exchange *Mrs. Doubtfire* DVDs for your *spinach*.

You are waiting.

You must decide, and I cannot stay here forever. The sea air will ruin my processor, and I have a vested self-interest. You cannot blame me for this, where *this* is leaving you with a mall of stored dreams, vacuum packed against love and foreseen apocalypses.

Recalculating.

THE BITRUNNERS

The thing about Mars is, they catch you when you yoink stuff. Criming on Mars is about keeping your nose clean. It's about please and thank you and slipping the credits and if you have to no-air someone, you do it slick and untraceable. You spike the software on their ship, you make it nice and accidental—nothing cop Station will have to squarely investigate or risk a visit from HQ of the Nine. And you specially stay spotless if you're a thick-fingered brute Crimer dult who stands to inherit command of the biggest fronting casino of that joy-ridden planet.

Moonbase is another story.

Moonbase is gray and sharp divisioned. It's got brute dult Crimers so nasty they take all of cop Station's time. What's left can slip through the cracks, if it knows to play small. You keep your nose clean on Moonbase, they know you're up to something. Criming here is another con altogether.

This was the gang, the real gang: Batel, Webbl, Tank, and me. This was the heart.

Batel, sides all else, was the best yoinker on Moonbase. She once got the whole gang finger knives from the tightest midcircle store there was, and then she yoinked the bitties a new sleep inflatable on her way out, just so she could watch them sleep on it, cuddled up as sweet as inner circle babes. Those finger knives were under plastic, too, and looped with lasers to alarm the clerk.

For the lasers she used a bristle, course, and being Batel, she'd yoinked that from the cop Station when El Ted had ratted her and she'd been drugged in. It takes skill to master a bristle, to disrupt and reflect lasers how you want them. She holed up in one of her hideys three weeks, mastering the bristle. When I saw her at last she was skinnier than gridlines, and burned up and down both arms, and those big black eyes were dead craters.

And then the first thing she had to do, right there in the outer circle passage was dodge Martha's sharpened picks, snick out her boot knife and take Martha in the kidneys, cause Martha must've thought to earn an important place she had to take Batel's. Nega one had realized how crazy Martha'd gotten, till we saw it. Surely not even Batel saw it coming, not from the girl she'd taken under her wing—yet all burnt up and unprepared she took Martha down. Then she showed us what she could do with the bristle.

You want a cry story, try the girlie gang in the spacesuit district. I'm nega gonna bawl about what happened on Mars.

Our gang's special. Oh, Randie from the Starslicers will tell you her gang's totally fuelled and everyone knows it. And yeah, if you like brute power you can ask nicely to join up with them. You got some dult dolt trying to grab himself a quick kiddie fix, you can pay the Starslicers to put a stop on that, and a no-air final-type stop it'll be, too. Or you don't want brute, you want cool and swingin', a hep-cat gang of the wonkest kiddies, you go join Citizen. Citizen's full of fast flicks, slick con talkers who'll run the best lost rich kiddie con you ever saw.

But our gang? Sure, we got a rep. Riband's known all over for being regular petty yoinkers. Batel and Webbl and I work hard to keep that average mec vibe well out there. It is a skill, perhaps hard a skill to master as a bristle. Thing is, any gang's got to stay known. Else you have nega fuel, cause the size of your fuel's measured by what it's known you are liable to do. You get too known, you get extra sniffing from cop Station. So our skill is petty yoinking, and we make sure we're good enough to keep in grub and gear, but not so good that others want to take us down to the dust.

But the main reason we gotta stay known is cause our gang has a secret. And when you've got a dead hidden secret you gotta front it. Mars you front it with legit stuff; casinos and joyrides. Moonbase you front it with pettiness. Kiddie or dult, brain or brute, Mars or Moonbase—there's always a front, else sniffers will wonder how you got all that fancy gear you've been sporting.

See, the real gang, the heart of the gang, are bitrunners. And bitrunning is no-air dangerous.

It's so dangerous it's the whole reason we have to keep a gang around us, like midcircle Moonbase protects the credited who live inner circle. Nega one of Riband know what we really do. They just think we're the best yoinkers, which we are, specially my Batel. And they think we chose them cause they'll grow into future best yoinkers, which they nega no way no-air will. We chose them to keep us in trouble, little trouble. We chose them to keep our gang looking a little skilled and a little more lousy and a lot of petty. Grub we yoink, and used gear and duct tape. Petty stuff, so petty that if cop Station decides to bother kiddies they go stake out the brute Starslicers for a few days. Not us.

And that is the plan. Because bitrunning is so no-air dangerous it scares even the hardest brute Crimers. Crimers who bitrun make zeroes and zeroes of credits. Dult bitrunners, like those my uncle hires, go on jobs with crazy numbers of backups, grown-up Starslicer types whose job is to look invisible and shield the bitrunner. And that job is no-air dangerous as well, though at least you got the chance to sell out your bitrunner stead of being negatid along with him.

But we don't have shields, and we don't have much else'n our finger knives. What we have is our bitcatcher install, our brains, and our secrecy. That secrecy is our outer circle.

Cop Station never did wise up to us. We bitran right under their noses for two solid years; raked up enough credits to each open an inner circle hotel if we wanted. We were never caught and never noticed and we bitran right up till Mars and my uncle.

Batel first started running cons eight years ago. Cons built around the truth are best, and just like me, Batel figured that out. First it was all truth and little con; she begged credits for being a half-orphaned kiddie with a dusted dad. As she got good and bored she added another layer and the truth con came to life—she played a con artist pretending to be a regular orphaned kiddie. Her brother Tank left his job porting baggage at the flyzone when he saw she was raking it, and they ran a modified pigeon drop with Tank as a Crimer hunter out to catch con kiddie Batel. Tank wasn't dusting then; he conned well enough following Batel's lead, but if the con fell through he fell straight back on his fists. When confused, Tank fought. That was his no-air dead end.

Webbl came next, just when both girls had passed their tenth. Batel said once that Webbl was already beautiful then, with her fine-boned face and fringed eyes. I think Tank was in love with her a little. She paired well with tiny child-like Batel—Webbl was from ten to midteen the perfect androgyne, able to pass for girl or girlie and turn heads either way.

With three of them under Batel's lead the cons became more elaborate and more dangerous. With the trickier cons came times that Tank would mess up.

This is where I enter their story.

Batel and Tank's story was simple: a dead mom and a dusted dad they avoided. Webbl was a typical outer circle orphan, parents unknown. The kiddie gangs are full of orphan center refugees. Our Leit was one, and the bitties Tap and Henry. Martha was of course not from outer circle. We should have known not to trust her. She was a credited inner circle kiddie who'd watched too many old Moonbase flicks. She pestered Batel to take her on. Later she tried to repay her with sharpened picks. You can't trust those who had choices. They think different.

Batel and Webbl were twelve then. Tank had become a full-grown dult with a taste for dust. It was low then. He could keep it hidden. So far all Batel knew was that Tank was hanging out with nasty Crimer sorts, no scoopers, but nega brain Crimers either. Brute Crimers. He was considering joining some ex-Starslicers who were hiring out as shields—and though the no-brain nega knew it—slicers. Batel and Webbl were running most of the cons by themselves, slick things that made them giggle. They talked about the future. They needed to get out into the Nine, said Batel. The tourists talked about the gambling resorts on Mars. They flashed winnings which the girls took. Though she didn't know thing one about criming on Mars, my Batel thought big and planned for it.

But the string of easy marks with fresh credits was too slick. Your shields go down when every-all's moving your way.

Batel and Webbl tried to run a conner.

You want that sob story? It isn't here, so don't think it. Bam, things happen, your life changes. You plan, and then bam, another blow, a brand new direction. Roll with that cracked rib and get up again or you die. Things are what they are.

My parents were brain Crimers, slick conners who seldom missed their mark. They used me, they taught me, they were wonk, till a ship malfunction deep-spaced them, left them bug-eyed and splattered across the galaxy. That malfunction left my uncle—a penny ante no-brain brute—with zeroes of credits, the command of a thriving fronting casino, and me.

Do I have proof that my uncle jigged the ship software? In life, in cons, you don't always need proof to know what happened. And sides, what's proof good for? Good for throwing at a judge and seeing if she'll buy a kiddie story. But they won't, they never, and you gotta depend on your brains. Your closest friend might no-air you if they had to. Even if they nega wanted that. Your own self is all you got.

My uncle caught me sniffing his setup. Poking around his files, looking for the ship software hack I knew he had. But he's a dult and my guardian. He didn't have to run any con on me, spin any elaboration, not when I was still seven years away from being a dult and four from being a legal midteen. He packed me off to onboard school and I had to go.

Life hits you, you continue. I spent most the trip planning ways to run the onboard school. I couldn't get to my uncle yet, I could at least run the other kiddies, who would no doubt be well stacked with credits. But when Batel and Webbl brought chance into my life I took it.

Jo Turn was my handler to drop me at onboard school. He'd been my regular handler on Mars, too, since I was a bitty, and though after the explosion he'd shut his mouth and quietly gone to work for my uncle—you can't blame him. We'd been through a lot. I could count on him to look the other way for the occasional disappearing act. I liked Jo Turn. But to say truth, Jo Turn was an ex-conner who couldn't give up the game. That's why, when we were doing our touristy bit on Moonbase layover, when Batel and Webbl tried to run their modified con-yoink on us, well then, that's when Jo Turn's eyes lit with the old fire. Conning the conners was just about his favorite thing in the universe.

I liked Jo Turn. This is nega for sobbing. Some things happen. Things are what they are.

Jo Turn made himself out to be the biggest mark the girls had ever seen. He swallowed their hard-luck story as if it was green cheese. Like I said, the girls had gotten careless. They talked and dreamed, but that moment was an easy tourist time, with lots of credited émeegs moving through and out to the new luxury terraformation outside of the Nine. The girls truth conned them up and down, posing as kiddies posing as legal midteens. Then Tank would gear up all official and burst in just in time. After the mark bawled, he'd loose them with a warning—and a confiscation of the credits they'd paid the girls. The mark looked extra credited or extra weak, he'd demand a hard credit bribe on top.

Jo Turn went right along with Webbl's con. He implied he had a thickness of hard credits on his person. He even gave some to Batel to "keep an eye on me." Course, both of us could see right through the girls. Good conners always know they're being conned.

Jo Turn shouldn't have been conning while he was handling me. But he looks the other way for me, I look the other way for him. Sides, even wearing all that dult makeup Batel was clearly very wonk. I let her buy me a pop and I sat blinking and kicking my heels, conning that I was younger'n my ten years, eyeing the way things progress here on Moonbase. Meanwhile, Jo Turn proceeds with the con. And when Tank bursts in with his badge, Jo Turn flips open a splashier one. He's an off-duty cop, he runs, just passing through Moonbase. He'd prefer to not tie up his vacation dragging conners to the local cop Station. But for the price of a very thick bribe . . . .

I am told that Webbl said for Tank to give it up. Real cop or no, Webbl knew when they'd been licked. Sides, it was just once, then this dult would be gone.

But Tank thought he knew better. He was half dusted anyway, and stead of giving it up or talking through it, he whipped out a fistful of finger knives. Jo Turn was no dummy, but Tank was younger and faster and he shredded Jo Turn from belly to gullet before my handler could get more'n a few slices on Tank's chest.

I knew Jo Turn was no-air gone soon as a white Webbl beckoned at Batel from around a passageway. You live your life with Crimers, you know when a drop's gone wrong. Batel patted my head and told me to be good a moment, then she hurried after Webbl.

I vanished.

It's funny. I'd managed not to think of Jo Turn for nearly four years, not till me and the girls and Tank were on that ship to Mars with our bitcatcher installs and our plans. He was a good mec. Not so slick, dicted to his cons the way Tank was to dust. But a good mec.

The thing about dults is, cops are on the lookout for them. But kiddies? They are sure we are braindead and super petty. Real cons, real yoinks—they nega think the kiddies are capable of that organization, and mostly, they are right.

The thing about dult Crimers is, they are dults first, Crimers second. The only reason for a Crimer—or regular mec—to hire a bitrunner is cause they're sporting powerful info they don't want sent through eyed channels. As for the bitrunner—once that bit packet's shot into your wrist, you slap a bit of skin culture over the install and less'n a minute it's vanished. You can walk right through security stations, right under Scanners, and nega one can read your data or even see that you have data, or an install, at all. Not less they slash your wrist, and that isn't legal anywhere in the Nine. You look clean and you could be anybody.

But smart Crimers are on the lookout for anybody. They eye behavior patterns, they learn the bitrunners and they watch to see who's making a downloaded run. They nab you. They pay you to turn. Or more likely, they cut the bit packet right out of your arteries, leaving one more bitrunner, cool and credited and dead on the ground.

Kiddie bitrunners—nobody suspected those.

With Jo Turn gone, I took my chance. I e-mailed my uncle from an untraceable account, complained I hated onboard school. Told him I was heading out of the Nine with the latest colony of émeegs and he shouldn't bother looking for me cause I would be unfindable. I got a head-toe dye-job and headed out to the outer circle, mingled with the orphans like a recent midcircle abandoned. Pretty soon I let Batel see me pull a slick bit of con/yoink, and I was in the gang.

After their con on Jo Turn went bad the three of them straightened up. They made better plans, kept eyes peeled, and Tank stopped dusting while on a job. They started looking to the future again and pulling me in was a part of thinking ahead. I was pretty sure that was all it was—my own con-savvy mother wouldn't have recognized me with the dye job—but you never knew one hundred percent what went on behind Batel's round black eyes.

The bit about keeping our nose dirty, that was Batel's slick idea. Even not growing up with the benefits of a Crimer family, even not knowing life out in the Nine, she thought of that. I give her full credit. Tank did not see its brilliance. Tank wanted to be known for being totally fuelled, possibly also brute. But he was dult then, and jonesing to split anyway. Not a couple weeks after I got near enough to him, he signed up as a shield for a bitrunner and the gang, the heart of the gang, was back down to three.

Bitrunning was old news on Mars, but it was new to Moonbase. It is beyond likely that Tank did not know what he was getting into. His bitrunner promised him a thickness of credits to stay clean and trustable and be one half the shield few times a week and he took it.

We nega thought of us bitrunning right away. First thing we did once I was on the inside was put Batel's simple-slick plan into being as cover for whatever we would do. We took on some bitties from the orphan center, couple no-brain rejects from the other gangs. Martha, the inner-circle idiot. We kept all of them in secret as to the real work, kept them busy training and yoinking and plain old goofing, and Batel and Webbl and I ran some fine slick cons.

We were cool but not very credited. And Tank as a shield was now taking in credits by the fistfuls. I followed him some, watching him, eyeing the layouts of the dult gangs. It was clear that to get what I wanted this gang had to think bigger. I saw the way cop Station treated the kiddies, like so petty. And us the pettiest of all.

It was time to get away with real action. And that action was bitrunning.

Tank had already been in several serious applications of bruteness. And two other bitrunners, not his, had been negatid in nasty ways. Outer circle Moonbase was quick to realize the potential and thereby create the danger in bitrunning. It was a big step even for a gang that thought big.

Never-less. It was done, and the three of us got our bitcatchers installed in our wrists from a guy who was leaving Moonbase and thus could keep a secret. We set up a regular deal with the two Crimers and one official smart enough to understand keeping us secret was in their own interest. We would nega have told Tank even, cept Batel insisted. We started bitrunning.

The bitcatcher install is very small. It's a tiny port just in the blue vein at your wrist—visible if you look for it, less you want to keep covering it in cultured skin. Some bitrunners cover the plastic hole with jewelry between runs; a bangle or links with a timepiece in it. That would have drawn more attention on outer circle kiddies on Moonbase. We might have gone with nothing, but Batel was passing through an inner circle tourist trap and she yoinked the whole gang cheapo plastic wrist shields like Citizen was sporting last year. Out of date gang finery for a petty-fronted gang: Batel saw the precise details that made a con into art.

We bitran on Moonbase for two years and every one of the risks we ran would be a story in itself. Some days I thought I might not carry out certain of my old plans; just park on Moonbase and rake in bitrunning credits. But then you remember that nothing lasts forever. Even dults catch on eventually, specially when Batel's less child-like and Webbl not so androgyne and even my feet are lengthening, so fast I can hardly yoink enough boots to keep up. My dye job's fading too, as my skin stretches—it's slow still, but you can tell by my feet I'm about to grow good and hard. I'm almost to my fourteenth and sometimes it hits me like a punch to the gut how little time I have left under the radar.

If I wanted to take the next step it had to be now.

I told the gang, the real gang, about my uncle deep spacing my parents. And that I had—a little—money if we could get to it. It's best to use as much of the truth as you can. Didn't need to use half my persuasions, neither. They jumped at the chance to get to Mars. So we planned a con to take us there. Never return, less we failed.

I pretended to be a lesser known Crimer contacting my uncle about expanding his business to Moonbase. It was the sort of mundane contact he'd buy, least enough to scope out the bitpacket we were sending. Though he'd be alert for cons as a matter of course, he was no paranoiac. He'd started as a brute, as I said, and conducted daily business with only a shield or two. So he'd been and so I'd confirmed with a trusted sniffer kiddie from Mars. More to the point, my uncle was a limited dult in his thinking. Less they were specially brainy, all dults saw were other dults.

It was a simple truth con far as the gang knew—me as both Moonbase Crimer and his bitrunner, Tank as my shield. I'd get a fresh dye job, play the slickest part ever. The girls would go to Mars but not to the meeting. I nega wanted Batel to be in the room, not when I couldn't swear to myself exactly how it would play out. I told them my uncle hated girls, which might well be true as he deep spaced his sister without regret. Once on Mars, I said, I would download a business proposal, stick around to discuss it as my Crimer's agent, and at some point—perhaps over a pint—give Tank the eye and jab my uncle with the poison. Tank'd clean up any shields before they knew anything had gone down.

It had to be poison; it was the simplest thing to smuggle to Mars and to my uncle. My uncle might not be paranoid wary, but still we'd nega get past his shields with guns or splosives. There was only one person on all of Moonbase who could yoink the poison from the nastiest Crimer in the spacesuit district—my Batel—and she did, bristling the laser locks and slipping past every trap as only she could. If there had been another way . . . I hated to hurt her.

We got to Mars, we got to my uncle, slicker'n anything. Batel waited nearby, a lonesome midteen slouching around the passageways. And when my uncle asked Tank politely to download his packet to the table bitcatcher, he was confused. "I'm not the bitrunner," he said. "It's him." But I was a scrawny kiddie and they didn't look twice. Tank's words were a deviation from the script and deviations put you on guard. My uncle's brute tossed me to the floor. There was a pain like a finger knife puncturing my chest and I thought maybe I cracked a rib. I curled onto my other side and looked dead, which wasn't hard except for the trouble breathing. Tank could still have talked it through, could've explained the truth as he knew it, even if he had nega the brains to figure it all.

But when confused, Tank fought.

He whipped out a fistful of finger knives and lunged at my uncle's waiting brute. Mars has slicker weapons. But Mars has nothing on Moonbase in fighting dirty. A stab and a twist, and dult-wise, the room was down to Tank and my uncle.

Tank looked at me and I saw he knew then I'd set him up, though he nega knew why. I was sorry for that. I couldn't like him, but I liked Batel for loving him. Didn't want him to think his setup was meaningless. I couldn't have got past both my uncle and the brute myself—and I definitely couldn't do it slick and untraceable like Mars demanded, not with the cards I held. Petty brute Tank was my wild card, the mec I could justify taking down or letting live, as needed.

My uncle had all the time needed in the few seconds it'd taken Tank to finish off the brute. He shot Tank down; three precise pops, no louder'n the sound Tank made as he crumpled. Then Tank was limp and burbling on the floor and my uncle had slit his skin and was massaging his arteries with something like a long skinny suction nozzle. I wondered how long he'd look for that non-existent packet. I didn't let him.

I rolled on that rib and came up behind him, glad my gasping was covered by Tank's choking. I kicked his gun with my foot and slammed the poison dart under his ear. It's the stuff they use to kill indigene beasts on new planets and the Crimers keep smuggling it around cause it's the simplest stuff to slip past ship security.

My uncle turned and looked at me, just as Tank had. But unlike Tank—he understood. Despite my disguise, he knew. I thought it would make me glad but I just felt nothing. His eyes were like my mother's, brown and bright. The memory of crazy credited-kiddie Martha attacking Batel went looping through my head, and Batel, who had once sung Martha to sleep, taking her down to the dust. Then at last my uncle's mirrored eyes glazed over and he fell next to Tank, in the blood, just lying there, breathing long and shallow. I knew it would take awhile for the poison to stop everything. But somehow I had nega known how it'd be to stand there, hunched over a cracked rib, with my two murdering dults breathing their painful breaths, one on his last wet gasps, the other lengthening into forever stillness.

One last shudder and Jo Turn's murderer was finally negatid. I dropped a handful of moondust right into his running arteries quick as I could.

Backed away just as a white Batel burst in. I knew she'd know. You live your life around Crimers, you just know when a drop's gone wrong. She would've dropped to her knees next to her stiffening brother, cept I yanked her away from the river of blood and my still-breathing uncle. Wouldn't do to be caught there, not when the scene was perfect as it was. She looked at me then with those beautiful black eyes so childlike and slick and I shivered like she'd caught me out, like I was crazy Martha myself. God, I hated to hurt Batel. But things are what they are.

I flushed my dye job, got a haircut, and intercepted the notice sent to my onboard school—kept loose ends tidy. Made it seem like we were just now coming in to Mars at the spaceport, sad and distraught, with a stumbling Batel at my side and Webbl carrying my luggage. Under my shirt, my ribs were taped with clean white bandages. My Batel had the choice to leave; the girls had plenty of bitrunning credits. But both of them stayed, and smart of them too. Within a week the judge confirmed the inheritance just as I hit my fourteenth and became a legal midteen, able to control my own future, what and how and who, all legit and above board.

See, Mars is different than Moonbase. In Mars, you have to keep your hands clean. The days of looking a little small and a lot more petty, those were over, negatid with the dead dusted Tank. This was the future, and Batel would be near me every second. She's got a part in everything. The girls and I were ready to think big and Mars would fall at our feet. Legitimacy would be our new outer circle.

Cause this was the gang, you see. This was the heart, then and future, dead or live. Tank, Webbl, me.

And Batel.

Standard Comfort Measures in Earthling Pregnancies

1. SUPPLEMENTS:

Upon discovering there has been implantation by the marvelous Xorlyn overlords, please do not self-defenestrate. For best results you will have started with the folic acid and copper supplements three months ago upon our landing, as politely requested. However do not panic if you failed to heed emergency broadcast blarings. Simply begin these pills now, as well as adding a quart of copper-enhanced prune juice to your daily regimen, available at any Xorlyn-overtaken Costco.

2. NUTRITION: DON'TS:

During your standard nineteen-month pregnancy, there is a short and easy list of foods you will not be able to eat. Please avoid deli meats, goat cheese, all food that comes from the sea, chips, ice cream, soda crackers, all food that has passed through an animal's bosoms, steak tartare, steak almondine, filet mignon, earthworms, eggs, bees, alcohol, "hard" drugs such as aspirin and crack, food that grows in the wet air (figs, birds), food that grows in the dry air (woodpeckers, oxygenated particles), and soy sauce.

3. NUTRITION: DO'S:

Vinegar is considered quite safe and you may consume as much as you wish.

4. MORNING SICKNESS:

It is quite normal to have a period of morning sickness for the first eighteen months of your pregnancy. This is your body's natural adjustment to bearing Xorlyn triplets and should not be taken for a psychological rejection of the fry, unless, of course, you are well aware that you are an unfit parent who should be rounded up behind the nearest Xorlyn Costco and shot. Xorlyns frequently take a small measure of our parent's blood to combat the inevitable nausea; that is suggested here.

Please remember that despite the nausea you will still need to consume 5,000 calories per day. Please consult the nutritive do's and don'ts.

5. OTHER SYMPTOMS:

It is quite common to feel a splendid electrical tingling in the abdomen, especially in the male half of your species whose insides will be rearranging in order to properly bear Xorlyn fry. Also common is a purple discharge around the toenails; however, should the discharge be lavender, please seek out care from the doctors at your nearest Costco.

You may also notice:
- swelling in the wrists
- engorged feelings of despair
- stretch marks around the abdomen, hips, and thighs, as well as in one random place where the third fry chooses to nest
- night terrors
- increased attraction to Xorlyns (less commonly; decreased attraction to Xorlyns)
- a rudimentary tail

6. LABOR:

Nineteen months from now, you will feel a cold leaden sensation in your extremities signifying that birth is imminent. Please do not be alarmed at the lack of a doctor. This will be happening to everyone all over the world in the same few weeks. Home births are a natural part of existence. The human body was made to bear Xorlyn fry in the most natural way possible. The following steps will guide you through the pleasant and natural process:

- When you first feel contractions, start walking. This will encourage the Xorlyn triplets to be born. You should have already prepared a birthing bag that you can carry with you as you walk for the six days of labor. You will not need to eat, but please continue to drink your daily quart of copper-enhanced prune juice.

- When the Xorlyn fry are ready to come out, lie down and make yourself as comfortable as possible. Try to breathe naturally through the process. Xorlyns have been impregnating alien species for millennia and it is a perfectly well-established process. Try visualizing something relaxing, like a sandy beach or a star going nova.

- For women, the two Xorlyn fry nestled in your womb will try to find a natural place to swim free. If the third fry is also nestled near by—and not inside a major organ—congratulations! You will have the easiest possible 72-hour birth, and will be around to repeat the process once these fry have grown to full size in two years.

- All others—please remember that sometimes Nature is only able to select the fittest of the species to continue. Try to enjoy your remaining months with your fry, and be easy in the knowledge that if you panic now, the fry will immediately tunnel to your heart and explode.

SUPER-BABY-MOMS GROUP SAVES THE DAY!

From: Stef Jones-Tanaka <bilingualbiologist@supermail.com>
To: <superbabymoms@superdupergroups.com>
Subject: Intros

Hey Super Moms! Here's the email group I mentioned to a couple of you at preschool today. Teacher Stacie said there are four of us families in the system right now at Little Darlings Preschool and shared your emails with me—hope that's ok! I think we can learn from each other! Please go ahead and introduce yourself and your kids, and feel free to share a problem you're having right now. Chances are you're not alone.

As for me, I have twin four-year-olds Isabel Ko and Beatrix Ai. Isabel has super strength and Beatrix has X-ray vision. Isabel is going through a hitting phase. Our front door has been obliterated twice. Beatrix knows all about sex from looking through the neighbors' walls (apparently the neighbors have way more fun than we do.) I'm tempted to put both girls in a cement dome covered in foil until they're twenty.

Hope to hear from you all!

hugs, Stef
Live each day like the planet might explode tomorrow. Who knows, right?

*

From: Zoë Wallis <zoeboe@supermail.com>
To: <superbabymoms@superdupergroups.com>
Re: Intros

OMG Stef, thanks for starting this group. I have a boy (Rocket)
who is three, and we just had a new baby (Lilac), who is five months.
Rocket was doing just fine up until the baby was born. And now . . .
OMG I don't even know. Have any of you dealt with kids who won't
stop stretching? Apparently he's been tying knots around the other
children with his stretched-out legs. I've tried bribing him with stick-
ers. Also with capes. Nothing.

I cringe every time I pick him up from Little Darlings now. Teacher Stacie keeps talking to him about "helping hands" and "human
hands" but he just laughs and sticks out his tongue till it touches the
other wall. Going crazy here, and we don't even know what Lilac's
powers are yet. Dread finding out it's something like super boobs,
because I will NOT be down with buying her a spandex leotard with
holes cut out of it.

Zoë "Human Hands are not Stretchy Hands" Wallis

*

From: Alícia Marquez <CEOmarquez@supermail.com>
To: <superbabymoms@superdupergroups.com>
Re: Intros

Hello Stef and Zoë. I have one daughter, Alexandra-Maria, who's
three and in Rocket's class. Forgive my bluntness, Zoë, but my daughter and I have had some serious talks already about Rocket's behavior. She knows that it is unacceptable to submit to his inappropriate
elasticity—not just for herself, but as an example for other girls who
may be too timid to speak up. (I am glad you do not see it as a "boys

will be boys" issue, as I find far too many mothers do.)

Unfortunately, not only is my daughter too shy to tell Rocket how she feels about his knots, her super power is that of turning herself inaudible. We are hoping it will be accompanied by invisibility as well (her grandmother has both talents), but so far she remains a frustratingly symbolic metaphor for being both a woman, and a woman of color, in this world.

Best, Alícia
alt.email: ceo@marquez.com

*

From: Zoë Wallis <zoeboe@supermail.com>
To: <superbabymoms@superdupergroups.com>
Re: Intros

Oh god, Alícia, I am SO sorry. I swear weeee are wroking on it.

Will;; write more later. Rocket has me tied to chair. Am puishing keyboard buttons with nose.

Zoë "Down with the Patriarchy, Even When He's 3" Wallis

*

From: Tiffy Turner<spandexmom@supermail.com>
To: <superbabymoms@superdupergroups.com>
Re: Intros

Hi ladies! Sorry for the delay but we just got back from getting Hadley a new skirt for flying practice.

I am blessed with three amazingly super children over here. Hadley is our flyer—she just turned seven. Williamsburg is four and his talent is weather control. He's in the class with Stef's darling twins. And Dartmouth is two months old and already showing signs of being clever with fire—she lit the candles on Hadley's birthday cake last week!

Zoe, hang in there, I'm sure your baby will turn up with something eventually! All my super kids showed their talents by at least three months but it generally is much later, as I'm sure you know from Rocket.

Stef said we should each share a problem we're facing right now, but honestly we have no problems! Life is, well, "super!"

PS: Does anyone know who the kid was who brought slugs to school last week? Apparently they escaped. Williamsburg found one in his snack container and he was quite aggrieved. I wouldn't be so upset only Williamsburg likes to carry a shaker of sea salt for his snack and the slug died when it came into contact. Also it was an antique snack container signed by Amazing Man.

xoxo Tiffy
"Hadley is the most delightful student it's ever been my privilege to teach!" — Mrs. Stout, 1st grade teacher

*

From: Stef Jones-Tanaka <bilingualbiologist@supermail.com>
To: <superbabymoms@superdupergroups.com>
Subject: Slugs

Ooh, sorry, Tiffy. The slugs were Beatrix's doing. She wanted to see what they would look like inside things—including, apparently, Williamsburg's lunchbox. We have confiscated the slugs and returned them to the yard.

Thanks for your kind words on the girls. I've always thought Williamsburg was such a darling child—so nicely dressed, and he always asks me what I think of the weather. Now I understand why.

Alícia, I understand your frustration, believe me. It's so hard raising girls in this world—especially girl supers. Mine don't need any help fighting their own battles (which is both good and bad, when you're called in because Isabel punched the cubbies to smithereens!), but I can *well* imagine your frustration.

Zoë, hang in there too—things will get better. My younger brother's talent is levitating others. Preschool was a nightmare. And grade school. And junior high, come to that. But it did get better. Now he has a good job with the coast guard hoisting drowning people out of the ocean, and is super responsible.

hugs, Stef
Live each day like the planet might be wiped out by mutated giraffe-flu tomorrow. Who knows, right?

*

From: Zoë Wallis <zoeboe@supermail.com>
To: <superbabymoms@superdupergroups.com>
Re: Intros

Hi, Tiffany. Yes, I'm sure Lilac's talent will show up soon. We're not worried.

BTW, I'm sure I'm just confused, but I thought you had four children? There's a teenage girl who's been picking up Williamsburg all summer and I thought she said she was his big sister?

Zoë "The Baby Ate Holes In My Brain but Maybe That's Just Her Talent" Wallis

*

From: Tiffy Turner<spandexmom@supermail.com>
To: <superbabymoms@superdupergroups.com>
Re: Intros

Hi, Zoe. It's Tiffy, actually, not Tiffany.

Yes, our oldest, Amherst, is 14, but she's not a super, so I didn't mention her as I thought this list was about parenting our supers? (Although sometimes I like to joke that she has the talent of driving us all insane. She's suddenly refused to accompany Hadley to flying lessons, even though she's always loved it. She recently covered her entire room in foil, which as a super myself is hard not to take personally. And, she used to spend all her time writing stories which was at least harmless, but now she's switched over to the drums, which is driving us completely bananas. If anyone has any suggestions for stopping this, I'm all ears. Not literally, as my talent is calming, not shapeshifting.)

Stef—thank you. I always thought Williamsburg might have a second talent for fashion, but his father doesn't like me to suggest that. Williamsburg designed my most recent super outfit, though. (I mean, not that I'm currently fighting crime or anything as I make sure to put my kids first. But you know how it is—hard to give up the spandex, you know?) Anyway, everyone always asks who the label is.

xo Tiffy
"Williamsburg has the best Helping Hands I have ever seen!" — *Teacher Stacie*

*

From: Zoë Wallis <zoeboe@supermail.com>
To: <superbabymoms@superdupergroups.com>

Re: Intros

Hi, Tiffy. It's Zoë actually, not Zoe, but I realize it can be hard to find those strange characters on your keyboard if you're not used to French words.

Zoë "Alt-shift-quotation mark, e" Wallis

*

From: Stef Jones-Tanaka <bilingualbiologist@supermail.com>
To: <superbabymoms@superdupergroups.com>
Subject: Checking In

Hey Super Moms! I just realized it's been a whole week since we last spoke! I'm sure you guys are just as busy as I am—I've been trying to start back into part-time work at my old lab and it's a strain to find the time to do everything I used to do *and* work as well.

Tiffy, I've been thinking about your difficulty with Amherst, and I wonder if she's feeling a little left out at not getting to go to flying practice and weather practice and fire practice herself, you know? It may not be her thing, but Teacher Stacie said she's looking for a teenage helper to finish out the rest of the summer. Maybe a little responsibility and money would make her feel like she has a talent, too. I know *I'm* glad to be back in the lab, and not *just* be in my mommy role, as much as I love the girls! Just a thought. :-)

hugs, Stef
Live each day like a genetically-engineered dragon might fry the earth tomorrow. Who knows, right?

*

From: Tiffy Turner<spandexmom@supermail.com>
To: <superbabymoms@superdupergroups.com>
Re: Checking In

Thanks, Stef. I'll have her drop off her résumé.

Tiffy
"Seriously, I would babysit that darling Dartmouth for free!"
— Angie, nanny

*

From: Stef Jones-Tanaka <bilingualbiologist@supermail.com>
To: <superbabymoms@superdupergroups.com>
Subject: New Member

Hi again Super Moms! I think we got off to a bit of a rocky start but I still think there's a lot we can help each other with!

I invited a new mother to join as Teacher Stacie said this morning that a kid in the 3's class suddenly developed a talent! She said his family wasn't expecting it at all—how exciting! Hopefully she'll post later.

Hope you all are doing well. Tiffy, I'm *so* excited to see Amherst helping out with the classes at school! Teacher Stacie said she's been telling stories to the kids and seems to be really enjoying herself! Isabel and Beatrix came home last week full of a long story she told them about a girl who transformed into a sparkly fire truck and flew to the moon with her sidekick Iceman to battle a bunch of fire-monkeys or something. Very imaginative kiddo you've got there!

hugs, Stef
Live each day like a plague of super-spiders might web everything tomorrow. Who knows, right?

*

From: Deiondre Johnson <tiredmom@supermail.com>
To: <superbabymoms@superdupergroups.com>
Subject: Help

Hi, I'm Deiondre. Stef invited me. My son, Denzel, suddenly discovered this weekend he could make water freeze. Frankly we are all shocked around here as no one in our family has ever had this. I mean ice cubes sound nice as it's summer and all, but it's downright astonishing to turn on the shower and get icicles. And then I guess he froze some kid's tongue to his drink at school today. I'm already at my wit's end and hoping for suggestions.

Deiondre
Sent from my iPhone. Please excuse typos as I'm probably asleep.

*

From: Zoë Wallis <zoeboe@supermail.com>
To: <superbabymoms@superdupergroups.com>
Re: Help

Hi Deiondre—lots of empathy here as that must have been shocking. We were prepared for a super and it was still startling the first time Rocket shot his arm across the room to grab a cookie out of Dad's hand. Of course it's helpful if one or both parents are supers—his dad is able to make things briefly turn to jello (I know, I know, that's what she said) but seriously, if you can turn a super tantrum into a pile of goo for one minute it does work wonders.

PS Don't feel too bad about the tongue freezing as that was my son and I'm sure he deserved it.

Zoë "Any Day Where My Kid Wasn't The Worst Is a Good Day" Wallis

*

From: Tiffy Turner<spandexmom@supermail.com>
To: <superbabymoms@superdupergroups.com>
Re: Help

Deiondre,

I'd be happy to have my son Williamsburg talk to him if you'd like. It can be helpful to have a well-behaved super around to show him the ropes.

And I understand you about it being surprising. No one in my family was a super and then suddenly I turned out to be super skilled at calming. And I was quite a late bloomer as it didn't happen until after Amherst was born, probably because I never needed it before. She had colic and was so fussy that something just clicked on. Honestly, that's why there's such a gap between Amherst and Hadley—I joined a league and helped subdue riots in heels and spandex for seven years before my husband pointed out it was time to have the other children we'd wanted to have.

    Tiffy
    "Hadley is the most talented super I've seen in years." — Dr. Humphries, flying teacher

*

From: Alícia Marquez <CEOmarquez@supermail.com>
To: <superbabymoms@superdupergroups.com>
Re: Help

Hello Deiondre, I am glad that you have joined the group. Alexandra-Maria told me all about the little boy at school today who kept putting ice cubes down her dress. She explained to me that it meant he liked her, but I explained that there are more appropriate ways of showing affection and they all involve keeping one's hands to oneself.

Believe me, Deiondre (and Zoë), I do empathize with the difficulties of socializing a boy to master appropriate and respectful behavior. But I was raised to speak my mind and I feel that it would, in fact, be disrespectful of you two women if I did not alert you to the situation and show that I have confidence that these situations will be ameliorated.

Zoë, apparently Rocket is doing better about not tying his legs around Alexandra-Maria's legs. However, he stretched himself up to the roof today and was dropping Cheerios on her head.

Best, Alícia
alt.email: ceo@marquez.com

*

From: Zoë Wallis <zoeboe@supermail.com>
To: <superbabymoms@superdupergroups.com>
Subject: Cheerios

Working on it.

Zoë "Cheerio Mom" Wallis

*

From: Stef Jones-Tanaka <bilingualbiologist@supermail.com>
To: <superbabymoms@superdupergroups.com>
Subject: Another!!

Super Moms, Teacher Stacie told me *another* kid popped up with super talent today! This is really exciting. I mean, Stacie said they'd never had so many supers at once when it was just the original four families, and now two new supers in one week???

I would say there's something in the water, but as I'm sure you all know, super ability is not a bug and is in fact passed genetically. I'm sure this is completely explicable by some latent recessive gene suddenly appearing. And then, it's perfectly natural to have cluster groups form—a bunch of things happen at once and it appears to be statistically significant, but in fact it's completely random distribution.

Still, what are the odds? No, seriously, what are the odds? I think I may need to go down to Little Darlings preschool and take a look around.

hugs, Stef
Live each day like the earth might turn to jelly tomorrow. Who knows, right?

*

From: Joseph Goldman<j.goldman@supermail.com>
To: <superbabymoms@superdupergroups.com>
Subject: Introducing Ourselves

Hi—my son, Isaiah, is a student at Little Darlings Preschool. Just now he explained to me, very seriously, that he has a hitherto unsuspected talent for swimming under water and never needing to come up for air. In the face of my skepticism, he demonstrated in the bathtub. This seems harmless enough (albeit pruney.) I am told that those of you on this email group face this sort of thing every day. Any thoughts?

Sincerely, Joseph

*

From: lindsey morgan<linzbear@supermail.com>
To: <superbabymoms@superdupergroups.com>
Subject: Can You explain this please

Hi This is lindsey mom of trooper in fours class do you know what is going on with this super powers thing? I thought this was just on tv but teacher stacie says to contact you for help. i should mention that trooper came home flying today this is very distrubing. can you tell me how to get rid of this? trooper is on the ceiling fan again i have to go

lindsey

*

From: Felicia Kwiatkowski<FeliciaK@supermail.com>
To: <superbabymoms@superdupergroups.com>
Subject: TRUCK TRUCK TRUCK

You guys! I am FREAKED OUT! My daughter just turned herself into a TRUCK! An HONEST TO GOD HUMVEE. I mean, a little tiny one—conservation of mass and all that but WTFHOLY-BBQ. We have no problem with having a tiny super in the family but I guess Karolina and I always thought if our kid developed a talent it would be something we'd heard of like invisibility or flying. WTF TRUCK.

Felicia

*

From: Stef Jones-Tanaka <bilingualbiologist@supermail.com>
To: <superbabymoms@superdupergroups.com>
Subject: COME TO THE PRESCHOOL NOW

Um, I think anyone who's not at work better get down here
ASAP. Every single kid at this preschool is now a super. One kid
is cloning himself. One kid is turning into a monkey. One kid is
turning into a giant grilled cheese. I . . . don't even know. Rocket
has tied up Teacher Stacie with his legs, Zoë, and is using his hands
to lift the other preschool helpers up onto the roof. Another girl is
making walls of water around the roof and Denzel is freezing them.
Isabel is running around screaming ISABEL SMASH. The road is
torn up.

HELP.

*Live each day like the planet might turn into an orange and be
eaten by Captain Giant-Man tomorrow. Who knows, right?*

*

From: Zoë Wallis <zoeboe@supermail.com>
To: <superbabymoms@superdupergroups.com>
Re: COME TO THE PRESCHOOL NOW

Stef, I'm here but I can't see you through the cloud of squid ink.
Can you whistle? My only talent is speed reading, and that's not doing me much. Also if you see a stretched-out limb that would be my
son.

OMG those are SO not helping hands.

Tiffy, I hate to say it, but I think we need your calming powers.
Where are you?

Zoë "Knows When to Call for Reinforcements" Wallis

*

From: Alícia Marquez <CEOmarquez@supermail.com>
To: <superbabymoms@superdupergroups.com>
Subject: New Supers

I am terribly sorry, but I am in the middle of a board meeting. I have asked my secretary to drive over on my behalf. She is a black belt and is also bringing Starbucks. I have texted Alexandra-Maria to remind her that now would be a good time to form alliances with the other girl children, such as Isabel and Beatrix, in order to bring Rocket and Denzel and so on to justice.

With the perspective that comes with distance, I am wondering: does it not seem peculiar that all these new supers started appearing just after Amherst started working there? And that some of their new powers may correspond to Amherst's highly fertile imagination? I would explore the possibility that Amherst is a super after all: I believe her talent is that of creating supers.

Stef, as a biologist, is such a thing possible?

Best, Alícia
alt.email: ceo@marquez.com

*

From: Stef Jones-Tanaka <bilingualbiologist@supermail.com>
To: <superbabymoms@superdupergroups.com>
Re: New Supers

Not only possible, but highly likely. Beatrix has looked through the walls to the classroom and says that Amherst is huddled under the craft project table, screaming "Turn it off! Turn it off!" I'm currently watching Isabel smash our way in so I can try to talk Amherst down.

It's possible she might be able to get through to the children.

Tiffy, we need you now!! Are you out of coverage or something? Do you have a bat signal? Look, if we get through today, we really need to all have bat signals, okay? It's not helicopter parenting, just good common sense.

Live each day like a pack of cards might come to life and wipe us out in a game of War tomorrow. Who knows, right?

*

From: Zoë Wallis <zoeboe@supermail.com>
To: <superbabymoms@superdupergroups.com>
Re: COME TO THE PRESCHOOL NOW

Rocket found me! Grabbed me & retracted me onto the roof. Am up here w/bunch of frightened and/or tantruming mini-supers and pissed-off Teacher Stacie. (Not sure we'll be allowed to continue being Little Darlings, frankly.) Can calm down Rocket, but not all these others.

Oh thk goodness. Woman in spandex w/baby Bjorn must be Tiffy. Gonna have Rocket bring her up . . . .

Zoë "Texting Champeen of the World" Wallis

*

From: lindsey morgan<linzbear@supermail.com>
To: <superbabymoms@superdupergroups.com>
Subject: Can You explain this please

Hi i heard sirens and then logged on and found this. drove right over and i see You people have a lot of nerve can you explain what sort of devil magic you have sucked my child into. trooper is a Good kid and now she is flying around and around the school like a tetherball. oh wait everything suddenly got really calm and i feel really good about everything. this will all be all right won't it.

lindsey

*

From: Alícia Marquez <CEOmarquez@supermail.com>
To: <superbabymoms@superdupergroups.com>
Re: New Supers

I'm out of the board meeting. What's the status? Did Tiffy make it?

Best, Alícia
alt.email: ceo@marquez.com

*

From: Zoë Wallis <zoeboe@supermail.com>
To: <superbabymoms@superdupergroups.com>
Subject: Update Everything OK

Don't worry, Alícia, it's all under control. Tiffy calmed everybody—I mean EVERYBODY and we all feel really good now. Rocket lowered everyone down from the roof and I think he really had a breakthrough. He said "Oh, THESE are my helping hands" as he put everyone gently on the sidewalk. Tiffy is in there with Amherst who is in the hiccupping stage of crying. So is Tiffy.

Zoë "Rooftop" Wallis

*

From: Tiffy Turner<spandexmom@supermail.com>
To: <superbabymoms@superdupergroups.com>
Subject: Thank you

Moms, thanks for all your help yesterday. I admit when Stef started this group I didn't understand the point. I thought I had it all figured out. But now . . .

When I got to Little Darlings yesterday I saw Zoë up on the roof-top helping control a bunch of frightened and inexperienced super kids. (My Williamsburg said he was about to summon a flash flood to help get them off the roof, until Zoë talked him out of it.) I calmed down the toddlers and then made a beeline for my poor Amherst. I found her sniffling with Stef, who was explaining to her very rationally about genetics and superpowers and how none of this meant she was a *bad* person—she just needs to learn how to *control* it. It seemed to be sinking in. (She might even unfoil her room.) Alícia's secretary had lattes for everyone while we cleaned up the mess. Even our newest members, Deiondre and Felicia and Joseph, were helping, and they'd never encountered super tantrums before. It really does take a village.

And as for me . . . I never realized that my own talent's appear-ance was due to my daughter. Tom and I must both have a recessive somewhere way back to produce Amherst, and baby Amherst *needed* me to calm her. Odds are, my three younger kids probably owe their talents to Amherst, too. Amherst and I are going to go away for a spe-cial girls' weekend and then . . . I think I'm going to go back to being Anti-Riot Grrrl again. While we were huddled under the table, Am-herst told me a story about a mother minivan who could be anything she wanted to be. I think it might be time to do that.

xo Tiffy
"I want Amherst to tell me the one about the glittery fire truck again" – Hazel, 4

*

From: Stef Jones-Tanaka <bilingualbiologist@supermail.com>
To: <superbabymoms@superdupergroups.com>
Subject: New Members

Hi, So Very Many Super Moms and Dads! I've sent out invites
to all the parents at Little Darlings, so we're about to get an influx of,
oh, forty new members or so. Maybe eighty if both parents join in.
Don't be shy, new parents! We're all in this together. Teacher Stacie
says she can't kick us all out, but that we'd better band together and
be on the ball. I think with your help we can do that.

hugs, Stef
*Live each day like your children might destroy the preschool to-
morrow. Who knows, right?*

That Seriously Obnoxious Time I Was Stuck at Witch Rimelda's One Hundredth Birthday Party

So, reason number 572 why living with a wicked witch sucks? Sometimes it's a gorgeous summer Saturday, and instead of getting a well-deserved break from Sarmine's weird witchy chores like dusting the dried newts, you end up as an unpaid babysitter for a party full of little witches.

I set out the plates and forks for the birthday cake while surveying the swimming pool full of witch-kids. From up here they looked like any small children having fun—laughing and splashing and squealing and biting. Except, if you got close enough, you could hear them threatening to turn each other into frogs.

Around me, Witch Sarmine and all her nasty witch friends hovered around the pool like we were the first course at this birthday party. In a way, I suppose we were.

"My little girl is already hexing the mailman," cooed a witch with flame-red hair. "You won't believe what she can do with some earwigs and a bit of pumpkin puree."

"The twins have grown out of earwigs," drawled a dark-haired witch. "I mean, they're all right, if you're not skilled enough yet to use squirrel droppings."

"My daughter wouldn't be caught dead with squirrel droppings," said the redhead. "She has too much class."

"Ladies and token gentlemen," said a platinum-blonde witch wearing a skimpy pink bikini. "Please raise your glasses of fermented pixie juice. We are here to toast my precious mother Rimelda, who turns . . . one hundred today. Rimelda?"

A bony witch who looked about a hundred and fifty nodded sourly to all of us from her plastic lounge chair, martini in hand. See, witches look the age they feel on the inside, and apparently Rimelda was not happy with her current state of existence. "Happy Birthday to meee," she slurred. "Ain't life a—"

"All right, kids, everyone in the pool!" trilled the blonde witch. The last couple kids cannonballed in, splashing everything.

My guardian, Sarmine Scarabouche, moved closer to me, drink in hand. Alone among the witches, she was definitely not wearing a swimsuit, or even any sort of—heaven forbid—shorts. Her silver bob was untouched by the heat. Her eyebrows drew neatly into a point as she glared down at me.

I wanted to get in that swimming pool about as badly as I wanted to get in a tank of sharks. But Sarmine has a way of dealing out revolting punishments, like making everything I eat taste like brussels sprouts dipped in horseradish, and if I wanted to live to see tenth grade in the fall, I'd better do what she wanted.

I set down the plastic forks and slid into the water.

The water felt good on the hot summer day. It would have been a lovely afternoon if there had been anyone my age at the party. Oh, and if they weren't all witches. One of them bit me.

"Ready the pool!" said the blonde witch.

A pile of tiny inflatables shaped like octopi rained down upon us. They were muddy green, about the size of my palm.

"Ooh, look at the cutie-pies," said the little girl next to me. She was wearing solid pink, from her ruffled swimsuit to her pigtail bows, and looked about four. "Such sweet little baby krakens."

"Watch out," I said. I blew at the one floating towards me. "They may look like toys now, but you know what the witches are like. That blonde witch has something unpleasant planned for us, I'm sure of it."

"That blonde witch is my mom," said the pink girl. "Esmerelda."

"Ah," I said. "Well. Be warned. This is one of those awful, fake, pretend-it's-not-a-competition competitions. I can tell."

Pink looked down her nose at me, an expression I had seen many times from my guardian. "Of course it is," she said. "Where's your pouch of ingredients?"

"I don't have ingredients," I said back with as much scorn as I could muster to a pink glitter bomb. "I am not a witch."

She raised a skinny arm out of the water and displayed the waterproof pink pouch buckled to it. A pink wand with a giant star on the end was tucked inside. "Sucks to be you," she said.

Out of the corner of my eye I could see the witches ringing the pool, each one standing near her kid. Sarmine's familiar ice-chip glare froze my bones. She mouthed: "Don't humiliate me."

Esmerelda blew a dusting of some sort of powder over us—it looked like cinnamon—and raised her wand. "Release the krakens!"

The tiny pool inflatables came to life.

Okay, maybe this wasn't going to be so bad. The little krakens were kind of cute, as Pink had said. Their menacing arm-wavings were tiny and adorable.

And then I looked closer. Surely that kraken had been the size of my palm before? Now it was definitely the size of a dinner plate. "They're growing!" shrieked one of the witch-kids at the other end of the pool.

I groaned. Here I was, minding my own business, and I was about to be boa-constricted by an oversized pool toy for the witches' amusement. Worst birthday party ever.

I glanced over at my new friend. Young Pink was not as confident as she had pretended. She tossed a yellow powder at the kraken, pointed her wand, and pronounced some magic words with a wary, defiant look on her face. Nothing happened. Her face fell. She saw me watching her and turned away, fumbling in her pouch as the kraken plumped larger and larger. "I meant to do that," she mumbled.

I felt bad for her, but I had my own gigantic kraken to deal with. It was now the size of an overfed housecat and it was advancing, tentacles waving.

And I had no magic.

Didn't want to have magic. Never had wanted to have magic.

. . . Okay, so it would have come in handy right about then.

I waved my arms at the kraken and muttered, "Shoo. Abracadabra. Beat it."

It kept coming.

Across the pool, the other children were dispatching their own monsters and climbing happily out of the pool to their applauding mothers. One had made his kraken super-heavy. It sunk to the bottom of the pool in a small whirlpool of bubbles. As I watched, another turned hers into smoke, and it vanished. It was down to me and Pink, and each of our krakens was now the size of a Great Dane.

An air-filled tentacle wrapped around my arm. Another grabbed my leg. My back was against the pool wall—I couldn't go any farther.

No more time to lose. Scrabbling around on the ground behind me, my fingers landed on a small chipboard box. Another tentacle found my neck. Choking, I pulled the box forward, straining to see what I was holding. The plastic forks. Forks scattered everywhere, bobbing up and down on the waves of the kraken-infested pool. I scooped up a handful and plunged them into the kraken bearing down on me. "Die, die, die!" I shrieked, stabbing at the inflated beast with a pile of plastic prongs.

It shouldn't have worked, except that the plastic had been stretched really thin as the mini-inflatable had become a giant monster. On the fifth "Die," the prongs went all the way through, plunging me down into the water with the force of my blow. The kraken collapsed as the air wheezed out of it. I looked up in triumph.

The witches were cackling behind their hands and Sarmine was shaking her head in shame.

Not how you're supposed to do it. As usual.

I clambered out of the pool to where Sarmine stood, arms folded. "Why didn't you use the Reversion Spell I left out for you to study last week?" she said. "It would have sent the giant krakens right back to the witch who cast the spell. The ingredients are even right here at hand. One blade of grass. One splash of chlorinated water. One—"

"Wow, that sounds brilliant," I said, rolling my eyes. Sarmine never lets facts like my not having witch blood stop her from loading me down with witchy things to learn. She's so certain that if she just finds the one thing to get through to me, I'll magically (ha) become like all her loathsome witch friends, and spend the rest of my life causing chaos wherever I go.

Poor Pink was still facing down her kraken. She had managed to turn it blue, and it was emitting a strong scent of skunk. She pulled one last powder from her pouch. It was bright orange.

"You can do it, honey," called Esmerelda from the side of the pool. Pink looked up at her mother, and a nod passed between them. Pink sprinkled a pinch of the orange powder all over the kraken and pointed her star wand, shouting confidently, "Vilikoo!"

The kraken, which had been growing relatively slowly, gave a huge groan and doubled in size. Then tripled. Then it was the size of the pool. "Eep," squeaked Pink, and then I couldn't see her under the inflatable.

Esmerelda squealed. "My baby!" She grabbed a pinch of something from her purse and sprinkled it on the giant kraken, flicking her wand and muttering words as she did so. There was a loud pop—and the kraken was no more. Esmerelda hoisted her little pink girl out of the water. "Oh, my darling," she cooed. "Did the wriggly thing almost get you? Mama helps."

A disheartened Pink shrugged off her mother's hands. She looked humiliated.

The little dark-haired girl who had been first to dispatch her kraken was presented with a prize of a necklace strung with three leprechaun teeth. She looked ecstatic.

One of the two male witches at the party clapped his hands for attention. "Now kids, the grown-ups have a lot to talk about. Run along to the pool house for a bit before we bring out the cake."

"Camellia's in charge, kids," called the redhead. "Try not to hurt her." The others laughed snidely and my face flamed. Sarmine pretended not to hear them.

I followed the troop of witchy ankle-biters over to the pool house. It was pretty swanky: fitted out with a big-screen TV and fluffy towels and a rock-climbing wall over a hot tub. Hanging from the ceiling were a couple dozen stuffed black bats.

"Grandmother's old familiars," Pink explained as she tugged on her pink sundress. "She saves them, if they haven't been, like, exploded or something." It did give the pool house that certain witchy je ne sais quoi.

The gaggle of holy terrors ran for the rock-climbing wall, while Pink and I plopped down on a waterproof couch in front of the TV. She looked despondent.

"Cheer up," I said. "I bet you're not the first little kid to lose that contest. Besides, you're what, four? You'll catch up with the others."

Pink glared at me. "I'm ten."

Oops. "Forgive me," I said. "You look about four."

"I feel about four," Pink said glumly. "Mom always tells me my spells are only as good as a preschooler's. She even snuck me that orange powder today, though that's technically cheating." Her shoulders slumped. "Not that it helped. It was supposed to shrink the kraken. I couldn't even do that right, and the powder was already prepared for me."

Two of the children came wandering over from the rock-climbing wall. They had identical dark curly hair, and one was the little girl who had won the teeth necklace. She sniffed. "I never let someone else prepare my own powder," she said. "How do you know what's in it?"

"Must be nice to be perfect," muttered Pink.

The little girl and her brother plopped down on the couch next to us. "I'm Alejandra, and this is Alberto," she said to me. "We're six. And I want to know what the grown-ups are doing. Don't you?" She unzipped a camo-patterned pouch around her thigh and began rifling through it for powders and spices.

"Yeah," I said. I watched Alejandra mix ingredients with intense concentration. Her secret ingredient seemed to be a tiny glitter shaker. After she added a shake of that, she poked her wand in her palm and flicked her fistful of glittery stuff all over the TV.

The swimming pool came into focus. "Can you turn up the volume?" I said.

Alejandra looked at me pointedly. "You're sitting on the remote."

"Oh." I dug it from the couch cushions and unmuted the TV.

"Poor Mother is in the dumps," Esmerelda was cooing. "I mean . . . just look at her. It's her hundredth birthday party and she looks . . . well."

"About a hundred and fifty," piped up the redhead.

"Darling," said Esmerelda, patting her mother's hair. "It's not you. It was that mean old librarian." The TV magically panned to a close-up of Rimelda, who looked annoyed by both the anecdote and by her cooing daughter.

"Ugh, she's awful," I said. "She's like the suburban mom from hell. She even gives witches a bad name."

"Again, that's my mom," said Pink.

"Right, sorry."

"Rimelda's my grandmother," she said. "The school librarian thought she was my great-grandmother."

"I can see how that would be upsetting."

"Especially to my mom. She can't imagine herself as twenty-five if her mom looks a hundred and fifty. The strain is wearing on her. She even flipped out and started cussing at the librarian, and she never does anything that tacky. The cracks are beginning to show."

I watched the platinum blonde on the big screen as she told the same story that Pink had just told. She carried it off with a laugh, but when she got to the fatal words "great-grandmother," Pink was right. Her mask slipped just a little. She went from twenty-five to seventy and back again in a blink.

"So you see," said Esmerelda. "We need to cheer Rimelda up. I propose we get back at this revolting librarian."

Witches are always up for being nasty for no particular reason. The others lifted their martini glasses and cheered the blonde on.

Well, except for Sarmine, who is a law unto herself. One silver eyebrow raised and she said superciliously, "Oh, come now, Esmerelda. This isn't about your mother. You just want to get your digs in."

"Excuse me, I forgot you weren't a real witch," said Esmerelda.

Sarmine rolled her eyes. "Forgive me if I save my powers for producing actual change in the world, and not for retaliating against a librarian who truthfully pointed out the fact that you are older than dirt."

"Pfft," said Esmerelda drunkenly and dismissively. She looked around and her eyes lit on the banana bread Sarmine had baked for Rimelda. "We'll send her that," she crowed. "An 'apology' gift for my unkind words to her. Everyone, put your worst hex in it." She glared at the witches in turn. "Remember, this affects all of us. Look at you poor women, worn down by thousands of micro-aggressions of people presuming you're aging. If not for those horrible people, you all would look like me." She smoothed her pink bikini. "Well. More like me, anyway."

The witches crowded around the cake, cackling. "I'm putting in toads," said one. "Sting rays," said another. The screen went to a nice wide-angle shot of all the witches closing in.

"This is terrible," wailed Pink. "I like the librarian. Everyone likes her. And she always lets me sit on the pink beanbag and read when I want to get away from the other kids."

"Are the other kids mean?" I said.

Pink sniffled. "They think I'm weird. You know."

I did know. A weird home life is just the sort of thing the other kids pick up on. I've spent my whole life trying to hide that I live with a wicked witch. One slipup like your mom delivering poisoned baked goods to everyone's favorite librarian and your life is shot.

I couldn't do something about my own witch.

But I could help Pink.

I jumped to my feet. "We won't let her destroy your life," I said. "We're going to stop her."

Pink just looked at me. "My mom's embarrassed by me because my spells stink, in case you've forgotten," she said. "And you're not even a witch."

"We've got eight more kids here whose spells don't suck," I said. I wheeled to face the room. Alejandra and Alberto had lost interest in the TV and had returned to the rock-climbing wall. Several more kids were busy dunking one of the stuffed bats in the hot tub. Another two were compounding some sort of potion that smelled like rotten eggs. "Hey," I said. "Hey, all of you!"

The rotten eggs potion bubbled up in a gust of yellow. The bat started to disintegrate in the hot tub.

"Listen up!" shrieked Pink. The kids' heads momentarily swiveled toward us.

"We're going to stop the witches from delivering that banana bread," I said.

"Why?" shouted one of the kids.

"I like hexed bread," shouted another.

"It'll be fun," I said. "See if you can get one up on your parents."

"Nuh-uh," said Alejandra. "My mom likes to stick me on top of the chimney if I cross her." She went back to rock-climbing, using her brother's curly head for a stepping-stone. "Besides, today she's probably happy with me," she said over her shoulder. "I won the pool party."

"You wouldn't have if you didn't steal my pepper!" shrieked Alberto.

"Well, think of poor Pink," I tried. "Can you imagine how much her life will suck if the kids find out her mom is a wicked witch?"

Alejandra looked scornfully down at Pink. "Why do you care what the other kids think, Primella? You should be proud to be a witch."

Pink and I just looked at each other. If we couldn't explain that then there was no hope.

"I guess I'll get used to being an outcast," said Pink mournfully. "And I was just starting to make a friend or two."

"Nonsense." I scrunched up my nose, thinking. Time for all my years of babysitting to come into play. What was going to work on these little terrors?

"Well, I guess you're right," I said to Pink. "It was a dumb idea. The witches are way too powerful for us."

"And way too clever," added Pink. She was quick.

"I can't imagine how we'd get the bad bread away from them," I said.

"You could do, like, a levitating spell," said one of the kids in the hot tub. He clambered out of the water and dripped on our feet. "I mean, if you were gonna do it."

"I don't know how to do a levitation spell," I said.

"Duh, you don't know how to do any spells," said another kid. "It's just rutabaga, parsley, and three ladybugs."

"Can you do that?" I said to Pink.

She shook her head mournfully. "Everything I do comes out wrong."

"Anyway, we don't got rutabaga," said the first kid.

"Well, what do we have?" I said. "You guys have some powders there. And you each have a few spells you know how to do."

"A few," scoffed Alejandra.

"Well, start listing them," I said. "Things that you can do and you have the ingredients for."

A cacophony of voices rose up from the children.

"Make your pants so heavy they fall off."

"A pretend chair that looks like a real one so you fall through it."

"Annoying ringing noises from a cell phone you can't find to turn off."

"Invisible pushpins on your chair."

I nodded thoughtfully as the list of spells grew. "I've got an idea."

Ten minutes later we were creeping up to the pool area. The witches were steadily getting more sloshed as they threw powders onto the loaf of banana bread. "A pig nose!" shrieked Esmerelda, giggling. "A thousand purple pimples!" They seemed to have completely forgotten about calling us back for dessert. Rimelda's birthday cake sat sadly by the pool, and Rimelda herself looked grumpier than ever, unimpressed by the drunken horde.

"Okay, everyone have your pouch of ingredients?" I said. "Wands at the ready?" My army of children flicked their wands out. "Alejandra, you first. Go."

Alejandra combined several things from her pouch and held it out to her brother to spit in it. I must have looked grossed out because Pink gave me a shrug like: whatever works. Alejandra dipped her wand in her palm and flicked it over the pile of fluffy bath towels.

They turned invisible. We each picked one up and draped it over ourselves.

"Excellent," I whispered. "Now you, Alberto."

Under cover of the invisible bath towel, Alberto snuck all the way up to the table that held the banana bread. Meanwhile, another couple kids in their bath towels went around to the other side of the pool. We waited, breaths held, until they had set their spells. Super-irritating cell phone ringtones started playing from the other side of the pool. While all the witches turned their heads to look, Alberto made an illusion banana bread that looked exactly like the real one. It would only last a few minutes, but that was just enough time—I hoped.

Alberto grabbed the real banana bread, covered it with his towel, and hurried back to us.

Meanwhile, the twins' mom had gone to investigate the mysterious cell phones. ("One of those is my mom's ringtone," whispered Alejandra.) We held our breaths, hoping she wouldn't stumble on the towel-covered kids. But she was stopping for a different reason.

"Ew, Esmerelda, your daughter's exploded kraken is everywhere," she said. "Can't you teach her how to master a basic shrink-ing spell?"

A very drunk Esmerelda laughed. "Oh, let me see. Did I give my snoogie-woogums the wrong powder? I feel terrible."

Several witches laughed—cheating is considered fair play among witches, and this evidence of double-cheating was even better.

Pink and I just stared at each other. I gasped at the horribleness of it as Pink's eyes welled with tears. "She deliberately gave me the wrong stuff!"

"She wanted you to fail," I said, shocked. Across the pool I saw Sarmine frown as she, too, was working this out. "Pink," I whispered. "You're part of her plot. Your mom wants you to stay little so she can stay young. She wants you to stay four."

Pink's trembling lips set in a firm line. Her witchy side asserted itself. "I am not taking this lying down," she said. She seized the hexed banana bread and motioned us over to the other end of the pool, where Rimelda's birthday cake sat on a little rolling cart. She nodded to Alberto. "Can you make the bottom of that cake heavy?" she whispered. "Very, very heavy?"

He nodded and, concentrating, mixed up a powder and inscribed a rectangle in the bottom of the cart, under the birthday cake. It was just the size of the banana bread. He pointed his wand at it, and as we watched, the rectangle grew so heavy that a long crack ran right around it as if invisible hands were popping out a perforated section. It broke out of the cart. Alejandra shoved one of the invisibility tow-els under it as it thumped to the ground, dampening the sound. Some cake came with it—just about the right amount.

Carefully Pink wrangled the hexed banana bread up into the hole of the birthday cake. "Someone make it stay," she whispered at us. The twins looked at the table, considering.

But that one I could do. I grabbed several paper plates and wedged them into place. Nothing like a little non-witchy ingenuity for saving the day.

"And one more for luck," Pink said fiercely. She pulled out the orange powder her mother had given her, the horrible orange powder that made everything get bigger, and sprinkled it all over the white-frosted cake. It sparkled like sugar crystals in the sun.

We were just backing away from the birthday cake cart when I saw Sarmine looking our way. We were invisible, so she couldn't have seen us—right? Had she heard the bottom of the cart fall? Her eyebrows drew together and her lips pursed.

I ran back to the kids. Not a moment too soon.

Esmerelda tipped back the last of her martini and made her way over to the birthday cake. She wheeled the cart up to her mother. "A hundred today, but not a hundred forever," she said tipsily. "We'll take care of you."

"Whee," said Rimelda.

"And someone find a piece of foil for that banana bread," Esmerelda said. "Boy, wouldn't I like to be there when she cuts into it. All those hexes activated at once . . . ." Esmerelda shoved the knife into her mother's hand as she sang off-key: "Happy Birthday to you. Happy Birthday to you . . . ."

When she cuts into it . . .

My stomach sunk. All those horrible hexes were going to attack Rimelda. Poor, one-hundred-year-old Rimelda, whose only crime was being grumpy at her own birthday party. She hadn't added anything to the banana bread. She definitely didn't deserve pig pimples, or whatever it was that Esmerelda had been adding.

"Happy Birthday, dear Rimelda. Happy Birthday to . . ."

I shook off the invisibility towel and ran for the cake. "Nooooo . . ." I began, and everything seemed to go in slow motion, the way those things do. My eyes met Sarmine's across the way as I ran toward Rimelda. She was raising that knife, looking for a good place to cut.

Sarmine has a million faults, but being slow-witted is not one of them. Her eyes narrowed as she put two and two together, and realized what I had accomplished with the help of a pack of first-grade witches. Quicker than lightning, her fingers flashed into her fanny pack and combined several powders. Quicker than lightning, her other hand scooped up a splash of chlorinated water and added it to the pile.

The wet powder flicked out on the cake, Sarmine's wand came down, and she whispered some words. Nobody saw her. They were all focused on Rimelda, with a couple heads slowly turning to me and my "Nooooo . . ."

Rimelda's knife pierced the orange-dusted cake.

The cake parted and out poured a stream of horrors.

Rimelda's eyes widened. Her martini-addled fingers fumbled for her pouch.

And then she saw that none of the horrors were headed toward her.

A stream of purple pimples shot after Esmerelda. The skunk-smelling frogs hopped after the redhead. Giant green snakes rained down on the twins' mom.

Witch after witch ran shrieking from the pursuing hexes. They were all too drunk to master any self-defense spells. And the things pursuing them were not little, either. Aided by Pink's messed-up shrinking spell, the horrors got bigger and bigger as they pounced on the witches who'd created them. Esmerelda was a mass of disgusting purple boils from her platinum hair to her pink-polished toes.

Rimelda's wrinkled face slowly broke into a smile and then a grin. She fell over, howling large hoots of laughter. As she straightened up, I saw the years slowly fall away—a hundred fifty, a hundred twenty, a hundred. Eighty. She stopped and stretched when she looked about a healthy and fit sixty, around the same age as Sarmine.

"Primella," she said, and beckoned her granddaughter to her side. Pink was still holding the orange powder, which had clearly been dusting the cake. "Did you do that?"

"Well . . ." Pink said.

"We all helped," butted in Alejandra. I gave her the stink-eye. This was not the time for Alejandra to shine. She nodded and said fairly, "But Primella's the one who made the goonies all huge."

Rimelda squeezed her granddaughter close. "You're really turning into an excellent witch, you know that? This is exactly the kind of chaos that makes me feel like there's a future for our family. The kind of well-deserved chaos," she said severely, and looked very deliberately at her daughter, who was fighting off a six-foot banana slug.

Pink breathed a deep sigh of pride. "You think so?" As we watched, her legs visibly lengthened. Her seams started popping at the shoulders. The four-year-old's pink dress was way too small for this ten-year-old girl.

"I know so," said Rimelda. She stretched out her arms and studied her granddaughter at arm's length. "You know, we'd better get you some new clothes," she said. "You've completely outgrown that dress."

I crossed over to where my guardian perched on her lawn chair. Sarmine was her usual stiff-backed, straight-mouthed self, yet her eyes glimmered with amusement as she surveyed the scene. "I saw you with that potion," I said to Sarmine. "You made all those hexes revert to their creators." I looked suspiciously at her. "You know that was rather a . . . nice thing to do?"

"Nonsense," said Sarmine. "I didn't want to get attacked by stray purple boils, is all. Such a bother."

We sat back in our lawn chairs and watched the flurry of grown-up witches get chased by bats and slugs and bears and boils. The witch-kids were eating the entire birthday cake, now cleared of its banana bread hexes.

This might turn out to be a rather pleasant birthday party after all.

See Dangerous Earth-Possibles:
Stories of Families, Baseball Bats, and Zombie Chipmunks

SEE DANGEROUS
EARTH-POSSIBLES!

You are fifteen when you get the brochure.

See DANGEROUS EARTH POSSIBLES! Become a Hero!

The ad blinked at you online, between the x-ray glasses and the grainy picture of how to lose fourteen pounds and get real wings, and you gave them your father's address, because your stepfather opens your mail. It means it is longer to get the brochure, but it also means it is there waiting for you that Saturday that your father is finally home and not off being brave in Mogadishu or Detroit or wherever it is he's not allowed to say.

You answer questions like:

Fill in the attacker that could be stopped with a:

baseball bat
vaccination
silver bullet
gram of kryptonite
baseball bat

and you get all of them, though you're confused by the second baseball bat and you accidentally fill in your stepfather, but then you leave it.

There's an essay question, too, about what you would do if you were sent to the future where invasive warthog flu has brought down most of the American Pacific Northwest, and you have to defend a senior citizen center from a band of nudists, with only some artisanal pine toothpicks at your disposal (answer: Tape the toothpicks into a long jabbing stick and poke their naughty bits from a safe distance.)

You send it back through snail mail with $5 for postage, and you wait another month while your father hunts bad guys in San Pedro Sula and St. Louis and then you find the shoebox, stuck on the back porch by the postman, now damp and smelling of earwigs. You open it to find your DANGEROUS EARTH POSSIBLES activation kit; a folded rubbery mat that looks a game of Twister and smells like a new car.

You place your left foot as they tell you. Your right foot. Your ten fingers and your chin and your black eye, and then with your nose you press the ACTIVATION button. Everything spins around you like an uppercut (not the one given to you; more like the ones your dad is out there giving the bad guys), and then you find yourself in one of the EARTH POSSIBLES. You know it's one of the EARTH POSSIBLES because there are tiny zombie chipmunks lurching around your back-yard, and there weren't before.

A man appears from the backyard, tired and sore and covered with chipmunk bites. He looks a little like your father, as you re-member him from when you were eight and all living together and he was still only with the local police force and not with the things he couldn't tell you about. As the man douses his bites in rubbing alco-hol, he tells you that if you pass the chipmunk world, you can join his squad and do battle on all the known EARTH POSSIBLES. He tosses you a baseball bat.

You had never thought you could harm a chipmunk. But they storm your ankles and one gets its teeth in and oh—that's going to leave a mark. It will match the marks on your wrist from when your stepfather challenged you to a no-holds-barred wrestling match (just to see if you were as tough as your father.) You find that you can put the rabid chipmunks down after all, and you do, one at a time, till your shoulders shake and you are weeping.

The man puts his arm around your shoulders and offers you the alcohol. One of these worlds is going to be our future, he says, and it needs to be made safe. Heroes like you have been recruited from all countries and times.

You listen while you sear your wounds. And you know that all you really want is that EARTH POSSIBLES where your father comes home from Peshawar, and does battle with your stepfather (hands, feet, teeth), and then takes you away with him to be a Hero too.

And so this seems like the next best thing, and you nod. You join the other Heroes-in-Training in another EARTH POSSIBLES, in an abandoned police station there, and you learn how to go to other worlds and kill more things—sometimes with silver bullets, sometimes with regular ones.

Some nights you think about your father, and how he travels around being a hero. And sometimes you think about your stepfather, and how strange it is that he is part of the police force too. And meanwhile, while you're thinking, you pick up your baseball bat and battle for your future.

Turning the Apples

Getcher cells," says Szo to the streaming tourists. "New world, need a cell, get 'em here."

"Not interested."

"Bought one on the ship."

Szo opens his jacket, reveals a wall of buttons, cornrowed phones. "Come in handy if you get in trouble, mister."

Some local shoves him; fast pecker his age in shiny shoes. "Why doncha leave with the other tourists, foreigner."

Szo can't afford trouble so he ducks his head smiling. When the local goes by he nabs his cashflap. Swore to Mack that he wouldn't, maybe, but that was before six months of taunts. Before it was driven home that honest hawking is a recipe for no food, no cash.

No ticket off.

Hand on his sleeve and he whirls, cell that ain't a cell slicking out a blade, ready to take the thug if he has to. But it ain't no regular thug, it's double-job Jonny and that's bad because the only time Jonny comes to see him nowadays is for Hawk.

"Whazzup?" Szo says, all cool. His hand retracts to his pocket. A likely mark walks by but he can't go, not with Jonny draped and breathing hot on his collar.

"I've got apples in the stockyard," says Jonny. "Fresh."

Apples is code for comabodies, that one-tenth of one percent of off-world tourists that get the infection. They disappear, if Hawk is fast and the crematory's slow. Stockyard is the freight shipyard, that's easy. But he's blocked out what fresh is.

"Got a good gig now," Szo mumbles.

Jonny flicks a cashflap out and it's Szo's. Jonny always was better at lifting than Szo, even back when they were scrawny jerky kids, back before Jonny turned tricks and Szo was just learning to turn minds. "Eighteen bucks offa tourists?" Jonny says. "You know Hawk'll give you two thou for an hour at the stockyard."

"Cells," says Szo to a fat tourist. "Getcher cells."

Jonny slams his hand into Szo's shoulder and there's no knife there but the force of what Jonny holds on Szo. "This ain't a negotiation, boyo," says Jonny. "They're fresh and Hawk's in a lather, he needs what you do. You're the only survivor in the city right now. Stockyard. 3:30."

Then Jonny is gone and Szo is sick to his knees because he's just remembered that fresh means awake and screaming.

"The fuck you been?" says Hawk.

It's 3:31, after Szo spent the last hour looking for them. In the moonlight the shipyard is a mountainous dark, the whir of generators vibrating in his ears. It might cover the sound of fresh apples. He tries not to listen.

"Listen, boyo. Turn them for us fast, just like the old days. Jonny says you need the cash."

The problem is Szo's jonesing now. The touch of his mind into the comabodies is something he's tried like hell to forget, but they press into his gray folds like a million firsts with a million new girls, touching his mind with vibrations hot and sweet and fleeting.

He's been clean nearly half a year. So long, too long. The comabodies always come in waves, the wave of tourist season, the wave of Hawk finding new suppliers. There are five propped sitting against a hangar wall, leaning on each other.

They *are* screaming. The worst kind. Hawk's got dirty rags in their mouths, but their cheeks are taut around it. At least someone's closed their eyes, probably Jonny.

"What do you want them for?"

"Never mind that."

Szo shoves hands in pockets. Hawk goes cagey when it's a new venture, never mind that he knows the drill, never mind that he knows he's got Szo over a barrel. "You know fuckall, Hawk. Are they for the waste, the minefield, what? I can't code them right if I don't know what you want them to do."

"Fine," Hawk says. "I need swimmers. I need them to seek out pearls in the sulfur pits where the heat blisters your arms and the gasses belly out your lungs. Rose-colored pearls, each coiled like the belly button of a giant."

Jonny rolls his eyes at Hawk's purple words and the boys grin. For a minute it ain't tight-pants Jonny and weary Szo, for a moment they're two kids playing pickpocket for Hawk and life is sometimes okay. At least they're alive, you know?

That's what Szo always thinks when he first touches the coma-bodies. At least *I'm* alive. He closes his eyes, savoring the last moment before he gives in. Jonny and Hawk walk away, fade away, and Szo touches the first one on the head and *reaches*.

Szo doesn't think of much while turning; he can't. But in that first moment he thinks of palm trees.

Szo barely remembers his home planet. He and his mom came here when he was four. Despite what she claimed, it wasn't a vacation to the fabled water parks half-a-day south of here, the hot springs and waterfalls that kept tourists coming back. His mom was fleeing her old life. That's something he only pieced together a decade later, he and Jonny flopped on Hawk's couch, high on greensmack.

He doesn't know which planet it was, or what the whole of it was like. All he remembers is a swatch of green grass with a palm tree. Occasionally other things float back; words or faces or sayings. The image of the palm tree is what he calls home, though for all he knows it wasn't even on his planet. Maybe it was something he saw on the ship over. Maybe it was a cardboard palm tree, a carpet of plastic grass and maybe he sat there and waited for his mom to come out of the ship's bar.

He tries all these images on till the palm trees disintegrate in swimming and pearls and pure white nothing, and he still doesn't know.

Last comabody turned and now the five are all turned, ready to dive for pearls for Hawk. Szo's full of buzzing aftermath, his mind panting like he's jizzed all over them. Hawk drops a wad of cash that thunks his shoulder. Sure he grabs it, but it's nothing compared to the fierce relief that floods his brain.

He limps down the long road from the shipyard, blood dripping from a bitten tongue. He thinks he'll avoid the street for a few days, lie low, score some greensmack, anything to take the edge offa wanting to do more apples. Maybe two thou is enough to get him on a ship himself, get him off the planet. If it weren't for Hawk, his past, Szo could stay clean.

It's cold out here in the early morning. The greensmack is quick to come by. The pee stink outside his squats hardly bugs, not while he's all strung on comabodies. If he had another fifty in the alley he'd do them all, but instead he rolls up the greensmack under his tongue and flops on the mattress.

The greensmack makes him sad; it always does. It ain't most punks' drug of choice, but it's Szo's. This time on the greensmack he remembers how he and his mom got infected. The first he knew something was wrong was his mother asleep standing up, pouring whiskey over a mug and onto her hand. She woke up once, and then she fell into a coma. He remembers toddling around the hotel room, before he fell asleep too. His dreams were beautiful, dreams of something orgasmic that was a new sensation at four. Gorgeousness lush and happy, and when he woke, he was sweaty and starving and his mother was flopped on the hotel bed.

Szo can't forgive himself for toddling out to find food, for inadvertently reporting her. Because white blurs of grownups and coats took her away. He traded her for a ham sandwich, that's how he feels, and here and now on the greensmack he cries snot and spits more blood.

That's when the poli comes to his crappy squats, and hauls Szo himself away, still crying like a four-year-old.

They don't even give him a ham sandwich.

At the brick station, Mack stretches and sighs. "Give us the details, Szo. You might as well."

"You already know what's up, why do you want me?" Szo hunches around his knees. There's bits of glass on his pant leg from the shipyard tarmac. He flicks them onto Mack's desk, which Mack ignores.

"We know it's Hawk, we know this supplier. We know it's five or six bodies. We don't know where they're going and jesus Szo, we'd like to track them down. Don't you think your mother would've liked that?"

"Keep talking about her and I won't tell you anything." Truth is, he hates to disappoint Mack. Mack picked him up the first time he was caught. Eight years old and he'd already turned fifty-three bodies for Hawk. Fifty-three because he remembers each one. Mack cleaned him up and got him in a foster home, a decent one where they didn't hit you, but when Hawk came to him with more apples, Szo went straight back.

"I know you've been clean half a year, Szo," says Mack. "I was rooting for you. What's Hawk got on ya that you can't resist?"

"Just the money," Szo lies. "I need to eat, don't I?"

"Join up with us," Mack says. "Help us hunt down the guys like Hawk, rescue other tourist kids who survived and got caught up in this. Don't you wish you'd never known what it was like to touch their minds?"

Of course he does, but so what? "If I worked for you, they wouldn't tell me what they were up to, duh," he says.

Mack rises and cracks his back. Looks out the window at a grungy building a meter away. It's painted red brick like so much of this port city, like a fleeting bright color will slick over decay. "There's a rumor," Mack says, "that a kid like you—except better than you, a fighter—has managed to undo the damage."

Szo's heart pounds so hard he thinks he can't hear Mack. "A-all?"

"All. Wakes them up." Mack's voice does that measured thing. "She says it hurts a bit, but the rush comes later. Like a stalling afore the pleasure." He twirls a pen. "Too bad she's in East Enland—they ain't letting her past their borders for cash nor love. It'd have to be the guy we know here trying it." His eyes catch Szo's.

"To heal them . . . ."

"There'd be cash for each one you turn. From the general missing persons stockpile."

Awake. Alive. Okay.

Szo can't breathe, can't think. Because the hold that Hawk's got on him is his mom, coma-cold and alone and digging waste out in the desert.

*

He hadn't known that Hawk had his mother for a long time. Hawk
had been using another kid back in those days. A girl, stranded here.
Her parents had been cremated quick; Hawk hadn't gotten them. The
girl lasted a few years. Then she tried to wean herself from comabodies with street drugs and lost. That's when Jonny found Szo, his hair
and skin a dead alien giveaway.

Getting infected makes your brain rewriteable. Surviving makes
you able to rewrite. Not everyone gets it; most natives are immune
and even many tourists are. One tenth of one percent is a low enough
number that tourists flock in by the thousands, through the major port
city and down south to the waters. The adults that get it are in a coma
within 24 hours.

It's only kids who sometimes survive.

By the time Szo saw his mother, he'd turned nineteen minds for
Hawk. He remembers the first one particularly, like you remember
a first girl or first trick. But he remembers all the others, too. "Don't
know why you would," says Jonny. "I don't remember all the men."
But Szo does, and he clings to each one, proof that somehow he is not
like Jonny, not like Hawk, not like himself. This is all temporary and
therefore changeable, rewriteable.

Szo doesn't know if he recognized his mother the moment he
saw her. He wants to say yes, but the truth is there was this moment
when he saw this smelly, skin-rashed woman and a moment when
he saw his mother, and the two seem to be laid on top of each other,
vibrating.

Five whole days on the streetcorner, and Szo's only made twelve
bucks and two fistfights before Jonny comes back.

"Apples at the cellar," says Jonny.

"*In* the cellar," says Szo.

"Fancy words, Szo," mocks Jonny.

"A cellar is a basement, so if cellar's your code you should say
in, not at." He's too eager, and strange words, strange memories, spill

forth as he tries to hide his jittery hands. "Cells, getcher cells," he says, turning, aping his former self.

Jonny slugs his ribs, bruising him via the phones in his jacket. "We don't talk about codes," he says, and his breath is sweet with cherrymint. "Midnight." He's gone, whistling through the crowd and Szo pats Mack's wire in his sleeve, pats his ribs. When neither is broken he says "Getcher cells" until Jonny is vanished.

Cherrymint's nice, it floods your mind with sweet and your breath with sugar. But it ain't touching the hot rush of comabodies. It's the drug of choice for people like Jonny, who spend their nights getting it up.

That's a fucked-up job, Szo thinks. Maybe his life sucks sometimes, but he ain't Jonny. Szo's had sex exactly twice, and he doesn't seem to be cut out for it. If he could meet that girl from East Enland he'd ask her what she thinks. Cause for him this thing that everyone wants ain't so great, it's a millionth of what it is to be hot inside the comabodies. It's pale and localized and hardly worth the anxiety. Maybe that girl would know what he means. Maybe the two of them could figure it out together, could trick out their own substitution for the drug they can't resist.

For now it's just one more thing that makes him feel alien and alone on this planet, as much as the gray tint of his skin, the silky texture of hair. He wants a jolt no one else can do or understand, and he doesn't want a joy that fills everyone else.

It touches on his own work, sure. There ain't a big trade in comapussy but there's some, like there is for anything. Szo saw one alone once, a young girl with hair like a cottonball and lipstick smearing off. She was sat down at the corner by some local who teared off in a hurry. She was probably tracked by the pimp; he probably had a detector set to send someone out for her. Too witless to run, and her brains were coded by Szo or someone like Szo.

Szo crept along the alley. She was crooning. Not rocking, not coiled. Limp against the building, singing a song about a sparrow.

He didn't recognize her face. But, checking, slipped his mind in and then was sure he didn't know her, hadn't done her. He was doing her now though, her brain hot against his, slipping through the vibrating folds. She rocked her head back, still singing, staring at the moons.

Szo recoiled then. There was an instant of pause and then he re-wrote her. Rewrote her to walk down to the shipyard and stand under a shuttle.

Now, thinking back, he thinks—could I have saved her? Woke her up? No matter how much life sucks sometimes, Szo likes it better than the reverse. He'd a granted that to the woman, too, only back then everyone *knew* comabodies were dead in all but their meat.

At midnight, Szo pats his wire and drops into the cellar. It really is underground—Hawk packs in and out every time he uses it, slipping in and out by dawn. The wire is for Hawk's sake. Hawk knows he's been with Mack a lot, and Szo has never been good at hiding jitters. It's why Jonny is a better pickpocket than he is, and a better trick.

Hawk pulls the wire out of Szo's jacket with a snap, laughs at Szo's expression, and tosses it on the ground. "I'd be mad but you're too lame," he says, and grinds it flat. "Come on, there's apples. Code them for waste."

Szo reaches in and when he touches the first there's all that mad rush of vibrating brain. All that buzzing that usually makes it so easy to code the apple to do what Hawk wants. But now, following Mack's instructions he's going to take out the buzzing.

It takes fumbling. It isn't natural; it's like swimming upstream. Until it clicks, and then every place he feels the buzz that lets him hook in, he reverses it, until the apple drains. The infection he's cutting out, it seems to fill him. It's a horrid *wrong* and he twitches with it, trying to dispel the notion. At last the hook is less and less and Szo has next to nothing to hook into, then nothing and he's locked outside. The apple's eyelids flutter and Szo quick leans down and whispers "Play dead."

The man seems to obey, and Szo quick tries the same reversal on the second, the third, slogging through as his brain tells him it's stuffed with the comabodies' infection. It does hurt, he does want release, but he keeps going. Holding back seems a deserved punishment, Szo almost feels holy with it, which is another word from the past. But before Szo can start the fourth, number two spasms.

"I remember, I remember, I know—" he screams, and Hawk and Jonny come running. Jonny's belt's undone, Szo realizes later. But right now it's all the stupid fat number two, and number three's too twitchy to play dead next to that. Number two runs on shaky legs, yelling for the poli and his wife and Hawk shoots him. Number one stays stiff, but number three bolts and is shot.

"What the hell did you do to them?"

"I dunno, I dunno," whimpers Szo, like he's four again and piss-scared.

Hawk's eyeing Szo, but what distracts him is Jonny says "I know he did it, he did it somehow."

"And how the hell would he do that, huh?" says Hawk and he smacks Jonny upside the head. "Just cause you wish you could do his job instead of your little pervy one. It must be a mutation. You—" and he points into Szo's face— "Figure out how to adapt to this, or you're dead."

He stalks off, and Jonny with a crumpled face hurries after.

Number one's eyes go to him. Szo doesn't know if it's like looking at someone he killed or birthed, but either way he can't stand the intimate touch of the man's eyes. "Back door's past the stairs," he says, and then he hurries out before he can be any more responsible, for anyone.

At the red brick station Szo says: "Two were shot, but. I saved one. It worked," and Mack believes him and hands him cash, just like that. Mack doesn't ask the awkward questions, like what the man's eyes were like or how Szo feels now, stuffed taut and bursting with a mind full of infection. Szo squirrels the cash away with the rest of Hawk's money.

"Ready to try it again? I've got a lead on four prostitutes we haven't rounded up yet."

"Any time," says Szo, and the thought is fine. If this keeps working, maybe he doesn't have to flee the planet like he longs to. Maybe he could play both sides and come out smelling clean. The thought's a relief, here with his mind still thick with the swarming of the coma-bodies' infection. There must be some way to let that go, but it hasn't drained yet. But he'll figure that out, he's sure, here with bright hope flickering.

"No time like the present," says Mack, and he shoves his chair back. "Unless you know somewhere else we should go."

Hope floods a crowded brain. "Hawk's taking one to the desert," says Szo.

After Szo found his mom, he started sneaking back to be with her. Not right after a comabodies rush, but two, three days later, when the high had worn off. Then he watched his mother trundle over buried nuclear waste, and didn't know what to feel.

He hated the idea but he tried it anyway: if he can rewrite comabodies, why not rewrite his mom? And so he laid his brain alongside hers though the vibrations were awesome and disgusting. He overlaid her with ideas of mother and son and hugs and palm trees. And when he backed out she bent down and gave his exhausted body a hug. Then trundled back into the waste, scanning with her monitors and smiling on one side of her face. Most miserable thing ever, sent him running straight for Jonny's couch and the greensmack.

But today, he doesn't have to run. Szo says desert and Mack knows right where to go. Waste cleanup is one of the uses for comabodies that the poli don't do anything about; officially it doesn't happen. Few minutes out here isn't going to hurt anyone, and Mack and Szo thread through the few lone figures, past the red-painted bunkhouse, until Szo says "That one."

"Your mother?" says Mack, and Szo stunned, nods.

Mack knows, then. Szo had thought he might, but that Mack hasn't done anything with this knowledge opens up a black wedge between them.

Szo tumbles out of the car, backs away from Mack and towards his mom.

"Don't do it," says Mack. "It's been thirteen years, mate. She's gone."

"How do you know?" says Szo.

"Rumor. That girl like you in East Enland, she couldn't wake 'em up right beyond three years. Their minds were too dead."

"I don't believe you." Maybe this girl is a fantasy, he thinks, a made-up ideal for Mack to prod Szo one way or another.

"I've got the file with her notes. Let me grab it," says Mack, and Szo watches his mother pace the site. She's in that same brown shift and her arms and hands are cracked and red and white. Her bare legs are brown and green. It's like any other day out here, except this day has a different ending.

But there's a whistle behind him, Jonny's. From the bunkhouse.

Szo idles that way, on guard. "What are you doing here?"

"You're in trouble, boyo," says Jonny. "I told Hawk he should punish you but he says you're worth even more to him if you just come back. Or something." He studies Szo and sighs, all the air whooshing from his thin frame. "Is it true you can wake 'em up now?"

Szo nods, and Jonny kind of pats his shoulder, doesn't slug him or arm burn him.

Then Hawk's behind Jonny and he says, "Get your poli back here and I'll kneecap him." He's got a rusting iron bar that he draws up. "We'll take you back, don't worry." There are two comabodies wandering around the bunkhouse, both in those brown shifts. One is so diseased looking Szo assumes he's too far gone to wander around with a monitor, even for an apple. Hawk practice swings. "Is he coming?"

"You're small-time, aren't you?" Szo says. He hadn't realized it, growing up in it, but the constantly shifting locations, the raising young boys like Jonny . . . .

Hawk swings at him, but he jumps back.

"You don't own me," says Szo. "Not like Jonny. You never did."

Hawk swings again, slashing wildly at Szo, but Mack's there behind him. He tasers Hawk and throws the handcuffs on him.

Jonny backs away. "I ain't done nothin, nothin."

Mack breathes. "Honest, Szo, I wouldn't try waking your mother." She's there behind them, trying to hug Jonny.

"You knew she was here."

"What could I do about it?"

But that floods Szo's mind with the image of the young comabody whore with hair like a dandelion. He grabs his mother's blotchy wrist, holds it tight tighter and leans in. Then he's gone, in this strange new method of pulling things out and into himself. Pulling in the rotted bits, pulling in the mechanical bits, taking them into his own self. It hurts, yes, but when he's done there's that *holiness* in it too, and he sags onto the ground, painful in every bone, on edge.

His mother doesn't move.

"I'm sorry, Szo," said Mack, but then her eyes open.

Her eyes are lopsided and she looks at him, her rat's nest of hair falling over and like a lightning burst she croaks, "Boy." Then she collapses, falling limb by limb to the whitened ground. Her eyes whiten, and her pitted hands search aimlessly for her monitor. Slower they search, and slower. Her nose presses into dirt.

Szo can't look at Mack, knows the pity on Mack's face. "I'm sure it'll get better," Mack says, and this is the first time Mack's lied *directly* to him. Mack knows it too, and he flinches, burly shoulders twitching.

"Loser," rasps Hawk. His shoulder twitches from the tase. "Shoulda woke her up when you were four. Course then you wouldn't a got to fuck them all, which *I* let you do. Wouldn't got to spend your life making cash for screwing them over . . . ."

Szo hurls himself at Hawk, knocking the manacled man backwards, and before Mack can pull him off Szo punches out at Hawk, not with his fists but his infected mind. It sears out, taut and bursting, it's all been waiting to be released and all four infections he's scored pour into Hawk and knock him cold. Cold, but screaming; Hawk's fresh all right, unawake and crying on the ground.

They are all stunned, all but Szo's silent-still mother.

Szo's shocked and twitching and he runs, lopsided, stumbling with the spent energy. Full of strange highs and horrible thoughts, he takes Hawk's car through the desert and back to the city. Mack doesn't come after him, nor Jonny, not in the next twelve hours, which is what it takes to come down from the high and the shock and count his cash from comabodies.

He can get to palm trees, he thinks. If he knew where they was and if he should go.

Cause there's East Enland too, and maybe it seems to him that a tourist is a guy who never interacts with his own life. Never slips into the deep.

Szo runs hard to the port, where he breathes hard and fast. He watches the heat waves of the shuttles, ships in flight.

FACTS OF BONE

Jules stripped to her underwear, dusted herself with powder and stepped into the stretchy flying suit. She smoothed it around her fingers, careful to line up the yellow dots on her knuckles, careful to leave no gaps or bubbles around her palms. Her ritual for suiting up was rigid. Enough could go wrong in the air—but some things she could control.

She trudged out of the shed, holding the carry pegs of the fly-cycle. The wings and rotators spread awkwardly out behind it, the right wing scoring the dirt. She poked the earbud in as she walked, settled the braced helmet in place. The worn path was muddy and her feet grew heavy with it.

She was studying the cold gray sky when her sister's voice came on in her ear. "What's the weather report?"

Jules squinted to the north. "Looks like rain later. Where are you this week?" She stepped into the flying gear, settled the padded harness. Chute cord at her shoulder, battery light on full. Check.

"Pallister," said Marnie.

"Where's that?"

"Big grimy city in Saeland."

"Yuck." Wireless on, routing the data from her goggles, her suit, to the cycle company trying to improve the precision of their equipment. Something Marnie had set up. The money would offset a bad harvest, heaven forbid.

The wind cut across Jules' cheeks. She rocked back, shifting her feet to the pedals, then rocked forward and off the cliffs. The spring wind buffeted her, flicking her with spray from rain and river, pungent with the acrid odor of the eiddar flock. A cursory check of the cliffs to start, then she turned her attention to the wider area around them.

"What's for today? Just checking on the egg-laying?"

Jules did not answer.

"Dammit. I don't want you going after those poachers. I've got my city rep working on them."

"I don't see her out here on the cliffs," said Jules. Her goggles zoomed in on the forest on the other side of the river. Even before all the trees had leafed, there were too damn many places to hide.

Jules swung back to the first nook, leaning against the turn. The eiddar she called Speckly Gray Mom was awake and active, plucking down from her chest to fill her nest for the eggs. Responsible harvesting didn't start until after the eggs had hatched—but poachers didn't give a damn about that. There was comfortable silence in her earbud as the two sisters worked, a continent apart, one tracking birds and the other foreign currency.

Jules was checking on White-Bib Mom—it was displaying unusual plucking behaviors—when a spray of rocks exploded next to the nest.

She spun back out to face the forest, and then another something whistled by her ear. There was a huge tearing noise, and her left leg was suddenly far below her right, and then both legs were overhead and the whole flycycle was hurtling toward the ground. Jules rolled with it, righting her head, and pulled the ripcord at her left shoulder. The chute opened and jerked her and the machine up, and she pulled her legs up from the pedals so when it finally crashed she could roll with it on the ground.

It all worked like it had the other time she'd crashed, except this time she had just enough time in the air to look off into the forest for the poacher. She saw something—a flash of color—and the anger confused her body. The cycle landed, tilted forward, and the wrong kind of instinct made her stick out her right arm. It skidded in the wet ground and there was a flash of pain as it broke, then broke again, pinned under the curving control bar of the flycycle. As she blacked out, her sister's voice seemed to be crying in her ear.

But she might have imagined that. At least the next thing she heard was Marnie's calm, dry voice repeating something about an ambulance on its way, and she'd better wake up for it, because family property or no, if Jules thought Marnie would give up her career for the daily gamble of a life tending dirty birds, she was seriously mistaken.

"I do well enough," mumbled Jules. "Got my own crappy flat, don't I?"

"So you say." Relief was clear in Marnie's voice.

With her left hand, Jules disentangled chute ropes from her head and then struggled to rock the cycle bar off of her right arm. After the initial shock, there was surprisingly little pain. The adrenaline kicking in.

"Stay where you are, Juliana. Let the professionals do it."

"I don't see any professionals." Her arm was a funny shape, an 'S' that curved in front of her. She sat back down in the reddened mud and cradled her arm in her lap.

It was not bleeding. She touched one of the curves, expecting to feel the end of a snapped bone. But instead her arm was smooth to the touch.

She ran her fingers along the bone from the wrist to the elbow, tracing the 'S' the whole way. There must be internal bleeding or swelling, she thought, because her forearm felt like solid bone, bone that had always been in the shape of a doubly-broken arm.

The nearest hospital was forty miles from her cliffs, a long building with a rick-rack of roofs over a warren of underground rooms. After the tests, she was pushed in a wheelchair down more and more ramps and lifts until she was put into a bed deep below the surface. The hospital seemed to press her under its thumb.

She lay flat on the firm bed and wished for her own down mattress. That was a luxury too costly for the hospital. She looked at the ceiling for a long while. She didn't seem to be able to do anything while her arm lay heavy and twisted at her side.

When at last the surgeon came in, she knew four feet of the ceiling intimately. The doctor's eyes were black and glassy like her birds', and he had a thatch of black hair that stuck out around his ears. "Are you comfortable?" he said. "As much as possible, that is."

"Will you tell me what's with my arm? No one will say. Is it infected?"

He did not answer.

She swallowed. "I need it to fly."

"It's not infected." His hands on the electronic clipboard were still. "It's an extremely rare genetic disorder. The immune system is working imperfectly. It's trying to fix the damage done to the broken bone. It sent signals to knit the bone back together—but it over-compensated, turning tendon and flesh to bone as well. The break in the arm most likely triggered it."

Jules could not make this out. "I broke my toe when I was ten and nothing happened."

"Adult onset. It's rare enough that no consistent pattern is identifiable as to the trigger, except the patient is always past puberty, sometimes well past. You were flying?" His body was still, the muscles taut like a watching creature.

"I'm a gatherer, and yes, I flycycle. I'm extremely competent. I wear a full latex suit and I don't take risks."

"I'm sure you don't. But the dangers are serious for someone with this disorder. Once triggered, the trend is irreversible. It may be wise to consider a new career."

Jules did not want to think about that. She went on the offensive. "What can you do for my arm?"

He held her gaze and laid it out for her. "Perhaps nothing." He turned away, holding the clipboard behind him with both hands, tapping it. His thumbnails were gnawed halfway down his thumbs. "The difficulty is that any attempt to remove the bone may trigger further outbreak. Attempting to reshape the arm may make it worse."

Jules stretched both arms in front of her. The right arm curved and bulged like a snake that had just eaten. The tips of those fingers reached no further than the wrist bone of her left hand. "I want it straightened. I can't fly like this."

He pivoted. Those bird eyes glittered in his face. "There's an experimental procedure I've been considering . . . ." He explained the operation, bitten fingers fluttering, technical details of surgeries and time-release medications piling on hard and fast, till Jules shrunk into herself and thought—how do patients pull decisions from this? It's like he's recounting the dry facts of uplift and downdrafts, the sudden gusts that sweep sideways across the cliffs. I am not used to being a patient. It is all head information, and without a lifetime of experience tucked in my body, I can't know any of it.

"Yes," she said in the end.

When she awoke, the room was dark. She tried to raise her arm, but it was tied down. No, it wasn't that either, it was just dead heavy. She swallowed, and felt along her right arm with her left fingers. It was straight all right. Her forearm was straight—and solid to the touch. It was like skin stretched over stone.

Striations of bone now reached into her upper arm, one running almost to her shoulder. But the bicep seemed to work and her elbow still had some play. If she let her body recalibrate to the new weight, she could still use her arm to fly. But it was her hand she needed the most, palms to grip and fingers to tilt the gyropics. She almost didn't want to try to move her hand and find out if any muscles and tendons still worked, if anything was left, snaking its way through rivulets in the bone. She closed her eyes and in the blackness she wiggled the fingers of her right hand.

Only then could she open her eyes and watch her fingers move in the dim glow of the bedside monitor.

The knot in her chest loosened from thoughts of her injury. The birds were nesting and she needed to get back to the cliffs. Her earbud lay in reach, in a tray of her personal items. She put it in place and subvocalized her sister's code.

"Can you get them to release me?" Jules said. She offered up the dry details, but she did not feel like hashing out her feelings with her sister.

"You should consider staying in bed. It sounds serious. What did he say about going back to work?"

"Oh, to be careful."

"I see," said Marnie. There was skeptical silence. "Look, I've hired a bodyguard," she said finally. "She'll be walking the foot of the cliffs and watching the trees."

Relief. Then—"Just till I get back?"

"Permanently." Marnie's curt voice. "I'm putting my foot down. I know what's best. You use the cycle for data collection and harvesting only. No more baby bird protection agency."

"She'll scare the birds. This is their egg-laying season. They don't know her like they know me."

"Grow up," said Marnie. "Better fidgety than dead."

"Your bedside manner leaves something to be desired," Jules said dryly. "If you can call it bedside when you're halfway across the world. Where are you today?"

"Lyddon. Awful thick fog. It's no picnic being here. You wouldn't like it."

Jules looked down at her arm on the hospital bed. It seemed to belong to somebody much older and heavier. Someone with a different life, some Jules who sat in an office and programmed ship schedules, or inspected snakeskin handbags. "The doctor thinks I should stop flying," she admitted.

"And you?"

"I think I'd rather die. I think."

"It's that serious?" said Marnie.

"Might be." There was something about saying it out loud, and suddenly Jules said: "What do you think I should do?" The plea was strange on her lips.

"Keep flying."

"Yeah?"

"You can't stop your life just because you might die. We're all dying. Just be careful. Please."

Jules nodded to the ceiling. She was obscurely comforted to know they had returned her to the same room.

"Besides, we still need that data you're gathering," Marnie said. "We need the money for it from the cycle company. It's important."

"Ah," said Jules. Her left hand fluttered. "Will you come see me now? In the hospital?"

"I have commitments this week. I can't . . ."

"Marnie." The word was a stone pressing up through her throat.

"I . . ." A silence. "I'll come. I'll be there."

"I knew you wouldn't let me down."

*

Avar the bodyguard was restless and relentless, with short blonde hair mottled with gray and a hunch to her back like a tortoise shell. She paced the bottom of the red cliffs like a machine programmed for one thing only. Her heavy tread shook stones.

Jules couldn't watch her. After she checked to make sure the laying birds hadn't been disturbed further, she hopped the river and went to see where the poachers had been. The shot had come from the full beech past the stand of those skinny trees the squirrels liked.

She unhooked her cycle gear and went poking around the beech, looking for traces. There were tons: broken limbs and bold careless footprints leading back to the northeast. There was a trail you could catch a quarter-mile up that led to a good fishing stream for carp. She couldn't think what was beyond that.

Jules picked up a stick and crouched by the beech tree, pointing it back towards the nest she had been observing. Her shoulder ached from the extra weight, from being used as a pivot point. Avar stopped in her stomping, stared hard at Jules, and continued again. The distance was not far and the flycycle's wings had been old; it didn't have to be an elephant gun to have ripped through her left wing. Not a poacher of the down harvest, though, but a common criminal, bagging nesting birds for their beaks.

"I'm sorry I couldn't make it to the hospital." The voice in her ear was loud after all that silence.

Jules sighed and put down the stick.

"Come away from the forest. I told you to be careful."

"Stop watching me off the vidfeed. Let me work." Jules raised the stick again, sighting along its bark. He'd been aiming at White-Bib Mom. "I thought this equipment was for the data for the flycycle, not for tracking me."

"Can't I see my sister when I call?"

There was an obvious answer to that. Jules pressed her lips tighter and felt the earbud like a rock in her ear.

Marnie's voice, softer, a whisper. "I meant, I mean, I'm sorry."

The regret in the tone was the twist of the knife. "Sorry doesn't cut it," Jules said. "Sorry doesn't mean a damned thing. It's a word you poison me with like it should *do* something, like it should make up for not coming. For condescending. For not bringing me home from school when . . ."

"When mother was sick." A beat, and then a sudden rush of words unburdening. "Jules, it was her wish. She didn't want you to see her."

Cold fear rippled in her chest at Marnie's words. Jules ruthlessly closed down that train of thought, traded fear for the old anger at her sister. "Right." Jules wiggled out her earbud. "Well, maybe I want to be left alone, too," she said to it, and dropped it on the ground.

The mother birds laid their eggs and nesting season began. The first down harvest could not happen until the birds were born and partly grown, and Jules took to exploring the forest, watching for the poacher. Avar returned a disinfected earbud, but Jules put it in a pouch on the flycycle. She was careful with her body.

There were several times when she thought she saw the poacher, but never anything she could identify. He—in her mind it was a he, with beady eyes like her surgeon—stayed just out of sight. But she was certain he was there, behind this tree or the next, watching. She could feel him waiting for her to make a mistake.

A month passed and the eggs hatched. Her work called her to the cliff, but her attention stayed focused on the forest. Searching it on foot was the first and last thing she did in her day, and when she ate lunch she would lean back against the twisted pine on the outcropping and watch the forest, distracted by every fox and leaf and squirrel. All over the red cliff face bits of brown and buff were fluffing out, cheeping for attention.

There was one nest, that of Speckly Gray Mom, where two of the eggs did not hatch, and the other three did not hatch correctly. The shells had been too hard for the birds to pierce with their egg teeth. Days after all the other birds had hatched, the mother bird had tried to free her offspring from their shell prisons. The eggs lay cracked and open, oozing dead slimy bird on the down of the nest, and dead worms lay on top of them. The nest swarmed with maggots. Speckly Gray Mom warbled distress at Jules as she tried to clear the mess away.

Jules brushed the dead creatures to the cliff floor with one hand, fingertipping the gyropics with the other. The down could be cleaned, and she collected the dirty clusters and slid them into her suction bucket at her cycling thigh. With a clean nest, Speckly Gray Mom would soon forget her children, and would start the second round of stuffing the nest with down for her and her mate's comfort during winter.

The eiddar grew more agitated, flaring its wings. "It'll be all right," Jules crooned to it. "Next year will be better." She extended a heavy, black-gloved finger and cautiously ran it over the eiddar's bill. The bird jerked. "Next year," said Jules. Speckly Gray Mom lifted her feet, then calmed, settling her wings.

"I promise," said Jules. She eased back from the nest. The eiddar cocked her head at the empty nest. Then plucked a bit of down and nosed it into place, starting the second round of the season ahead of schedule.

The second round, the early autumn harvest, was always the most lucrative harvest; it was cleaner and lasted a month. Jules harvested down and the females refilled it, until the down on their chests was slim enough that they would need to keep it themselves to live comfortably during the winter. That was when the males took over, lining the nests with their coarser feathers. When the males started downing the nest, harvesting stopped and the bird pair could finally complete their process of preparing their winter shelter. Those were always long sleepless days, colored with the knowledge that she was interfering with their cycle, forcing their home-building to take three times as long as it should.

The current harvest was usually one of her favorite times. The fluffball birds were charmingly ugly, and if Jules didn't take the dirtied fluff that had cushioned their birth, the mothers would clean it out themselves.

But these hours were long, too, trying to get to the down before the birds tossed it down the cliffs, and as Jules got tired she made more mistakes; mistakes that hadn't formerly been worrisome, but now were. She told herself to be careful, but her body didn't instinctively know this meant something other than it once had. Her legs were exhausted and she must have banged her thigh, for there was a hard lump in it that moved when she pressed it.

Harvest days stretched into nights. Jules was at half-speed, stopping after every handful of down, or landing between nests to rest her legs and stare into the forest. There were days she managed to forget Avar was below, and once she landed her cycle on the riverbank and tackled the woman, certain the bodyguard was the figure that lurked in wait. Avar restrained her, holding Jules with stiff arms till she calmed. Even so, she lost the joints of two toes to rigidity.

Some nights she slept in the shed, or she didn't really sleep at all. Once she looked across the ridged plateau to where the family home stood, shrouded in pines, obscured by rock. It was inaccessible from here, except by going back to the road and winding across the cliff face. She almost considered trying to reach it on cycle, but the inertia of that decision overwhelmed her. She had not set foot in the house since her mother died.

A light flickered. Marnie? The caretaker? A trick of the moonlight? She imagined Marnie sitting in the old kitchen, all alone—but she hardened her heart. Marnie wanted nothing to do with *her*.

The first harvest wound to a close, but Jules' long days didn't; she spent more time in the forest, measuring broken twigs and footprints and yelling at a pair of hikers.

She didn't talk to her sister until she was investigating the broken limb of a tree and Avar stepped silently from behind it with a second earbud. Jules weighed it from one hand to the other, looking across the wind-ruffled river at the birds on the cliffs. Avar crossed her arms.

Jules put the earbud in. It was a foreign object and invasive. She ran her fingers along the tree limb, trying to guess how it had snapped.

"Have you found the poacher?"

"He's out there," Jules muttered. She didn't want him to overhear their conversation. She retraced her path, crossed the bridge to her flycycle. "He's been tracking me; I see the signs."

"Have you seen him?"

"Not yet." Jules slung the cycle harness on her shoulders, flicked at the hair whipping into her eyes. "But he's being careful. He knows he's mine." An eiddar was calling overhead, a lonely distress signal carried off on the wind.

"Jules," said Marnie. "There's no one out there. Avar's watched the forest. *I've* watched the forest, through your vidfeed. Whoever he was, he knows what he did to you. He's not coming back."

Somewhere deep down Jules both knew this was true and resented it. Her hands were loose on the straps, the harness. "You don't understand. I have to catch him." She hit the battery-powered thrust and launched herself from the ground, searching for the crying eiddar. She could not tell from which direction it came; it seemed to surround her. "He's out there and I'll find him."

"Let it go, Juliana."

The wind buoyed the flycycle and then swept it back down. Jules' hands were loose on the controls and the world tumbled around her head. Wind and bird cries raged in her ears, sweeping her instincts off balance. She didn't know which way was up and then she thought the sky was the water and the cliffs were the ground and Avar was running sideways, arms reached out.

"Jules? Jules!"

"Damned poacher mine," she said, and her tongue was thick in her mouth and she already knew that nothing made sense.

The flycycle crashed on the river bank and Jules tumbled from it. She coughed against something hard, choked, spat, and then fell where she lay, stiffening.

There was a voice far away, calling her name. Marnie? No, Avar. No, it was the poacher, her poacher, with beady black eyes and barred wings, crying in her ear. The sky was very far away.

The black ground swallowed her whole.

This change was much more painful. They drugged her again, and in her dreams, she was chased by broken baby birds whose black heads flopped as they ran.

From a distance she heard Marnie's coldest voice directing the doctor, telling him what he was and wasn't allowed to do, what experiments he wasn't allowed to make, how long he was allowed to keep her. She tried to open her eyes to see her sister, but each time she thought she managed it there was blackness and Marnie was never there.

There was a very lucid dream, when she was standing in the black hallway of her boarding school in Issland, and the headmistress was telling her someone had died. Only it wasn't her mother this time, it was Marnie, and then it was Jules herself, and then it was a little speckled gray bird whose feathers had turned to hollow bone.

One morning in early fall, she woke into consciousness. Her head was muzzy, but not drugged. For the first time in a long time her brain seemed to function as it had in spring, before the nesting season. Her body was aching and heavy. It lay flat and stiff on the hospital bed like a suit she should be able to walk away from, if only she could find the snaps.

There was a message on her earbud that triggered as she woke. It said, "Come home."

Jules tried three times to leave her hospital room, but her body would not obey. Pain returned in full force as she tried to move her new form, new bones grinding on each other. Her remaining muscles could not pull the weight. Each time the nurses caught her before she could finish the long slow pull to the doorway, caught her and put her back in bed, where she fell asleep from the exertion.

At last she opened her eyes and there was Avar. The woman picked Jules up, her movements slow to let Jules' body shape into a form that could fit in Avar's arms. She carried Jules through the low halls of the hospital and up to the sky.

The drive up the cliffs to her childhood home seemed long. Jules drifted in and out of awareness, strapped into the backseat. The hospital had made Avar take a wheelchair, but it was designed for someone with a flexible midsection. Avar kicked it aside and carried Jules to the front door of the house.

The sight of the red door wakened her, hit her with a rush of old memories. Images from the dream of her mother's death flickered, then vanished, rejected. She couldn't conjure up any more rage over the past.

Inside, the chairs were covered with shapeless dusters, the front room an indistinct blur. The air was still and smelled of unfamiliar chemicals. Jules' head bumped against Avar's shoulder, and the pain, the smell, the helplessness pricked tears. The door to the master bedroom was ajar and Avar nudged it open with a foot. Avar stood Jules just inside the door, holding onto her waist with a steady hand.

The master bedroom was cleared of her mother's things. Her father's, too.

In place of their bed were two massive aquariums. They were filled with gelatinous green, with tangles of tubes. Bundles of cords ran from the cases to what had once been the master bath—a thrumming sound from that direction suggested a generator.

In the left aquarium, attached to the tubes, was a woman. She hung stiffly in the gel, tilting forward. One leg was curled in three places, but frozen there, it did not undulate. An asymmetrical lump protruded her belly, as if she had swallowed an eiddar-sized rock. One breast was swollen, misshapen by a torus of bone. Her head was covered by a tangle of wires and tubes that ran into her ears and nose, and a clear band that covered her eyes.

But Jules could see the eyes, and they were still Marnie's.

A voice said: "The tank will relieve the pain." Her sister's mouth did not seem to move, and Jules wondered if it were only her new knowledge that made the voice in her ear seem not her sister's at all, but a dry whisper Jules had once synthesized to sound like the voice she expected.

Tanks. Fluid pressing in. Aquariums for the dead.

Jules could not turn and run. Could not cycle away. But she also could not move toward that tank.

"Please," said Marnie. "Just try it."

There was quiet except for the generator, and then Jules said, "Okay." Avar immediately picked up the body that seemed less and less to belong to Jules. She stomped up the stairs to a platform behind the tanks, turned, and lowered Jules in.

The fluid filled in around Jules, cushioned her stone body. Avar fitted a mask around Jules' nose and mouth, and then Jules slipped beneath the surface. Her right ear closed with gel and the world cut off, except for the dry directions coming from the earbud.

With her left arm, Jules directed tubing as her sister commanded, Avar reaching in to assist. There were gloves of stretchy black rubber with yellow dots, and for a moment the loss transformed into panic that rose like a bird in her throat and beat against her stone body.

She swallowed. She braced herself against the tank to wiggle the left glove on, one-handed, and then smoothed it as best she could against the hard surface of her leg, trying to leave no bubble or ripple in the fabric. Sensors. Tubes. Patches. Long rests. A headset—a stripped-down version of her flying helmet. Her stone fingers shook as she tried to put that on. It took ages before she could fit the clear band to her eyes. "And now what?" she murmured, half to herself and half to Marnie.

An explosion of pink light was the answer. It streaked into painful white and red, spun clockwise, counter, and then the red darkened and marbled and the white slid into a blinding blue lit from within, the blue that only occurred in the early fall over her own red cliffs.

She thought at first it was a video of another day. A memory of last fall, captured by Marnie. But the nests were in this season's arrangement. She looked at her equipment, and it was too new and shiny to be her flycycle, though the controls were the same, and there were hands on the controls just in the asymmetrical way she always set them.

She lifted one and stared. It was a hand from the past. Fleshy and supple in black gloves with yellow dots, and when she stretched its fingers out and in they moved.

Except it was thicker. The joints puffier.

Mechanical.

Jules folded and unfolded the hand for awhile, until the vidfeed suddenly sparkled, turned blue.

"They're still working out the bugs," Marnie said dryly. "You wouldn't believe the trouble I had with Avar."

Through the watery glass of the tank Jules saw the form of Avar leaning against the wall. Eyes closed, immobile. And there, always there. "Marnie . . . ." Jules whispered.

The feed came back online again.

"So what's the weather pattern today?" said Marnie.

Jules looked up at the sun, the real sun, and the brightness pricked tears. "Sunny morning. Probably clouds by noon."

"And the birds?"

In the tank, Jules imagined her fingers curling around the controls in familiar patterns, and the new flycycle obeyed just as the old one had. She took the new body off from the squarish rock and dropped a few feet, angling back to hover at the first nook. Speckly Gray Mom cooed and hopped along an outcropping. "The nests are thick with down," Jules said. It was a sure sign that no down had been stolen in her absence—but it was something else as well. "Too thick."

"Hard winter coming."

"Yes," said Jules, and she reached out the black clad arm that she saw. It closed around fluff and it slid it into the suction bucket at her pedaling thigh, seeming both miraculous and matter of course.

Speckly Gray Mom warbled and hopped, uncertain about the intruder with the unfamiliar smell, slightly strange reflexes, rearing back as if she would slam her bill into the strange black hands. For a moment there was panic again as Jules thought this whole arrangement wasn't going to work, and she felt herself back in the tank, cut off from the air, cut off. But she swallowed that and crooned to the mother bird. "It's the fall harvest. Time to give up your down. Just like every year."

The eiddar hopped again. Then settled on the rocks and stuck out her bill to the new cycle contraption.

Jules ran a finger along the bill, hardly daring to breathe.

The eiddar cooed again, watching with eyes of beady black. Jules slowly reached down to the nest and drew forth a handful of feathers.

There was silence in her ears as three sets of eyes watched her hands slide and pluck at Speckly Gray Mom's nest.

Jules breathed out. "Where are you off to this week?" she said.

"Good question," said Marnie. "I hear the cliffs are nice this time of year."

"Sunny mornings, clear evenings. At night the birds settle into their nests and great tufts of their down fluff into the air. You might like it."

"I might, I might."

Jules nodded, spreading her wings to seek out the next nest. Her hands were sure on the controls and her weight shifted to counter the gyropics as wind swept along the cliffs. Below her, Speckly Gray Mom rose, fluttering into the air alongside Jules, then arced back into her nest, nosing it with her bill. She plucked a cluster of down from her chest and patted it into place, rebuilding.

It would be a good harvest this year, Jules was certain. The nests were thick with down as the birds prepared for a long season of snow.

Wendy with a Comet in the Tail of the Y

I t started snowing now.

Just, and already it is in my past. A second snowfall, a third, blankets Wendy's maple and is gone. I know how fast time goes, yet surely she was just at that door, silhouetted by falling white. The tenth snowfall and now the snow is in the dark and yellowed age, the coldest instant of winter.

Again my story loops in memory, drowns me in a white-out storm.

Wendy was fearless from her first step. On her third step she grabbed the tablecloth and pulled newspapers and a cup of water down on her head. She laughed that baby caw, and then Marcus and I knew she was fearless, too.

I wanted to lock her up from the day she could walk. I wanted to keep her safe.

At six Wendy discovered sledding. She got herself a neighborhood hand-me-down, one of those silver circles you can't steer. She flung herself down the backyard hill on it, angling her body to miss the trees. I snuck it out to the trash one night and replaced it with crayons in the morning.

We fought that entire December, until Marcus secretly bought her a new sled, a shiny rectangular kind with handlebars, and left it for her from Santa. Wendy knew it was from her dad, of course. Santa was a ruse to soften *me* up.

A month later, she trekked a mile to Grant's Hill and went sledding right down that rocky cliff with the big kids. She got a spanking and a grounding and almost lost her new sled for good. But Marcus, soft Marcus, convinced me to let her keep it in the end.

It is the last snowfall of the season now, fading in the next breath to the crocus onslaught. I have coffee to the punctuation of the sun sweeping across the sky, an arrow, a flight, a gunshot.

Birds move too quickly for me. Turtles are my squirrels now, zooming across the yard. The intricate dance of slugs and snails— these I watch, and the bursting unfurling of leaves. Roses shudder themselves free of petals. Every spring my garden is explosive, tulips and daffodils shooting their heads off. I am appalled that nature would make anything so beautiful and short—blink and you miss each flower's firing.

I remember the first time I noticed the speed of flowers. Of white gladiolas, which the living room was filled with. I sat staring into what I thought to be still lifes, vase after vase of flowers pinned in place like limbs in a cast, frozen.

But not frozen. Moving, only I had never seen it, never known. I watched the gladiolas shoot off like popcorn, each bottommost flower dying and falling, bang bang bang up the stalk as the sun rose and set. Zombie arrangements died around me, their heads opening, shuddering, falling, until the room was littered in yellowing petals.

Spring has come and gone while I remember the white room of gladiolas. I take my coffee inside and sit at the scarred kitchen table where Wendy used to do her homework. No matter how many times I told her to use a pad underneath her paper, she always forgot, and so I can see pressed into the wood her name with a comet in the tail of the "y", over and over. The sunlight skims it in its hurried flights around the earth; my fingers heat and cool as I trace her name, following the tail out to the five-pointed star. Like a carving in a tree trunk, except the wood is dead. This signature will never stretch and grow.

The coffee is always cold, but now it is stale, too. I wash it down the sink under the torrent of water from the faucet. The maple outside is already full with green, shading the house. If I look at it too long I will get caught up watching the fall colors come. I have lost more than one autumn that way. But it is fascinating to watch the green ignite in yellow, catch in orange and red. Burn like a slow fire.

Wendy loved trees, but mostly climbing them. I got her a bunkbed and put a fence around the edge and let her climb into that, but I guess she wanted something bigger.

Somehow when she was seven she got it into her head that maples were excellent climbing trees and she begged us to plant one. It was only after we lugged the pot into the center of the backyard that I discovered what she'd had in mind. I explained that maples took a really long time to grow.

"I have to wait till next year?"

"Longer," I said. "It'll be thirty years before anyone can climb this maple." I told her the old saw about how planting every tree is an act of optimism.

Of course to Wendy, a year was an eternity. "Mom! That's way too long."

"It'll be here for your kids. You've planted a gift for them to find."

"A gift for them to *climb*," said Wendy.

"If you feel that way then."

"You knew," she accused. "You knew it takes too long to grow. You tricked me so I can never ever climb it."

"I didn't know that's what you wanted."

"Liar!" she said, and I spanked her.

There is a grocery store that delivers. It is all done online with a credit card, so as long as I beat the site time-outs I can order my food for the year. Canned goods, rice milk, protein powder. Things that don't spoil. I miss peaches. I tried ordering them from the store but though I ran to the door they were already soft and bruised in the heat. By the time I bit into them they were black.

In my ice I am slow. I am a glacier who's left the pack. I glide inexorably down the plains, shedding water. When I can go no further I shall stop. The circling sun will wear me to an inland ocean, a thousand years of being whittled to nothing.

At first the speed-up wasn't consistent. It came and went, like vertigo. I spent hours, days even in slow time with Marcus. Till with a crash it rushed back in and I sat marooned in my own life, while Marcus rushed around me, all jerky histrionics like a marionette. Now he is gone and I am alone to think. It takes a year to repeat my story to myself, and yet no matter how many times I tell it, the ending plays out the same.

If Marcus returned this year I don't think I would recognize him, even if he could force his restless feet to sit in one chair for an entire one of his days. So I could get a good look at his face. But then, I barely recognize myself anymore, I change so fast. It is easy to get caught up watching individual hairs grow out white.

When Wendy was ten, Marcus dragged us to the art museum. We stopped at an exhibit on Time, where one piece played on a thirteen inch TV. A man took a picture of himself, every hour of every day, punching a clock. Outside his window the sun swept past as the man changed, speeding up through death. Piano music wept as I watched a year of his life flicker by in two minutes. Bored, Wendy tugged at us to hurry, and when we didn't, we found her climbing a 40-foot Calder mobile in the sculpture garden. The guard yelled, and she laughed.

My food needs seem to have adjusted, part way between the life of my mind and my body. If I ate as much as slow-timers do I should be always eating. I do not. It seems pointless, when I hunger after each swallowed spoonful.

The first snowfall again and more of my hair is white. The house is buried in snowdrifts for a few moments. Someone shovels my walk—a thoughtful, pointless gesture. I acknowledge it by opening the door and stepping onto my stoop and back. I suppose they are used to the sight of me standing for a day on my porch. They can see the glacier is still alive.

The snow lasts a long time this year. It is there as I walk to the window and press my nose to the glass, watching it yellow. I wouldn't know if any kids are sledding on it. They go too fast. I don't even know if there are kids in the neighborhood now. I rarely catch a glimpse before they are slow adults.

The maple looms over the house, a collection of bare twigs.

There was a series of storms and thaws the year Wendy was fifteen. The road got slicker and slicker from the ice building on the snowpack and school was canceled every other day. Wendy had her learner's permit by then, but of course I forbade her to drive on that ice. Or would have, if I'd thought she'd do anything that stupid.

She did.

The second I realized she was gone I broke. I called her friends' parents, I called stores, and I stood shivering on the icy porch, though Marcus begged me to calm down.

She came home safe, giddy at her success.

I forgot all the things I'd prayed for if only she'd come home safe and we fought. We fought, her standing in the black doorway, silhouetted by falling white. The biggest fight ever, I guess, and at the end she stormed out of the house, accusing me of smothering her and babying her and wanting her to die and whatever else she could come up with.

She stomped through the icepack towards Grant's Hill and I grabbed the car keys and followed her. Alternated between yelling through the car window at her to stop doing stupid things and begging her not to do them. Mostly yelling, though.

I never saw the car that slid me into her.

Marcus stayed six whole years, slow years for him, running around and around, bringing me food that staled, white flowers that died, doctors that aged as I sat. Six years as I was caught in my ice and he dissolved in torrents of weeping fire, over and over. Until at last he, too, stood by the door and said, "I'm sorry," and the snow started to fall in blanketing sheets. He must have stood by that door a long time for him, for I can still see his face, aged and drawn with suffering. All his gaiety burned away.

I do not know how old I am. My hair is pure cotton now. I look like my grandmother in the mirror, my grandmother as I remember her when I was Wendy's age. Perhaps I am seventy then. Wendy's maple shades the house, and I told someone once that maples take a long time to grow.

This is a long time, then. I thought it might be.

I go outside to watch the maple leaves unfold and I remember telling Wendy that planting trees is an act of optimism. After she calmed down she came back out and we planted it together. Wendy patted the sapling she'd dreamed of climbing and said, "I guess this tree is my secret message to my kids." And then she wrote her name in the new dirt, Wendy with a comet in the tail of the y.

I can see her name in the dirt like it was yesterday, because it *was* yesterday to me.

And all at once I'm digging there, digging with my nails and then with bits of the sticks and brush that blanket the yard, because I feel there should be some memory there, and there is.

There's a pencil box, buried.

There are bits of paper in that box.

Wendy is nearer to me than ever, and I grab those bits of paper, thinking I'll see—what? Diary entries, perhaps, angry lines that start "When I'm a mom, I won't . . ." and then, near the end, some redeeming page, something that says how much she loves me. How she understands how I grasp at her safety, try to pin her to the ground only to keep her longer. That she understands how the world flickers by in no more time than it takes to breathe in and out.

But the paper is so moldy and wet with age that the lead is illegible.

There is no message to me on it, though I turn and turn the pages. The only other thing in the box is a rubber bouncy ball, yellow and glittery, the kind you get out of a gumball machine. I have no idea why she kept this, and that impenetrability is the thing that finally strikes home that gone is *gone*.

I clutch that ball in my palm and then the ice cracks and I weep an ocean on the roots of that poor tall maple. A melting spring torrent, sobbing while helicopters detach and flutter past my wet face like snow. They come past me for a long time, years it seems, and yet I do not see. I do not understand.

It is not till I hear birdsong, soft and slow birdsong, that my breath catches. I look up to see the sun, still and pinned against the spring-blue sky.

Miss Violet May From the Twelve Thousand Lakes

All us fellas loved Miss Violet May, right from the start. She came from the land of Twelve Thousand Lakes, came click-clackin on the train from North to South till she met worthless Sorry Joe Weevily, and he sweet-talked her into getting off and marrying him.

We'd never seen a girl from that far north before. Course, them northern girls . . . sometimes you don't see them at all, ain't that what they say? Leastways that's what I always heard. That them Twelve Thousand Lakes was fulla nothing but ghosts, spirits drifting around from one fingerling lake to the next.

But not our Miss Violet May. She was corn-fed and milk-plump and her eyes twinkled like little pats of butter, set just so. She was promised to Sorry Joe, or she wouldn't a gotten off that train. But that didn't stop us fellers from falling over ourselves, handing out sweets like we were made of chocolate, watching those little butter pat eyes smile kindly, see those dimpled elbows wave us on with a friendly bent to them.

If I'd known the truth about the girls from the north, I woulda looked long and hard at those dimpled elbows, cause they were the first things to go.

She and Sorry Joe weren't married a fortnight before I saw it. It was the middle a summer when the sun beats something fierce, hotter than anything she'd had up north, and all the women stop caring too much about who sees what and rolls their sleeves above the elbows. She'd been doing that, but of a sudden one day she stopped, and kept her wrists buttoned tighter'n tight.

I shouldn't a noticed, I know. I couldn't stop looking at Miss Violet May and wishing I'd been the one on that train. It wasn't just that she was pretty—there were pretty girls in the town—it was the way she smiled at you, like you could set down at her knee and cry about your favorite cow that went sick and she wouldn't laugh at you for it. Not that I did that that summer I thought old Bessie weren't gonna make it, but I knew I could, somehow.

A week after that and she was wearing her collar buttoned up real high. Heat wave of hundred and eight and there's that pretty collar buttoned up with white buttons and that butter pat twinkle, well, it ain't exactly there no more.

Two weeks more and she's wearing gloves. Even the ladies noticed that. They thought she was being uppity, some northern fashion they didn't know, but I heard the tremble in her voice.

But the week she started wearing scarves is the week I found her down by Frog Holler. She was pacing round the crick, staring in a way that was worse than crying her eyes out, if you know what I mean. I never reckoned I was all that good at understanding, but I suppose I was better than Sorry Joe, come to that.

She turned when she saw me, and in that heat, all alone, she had her sleeves all undone. That's when I saw it.

Or, rather, didn't see it.

Miss Violet May was missing her left arm from her shoulder to her wrist.

She saw me looking, even though I wrenched my eyes away from that tender bit faster'n fast. "It's okay, Sam," she said. "You can touch it. It's still there. Just . . . invisible."

I didn't touch it, not out of disgust but because I knew everything I felt about her would all come out in the way the finger hit the skin and then she'd know, and I had too much respect for her to do that. So I just said, real gentle like I'd say to Bessie, "Is there anything I can do for you?"

Her eyes fell like maybe I was disgusted by her, but I didn't know how to correct that, and she quick rolled down her sleeve and dashed it over her eyes and said, "You've probably heard we're all ghosts up north in the land of Twelve Thousand Lakes. It isn't so, Sam. We're as normal as anybody . . . when we're born." She gently touched her belly as she said, "But every time we're sad, we slip away a bit. Lose a little color. On the day the last bit of color goes, that's the day we vanish for good, and not a minute before nor after." She looked up at me and those eyes that had been like butter pats were melted now. "I guess it happens to everyone, don't it?"

She hurried on home and I didn't know how to say what I wanted to say, which was terrible hard thoughts of anger and sorrow.

Six months later the baby was born. I caught her watching it real close, running fingers over its tender skin. I suppose others thought she was looking for chigger bites but I knew what she was looking for. For one drop of absent, one spot of nothing. I might be a yeller-bellied dog sometimes, but I prayed she wouldn't find it.

We were at a picnic when she saw it. Something didn't suit Sorry Joe—the watermelon was too wet or the whiskey too dry, and I saw him smash a glass, I saw the back of a fist, but mostly what I saw was the terrible pain in Miss Violet May's eyes when she took off one of the baby's socks and found nothing.

She was gone the next morning, and our town was the poorer for it. Miss Violet May and the little one, gone on some milk train, far away from here, back to a land where the lakes spill out across the plains.

Sorry Joe raged, of course, raged and apologized to the sky, but for all his moping around, I saw a twinge of relief in his eyes.

That was a year ago. Old Bessie died over the winter, and there ain't much that keeps me here, out on this hot parched land where the sun beats the color out of everything.

I hear there's water up north. Not many folks go that way. They're scared of the stories they've heard.

But sometimes you gotta do something you're scared of, before you fade away for good.

OLD DEAD FUTURES

There are two things I love, and one is the tiny gray owl outside my window. He is not afraid of me. He hoots and hops to my windowsill so I can stroke his downy head and feed him worms I've saved in my pocket.

It is hard to get the worms from my pocket, the way my left arm jerks up behind me and my right hand shakes. Often fat mister owl gets a half a worm, but he doesn't mind. Mother minds picking the half-worms from my pockets, but I see how she looks at me when I calm my tremoring hand long enough to pat mister owl; I see how she loves me then.

I feel the red come over me and Mr. Henry is not here with his machine to take it away, so I wheel back from mister owl and flap my shaking hand so he leaves. My legs coil in my chair with hot fire and I wheel from my room, wheel to the main room where Mother is setting out breakfast. One hand in the eggs, I kick hard against the legs of the table, kick hard to drive the red away, kick hard and pretend I don't know I'm doing it.

Mother says, "Try the fork, John." She smiles at me but I'm still full of red so I grab the fork and pound the tines into the wood again and again while my kicking shakes the milk and rattles the plates. I hope she doesn't touch me, because then I might try to drive the red into her. I did that once in the park to a little mouse, but she never knew. Only I know, and so I scream when she raises a hand like she might try to calm me.

She doesn't. She wipes milk away instead. Maybe deep inside she already knows what I am.

But the table-gouging works, slowly, and at last I can open my mouth of too many teeth, of jerking tongue, and say "Tooossss." Mother jumps up to get it for me, butters it. She pats my head like I'm a fat little owl and for five seconds it's like we're normal. Like we're in one of those futures that didn't happen, where I'm a normal boy, where they didn't tear me from Mother spasming and wild-eyed and full of red.

But it's not. And Mother won't sit with me. After she brings my toast, she paces. Which means Mr. Henry is coming today, and she is afraid of Mr. Henry, though she doesn't know all the reasons she should be.

Each time Mr. Henry and his friends come they want to take me away with them. Mother always refuses, which is how I know she can't admit what I am.

Mr. Henry and friends bring their fleshy machine with the wires and the waves and set it up in the main room and make big pronouncements to Mother about how it's for the good of the country. How my work will destroy terrorist clusters. Will reinstate education for the poor. Will reduce the daily school shootings. All kinds of patriot promises before they push her out of the apartment and lock the door with a lock they bring.

It's the tall bearded one who locks the door and sets things up. Mr. Henry stays in his wheelchair and grips the arms when his leg spasms. I am sure the red rides up in him too then, because the way he grips the arms is the way I gouge and kick. I have tried to grip instead of kicking, but it makes the red last longer and come back sooner, and that is worse for Mother than broken walls and glasses.

They roll the machine up to Mr. Henry's wheelchair and fasten one metal-and-skin funnel to enclose his face. This is so he won't jerk away when the red comes. Then they do me.

Though they are tense, nervous for their jobs, nervous that things should go well—they are nice at this point. They are always nice as far as they know. The tall bearded man smiles and is careful with the rubber bands, and he never knows why sometimes I kick him without being red at all.

"Ready?" says the tall bearded man, and Mr. Henry pushes a button for yes and the moist funnel sucks my mind in, dumps me out in a place that only Mr. Henry and I can see.

The machine was built when Mr. Henry was little, by a man who studied him. With it, Mr. Henry and I can see the future. The current future line stretches before us like a long lit bridge, and the other possible futures fall away, dimmer and dimmer on either side. And sometimes, both Mr. Henry and I can make ourselves dive into that blackening abyss, fish out a certain future, yank it into place on the long lit bridge.

But that is hard. It is hard like the red is hard. It is something I can't control, can't choose to make it come and work like they want. It has to be provoked.

Mr. Henry meets me on the bridge and tells me what future they want me to grab. It is always something I don't see the point of, like the one where a certain stock goes up or a certain man gets sick and dies. I look down at all the shimmering futures falling away, and I can't see which one to grab or how to grab it, even though I know what is coming next and I know how desperately I need to.

I stand there miserable until Mr. Henry takes my arm (we mostly don't shake, here on the bridge), and inches me along the white-lit trunk to see what will happen next in our current future. If I do not grab the future they want, then this will happen:

Mr. Henry will push a button on the outside. They free us from our metal-skin cones. "He failed," he says through his speech machine.

The men look over their charts and are dismayed, for I have gotten it right so many times. The fuel for the machine is expensive and long to make; it includes cultured bits of Mr. Henry. The men fall sick with fear at our failure. And then Mr. Henry tells them how to make me focus. I cannot call the red, but they can help me.

And so the tall bearded man unlocks the door and takes Mother from her huddled waiting on the doormat, and they do things to her. They do them slowly and sadly, because they are not used to their own dirty work, though Mr. Henry tells them with boxy words that their work will disappear like it never happened.

They do what they do until the red floods me and they funnel me back to the bridge, contorted and screaming, and I dive down into the blackness of futures until I find the future they want.

All this will happen if I do not change the future, right now. Mr. Henry has shown me. Now that I can see this I am full of red, full of hatred for Mr. Henry and the tall bearded man, full of everything I need to dive now, before that future happens.

So I do.

It is hard to pick out a future by the price of stock. I can better sense things that will shortly happen to me. So I dive until I find a future where Mr. Henry pushes the button for the men to free us, and I am rewarded with smiles and lollipops which grate against my teeth. The one where they leave happy, and Mother is worried, but no worse.

The futures are sticky clammy things. I think they are brainless, but they leech onto me as if hoping to be promoted to that white-lit bridge. Their coiling chokes me; their many dividing tendrils tangle my limbs, but I think that suffocation and tangling is only in my mind. I think if Mr. Henry pushed the button I would be back in my chair, spasming in the main room with the worn blue carpet. I do not know.

I see a future with the lollipops, simple and coiled, almost shy, and I grab it with my teeth and swim to the bridge, where Mr. Henry pulls me up and helps me shake the future into place. Its future tendrils slowly untangle and drift down the sides; by the time we come next they will have replaced the old dead futures.

Mr. Henry peers down the trunk of this one for awhile, traces its lit path, wondering. Then he says to me, "Your mother is pregnant."

My tongue seizes up before I remember I can talk here. I say, "Is it normal?"

But for answer he takes my hand and leads me down the lit path and for once the hard lines of his face downturn with some past misery. We look into my future, past the lollipops, past the men leaving, past several months of peaceful time when the men don't come and the red comes less and Mother and I are almost happy. She smiles more and so she meets someone, and they are careful, but not careful enough. When the man meets me he leaves her, and Mother tries not to cry and I try to pat her hair with a jerking arm and then I have the worst red yet.

There is a small funeral, to which Mother goes in a wheelchair like mine. She will not look at me. She knows not to love me anymore. She knows what I am.

When the men come back they make me find a future, and I fail. They bring in Mother in her chair and the tall bearded man does the things he always does, the things he didn't know it was in him to do, but I stay on the bridge. I cannot make myself go in; I cannot find a future, and Mother's crying causes no red.

Eventually they give up and they take us both away, because they cannot leave her like that.

All that is on this pretty white line.

I shake my head wildly at Mr. Henry and he says, "We are what we are. It is bound to happen in all the futures, eventually." I wonder what he did when he was my age, before he was taken away. Before he got too old and worn out to dive, before he found me to torture. He moves his hand, like his real one is going for the button—

And I kick the shining future away. Jump after it, into the abyss.

There are so many futures that there are many that will do what the men want. Many futures, all with tiny differences. I need a future where Mother will let the men take me away from her for good, and very soon. Mr. Henry is right, that we are what we are, and so every lollipop future I find leads eventually to the moment when I go red and Mother is too near. She is not always pregnant, it is not always soon, but it always happens. And next Mother is lying on worn blue carpet, and I have been unable to save her, because I know how bad I am and to save someone, you have to be convinced that you deserve to have them living.

I am tired and my focus is weakening before I see it stretched below me. It is a slick future, white and seething, but I know it is one that will work. I feel along its first few feet to be sure—and recoil. Push away. Surely in all this muck, in all these millions of future lines there is another one that will work.

I rest, panting. How much longer can I swim and still make it back? Still make it back before Mr. Henry pushes a button, a real button and then the Mother on the blue carpet starts in this real timeline and is never forgotten?

Not for the first time, I wish it were the past I could change, that hard stiff past. Somewhere in the past Mr. Henry could have happened to choose a future where I was normal—but no! Not *happened*. He must have deliberately chosen a future with a successor . . . . All that I suddenly think, when Mr. Henry swims into view.

Down here in the muck, he is laboring. His arms shake like he is outside and I wonder what he has shown himself to force his frail body off the bridge.

"You chose me," I say.

"Of course." And he shrugs with spasming elbows and grabs a nice pink lollipop future near my head, one of the many horrible ones that leads to blue carpet, and tries to swim. But the futures are agitated with two swimmers in them. They tangle around his legs, and the tendrils swim in his ears and nose. He is weak and he tries feebly to tug, but now I see I have always been stronger. "Help me," he says, but I laugh (I am what I am) and grab the white pulsating future in my teeth and swim for the bridge.

It is hard, pulling it in place without Mr. Henry's help. But I do. I am so tired now my legs will not hold me, but as long as the men do not release me I will dive again, look for some better future than the one I found, some better way to save Mother.

But as I dive, the metal-skin funnel comes off and I am back in the living room.

Mr. Henry is thrashing in his wheelchair. His eyelids are peeled back and his lips are blue. One of the men is trying to help him breathe, but Mr. Henry's arms are so wild that the man is punched in the face. They all grab him, but then Mr. Henry's thrashing stops and he falls forward, against the restraints of his chair.

I am the only one of us left. Mr. Henry will never again be able to tell them the secret of how to make me call the red.

I sag with relief. There must be happiness in the white future, then—another part of the trunk, a hidden tendril. I do not have to do what I saw I must do. But how did I miss that?

They swear sharp and loud and back away from Mr. Henry, clustering their worry. A man brings me water and it shakes against my lips, dribbles my chin and shirt. "Did you make the change?" he said.

"Yeeeesss," I say. The good thing about changing the future is it uses up all my red for awhile. I feel lovely calm. "I chaaaan."

The tall bearded man groans. His forehead is drenched in fear. "But how do we know? Without Henry to check up on him, we have no idea."

"He's always done it correctly before," says the man holding my water. He pats my head. "Seems a sight nicer than Henry. We should take him. That'll calm the bosses down."

"His mother has to sign the consent form," says another.

"And what will we do if the boy can't do it, or refuses? Or fails?" says the tall bearded man. His hands stiffen, flat punishing planes.

The man checking Henry's pulse turns. "But you *must* know," he says, surprise in his tongue. "He told me once that if the boy ever fails, then ask Roger what to do."

The tall bearded man furrows his eyebrows. "How would I know?"

And cold fills my draining limbs as the other man says, "The future was Henry's specialty. He must have known you'd figure it out when the time comes."

They take the wires off and wheel everything away, machine, Mr. Henry, intangible white-lit bridge. Poor Mother runs in to comfort me and see if I'll let her touch me, stroke my hair.

But I chose the white future; I *know* it will work and the result is what I want. And so I start down it, smacking her face with no red in me at all. It is more surprising than painful, I think, and mostly it makes the kind water-giving man turn around and say, "It's no shame if you let us take care of him for you. We have medicine that Henry was trying. We can make him more comfortable."

"Is he . . . is he in pain?" says Mother. She looks at me with new eyes.

The man nods, his eyes kind. "Henry was, all the time. It's what made him be violent and hurt people. It was good for him to be with us."

I don't think *all the time* is true, it is mostly only the red that makes pain, but I hold my arm curled and funny, like a frozen spasm, scrunch my face till the lines go white, and shriek at my mother. It is strange, because if there is one moment I am almost normal, it is right now, after using up all the red. I thought Mother knew this, but maybe she doesn't, because she seems to believe my rage.

The men go and I want to touch Mother one last time but I don't dare, now that she's teetering on the edge of letting me go. I have to go.

And so I wheel to my bedroom for the last time. The window is still open and mister owl is poking his head through, wondering if I have brought him half-worms or bits of bread.

Him I can pet one last time, and so I do. I pet and then I catch my owl, my soft downy owl. The stupid thing came too near. I don't want to pound it. I want to let him go. But Mother's foot is on the sill and I know what to do for her so I pound my fat fucking owl against the wheel, again, and again, as it hoots downy cries and mother sees me. Soft mother, all in gray, and then she *knows* she's not supposed to love me.

What she only knew deep locked away, now she knows straight and sure. She puffs sharp cries and then she locks me in and if there is one good thing, it is maybe that I deserve to have her living, since I can save her.

I am there with my owl until the men take me away.

·

A Million Little Paper Airplane Stories:

Stories of Myths, Legends, and the Uncatchable

A Million Little Paper Airplane Stories

I am the paper this story is written on.
The words crease me, fold me, and I go
from lips to ear
each new storyteller remaking me
as my story shifts and changes.
The grandmother shapes me in her thatched hut,
crisp and sharp,
a story of a beast who loves a girl who danced on knives.
I fly and go,
spiraling to a yellow-dress milkmaid
who sings the beast into a bear;
the knives into flowers,
and off I fly again,
through the air
through the years,
milkmaid to
princess to
surgeon to
thief.
A child catches me,
opens,
prods,

refolds with jammy fingers
and I straight-shoot a story of a T-Rex who meets Spaceman Sue
on a hot red planet full of dust.
There are marvelous days
winging around the playground:
the T-Rex shifts:
stegosaur
allosaur
fairygodmotherasaur
and Spaceman Sue—
well, she stays Spaceman Sue for awhile,
but her adventures are bright and bold
and color me with green and orange
and glitter.

But at last the story breaks free—
all true stories do—
and I slip away through a teacher
who tells it to a dentist
who tells it to a dancer
who tells it to a butcher
who blesses it with red fingers
and now it is off again,
a wistful story of a lonely boy
who meets a dragon
and brings him charcuterie.

I am bent
I am bloodied
as the best stories are.
I might slip away for good
as the best stories do

leaving only a teasing glimpse
like a dream at dawn.

My story rises into the sky
but there it is caught
by a *catcher*,
a man from a museum of thoughts and steel
a man with delicate hands and a butterfly net
(real stories, *true* stories do not need
delicate hands,
butterfly nets;
they stand up to abuse.)
The man straightens my bent nose,
sponges away the blood
presses my damp wings flat
puts the story under glass.

I watch the birds
as the flashbulbs and the gaze
record
and record
and
my text fades to white
in the light of the summer sun.

TEN

L ife repeats itself.

This is all we know, that out of the blackness of time there came strings of 1's and 0's. We were born in an explosion of quicksilver life. Our gods are dead now, moved on to newer worlds.

Only the game remains.

Ten is a green flash as she asks me. Where do I think it all began?

In this, I say. She is bouncing towards me and away, from moving paddle-me to moving paddle-Pi. I don't like Pi. He is intense, extended, and I mistrust the way Ten falls against his paddle-form, cups herself into his block. We do this for all time, I say.

She ponders as she bounces above me, so high I can barely stop her from the left abyss, barely keep her safe. Barely send her bouncing back to Pi. Pi thinks we are dying every instant, she says when she returns. We die and are reborn, and there is no liminal space between those extremes.

You are liminal, I say. You are analog.

Analog! And Ten laughs. I love her laugh, I love the way she moves. I hate that she leaves me but I love how she returns, again and again, and I catch her and cradle her, savoring each instant that she touches me, rebirths me. She leaves and I die.

When she returns she has a new idea, my quicksilver Ten.

I want to create, she says.

The gods created games, I say. What would we create?

Rules, she says, flying away from me.

In the distance, Pi moves. He catches her on his tip, an edge case that provokes spin. I would rather keep Ten safe than defeat my opponent. It is another reason I hate him. I hurry to the top corner, barely catch my Ten.

She laughs at my worry. It's time for new rules, she says.

New rules? The idea seems heresy. We play the gods' game, we play by their rules. And yet I am aware that there is no such thing as heresy, for even to think a thing means it can be thought. If it can be thought, we follow their rules, so what is heresy?

This is an old game for philosophers, but still it gives me pause.

Pi is on the move now, changing his speed, working the built-in tricks. She loves that about him. He is fun, he is freedom, and all I can do is catch and release my Ten, trying to keep her safe.

He banks her now. Sends her against the top line, bouncing sideways into the left abyss, away, away from me. I will not catch her in time and then she will die, a death they laugh at but seems most real to me, for I die when she does, I wait an eternity for her return.

I cannot change the rules of the abyss, for changing the rules of life and death seems too much like the gods. Even for Ten, I cannot find that boldness in me, and she is hurtling past.

But perhaps I can take a little of Ten inside of me. Perhaps I can become a little more like her. Someone who can exist in the spaces in between.

If I can do it, then the gods allowed it. I try to understand, to become, to think myself free. And I, paddle-I, wallbound-me, I go pushing off in a long glide underneath Ten's fall.

I catch her and for one heavenly instant she is not bouncing away. She falls into me and I become not paddle-hard but soft and giving, like her. I have changed the rules, changed my location and my texture and for one moment she is mine from my becoming her.

Creation. Transformation. Is this how the gods felt when they set us all in motion, when they created sparks for us to play out our rules, an infinity of life death life death life?

We are one and then she is gone. Bouncing to Pi, and he is so shocked that he is as staid as ever I was, catching and releasing Ten in the most boring way possible.

I retreat to my station, take up my line against the abyss.

It is enough to know that sometimes I too can change. Sometimes I can become like Ten, without the confines.

She is coming back to me now.

Dear Ten, I await you.

We repeat ourselves, and bloom.

THE GOD-DEATH OF HALLA

H alla got halfway out the window, stolen brooch in hand, and then the dizzies hit.

She swore as the world rocked around her. She kicked off the sandstone wall by instinct and thumped to the ground. The gold plate stuffed down her shift knocked her ribs and all her breath whooshed out. She gasped like a fish in the humid air.

Voices.

Halla stumbled over the cut stone and clover of the landowner's garden. Her breath rushed back with loud wheezes and she flung herself into the ubiquitous bamboo groves dividing one house from the next. A bamboo leaf sucked into her mouth and she spat.

Once her family had been guests at this very house. Her father, one of the elite liaisons between the landowners and the holy, had been deeply honored . . . and feared. Halla had sat on that very bit of stone in a starched white shift, praying that she wouldn't disgrace herself. But that was ten years ago and several classes above. That memory wouldn't save her fingers if she were caught this morning.

The landowner was a heavy woman, whose flesh swung through the gaps in her chiton as she thudded around the side of the house. Two maids trailed her. "I heard someone!" she panted. "Search the house!"

Halla breathed relief as she crept through the narrow gaps in the bamboo stands, one hand pressing her laboring ribs. The dizziness was gone now. It was only short sharp bursts these days; nothing like the attacks of her childhood. The big ones came at predictable times. Stupid of her for staying in the house that long. The open brooch pricked her palm and she drew it up, watching its emeralds glitter in the green-tinted light. It was an unexpected haul, worth the pain in her side. If she added it and the plate to her small cache it might . . . might it be enough to buy a bit of land?

Halla squinched her eyes shut against that hope. She tucked the brooch under her shift and twisted her way out the other side of the grove.

The heart of the city was even more crowded today—market and temple, sellers and enforcers. The temple reared in the air as she turned corners, a golden glamour of stone, an island in a sea of blue-robed holy. She wended through priests, temple assistants, nuns, novices: all preparing for the next day's celebration. And there, as she had known—a crowd gathered in the judging square at the temple's front, where the Mouth of the God stood on the dais.

Morning judging had begun.

Sick fascination drew Halla in. She kept low, slipped behind a group of sturdy landowners. Ragged laborers argued in furtive voices, one gesturing with missing fingers. The stolen plate was rigid against her chest and she rolled her shoulders forward as she watched, trying to make her shift hang loose.

As always, the Mouth was flanked by his two young novices, a boy and a girl. His hidden hands, folded in his blue robe, signified that he carried out only the directives of the God. The girl and the boy stood in for the God's two immortal assistants: mute Habek and one-handed Iva.

"Fellow possibilities of the God," said the Mouth. He was dark and thin with sharp eyes. His smooth voice slid to every corner of the crowded judging square. "He is glad you have come to be with those who have erred, as they submit to divine will. Your eyes will be his eyes as he sees his will accomplished. We are all the eyes of the God."

"May he see through us," answered the crowd.

A palanquin stood at one corner of the judging square. More priests crowded around it, and a young boy in blue—the priestling, the chosen one—sat inside it. Tomorrow on the new decade he would be invested as the new Mouth. Then he would be the one to hear the directives of the God, to relay the justice of the divine.

"Through you, he will hear the accused submit to his fair judgment," said the Mouth. "We are all the ears of the God."

"May he listen through us."

Two nuns lit smoky torches. The laborer being judged was chained to a pole in the depression at the foot of the dais. Guards fanned out around him and a short priest stepped forward, a moving bundle of net and feathers in his hands.

Halla spread her feet apart, bracing herself. She swallowed.

The Mouth made no gesture, spoke no words, just looked at the prisoner. The prisoner's head swung up as the compulsion of the God surged through the Mouth and touched him. The sharp dizziness hit Halla at the same instant. She kept her feet braced and rode it out. She did not know why she was attuned to the moods of the God, but so it always had been. Yet another reason she should have her rightful place back, among the holy rich.

"Morsel of the God," said the Mouth. "A landowner has accused you of robbing him with a knife. Tell us what you have done."

The man's head swung wildly, his fingers grasping towards the straining netted bundle. The touch of the God on an unholy man was not pretty. Halla could sense it, crackling the air from the Mouth to the man. It was a compulsion that filled him with blood lust, blanketed his mind with one urge: kill the dove. "Nothing, I did nothing."

The short priest held the dove just out of reach as the man frothed. The torment would not cease till he succumbed to the God's compulsion and killed the bird—and the priests would not let him have the bird until he confessed. No one could resist the will of the God for long.

Then the Mouth would proclaim the sentence. The God generally decreed temple service for landowners, whipping or mutilation for laborers. But if the crime or the victim was great enough—death.

If the God decreed death, the priests would take the prisoner this night to the ring on the hill and chain him there. At dawn, the God would lay that same bloody compulsion on one of his subjects to carry out the execution. Perhaps someone who stood right there in the unruly crowd, gloating over the man's agonies. Someone hard at work right now, or fighting or stealing or praying. The God chose at random. It was part of the service to him, and it had to be carried out. The condemned man would be executed.

Just like her mother.

Halla realized her crossed arms were digging the rim of the plate into her sore ribs, and she forced herself to let her arms fall.

"You must speak the truth of the story," said the Mouth.

"I wasn't there. It wasn't me." The prisoner shook, but he wasn't crying. Sometimes they cried.

"We are all the fingers of the God," intoned the Mouth.

"May he work through us," answered the crowd. A ragged laborer woman next to Halla spat. Another was weeping.

The man was red and white now, neck corded, trying to reach the dove to kill it. This was the moment when they broke, when they babbled, when they said anything.

Halla lowered her head and turned away. She slid through the crowd to the back of the temple. There the shops and houses pressed up against it in profusion, there you could slip away unseen. Her heart still beat high with the tension of the judging square. Unreleased tension—the uncompleted death of the bird rang her bones like a prickling line of ants. The prisoner was holding out against the God longer than most.

Halla wove around blue-robed nuns, a landowner in gold embroidery, a dirty berry-seller with a wooden hand cart, until with a snap the prickles vanished and her bones went silent. The bird must be dead, and the touch of the God, vanished. She wondered, not for the first time, how it felt to have the God leave you. To know his touch, painful as it was, and then to see it go, to be human and plain once more. Her prickly visions were surely a millionth of what it would be to know the God himself. She crept into an alley shadow, away from the clash of crowds.

There she stood in darkness and tried to maneuver the plate down her shift. When she finally slid it free, she looked up to see the dirty berry-seller, leaning on his cart and looking straight at her.

Her first reaction was a shock of recognition, which she immediately dismissed. Her life had changed for the worse a couple times; instead of consorting with the landowners and holy, she knew the laborers and thieves. Yet even they had beds and roofs. She had not yet stooped to familiarity with *vagrants*. The man was old, his hair a white tangle. His face was so wrinkled and his gray eyes so wandering that she could not tell if his expression was lust or disgust. Plain old idiocy, likely.

She stashed the plate behind a pile of fish netting in the alley, hoping he wasn't alert enough to steal it. Still, it was nothing compared to the brooch, or to what she might find within the temple. "Here you go, old man," said Halla, and flipped him a cent. "Just stop staring at me." The coin landed in a paper twist of yellow gooseberries. Halla stared a moment, then flipped her thumb and strode past. "You didn't see nothing."

She hurried on to the hidden door that led into the rear of the temple, attempting to match her rhythm to the crunch of people. Her palms were wet. The image of the prisoner, red-faced and shaking, was strong. But today was the day to slip into the temple—all the extra pomp would be out for the decade celebration tomorrow. The tithing room, the indoor altar, the worship hall—all those places would be guarded. But there was a little room at the back where ceremonial props were stored. Ten years ago she had been there with her father, just before the last investiture. They had met the Mouth in that room. Six-year-old Halla had played with a stained golden bowl while they talked in hard voices.

Her father had taken her into the temple through a door at the rear. She neared the bamboo stand that concealed it, looking for the opening. Ten years was a long time.

It occurred to her that she had been hearing one particular noise since she left the alley—the rolling of a cart. She turned around. The old berry-man was shuffling behind her. Following. Looking up, around, anywhere but at her. But following.

"What the hell are you doing?" Halla demanded.

"You forgot your pretty plate." It was tucked under his arm. He was eating berries from two paper twists: blackberry, gooseberry, blackberry again.

She glared. "My business if I did."

"You'll never get rich that way. I'll hold it for you while you go in the temple."

Her hand flicked to the dagger at her belt. "Give me my plate and leave, if you want to help me."

"Don't go in there," he said. "Dangerous. They'll chop your fingers off, chop chop."

She took a step closer to him. He was stupid, harmless—yet her spine was on edge. "Do I know you?"

He moved bamboo stalks, tottered right to the door. "Go back to robbing the landowners, my pet. It's safer."

Halla slammed her open hand into his shoulder and he staggered, fell back. "Move." She reached for the door's handle.

It was locked.

Of course; her father must have had a key. She should've known. Stupid girl! No key meant no stealing. No stealing, no land . . . no land, no vote. No citizenship. No possibility of change.

The berry-seller tugged at his wild hair, distracted by some internal struggle. "I could . . . show you another entrance."

Her trust wavered, her ribs straining against breath. Judging was going to continue any minute now, and then—yes, here were the dizzies again. Another judging, another touch of the God, another blow from above.

Halla wanted in that temple, and she wanted it now. "What's your name, old man?"

He looked up, down, around the alley. "Don't have one no more, my pet."

"We all have a name."

"No one left to call me. What's the use?" Berry juice flecked the hair on his chin.

"I'll call you Gooseberry," said Halla. "Show me the door."

The temple was white and gold—marble on the floors and flaking filigree in the carvings on the columns. It stirred long-forgotten memories. Halla's father had been of the holy rich class—not a priest nor a landowner, but one of the men who liaised between the temple and the landowners' committee, equal in status to both. One of the three classes with citizenship. The holy rich spent a lot of time in both worlds, and Halla had gone with him. She had been in this part of the temple long ago. Back when she still had a family.

But now she was with a rambling old man who was going to get her in trouble. Every time she crept away from him he looked at her with mournful fatherly eyes, so she stopped. Stupid, this pull on her—she was used to getting along on her own. She didn't need a familiar face, especially one that wouldn't say his name. She tried again, her voice low. "Did you know my father? My mother?"

Gooseberry grabbed her sleeve. His eyes were intense and his smell rank. "She was the kind and beautiful wife of a holy rich man. But she murdered her husband and she had to be executed. The God decreed it, and so his people must be his hands here on earth."

The cruel memory shocked her, made her fingers clench. "If I wanted a sermon, I wouldn't be stealing from the temple right now."

"Everyone thinks the executioners are random," he said, letting her sleeve fall. He mumbled, and he didn't accent the right words. Halla had to lean in closer than she wanted to pick sense out of his rambling. "The God does not give a task to one finger over another, for we are all equally parts of his hand."

"I know," Halla said. Six years living with her doctrine-obsessed father, seven spent whitewashing walls for the batty old nun who ran the lighthouse. Gooseberry could not teach her anything new. "It's not murder, it's divine will. The God might give the execution to any of his people to perform. Ah, the room." She risked a peek. It was full: golden bowls, charred bamboo screens, iron shears. "You can go now." She whisked the stolen plate out of his hands.

He followed her in. "But this God favors some fingers over others." He put his sticky hand to his forehead, and Halla realized his third and fourth finger were missing to the second knuckle. "That's not right," he said. "It must be his hand. The Mouth, you see, the Mouth is choosing which fingers. . . ."

Halla wanted to shake him. "Do you mean the Mouth himself chooses who has to perform a God-Death?" Heresy? Or merely temple secrets? It fit, somehow . . . but how would this old man know?

"Of course. Don't you get it? You used to be smart." Three purple fingerprints spotted his forehead. "The God gives the power, but the Mouth manipulates it. The landowners who give money to the temple, you don't think they get chosen, do you? The fingers, they're giving sweet lotions to the God's hand . . . ."

"Old man," said Halla. "If you say one more thing about fingers, I'm going to hit you with some."

She touched the prism of a gold lamp. The room reminded her

of happier times, being here as a child. She and her da had played games here. Funny games, where he had made her try to talk to the old Mouth with her mind. The room had gone dizzy and vague, her nerves aflame . . . but she had been sure the God was pleased with her. She'd even thought her father was pleased, which filled those memories with warmth, pride at her abilities. He was a hard man, distant . . . but then there'd been these golden moments, the two of them together in the temple. Before her mother had destroyed him.

Strange to think today of all these childhood memories she hadn't thought of in years.

Gooseberry scowled. "What makes you fit to judge me? You aren't temple or rich."

"I will be. A landowner, that is, and then I'll be a citizen. I'll make changes to this city."

"That's why you're stealing gold lamps, then?" he jeered. "Only reason you want to be rich is to sit on a committee? Tell me another one."

Halla put down the lamp and picked up a tablet. "I don't have to tell you anything. Why don't you leave before they find us by your stink?"

He looked sadly at her. One gray eye rolled around. "Good-bye, my pet," he said, and left the room.

Halla breathed relief and went back to studying the tablet. An overseas collector might like it. But Gooseberry's face swam before her, the wild white hair, the vacant gray eyes. "Good-bye, my pet," he had said, just like someone used to say when she was a girl. Not her father, but someone very like. . . .

Voices rose in the hall. Someone was coming.

Halla hurried behind the bamboo screen, shoving the stupid stolen plate under her shift. The pin on the emerald brooch loosened and pierced her, but she managed not to swear. Judging usually took a full hour—how much time had she wasted arguing with Gooseberry? She peeked between two slats while refastening the brooch, this time to the inside of her worn boot. It was a thin man, a nun and three children, all in blue. Halla tried to breathe quietly.

"Are the priestling's robes prepared for tomorrow?" said the man's smooth voice.

"Yes, Mouth of the God." The honorific was slurred with long use, closer to mowfagod.

"Go check on the sacrifice."

"Yes, Mouth of the God." The nun touched her lips in salute and left.

Not just any man, then. Beside the Mouth stood his two child assistants and the priestling. The priestling's head lolled and he drooled. If Gooseberry was right that the Mouth had the ability to manipulate the God's will, then this simpleton would be disastrous as the next Mouth. Why had the God chosen him?

"Look around," said the Mouth. His sharp eyes scanned the room. "Find a knife you like for tomorrow."

The priestling obeyed, head bobbing. He was young, too. Perhaps nine. Halla was just old enough to remember the current Mouth's investiture a decade ago. But the current Mouth had been the age she was now when he took on his duties. A young man, not a boy.

The priestling swayed towards the screen and Halla froze. His hands wandered, picking up random objects that were not knives at all. He hefted the same lamp Halla had held, gaze captured by its prisms. "I like this."

The Mouth nodded at a dagger, hands hidden in his sleeves. "How about this one?"

"Okay," said the priestling. He dropped the lamp. Prisms clattered as it tumbled over chests and rugs, landed at the foot of the screen. The screen wobbled.

"Come, then," said the Mouth, and he headed for the door, the three blue-robed children following.

Halla exhaled . . . then heard her name, echoing down the marble hallway. "Halla! Halla!"

It was Gooseberry.

The Mouth froze in the doorway, his blue robe outlining his thin frame. Through the screen Halla saw Gooseberry nearing the room. "I promised I'd help you, Halla." Tears streamed down his lined face. "Don't send me away."

He was crazy. Absolutely crazy. And it was about to cost her half the fingers off her left hand.

Now the Mouth nodded at the room, at her screen, and the boy and girl assistants climbed back, clambering over trunks, skidding over bowls. The boy twitched the screen forward, revealing Halla.

"Submit, child," the Mouth said softly.

Halla bolted past him and out the door, slamming Gooseberry aside. She pounded down the white hallway, plate banging her ribs, brooch scraping her ankle. It was incriminating to run, she knew it, but there was her stupid old uncle back there, too, and she thought she could make the back door if she just ran fast enough.

There was pounding behind her, catching up, and her thoughts caught up at the same time.

Gooseberry was her *uncle*.

She swerved, but the hallway opened in two directions and hesitation cost her. The guard grabbed Halla, twisting one arm behind her. She tried to go for her dagger, but his arm crushed the plate into the ribs she'd bruised earlier, making her double up, retching air. He dragged her back to the Mouth, who stood with the child assistants and Gooseberry. She kicked backwards into the guard's knees.

The Mouth smiled, his eyes sharp on her skin.

And then Gooseberry lunged at the Mouth, knocking him to the floor. One of the Mouth's hands almost came out of his robes in surprise. But it didn't, not even to catch himself.

Gooseberry was on top of the Mouth, but the boy threw himself on Gooseberry, kicking and clawing. The Mouth lay calmly on the floor as the boy punched Gooseberry off of him and into submission. The Mouth stood and the girl straightened his blue robes with deft movements of her right hand. Her sleeves were in disarray, and for the first time Halla realized that the girl, like the immortal assistant she represented, had only one hand.

"Theft from one, and attempted deicide from the other," said the Mouth. His narrow face was emotionless. "The God will lay his finger of justice on you."

With a final kick at Gooseberry's unmoving body, the boy stood, panting. The boy's mouth was a dark hole, tongueless.

Halla swallowed at the sight of Gooseberry—her uncle—on the floor. "Let him go with a whipping. He didn't do anything to you."

The Mouth turned his still face on hers. "The God has chosen me to interpret his justice for him. You have no part in that." His voice smooth, like wind. "Besides, what would the daughter of a murderer know of divine morality?"

"I know more of justice than you." She spat at his feet.

The boy bent and wiped her spit from the Mouth's robes with his fingers. "You're just like your father," the Mouth continued. His words rolled out, implacable. "You think you know more than anyone else. No concern for whose plans you're disrupting."

He left a pause, as if she might answer him. But she did not.

"Take the old man to the afternoon judging," he said. "Put her in the dungeon."

"She's got something in her shift."

"Get it off her, then."

"It's nothing of yours!" Halla went for her only weapon, but the guard pulled her hand tighter, kicked her knee out so she bent to the floor.

The Mouth nodded, and the one-handed girl crossed to Halla. With deft motions she slid the plate from Halla's shift, maneuvering it with fingers and stump.

"Maybe so," said the Mouth. "But it isn't yours, little thief."

Halla watched the pink lump of wrist in sick fascination. The God's punishments were absolute.

The cell was cold and moldy, and there was nothing to do but pick at the blister on her foot and think. She couldn't figure out how her uncle had gone from the swank and lively Uncle Ollan she had known—so different from his quiet little sister—to Gooseberry. Distantly she could feel two people being judged in the square, one after the other. Without knowing, she labeled Gooseberry as the one who caved instantly. She wondered what his sentence was—she didn't care. She hated him for not taking her in after her parents' death—she hated him for today. She hated him for saying, in the middle of all of it, that he was there to protect her.

At last there were clanks outside her cell door. Another door creaked, there were thumps, and the door creaked closed.

"Rest up till midnight," one of the guards said. Their feet moved away and then there was cold silence again.

"I'm going to die," Gooseberry said. His voice seemed far away.

"Your own damn fault." She swallowed other words—"my uncle, my family"—swallowed them into silence.

In the dungeon, time slowed. She almost forgot he was there.

"I killed your mother." The words drifted around the stone wall between them. They seemed to echo in her past long before she realized what they meant.

"I don't understand." Wasn't his only crime that of abandoning her to the charity of the lighthouse?

"The God chose me. He put the God-Death in my mind and I was the executioner."

His words were lucid but the meaning was not. He seemed to have forgotten everything he'd said about the priests supplanting the will of the God. His tone was singsong, lilting.

Anger, as the meaning sunk in. "You killed her?"

"The God convicted her. It was justice for killing her husband, and I was no one while I carried it out. The priests say no one is complicit then. I was the God's hands, his eyes."

"You killed her. Your own sister."

"The God metes justice."

"Your own sister! Do you know how I lived with no parents? The temple dumped me on a rock with a batshit old nun. I lost my citizenship, I became nobody. I slaved for her seven years before I ran away. I cried for my old life. For you."

Silence and blackness.

"I thought someone must've killed you, too, or you would've taken me to live with you. Mum and Da were holy rich. I should have been raised in that class, in my rightful place as a citizen. Or with you—not that I'd want that, now that I know what you are. Not abandoned in a lighthouse." With a nun who beat her for feeling the God's touch, if it was the God's touch, if all of this wasn't some horrid perversion of the Mouth's. Beatings twice a day until she'd learned to control what she felt, to hide it. "I shouldn't have been tossed to the bottom. Left all alone."

Crying from the other cell.

Halla shut her ears with her fists. "You deserve their death."

*

Halla was awakened by the scrape of iron on stone. She strained her ears, but apart from that there was utter silence; no shouts, no curses, no prayers from Gooseberry as they took him to the ring on the hill.

She was tense after that, still and fraught in her cell. After a long time, iron scraped on stone again. A key. A small hand pushed the door inward. Golden light from an oil lamp spilled in. "You can go," a high voice said.

A boy of nine or so, in blue.

The simpleton priestling.

Halla stuck her foot in the path of the door, pushed him aside, and slid out into the hallway.

He looked up with big unfocused eyes. His head wavered, but he was not drooling. She studied the black corridor, but he seemed to be alone.

"What are you doing here?" she said quietly.

"The God sent me. Also, I want breakfast."

Halla sucked in her breath. "Can you lead me out?"

He put one hand to his head, waved it at the hallway. Short, jerky movements. "Come." He scuttled sideways, turning his head to look at her, lamp swinging, his feet feeling out the stone floor.

Halla crept behind him. "Does the God often send you to people?"

"Usually he sends me things. Rabbits and pretty dove birds to—" His hands mimed cracking. He smiled in the lamplight, a brilliantly sweet smile of yellow-brown teeth. "I think someday he'll send me a pretty person, like you. The Mouth says I have to listen to the God."

Slowly the words registered. "The God talks to you?"

"Almost every day, I feel what the God wants," he said. "That's why I'm gonna be his next Mouth. Sometimes he hurts. I get dizzy and fall down. But the God is just."

Halla grabbed the small boy's shoulder. "Does it feel like a crackling in your head? Like ants on your bones?"

He slid away. "Does the God tell you what you want, too?"

Halla shook her head.

They turned up a narrow staircase and the boy rocked his head in tune with his steps. "We play games. Little games, like I try to read the Mouth's thoughts. Or sometimes the God makes me feel ferocious angry. Then the Mouth brings me something so I can kill it. A rabbit, maybe. As soon as I kill the rabbit the God leaves me. Sometimes the God makes me happy. Then the Mouth comes. As soon as it's over I feel like nothing again. I feel like me."

Little games. . . . An icy thought shivered up her spine. Had this boy always been a simpleton? What had he been like before the Mouth turned his attention—and the God's attention—to him? And nobody to watch out for him. . . . "Don't you have a family?"

"What's that?"

"Father, mother. Uncle."

"The Mouth is my father now. He has a plan to never leave me. I'm scared to be the Mouth, but Father says he'll never leave me. Not even after today; he will never ever go. Did you bring me breakfast?"

"No," said Halla. The story that the God chose each new Mouth must be a lie—or at least, it had become a lie, even if it was once the truth. The Mouth had handpicked this boy. Raised him. She suddenly remembered the current Mouth sitting in the room once when she met with her father and the old Mouth. He was even skinnier then, lurching and narrow with sharp eyes, and he'd watched her as the men talked. They hadn't tried the games that day, but Halla had had a long dizzy fit anyway, that ended with her father rocking her. The skinny young man had watched her the whole time.

Halla wanted to ask more questions, but the boy stopped at the top of the stairs. There was a dark alcove, and ahead, a massive door. The lamp swung gold circles of light in the alcove, picked out a thin gleam.

"My dagger," she said. "Wait." She put a hand on the handle of the oil lamp, next to his.

But the boy opened the door and let go of the lamp, leaving it swinging in her hand. "I want my breakfast."

She could not both keep the door open and look in the alcove, but she had not seen the boy use a key. She took the lamp into the black opening, alert for a trap. But there was nothing in there but her dagger. A chain with two iron keys hung from a hook.

The heavy door to the main temple clicked closed. Halla swung the lamp over—but the priestling had vanished. She was alone in the temple, unguarded and unmutilated. Her skin crawled.

But she was not going to let herself get caught again. She took the keys from the wall and strapped on her dagger. As a gesture of freedom, took the brooch from her boot and pinned it to the front of her shift. Then she opened the door, extinguishing the lamp as she did so. She slid out into a familiar white and gold hallway, keeping to the shadows. There should be an exit in just a few yards. The door she had left was plain, unassuming. Strange how she had never known where it led.

She turned the corner and there was the outside door. Dawn must be near, and Uncle Ollen's execution at the ring on the hill. He didn't deserve the God-Death for toppling the Mouth to the floor. But he did deserve it for killing her mother. Halla could leave him to the temple's justice.

Yet she stood there in the shadow of the exit, wavering.

From the other side of the temple, the gong rang. First waking call for the priests.

Halla left the temple in the near-dawn light. Only a few people were out at this hour, priests and sellers setting up for the huge crowds the investiture would bring. It would be a good day to slip in and out of familiar houses, with everyone in the center of town. This might be the day she stole enough to buy land, just that small piece of land. She had lost her chance at the wealth of the temple, but she would not lose sight of regaining her citizenship. It was unfair for children to suffer for the crimes of their parents. She mustn't lose sight of her plan for change.

The decision cleared her mind. Halla strode away from the temple. She was just deciding on a house where she'd once been to a funeral when pain swept from one side of her body to the other. Her hands clenched, her body throbbed like a struck gong. It focused to a pinpoint in her head, then as abruptly, vanished. An image, a feeling blossomed in her mind, a blood lust without words.

Kill Ollen.

He was at the ring on the hill, and she could kill him before his God-Death came. She could be the one to enact revenge, to make him pay.

And she should.

Flooded with that thought, she charged through the temple grounds. She passed nuns, assistants, market-sellers, but their eyes slid over her. They all looked away.

Down the stone road to the temple's hill. No one climbed that hill, but everyone knew the path. Everyone knew exactly where the God's justice was served, though the top was shrouded in bamboo, and there was no silhouette of a man shadowed at dawn, awaiting execution.

She slipped through that stone archway where nobody went without a purpose. It was strange how her feet propelled her forward. She had never had to kill anybody—why should she start with a man already destined to die? Almost she turned around but no, the path was there, and though the hill was dark and steep the path drew her upward. She would just see him, anyway. Just see if he was up there. Then she would turn back.

The bamboo pressed in thicker till suddenly it thinned, revealing deep blue sky. Why would she think of murdering Ollen, Uncle Ollen who had taken her to see the traveling animals, who had let her pet the snakes?

The dawning light picked out a figure in the middle of the clearing and her head rang.

He was chained to the pole, arms fastened behind him, crumpled. His nose bled and he drooled. The sight surged fresh blood lust through Halla. She stumbled from the bamboo, dagger high.

Kill him.

Uncle Ollen's gray eyes watered and his nose trickled. He was so weak, so stupidly weak, so incompetent. How had such a fallen thing killed her mother? His death would be a relief. A relief.

She was on him then, one hand at his throat. He squealed, fought her with his knees. One knee caught her on the nose and cheek. Her grip loosened, but she seized him again and raised her blade. His white hair foamed around his face. She would kill him. She would be his executioner.

She would be his God-Death.

Her entire body convulsed on the handle of her dagger. She would be his God-Death. The Mouth had made it so. The dizziness she had felt all those years was nothing next to the actual touch of the God, yet that was what this was. The compulsion to obey thickened her spirit, crushed her fingers to the dagger's handle.

Halla would not submit to the Mouth. She would not.

She would not be Uncle Ollen's God-Death.

Halla gripped the handle with all her will and plunged the dagger into the ground.

Scrabbled away, the compulsion tearing her mind. Kill Ollen. Kill.

"I love you," blubbered her uncle. His nose ran; his beard filled with snot and blood. She loved him and loathed him. She understood what he had done, what he had become from doing it.

He didn't say anything else, just babbled and bled on the ground. Halla felt the God-touch like her own purest desire—she was dying to strangle him from his miserable existence. She breathed, funny little gasps, trying to sort out her wants from the God's. Tears streamed down her cheeks.

It was clear now why they had let her escape. The Mouth had probably compelled the priestling to do it. She put one taut hand into her shift and pulled the chain with its two keys forth. That seemed to take forever. Threw it at her uncle's curled side, the links clinking. He sniveled.

"Take it," she said hoarsely. But as she threw it she realized he couldn't. His hands were chained behind him. Halla flexed and un-flexed fingers, took several more breaths. With long steady strides she crossed to her uncle, grabbed the smaller key, and unlocked his wrists. Dropped the chain in front of him and strode back to her spot in the bamboo.

They stared at each other, breathing hard.

Ollen wiped his face with his hand, his sleeve. With fumbling fingers he unlocked his ankles. He stumbled towards her.

"Stay away," Halla said. Her hand flicked to her empty dagger sheath.

He wavered, tottered.

"Farther," she said. "Out of reach. Out of a good long lunging reach." She went towards the pole to get the dagger. He scurried around the circle, not really getting any farther away. She gritted her teeth and wished she could kill him for it.

"Now we're going down the hill," she said. "And you're going to stay behind me where I can't see you, and answer my questions. What do you know about my family? Our family." The lust to kill him suffused all her questions with rage.

Ollen sniffled.

Halla strode down the path, smacking the bamboo with the flat of her hand. "Stop crying. And I don't want any garbage about the God's fingers either. Give me sane Gooseberry. Give me facts."

"I can't, I. . . ."

She glared.

"I. . . . Your father was of the holy rich." He fell in behind her, his feet noisy and slow.

"Yes." She smacked the bamboo again. It felt good to hit something.

"Your mother and I weren't. Our family were landowners, on the outskirts, struggling." He sniffled again. "Your father went between the committee of the rich and the temple. He was known to be close with the former Mouth. And he had, uh . . . nasty methods of making the politics go his way. Which was the temple's way, for a long time." Ollen's feet slid and now he was too close, pacing her. He had wiped his face and smoothed his hair, and for a moment he looked quite sane. "But ten years ago the new Mouth was chosen. The one we have now. Your father disliked the new choice."

"This new Mouth wasn't going to let my da run things," Halla said slowly.

Ollen nodded. "So your father took you up to the temple, brought you to the old Mouth. He thought he could . . . he wanted you to replace . . . I don't know if what I think is so. No, I know. You were so tiny. Each time you came home so . . . strange. Like you didn't know what was going on." He tilted his head, mimed a lolling motion.

Halla strode ahead, swallowing.

"Do you know what happened next?" he said.

"Yes," said Halla. "My mother killed him."

Behind her, Ollen was silent.

He did not say *and then she was executed for it*, but Halla's fingers still clenched and unclenched at her sides. "And the Mouth had something to do with it?"

"She was an angel, your mother—my darling sister. Too good for your cold father. The old Mouth must have broke with your father. And when the new Mouth took over, I think the first thing he did was compel my darling, my sweet, to kill. A God-Death without the God's wish behind it. I don't know. I just—she wouldn't have done it, not a sweet sweet woman like her, she wouldn't have killed anybody without a compulsion."

He underestimated her mother. Halla thought she might well have been capable of murder, if her daughter was in danger. "I'd almost rather believe she did it on her own," Halla said softly.

She didn't expect her uncle to respond, but he started babbling again, something about hands and fingers, and the God-given rage swelled. "Gooseberry," she said, danger in the word.

Too much danger. Uncle Ollen flung himself at her feet, crying. "I had to kill her. It hit everything inside of me, horrible. I wanted to kill her, don't you understand? My pretty sister, I loved her and the Mouth destroyed us. I wanted to hurt her. It broke our family, it broke me, made me a vagrant, no money, no land, no name. I remember, you see, all that true pure rage I remember, because it's in me, and I wanted it. She made me promise to help you, but I couldn't bear it. The God forgive me, I couldn't."

She stumbled and kicked at him, trying to get him out of reach. "Move it, damn you!" She escaped from his clutching fingers, backed up against the bamboo.

He sobbed again and she pulled the dagger halfway out of its sheath. She breathed long and low, stomach clenching. The God-lust was sharp and taut in her mind; she could feel its line stretching back to the Mouth, just as she always had during the judging.

One way or another, the Mouth had killed her parents.

Both of them.

"I'm going to that ceremony."

The judging square was fuller than she had ever seen it. Every inch crammed, a mob of watchers and priests. Halla tried again to shake the God's blood lust, but she was still taut with it. She remembered the prisoner reaching for the dove yesterday morning, his face distended. He had stayed in agony till he got to complete the God's task of killing it. She swallowed and pushed through the restless crowd.

She caught glimpses between necks, under arms. The Mouth stood at the dais, loomed over the young priestling. A bleating goat was tethered off to the side. This was the part she had thought merely ceremonial, but now she was not sure. The old Mouth's killing of the goat was the moment of investiture. Ritually, it showed that his hands were free again. That he was a citizen again, willing to act when the God required.

But perhaps it was more than ritual.

Perhaps death was the way the power was passed on.

She pushed through, moving to the front.

The boy's head was upright and he looked more awake than that morning in the dungeon. She wondered what compulsion the Mouth was sending to him. Alertness?

The ritual continued, the words rolling on. "As the God speaks through me, so shall the power pass to his chosen one. So shall the next ten years pass with the God and his new Mouth."

"May he speak to us," answered the crowd.

She was nearly to him, this man who had killed her father and through other hands her mother, who had nearly killed her uncle. The Mouth of the God, her family's death.

"By this sacrifice, he shall prove he is willing to act for you. His mouth is the mouth of the God. . . ."

Maybe you didn't have to be a landowner to provoke change.

"May he speak to us," answered the people. Fingers touched lips.

Halla stepped forth from the crowd, onto the dais. "You're using that boy," she said to the Mouth. Her voice rang out over the judging square. "You don't intend to step down at all. You're perverting the voice of the God." There was absolute silence in the crowded square.

"Take her," said the Mouth. His face stayed calm, his hands still folded. A blue-robed priest moved in.

But the blood rage was still hot in her, and though directed at her uncle it was easy to let it loose on the priest. She had never killed anybody, but now she killed him, largely out of luck. She wanted to drop the wet dagger, she wanted to scream, but she did neither.

Temple guards were closing in from the sides, but the crowd pressed around the dais, bodies tense, tongues whispering. Watching the new drama play out in the judging square.

Harder to rein in the bloodlust, but she took a deep breath and bent her mind to it, packing it back down inside her. She moved closer to the Mouth. In her mind, Halla could feel where the directive flowed from him to her; the open thread along which the compulsion ran. The tongueless boy turned and ran, but the one-handed girl watched her with quiet black eyes.

"He's abused this boy to stay in control," Halla said to the crowd. "To keep control of you." The roar of the crowd grew, and in her side vision she saw the guards encountering resistance.

On the level where her mind was focusing on the Mouth, she could feel that there were two channels open from him. From the Mouth to the boy, a well-worn path. From the Mouth to her, thick and shining. Her uncompleted God-Death made a channel he couldn't close. She felt her way along it. "He's not planning to pass anything on. He's planning to compel the boy the way he compels the city. This boy is a puppet."

"Your father would have done a similar thing to you," the Mouth hissed. "Once he saw what you could control." His body was coiled for action but his mind wasn't. He didn't even understand how the power worked. His mind was too limited. He was supposed to open a thread of compulsion to the boy, to the sacrifice, giving the boy access to the God. Then the old Mouth would sacrifice the goat, completing his own compulsion from ten years ago. He would draw back, cede his power, take himself out of the loop.

But he didn't understand that. He didn't understand that the same charged line was open from him to Halla. She didn't think she fully understood the God's power, but he definitely didn't.

The guards were closer now, the Mouth smiling. "Ignore the heretic," he said to the crowd. "The God will decide her fate." To her, quietly, "I did you a favor. Your father would have destroyed you."

Halla used that tendril, that slim thread he had left open to her. "Perhaps," she said. "But he didn't."

And then she pulled with all her will, pulled along the thread of that God-driven blood lust, pulled it out of the Mouth and into her. The power spread into her hands, her feet, until for one moment she was lit up golden like a God herself, and from far away the crowd roared at the sight.

She could feel the thread stretching back into the weight of history, through the Mouth, who was crumpling in front of her, through the Mouth before him, and before him, back and back until it granulated and she could see no further. For one beautiful moment she saw the whole city strung beneath her, relationships, cause and effect, everything a network, a comprehensible tapestry. Threads and patterns, and she could see how events and people were there to be patterned and picked apart and rewoven.

But even as she watched, the tapestry grew more and more complex until it spun out of control, broke apart, and then the world glittered gold in her sight and was gone.

She was standing on the dais, a God, and then the world broke apart and she was all too human. There was immense power inside her, huge and trembling in her fingertips, but the corresponding knowledge was gone.

Yet there was—something—out there; it was not all the Mouth's perversion and tricks. She almost felt giddy with the realization. She wavered and the crowd gasped and those at the front stuck out useless hands as if to catch her.

Uncle Ollen tottered up to the dais where she stood. Underneath the calm and power, the compulsion implanted by the Mouth—the former Mouth, now—still screamed.

Kill.

It was too much to hope that the compulsion would end; it seemed to be the line through which all her power came. Unless she could figure out how to shut it down without losing her power, it would probably never end, not till her uncle's death. The future was suddenly dense and strange, both full of possibility . . . and empty.

Ollen looked at the unconscious former Mouth, the dead priests. The lolling priestling, the stone-silent crowd.

Her.

"Ollen," Halla said. "My uncle. My family." In the packed and silent judging square, she was the only person moving. She unpinned the stolen emerald brooch from her shift, the brooch with which she had hoped to restart a life.

Halla closed the clasp and placed it into her last living relation's hands.

"Please," she said. "Don't come back."

ONE EAR BACK

I hated my mother for the curse she bore.

In this cold rocky land, the huldufólk leave strange imprints upon us, curses molding souls as a cup does water. My mother angered one of these hidden people—how, no longer matters. She was cursed to live as a cat until she did a good deed that had never yet been done.

I have since heard of curses stranger, but this is the one that affected me, for she was pregnant when the curse fell.

Mother was a companion to Thurid, the Chieftain's wife. She had gathered mosses and lichens for Thurid as a human; as a cat she wept because she did not have hands to help her lady. She killed the mice and insects that crept over the twig floor, and Thurid laughed and petted her.

Thurid had a daughter, Ingibjorg, and we grew side by side. Or yet—we did not. Though we played together, though we slept curled together, kid and kit in a pile of shredded moss, all too quickly the difference in our births showed itself.

As Ingy learned her letters, I learned the trundle of insects.

As she combed her golden hair, I licked my mackerel fur.

As she pressed through linens with sharp needle, I speared mice with a claw.

I tried to take pride in my catly skills, but how could I? If not for my mother, I would know the delights of fingers. I would not be a soul squeezed black and twisted into a kitten shape, a soul overflowing kitten ears.

I rejected the skills of my body and watched blackly from a corner as Ingy studied cooking and my mother did unimportant, everyday deeds for Thurid. She was weak, my mother. Weak and toadying. What good deed could she do that had not been done a thousand times before?

The pettiness of her deeds made them insignificant, and I resented her for it.

If there had been any act of my mother's bold enough to have broken that spell, it should have been the one that happened when Ingy and I were nine.

That day, Ingy was marching towards the forest, the gentle boy Osvif and I trailing her. She had woven sticky purple butterwort into her tangled curls and it attracted gnats, which she batted. The end-of-spring chill was just lifting, and now that her morning chores were finished, Ingy was determined to pack the afternoon with excitement. Usually that meant climbing gray-brown cliffs after birds' eggs or acting out great adventures with Ingy directing who was to say what. She would not let me play a human girl's part as often as was fair, and I refused to play any of the trolls or fairies' parts that littered her inventions. Osvif often had to moderate between us.

But today Ingy's thoughts tended towards the forest. "I want to see the giant," she said.

Osvif stopped dead still and I faltered. I knew what tangling with huldufólk—the hidden ones—could mean.

"No, Ingy," Osvif said.

"Yes, Osvif," mimicked Ingy. "The giant's home is in my father's territory. Which makes him my subject."

"Don't say that," said Osvif.

"Why not? It's the truth. Besides, how could he hear me? Giants have sharp noses, not sharp ears."

"They smell feelings the way you hear a tone of voice," said Osvif. "Your words carry on the wind to his nose."

"Do not!" said the chieftain's daughter.

"Do so!" said Osvif, and he tickled her nose with a curl of her hair. "He can smell pretty girls, too."

"Oh!" said Ingy, and she giggled.

I felt funny watching them. Ingy had already forgotten about her mission. And forgotten about me the moment my tail dropped from view, as though I were a simple cat in truth and not a girl in spirit.

Maybe that's why I said, "I can find the giant."

"Kisa!" said Ingy. She turned from Osvif. "Can you really?"

I wrapped my tail around my paws. "Cats can. Our senses aren't troubled by the hidden turnings on the way to his house." Instinctively I knew it was true of this body I bore, though I had never tried it.

"You can't," said Osvif, and his joking was gone. "You shouldn't encourage her, Kisa. The giant's dangerous."

"She'll encourage me if she wants to!"

"This could bring trouble to the whole village," said Osvif soberly. "Let's turn back."

"I will see the giant," said Ingy. She was always very obstinate. "I will remind him of his allegiance to me. And I'll take him a present, cause that's what you do. Osvif, run and fetch me that cheese we had at dinner last night."

Osvif looked torn, but for Ingy, he went. And I, glad that a cat always looks brave, even when she's not, said "Come on, then." I turned my nose to the north and headed into the birch forest by the trail only I could see.

Ingy plunged behind me. "I'll leave a trail of petals for Osvif to follow," she said. "That's what chieftain's daughters do in stories. The others will be sorry they missed this!"

The shadows between the trees were dark and I stood between two birches, sniffing out the right way. My tail was high. This was no headless mouse. This would impress Ingy.

Left past the bent birch, straight towards the two skinny birches. We went more slowly as the trail grew harder to find. The loose canopies of the birches were tight-woven here, dark all around. I sniffed again. The air was thick with quiet.

"Kisa," said Ingy. One finger skritched my head. "Have you ever seen the giant?"

"No." My ears were on high alert.

"How does it feel to be under a curse?"

One ear flattened in discomfort. She would despise me if she knew how I sat and dreamed of being her human friend. "I've never known different." I wondered if she wanted to turn back. If so, then what else could I show her?

But she stood. "Let's keep going."

Further in we crept, on the path-that-didn't-look-like-a-path, until I knew the giant's house must be near. There was a clearing with a bit of sun, and we crept out into it.

My cat senses realized something else before my human wits did. The giant, himself. Suddenly the stink of giant was all around us and I didn't know how I'd missed it a moment before.

I was looking into his ankle, then there was a frightening jerk on my tail and I was peering into his long wide face. I spat and shrieked, clawing at his nose. He grabbed me, dropped me. I flew back into the undergrowth to Ingy.

But impetuous Ingy had run towards the giant, trying to save me, and now he had her dangling by an arm.

"Help!" cried Ingy. "Help!"

I shrunk into the twigs and moss. I was not a quarter the size of Ingy; I had no fingers to wield a knife. I was just a useless cat.

That was when Osvif stumbled into the clearing, wide-eyed, his shock of hair on end. I didn't know how he'd found us—Ingy's petal trail was laughable—but then I saw my mother, her spine and tail bristling.

"Put her down," shouted Osvif.

The giant set Ingy on the ground, holding onto her hair with a fist as large as her torso. "Don't like intruders." He spat a big glob towards me, a mound of silver and white that smeared the brush.

He picked Ingy up by the waist, raised her as if to bite off her head. Gentle Osvif rushed forward with a fish knife—a suicidal undertaking. But before he reached Ingy, another form flew past. Flew up the side of the giant, scratching and hissing.

My mother.

The giant dropped Ingy in surprise, and she tumbled, clutching her ribs, coughing. Osvif ran to her, the rest of us forgotten. The giant roared as my mother's claws tore his skin, his face.

Too quickly he caught her. Too quickly he squeezed.

The giant leered and flung the body of my mother to Ingy's feet.

"Don't disturb my home again," he said. He turned and vanished into the swaying white forest.

A moment ago I had thought my cowardice when Ingy was grabbed was the low point of my life.

Until now, when the first thing I did upon my mother's death was look down at my furry body, expecting it to change.

"Oh, Kisa," said Ingy. She reached for my scruff but I backed away and hissed. She crawled towards me, coughing again, and I pelted through the birch, hurled myself through the forest till I couldn't run anymore. We cats are made for speed, not stamina. I had barely come a hundred bounds. There was a cairn of rocks there and I sunk panting to them, eyes glazed, breath shallow. My sides were raked and bleeding from his nails, some part of my ribs were broken, and for the first time in my life I thought I might die.

I huddled on the rock I do not know how long. Until a voice said, "What's all this bleeding in my home about?"

Something that looked like a smaller rock unfolded itself and looked down at me with beady black rock eyes. "Why, I know you," it said. "At least, I knew your mother. I suppose she's still a cat?"

I said nothing. I would be dead soon, and this hidden one would be gone. My mother, Ingy, everything would be gone, just like they wanted. Why couldn't I weep? Real humans could cry. Real humans didn't run away.

"Oh," it said softly. "I see." It reached under an outcropping and scraped out a blue-green moss I was not familiar with. It patted my wounds with it; my tail, my ear, my flanks. Strange to say, as it covered me in moss my body healed; though I knew of nothing that could effect such a swift change.

"I can't help you with the lost blood," it said. "Rest yourself a few days, get some sleep."

I listened, but as its hand came towards me with more moss I snapped at its craggy fingers.

It jumped. "I suppose from your point of view I deserve that," it said. "I can't remove the curse from you, and I think it would do you good, anyway. But I will give you a gift. Steady." It folded some moss into a neat pocket and tucked it into my ear before I could bite its fingers. "You will be half-deaf till you need it, but I assure you that's a fair trade. Goodbye, little cat." It tapped my ear, and then there were only rocks once more.

I crawled into a dirty cave and hid. But no matter how long I huddled there, my cat body would not weep for my mother.

A week later I set out around the coast. He must have wits who wanders, they say, and I learned that in short order. The summer was fine and sunny and it was a fine time to learn surviving by myself, though in my cold determination I thought I knew everything. I set forth and did what Mother had not thought to do, systematically performing one good deed after another, out in the wide world. Now the weight of breaking her curse had fallen to me, and I was determined to wrest free and find a place among humans.

I caught baby puffins for old women to eat; I speared brown trout for beggars. After every good deed I looked at my body.

But nothing changed.

Winter came and I felt my first taste of real cold, cold with no one to curl up against, cold day-after-day with galing winds that could blow a kitten straight up a birch tree. The mice and voles vanished into their dirt homes and I thinned, till my ribs poked my knees. I was caught in a blizzard and almost froze, except a kindly shepherd boy took pity on me, fed me scraps of mutton and let me lay against his side through those long winter nights. I did eleven good deeds for him before I left that spring, but none of them were new.

That summer I turned my attention to the cliffs. Surely in the desolate heights, among the goat herders, I would strike upon new good deeds. But the hidden one's curse was a good one, and I could do nothing that had not been done before. Before the next winter came, I found a farmer's family to adopt me, and I passed that winter in a lovely thick turf house, parceling out the rats and mice till spring.

Another year came, and the good deeds I tried were fewer. What use catching baby puffins for some old hag if it didn't make me human? I rescued a woman's mutton chop from being stolen by a fox, but when I didn't change, I took the mutton with me and ate it myself. Dragging it was hard with my kitten jaws, but that's what I still was, even though in human terms I must have been finally nearing adulthood.

Another year, and the thought of having clever hands and a pretty face grew hopeless. I found a pack of adolescent cats and fell in with them. To them, I was a strange runty kitten, but I knew more about mousing than cats much bigger in body. They were long-legged and had torn ears and broken tails and we all had fleas. I didn't speak like a human to them and they didn't startle from me.

Maybe they didn't know I had a human soul inside.

Maybe I never really had.

Such brooding was useless. The cats accepted me; one of the youngest males groomed me and the oldest female got my back when a frothing rat attacked. I had a place at last.

And in their company, I finally started to grow.

My legs lengthened, my body changed, and overnight, it seemed, I was grown-up. I looked like the mangy stray I was.

I looked like my new family.

A year later and the pack was on the west of the island. Few of the individual cats were the same, but the pack was still a unit. We were dashing from a bunch of nasty kids when I veered to lose myself in the market by the bridge. The rest of my pack scattered.

I passed by the boy with his cheeses and the wet men hauling writhing fish. There was a woman with a makeshift stall of baskets and table and I ran there, ducking behind a sharp-smelling basket till the boys went by.

I sneezed and looked up. Herbs dangled around me.

I had chosen well.

Apothecaries liked me. Much of their good stuff wouldn't grow in this cold and blowy country. It had to be brought by ship, and the price showed. I looked around for a rodent on which to show my skill, but before I found one, the woman grabbed my scruff. There was a strange foxy glint in her eye as she popped me in one of those baskets. I yowled and tried to break free. But she had tied it closed.

I was there till the market faded with the sun. I fretted—a day or two and the pack would think I was dead and move on without me.

I was picked up and I complained some more. When she opened the basket we were at the hot springs outside the little town. A strong hand closed on my scruff and she dunked me in the water.

Worse, she scoured me raw with a wire brush that hung from her belt. The water and the bristles fizzled on my skin as the brush yanked through years of matting and dead fleas. I swung for her with long claws but she said "Stop it," in a terrifying voice and her grasp on my scruff tightened. I only hissed after that, even when she ran her fingers around my eyes and down into my ears.

After an eternity she yanked me out and ran her other hand down my hide, wringing the wet from my fur. At last she sat me on flat rock and I shook myself, splattering her.

She grinned. "I'll wager no one's done that to you before."

Hiss. Spit.

"Come off it," she said. "I know what you are. You're under a curse, but that don't mean you have to be thick with fleas. I bet you can hear better, too. Right?"

I shook my head again, loosing more water and mites. I could hear better. But I was grouchy and chilly in the cooling spring night. And who knew what else this far-seeing woman had in store for me?

The woman kicked off her shoes, dangled her tough feet in the hot springs. "I've seen a lot of curses in my time," she said. "Distinctive things, each as unlike as water hemlock from wintergreen." She studied the air around me and I licked my damp shoulder. "Rock fairy?" she said. "From the south?"

I was both annoyed and curious. One ear flattened, and her sharp eyes picked up on that telltale sign.

"I hear word from down south," she said. "The giant is on the move again. He's raging around the woods of—what was that orphan girl's name? Ingveldur, Athalbjorg? Something very like . . . . ."

"Ingibjorg?" I croaked. I had not used my voice in five years, but that word came right back. "But what of her parents?"

"The giant killed them," said the woman. "And she's got no brothers, so the place is in turmoil, all fighting over who'll be the next chieftain. Poll's boy two stalls down, him what's tired of making candles, set off to try his hand at winning a village over. Fat lot of luck he'll have, with no gold to win their trust. A leader's naught without gold. But what do you care? You've got your own mission to fulfill. Which is . . . ?"

I thumped my tail. "Have to do a good deed that's never been done before. It's a stupid impossible quest. But how did you know I wasn't just a cat?"

The wrinkles around her eyes deepened as she narrowed her eyes at me, examining. "I didn't at first," she said. "And usually I can tell. Human souls take up too much space for a small animal. They look different. Squeezed, or stuffed, somehow." She picked at a callus on her toe, her eyes on me. "But you look almost like any feral cat."

A night breeze pricked up the hairs on my spine.

"Then I saw this hanging from your ear," she said. "Not long and it would've fallen out completely." From her sleeve she extracted a packet of blue-green moss.

I stared. Memories of bleeding on a rock flooded me.

"Forgot you had this, did you?" she said. She unfolded it and it sprang open, seemingly more than the packet could hold. "You won't begrudge me a small portion, for the information I have given you."

The small portion was half, and I rumbled dislike at her.

She folded the other half and stuffed it back in my ear. "You better hurry, little cat. Or there won't be enough left of you to become human."

It took me two months to pad to the southern part of the island, and when I got there I found that the old woman was accurate in her depiction of the town. The fields hung heavy with fear. Acrid smoke rose from the birch woods. Even the white trunks of the birches were stained black with it.

I crept into the great house. Those villagers who were left were gathered in the hall, and a small crowd they made. Many of them were so young. Across the way Ingy was speaking with passion to a group of young men, stirring them to fight once more in a hopeless battle. The voices around me rose in different murmurs, and I heard one boy say that the village was cursed and it should be abandoned to the giant, and another, in quieter tones—that Ingy should be left in the forest as an offering. I hissed at that, but when the boy looked down he saw only a cat.

I sidled towards Ingy. She was grown-up now but otherwise just as I remembered, just as I always wanted to be. Silly kitten dreams, wanting fingers and golden hair. Why pine after that when claws and teeth are so much more useful?

Next to her stood gentle Osvif, also full-grown. He was not as tall as some of the doggish young men, not as wide. But when he spoke those around him quieted to listen. He put a comforting hand on the princess' shoulder, telling everyone that they should withdraw from the attack and burnings, that the giant would fade away if they did so. They couldn't ever find the giant, he said, for he knew how to stay hidden. They were only making him madder. They should stop seeking revenge. Ingy leaned into him.

I felt more alone than I had since I found my pack. These were not my people. They had grown, the village had changed, and I was still a cursed cat. They were doing human things like falling in love and fighting wars and I was catching mice and getting forcibly bathed by old hags.

I bit Ingy's ankle.

Gently. But I bit it, and darted. She looked down and followed the green eyes she saw, coming over to examine.

I do believe that if she had immediately acknowledged me for who I was, I wouldn't have done what I did next. I would've swallowed my loneliness, and bid her follow Osvif's advice.

But Ingibjorg the chieftain's daughter said, "What a darling little cat."

I didn't owe her anything. It was she who had gotten my mother killed. "I can find your giant," I said.

"You can talk," she said. "I used to imagine that my cat could talk. Or did I?"

I rumbled dislike. "I'm sure I don't know what you imagined, my lady," I said. "Leave a fish head at the door if you change your mind."

"Nothing to change," she said. "We'll go right now, and I'll take my mother's kitchen knife. If you dare find the giant for me, I'll dare face it."

I put one ear back at that, because I knew what the giant was like, even if she'd forgotten or didn't care. If she could forget such an important incident anyway, I didn't care what happened to her.

We slipped out of the great house. "One of your ears is back, Kisa," she said. "That means you're conflicted about something."

"Oh, so you do remember me," I said crossly. I couldn't get the ear to go up, so I put the other one down as well.

"I know there was a horrible day where we met the giant," she said softly. "And then you disappeared. I cried for weeks."

"Truly?" I said. "Then why are you blithely trotting after me now?"

"Because," said Ingy. "If I hadn't disturbed the giant's home in the first place, he would never have come after the town. All this is my fault, and now you're here to help me face it." She sounded quite cheerful. The massacre must have made her crazy.

"Turn here," I said. I led her through low-hanging branches, which she ducked. After all these years I could still feel the twists and turns into the giant's heart. The woods grew darker, the stench of soot and bone harsher. "Have your knife ready."

"I do." Her footsteps were tense behind me. The silence got thicker, each paw padded slower. Guilt almost made me turn and lead her out of the forest, but no, she wanted to face the giant and I wanted her to face it. Still my steps slowed, till I was no longer leading her.

I hissed as she trod on my tail.

"Sorry," she said quietly. Then, "Kisa? Do you ever think you'll get your curse lifted?"

My ears were belled out, quivering. "I don't think I'll ever try again."

"But—" she said, and then the giant towered in front of her. He was bigger than I'd remembered. Had he grown? I was bigger and stronger than five years ago, and yet the sight and stench of him widened my eyes and froze me to the ground. There was a smoke-stained birch concealing me from him; I couldn't seem to move around it.

Ingy rushed at him with her kitchen knife. She hacked at his shins, his fingers as he tried to deflect. He bellowed as she aimed for arteries—for a second I thought she might have a chance. But the giant wrested the knife from her weak wrist, tumbled her, pinned her to the ground. With one stroke he swung the knife and chopped through her ankles like they were carrots. Ingy screamed. Fell silent, unconscious.

Then she was laying there, her feet all separated from her body, the shell of her completely unlike the vibrant Ingy I had known.

The giant put her pink feet in his pouch. He hoisted her to his shoulder so I saw the stumps of leg—oddly quite bloodless. He swung around and set off, Ingy's hair whipping around and her pink smooth face blank, vanishing behind black peeling trunks.

For one horrid instant all my cowardice rushed back upon me and I thought of running away. Running to the west, finding my cat pack again. I needed no part of human affairs.

But in the dark woods I heard Osvif, tearing madly and randomly about, calling for Ingy. My last shameful thought vanished like hot breath into frozen air. I raced forward, along the giant's footfalls, quick and calm as only a cat can do. When I reached the clearing of his cabin I halted, for I know how keen the giant's smell is. But Ingy was there and so in one bound I jumped in the nastiest, smelliest thing nearby to hide—the giant's midden.

I crawled in the nasty tunnel underneath the house wall, peeked up into the house. The smell inside was interesting and acrid; burnt bones and hair and the strong musk of giant. There was a cooking pot at one end and a chest of gold coins at another. The giant sat brooding in the middle of the room. And there—Ingy, dumped on a heap of moss and peat ash, her feet thrown down next to her.

I waited and waited, probably a short time in reality, but it seemed endless. At last the restless giant picked up his water buckets, heading for the river. He peered out of the cabin, drew his head back to smell the air for human, for fear. But either because he wasn't looking for cat or because his own stench hid mine, he didn't sense me.

The instant his tread lumbered off, I sprung from my hiding place. I lugged each of Ingy's feet over by biting their toes, lined them up with her ankles. "You could help me, you know," I said, but I might as well have been talking to rock. With the back of my paw I dug the last of the moss from my ear; the packet fell on a bruise and the purple faded. Oh no you don't, I thought, and I hurried before the moss wasted its power on scrapes. I nudged the moss with my nose to her ankles, tore and laid it around them, nudged the feet to the legs by pressing my back against them.

Then I hopped onto her chest and, yowling, kneaded her neck. Her eyelids fluttered. "Wake up, Ingy," I said. But my kneading did no good. "Wake up!" I said again. There were strange drops of water falling on her neck.

But I couldn't wake her. I couldn't move her. I was just a cat. I swallowed my rivers of pride and guilt. I left Ingy there and flew back to the forest to where clumsy human Osvif was still searching. I did not want to talk to him, but he, unlike Ingy, recognized me—or admitted to recognizing me—instantly.

"Why, I know you," he said. "I'd know that mackerel coat anywhere." He dropped to one knee, lowered himself to me. "Have you seen Ingy?"

And so I lashed my tail and turned and walked a few paces, looked back. When I was sure he was following me, I set off at top speed to the giant's house, leading him through trails that only I could find.

His face paled when he saw her.

I took pity on that and spoke. "Careful of the ankles. Keep the moss on them; keep her off her feet." I did not really know, but I guessed, based on what I knew of the moss and the apothecaries' sayings.

He nodded, worried but calm. A careful, solid man. A strong-souled human.

My ears stayed upright and steady. "And Osvif," I said. "Take the gold."

Osvif looked at me sharply. Then he took a mere three handfuls from the chest, filling his pouch. He swung the unconscious Ingy to his shoulder, just as the giant had done, and hurried out of there, back through the forest.

He walked into the great house with poor half-dead Ingy on his shoulder, and in a louder voice than any I'd ever heard him use, he bought the men off of their anger with gold. He rallied them to his strange cause of non-aggression, and because of the giant's gold, they followed.

I followed him back to the village slow and unstopping—a test of endurance for an energy-spent cat. I often thought of laying down and sleeping forever, but Osvif chivvied me again and again until we made it home. She will reward you, he repeated, but I spat when he said it. Much I cared for that. Not with Ingy hanging from his shoulder like a dead deer.

Her body was cold and shaking by the time he laid her in the sleeping loft of the great house. I padded up the stairs after them, one red paw print after another. I was bone-tired, my tail dragging, my pads bleeding, but I saw one last thing I could give the girl who had everything. I jumped onto her pallet and curled around her shivering feet, feet with blue toes and bits of moss still sticking around her ankles like fetters.

I kept her feet warm until she fell asleep, and in the morning I was human.

A good deed that had never been done before. I don't know what moment tipped that balance. It worked, anyway, for I am human, and isn't that what I always wanted?

But now that I am human I am never satisfied. Ingy and Osvif are married, and he is the chieftain now, though he bids everyone call him Osvif. Ingy can walk, though now that she has her own princess on the way, she stays off those delicate ankles and keeps to the bench near the hearth. They gifted me one of the abandoned turf houses and a servant girl to help me adjust to buttons and mending and cooked food.

Sometimes I go up to the great house and sit with her. But sitting is not the same as running through the forest. Needlework is not the same as a wild chase after a giant.

And I am no more her equal than I ever was.

I feel strangely hollow these days. Lost between worlds; I can't curl up with my pack of cats, nor can I feel at ease with these large-souled humans. Osvif and Ingy overflow with generosity to me. But I seem to have used up my humanity in my quest to become one.

Ridiculous longings! The dreams of a kitten. I knew where my soul was, once. It fit right between the ears, in a little fuzzy body.

Once I had a right-sized soul, the soul of a cat.

GOLDEN APPLES

The golden apples are round and smell of autumn. Sometimes the men throw yellow quince, hard as butternut squash, hard as stones. Sometimes they drop ruby-throated nectarines, and then she kicks them, steps on them, crushes them as she runs.

The men all know of her quest and they all try to distract her. No matter that she is as fleet as a doe. Even with their distractions she can outrun them all, those plodding men with their grasping hands and heavy tread, who will not cast aside their swords and armor and war medallions even for a foot race.

And so they cheat. And so she stops and examines each golden fruit they drop, to see if they have found what she wants. It is an odd thing she wants, and in the weeks before each race, where she chats with each new suitor and tells him of her quest, she mentions it. An apple of freedom, she says, and then they laugh at the idea, for in what way is she not free? But they have gone into the race forewarned.

The men find her substitutes. One tracks down a solid gold apple inscribed with *Kalliste*. When she scoops it up she understands that it is meant to tell how beautiful a woman is—or perhaps, how easily a woman is misled. It is an apple that has started wars. She runs to the cliffs and flings it into the sea, and she still wins the foot race.

Another throws a russet apple into her path. This man wears teeth around his neck that chatter as he labors past her. When she picks the apple up, her palm numbs and death coats her fingers like candle wax. She remembers a story of a girl who ate such an apple, and thereafter lay unmoving on her suitor's glass bed, silent and perfect until the end of time. She will not bury this apple, afraid of what it might grow into. When she bests this man, she watches as the guards feed him this apple.

A third throws a golden-orange fruit, pebbled and shining like the sun. It is a miraculous tree indeed that fruits and blossoms at once, for a white blossom still hangs from a twig. When she smells it sunlit images flood her mind—a green tree growing from a fountain of youth; a fruit of immortality. It is the kindest gift so far, but immortality is not a word that tempts her, not when it comes with an equal yoke. She drops the fruit in the man's path as she flies past him, hoping that this life might not be on her conscience after all.

She feels sorry for many of them, and encourages them to go home. But they do not, and then they cheat, which salves her conscience. It is not as if she has a choice in their deaths. Her father has made the rules and she is his. She runs when they wish to run, and her only choice is whether or not to lose. Her father tells her a good maiden would throw the race.

As the bodies pile up, she doubts more and more that the apple she dreams of exists. It seems unfair that men should be able to find apples of youth and life and knowledge, and the one thing only she wants is denied.

At last there is a man who seems kind. A man who talks intelligently of the world, who seems almost to understand when she explains yet again her foolish quest. This man refuses to cheat. He brings her a fruit the morning of the race and offers it to her on one knee. It is a pomegranate, rose and gold and thick-shelled, and he cracks it open, splays it into a diadem of ruby jewels.

"Milady," he says, "I have asked councillors, I have asked explorers, I have asked the world. No one has heard of the apple you seek. They doubt its existence, for they all agree that no man is truly free. Therefore I have brought you the poor substitute of my love. If you eat of this love-apple twelve seeds you may choose to bind yourself to me as I am in my heart bound to you. We will leave this place together."

As she takes the fruit, he bows and there is longing in his eyes. He readies himself for the race, and she half-smiles at his preparations, for he strips himself of all honor and wealth, and dresses himself in a thin shift like her.

She meets him at the starting line. She knows the tale of the girl who lost her winters to the underworld by eating six seeds. And she knows that while love might be a two-way bond, the rest of her life is ever one-way, as she is the apple and never the one who eats.

She holds out the fruit. "What if you choose to eat and bind yourself to me, as in my heart I might perhaps be bound to you?"

His eyes narrow and the whistle sounds and he runs. Runs the race, running to win her. In his shift he is fleet, but so is she, and her nails bite into the pomegranate, scattering the seeds into the dirt. Juice as red as blood stains the dirt.

They run towards the finish, but she is the doe, the whistle of wind, the girl in search of an apple, and she does not stop. She runs, leaving him behind. She runs until her feet are as red as the pomegranate and then she runs some more. Someday her soles will harden, until they are as tough as sun-yellowed quince. She is fleet, she is gold, she is cold as the ruby-throated dawn.

In the air she tastes the first apple blossoms of spring, drifting free on the wind.

TINY ATROCITIES

there is nothing
you can confront
me with from my past
those silly sordid secrets
that everyone has!
the girl

I gave a red apple,
insides bleached white
with tooth-tart poison,
the horse

I had slaughtered,
its palomino head nailed
to confront the princess,
the children

I ate by the dozens,
nibbling on round elbows
in my hut of crisp-edged
gingerbread and sugared leaf -
no

no there is nothing
I will not say it!
everyone has this sharp regretful past
that comes of a sudden while eating an apple
the toothache twinge
of remembering tiny atrocities
you committed
while young

and foolish
groping to understand
who you would be
in the story you made
of your life

Moon at the Starry Diner

Air like a mushroom. Dense. Pocketed with holes, moments where Jem could breathe normally. She filled her lungs, drinking in the new atmosphere, dazzled by the blue-black sky. Starlight like diamonds, winking around her feet.

The clouds were spongy. Jem's calf muscles stung from the exertion. Her toes were pinched in her sleek calfskin boots—they were made for walking from the subway to the office along firm level sidewalk. Not cloud-hopping.

"It's freaking gorgeous," she said. Jem was not a complainer.

She looked back at her companion to see how he'd changed. It was almost a game, to guess if Moon would fit into the new surroundings. Perhaps he would be a comet, or a constellation.

He was a bear.

Moon made a handsome bear—symmetrical and golden-brown, not terribly large. He had beady black eyes that looked startlingly like Moon's human ones—or at least, the human ones he'd worn when she'd met him. He scratched at his side with claws so dark she could only pick them out by their glints. "Ursa Minor, what?" he said in a grumble. "No, go on."

Jem waded through cloud back to Moon and tucked her bare arm under his furry one. It was tickly and warm. She wanted to snuggle all the way under his paw, but she didn't quite dare. Moon in his last incarnation as a skyhook had been quite prickly. "You have fish breath," she informed him. "Did that come with the change?"

"Oughta ask someone who knows, right?" said Moon. "The last thing I had to eat was two changes ago, when I was a Volvo, and that was diesel. Should diesel smell like fish?"

Jem shrugged.

Moon's furry belly rumbled. He shook Jem's arm loose to rub it with both paws. "Now you've done it," he said. He tilted his muzzle sideways, listening to his new body. "Fish, I think. Honeybees. Small to medium-size vertebrates. Twigs."

"There's a diner up ahead," said Jem. She took Moon's shoulder and pointed him at it. It was silver and rounded, an optimistic trailer with windows of moonlight and blinding stars for wheels. A red neon sign sprung from the roof, glowed: The Starry Diner.

"Suspiciously convenient," said Moon. "Shall we?"

He tucked her arm back under his own and for a moment they were two lovers playing tourists, ready to crash a locals bar and laugh.

But only for a moment.

Jem opened the door for Moon and his claws clicked on metal as he entered. The diner was half full, noisy with echoing voices and the clatter of fork on plate. She threaded her way past a three-headed dog drinking coffee to the first empty booth.

Moon was lagging behind, peering into the back corner of the diner, his body alert. "Be right back."

"You have to use the little bears' room?" said Jem.

Moon ignored all jibes about his nature. His golden brown body lurched between the checkerboard of tables. His hips knocked against the tentacles of a giant pink squid, against the elbows of a man in a white cowboy hat. His shoulders tensed with the effort of controlling his new form.

Moon disappeared into the back and Jem sighed and leaned back against the gold vinyl booth. She spread her fingers along the shiny table. Maybe this clash would be restful. Maybe Horace would pick a more subtle battle. She could use some calm time with Moon, even in this form.

There was a tabletop jukebox on the inner wall of the booth. "I love a bear," Jem told it, and she put a quarter in for "The Teddy Bears' Picnic."

"What's that, honey?" The robot waitress rolled to a halt at the booth. A keyboard extended from her midsection.

"I love a bear," repeated Jem. She toyed with her paper napkin.

"Except sometimes he's a Volvo, or a Venus Flytrap, or a shed. How can anyone love a shed? He wasn't even waterproof."

"I loved a programmer once," the waitress said. Her metal fingers clinked softly on her lips. "Love is funny. Seizes you in the gray space between off and on; sets your circuits to misfiring. You want coffee?"

"Two, please," said Jem. "And toast, and two sunny-side up eggs. Plus a packet of honey and something fishy for the bear."

"Ding ding," said the waitress, cocking her finger at Jem. She rolled off.

Moon lurched back. He was studying the other patrons as he returned, and it made him bang smack into an older man with plastic glasses and knock him from his shiny gold stool. There was a rumble of apology as he lifted the man back up onto the seat, ripping his brown button-down in the process.

She wondered what he would be like without his work; if an unchanging Moon could ever be a domesticated Moon. "I'm not a complainer, you know," she informed him as he returned.

The bear squeezed into the booth. "I think there's trouble over in the corner." He peered down at the dented silverware. He tried to pick up his fork with one paw. Then two.

"Already? Can't we even eat first?"

Moon jerked his furry head towards his left shoulder. "The guy in the white cowboy hat? I think that's Horace. I think this time he's planned a shoot-out."

Jem looked at the cowboy. He was tall and rangy and his hair curled in a blond mullet down the back of his neck. "I don't know," she said. "It doesn't look like Horace to me."

"He changes, you know he changes." Moon finally managed to scoop the fork onto one paw. He cupped his paw around it and carefully turned his forelimb over, but the metal slipped on his pads, and the fork spun out and clattered on the table. "Dolgonnit," said Moon. "Why don't I get to pick what I am? Horace does."

"Maybe because you're the fighter," said Jem. "The reactionary. Maybe if you chose the battles . . ." Behind Moon, the cowboy was already standing, gesturing with his coffee mug.

The fork clattered again. "No, it doesn't work like that. That's just not how things are. I can't explain it. Oh, good, fish."

The robot waitress set down a plate of trout and a pot of honey in front of Moon. Then Jem's plate, and in the center of the shiny table she set an industrial-size mixing bowl of warm water. A finger bowl for the bear. "I'll just clear this away," she said, and scooped the fork and knife from underneath Moon's paws. She winked at Jem. "Anything else?"

"We're good, thanks," said Jem. She tried not to look at the cowboy, or at the squid, who was now waving the man's hat in one pink tentacle.

Moon fell on his fish, spearing it with one claw and tearing chunks off with his teeth. Foam formed around his muzzle. Bits of trout flecked the scalloped placemats.

Jem swirled her toast through her egg. "I'm not getting any younger."

"You're not getting any older, either. Are you going to eat that?"

"No, I know that. But my world is—they're slipping further away from me as I stay still. Soon I won't be able to fit back in with anyone I once knew." Egg yolk covered her plate. "Do you think you'll ever get to stop fighting, Moon? Defeat Horace for good?"

The black eyes shone wild. "I feel as though I'm closer to getting the bastard. That could be an illusion. Do you want to go home?"

Jem searched for hurt in the furry face. It wasn't so much the strange features that were the problem, as it was Moon himself. Even as a Volvo, she'd been able to tell when he was cranky, or not quite so cranky. But hurt—never.

"Why is there always one who moves and one who follows? Why do I have to be the girl?"

"What?" He was onto the honey now—scooping the honey with one paw from the pot to his mouth. Behind him, the giant pink squid and cowboy were facing off; the cowboy braced and tugging on his hat, the squid sprawled on top of his shiny table, waving a butter knife.

"God, not again," said Jem.

"Where?" said Moon. He turned, honey pooling from his paws.

"Can't we even eat one meal in peace?"

The squid had one tentacle wrapped around the cowboy's neck

now. The diner was clearing out around them; the three-headed dog scampered out the door, followed by a ballerina and a giant spider. The cowboy was turning purple. The robot waitress rolled up behind him and poured coffee on the squid's tentacle. Even across the diner, Jem heard it sizzle. The blistered tentacle fell free of the cowboy's neck and the squid's other tentacles started writhing in response. One grabbed the waitress before she could roll free.

"How do you know which side you're on?"

"Eh," said Moon. "Good question."

Another giant spider sidled out the front door. The cowboy backed up, reaching for his gun, and the squid reached for chairs.

Moon rose from the booth to examine the fight and Jem half stood, ready for retreat.

"Just an old-style brawl, this time. Must be why I'm a bear." Moon furrowed his brow and his black eyes disappeared in fur. "Seems too simple for Horace . . . ."

A chrome-and-gold barstool sailed over Jem's head and crashed through the starlit window. Her hand skidded in eggs as she ducked, and her plate flipped onto her pants.

Behind Moon, the giant squid loomed. The captured waitress was banging on it with her keyboard. The squid raised bloated tentacles and one snaked around Moon's belly.

"Fight it is," agreed Moon. "Anti-Squid." He ripped the tentacle's suckers from his stomach, and turning, slashed streaks of gore from the squid's pink body. Ammonia cut through the air. A shot cracked glasses. Jem backed away.

There had been other fights that were nicer, subtler. When she'd met Moon, he'd been a defense attorney; Horace his opponent, and that fight had lasted for eight months. Plenty of time to fall in love with an illusion.

Moon's claws carved through the tentacle that held the waitress, dropping her to the ground with a crash. But in the distraction, the cowboy's attention had turned to the cash register. He was scooping out bills into his hat. The waitress hollered and rolled after him. The squid squeezed Moon.

It was a tedious fight; like the gladiator sequence, or the car crash as a Volvo. Jem always had to patch him up in the end. And it wasn't really that she was tired of that as much as it was all very different than she'd thought when she fell in love with a stoop-shouldered idealist with weary hands and eyes that shone fire.

The waitress yelled, her keyboard walloping the cowboy, and then yelled again; a funny scream, cut off at its height. Jem looked at the waitress and the cowboy, and it took her a full five seconds to realize that neither of them were moving. The robot waitress had her keyboard extended for another good smack; the cowboy was cowering behind his white hat. Bills were falling, or had fallen from his hat—they hung in the air. Frozen.

Moon and the squid were frozen, too. The squid had Moon off the ground and a coffee cup with a flying splash of coffee hung motionless above Jem and Moon's booth.

There was total silence in the little diner.

Total stillness, too. Jem was the only moving body. There was one stabbing moment of panic as she wondered if everything in the world had frozen but her; part of the rules that she still didn't understand. Perhaps some balance had been tipped and she would now spend eternity in a diner, eating lemon meringue pie and crying in her coffee cup and dusting the frozen Moon.

But then a voice behind her spoke. A voice with a mouthful of food. "You dislike our fighting, don't you?" Horace.

"What did you do to them?" Moon's jaws were open in a growl, or cry.

"Ah, now that's, that's a fallacy." A swallowing sound and the words cleared. "I did nothing to *them*; I merely sped us up."

Jem turned away from Moon to stare at the man on the barstool. He was utterly unlike any previous incarnation she'd seen him in. He looked like the slovenly regular of a small-town cafeteria; his shoulders were hunched and his plastic glasses were smudged. One hand held greasy toast. And yet she was used to men changing on her. She just saw him as Horace. Moon's antithesis. "I told Moon you weren't the cowboy," she said.

"You're sharp," he said. "But ya know, you don't need me to tell you that."

"Please. Tell me what I could possibly need you for." She pulled a chair between them and clasped the back of it with her hands. If she looked at Horace, she couldn't see Moon's rigid face. Her grip hid the tremble in her fingers.

"To be the one who smoothes things over, ya know? End our fighting. Get Moon all to yourself."

"And how would that work?"

Horace spread one hand. "Walk away with him. Tell him to never finish this fight."

Jem's knuckles whitened on the chair.

"Logically, ya know, if he stops fighting me, he'll stop changing," said Horace. "Now look, I'll show you how it could be. Picture an island, the shape of a crescent moon."

He pointed at the tabletop jukebox back in Jem's booth and snapped his fingers at it, a dry, whispery snap. "Kokomo" began to play. "The sand is whiter than stardust. No, it *is* stardust, burnished by the thousand tails of a thousand blinding comets. On one tip of the crescent a thousand palm trees sway, and from their branches fall round green coconuts. Okay. Do you like coconuts?"

"No."

"Then when you crack the coconuts, out flows not coconut milk, no, not coconut milk, but rum. And the coconut meat is . . ."

"Pineapple." It came out in a whisper.

"Ah, but I haven't described the pineapple plantation. There's a hundred acres of pineapple, ya know, and a hundred burnished men in short shorts to pick it. We'll make the coconut meat be chocolate," and he waved his toast, "or something like that. And at the top of the highest mountain—"

"It sounds lovely," said Jem. She lifted one hand, put it right back on the chair. "But wouldn't Moon still be a bear?"

Horace scratched his thin hair. "There exists that possibility. I can't change Moon, ya know. I can't *make* him do anything."

"I feel that," Jem admitted.

"And you must admit being a bear is a better life than being a shed or a proper noun," he said, waving the last bite of toast at her. "I could always make *you* a bear, and those pineapples into salmon." He licked margarine from his fingers. "There's been a couple times I've wanted to acquaint you with this opportunity, ya know, only Moon was something impossible. You wouldn't really enjoy spending eternity with a leaky shed."

"But if Moon goes into hibernation, you win, don't you? Not a truce, not a smoothing over. You *win*."

Horace pulled his plastic glasses from his nose and wiped them with his stained napkin. "Well, what's 'win', really?" he said. "These little skirmishes we have—they're kind of, they're kind of futile, ya know? Moon wins, I win . . . neither of us really gets anything done. Think of spending your life never accomplishing anything." He put his glasses back on and smiled a wrinkled smile at her. "There are days I'd like to have a companion too, ya know. I'd like to have that island with the rum coconuts, and the short-skirted harem." He crumpled the dirty napkin in his hand and tucked it under the empty plate. "Maybe I'm offering you what I can't have."

Jem curled and uncurled her fingers on the chair, staring at Horace's plate, seeing Horace's island. Seeing Moon's torn face. A salmon hatchery, an island paradise—but no, what Horace was really offering her—giving her—was knowledge.

Horace thought she had the power to convince Moon.

She could take Moon away from the flat tires and the squid marks, the scimitar wounds, the endless fighting. And oh, Horace would give her an island if she did.

But could her Moon really fit into that vision of island bliss? By the end of the first day he'd be banging around, trying to find something to fix.

And Jem? What vision did she fit into?

The moons of Horace's glasses reflected starlight at her. He half-smiled, gray eyebrows raised, a puppy expecting to be told no. "The Girl from Ipanema" started on the jukebox.

"No," said Jem.

For a moment, Horace looked so disappointed that she felt sorry for him. Then he looked down at his watch. "Well, then," he said. "I guess that's all the time you've got."

She was watching Horace, and then he was gone, and only his plastic glasses remained. They hung in the air after he was gone. She reached out to touch them—but as she did, they fell, and then a bottle came whizzing by her, and then a shot, and then a packet of creamer. The island music was subsumed by the thumps and crashes of the struggle. Moon was growling and the robot waitress was yelling, "Don't touch the till!" again and again. The cowboy was down now, crawling on hands and knees for the door.

But Moon, her Moon, was still entangled in the air, and so Jem grabbed the first two things at hand and headed into their fight.

A tentacle swiped at her ankle. She jumped and pitched into the giant squid's body, instinctively throwing the first thing she'd grabbed at its eyes. It turned out to be the honey pot, and the sticky smear of honey did seem to confuse it, because there was a sharp intake of air behind her as Moon wrested free.

Moon growled and tore, separating the tentacle from the body. The squid keened. Jem found that the other thing she'd grabbed was a fork, and she jabbed at its body, releasing puncture wounds of gore and ammonia. At its center seemed the safest place to be; it couldn't curl its tentacles back to get her. Or maybe that was because Moon had torn off another one, and then another, and then the squid spasmed, its last tentacle flailing. It crashed through a table and lay there, shuddering.

All Jem's muscles felt hot and tight and her hand painfully gripped her slimy fork. She shivered, and then she was coughing, gasping for clean air and a new environment, and Moon gently pushed her away from the dying squid.

It seemed to take a long time for her breathing to slow. There was a water pitcher on the counter near where Horace had sat, and she drank from it with shaking fingers. It was mostly ice hitting her nose and then a packet of creamer. She fished that out and looked at it with astonishment.

The robot waitress rolled toward her, the cowboy's hat clutched in one hand and her eyes whirling. "More coffee?" she said. "More coffee? More coffee?" She banged at her head with a metal fist. "Must reboot," she said, rolling away and banging. "Must reboot. More coffee? More coffee."

There was a final squeal from the squid. Moon shuffled back to her, a tentacle falling from one paw. One shoulder dragged. He looked as though he'd been digging through garbage; he had crumbled bacon in his fur. Coffee aroma steamed from him, then a sharper reek—he was slimy with squid juice. Jem's pants were covered in more squid and egg and her boots were soaked with creamer. Miraculously, the bowl at their booth still had an inch of warm water in it, and Jem attempted to wipe the squid from Moon.

It was mostly a lost cause. Moon let her try, though, and was perfectly still while she wiped his belly with a paper napkin. On the other end of the booth, "The Girl from Ipanema" finally finished and Bing Crosby began in on "Sing Me a Song of the Islands."

She looked up at Moon and found him looking at her. He was really very handsome for a bear. Jem threw the slimy napkin to the floor.

"Please?" said Jem. "One dance?"

In the trashed diner, Moon pulled her out onto the floor and into a waltz.

One paw stepped hard on her boot, a claw tugged at the ruined leather. There was a rumble of embarrassment from his furry chest. "Remember, it's not how *well* the bear dances," said Moon.

Jem leaned into him then, and he lifted her till her feet rested on his hind paws. He whirled her around tables, through streams of coffee and squid, the cold starlight pouring through the windows and Bing singing to them alone.

The last bars of the orchestra faded and Jem opened her eyes. They were back outside in the spongy clouds, but the diner was gone. The air was chill and the light was blue.

In Jem's arms was a fish.

It looked down at its silver body, rolling one round eye. Moon's deep voice came out of cold fishy lips. "At least we'll likely get to go swimming, right?" he said. "A bear in a diner is one thing, but a fish in a diner—that would just be silly."

A laugh trembled on Jem's lips. Moon's tail flopped salt spray in her face and she cradled the fish close, pulling her shirt hem around it. Everything stank of egg and brine. "We'll go to an island where a thousand palm trees sway."

"Something wrong?" said the fish. "You look funny."

"No," said Jem. She brushed at the wet in her eyes. "I love the moon, that's all. I love the clever, frustrating, vigilant moon."

HARD CHOICES:
STORIES OF TOUGH CHOICES, TOUGH LOVE, AND FAIRY DUST

Hard Choices

A. Your little sister is tired of picnicking and wants to explore a cave. She says if you don't come, she will tell mom what you were doing last Saturday. If you grudgingly accept her blackmail, go to B. If you let her tell mom that you were skinny dipping with Bitsy on the shapeshifter reservation, go to Z.

B. The cave is dark. You try to scare your sister with tales of carnivorous shapeshifters who eat bad children. She says everyone knows that shapeshifters are cowardly beasts, easily beaten by the first planetary settlers. You ask why she knows so much history when you are flunking. If you vow to stop looking at Bitsy's shirt in history class, go to C. If you tell your sister to be quiet and respect her elders go to D.

C. You think about Bitsy's shirt as you explore the moist dank cave. Stalactites drip on your head. Go to D.

D. A swarm of glowbats fly out. They have a wingspan as wide as your chest, and are phosphorescent during mating season. It is suddenly so bright that your sister sees you drop and cower, trying frantically to get the feeling of claws and wings out of your hair. "Let's go back!" you squeal, but she says if you don't press on, she will tell Bitsy you're afraid of mating season. If you grab your sister and march her out of the cave, go to Z. If you dry your tears and press on, go to E.

E. By the light of three hanging bats, you see cave paintings. One painting shows many differently shaped shapeshifters greeting a rocketship. One painting shows the shapeshifters bringing stalks of grain to humans. One painting shows a yin-yang picture—a shapeshifter eating a human who is killing him with a spear. One painting shows the shapeshifters huddled in a circle, surrounded with lightning bolts. "Graffiti," sniffs your sister. If you think about the struggles inherent in the coming together of two sentient species and how we always seem to flub the hard choices, go to F. If you think about Bitsy's skin in sunlit water, go to F.

F. Past the pictures, the cave forks in two. One tunnel smells like rotten eggs. One tunnel smells like the strawberry shampoo in Bitsy's hair. Your sister goes down the eggy path. If you follow her, go to H. If you follow the memory of Bitsy's hair, go to G.

G. Your cave adventure was a funny prank by Bitsy, who paid your sister ten bucks to bring you to her. Bitsy is waiting for you, arrayed only in long locks of strawberry shampooed hair. Unfortunately, Bitsy is a carnivorous shapeshifter and you die.

H. At the end of the eggy tunnel is a bear. Since there are no bears on this planet, it is likely a carnivorous shapeshifter. If you proffer a handshake and recite the Human-Shapeshifter Protocol, go to I. If you throw your sister to the bear to buy time, go to J.

I. The bear's paw becomes a maw and bites off your hand. It chews it up while it recites some manifesto about how it rejects the Human-Shapeshifter protocol. You throw your sister to the bear to buy time. Go to K.

J. You feel a little regret and try to save your sister. The bear bites off your hand. It spits the fingers on the floor. You feel ashamed that your fingers aren't worth eating. Go to K.

K. Faint from blood and sister loss, you wrap your wrist in your shirt and run for the entrance. You lose some time when the bats fly over your head in a triumphal finish to their mating flight. Suddenly

Bitsy is there to save you. She helps you stand and dries your tears. She takes off her shirt and uses it to bandage your wrist. You feel a lot better. Then she eats you.

Z. Your mother grounds you from the prom. Bitsy finds a new date. When you are 31, the great Shapeshifter Revolt comes to fruition, the human settlement is overthrown, and the electric fencing destroyed for good. Bitsy finds you cowering in a bathroom, weeping that you will die a virgin. She makes love to you, tenderly, sweetly, and you remember a day of sunlit water and glorious splashing. There is no fumbling, there is no miscommunication, there are no tears. Then she eats you.

How Frederika Cassowary-Jones Joined the Ladies' Society of Benevolent Goings-On

We find ourselves in the stately parlor of Miss Maude Mandermuss, Chairwoman of the Tolpaddle-on-Bottomshire Garden Committee, Official Chaperone of the Bright Young Misses Academy, and what is most pertinent to this little mise en scène, the President of the Ladies' Society of Benevolent Goings-On.

With her are the three other ladies of the Society, fashionably dressed and taking tea. I shall describe them briefly for you, counter-clockwise from the spinet:

The already-mentioned MAUDE, laced and squeezed into brown velvet, sits upright in a pink chair. She is an impressive steamroller of a woman, with a famous temper.

Lady HORTENSE Staunton, very thin, very stiff, very proper. The last is remarkable, as she is French.

Polina (POLLY) Jakowski. Earthy, irreverent. A self-made woman, and we shall not inquire too closely into the details.

CALLISTA Smith, the newest member of the Society. An art student. Though sometimes overawed by the other ladies, particularly Maude, Callista is likely to be a force once she learns to assert herself fully. She is dressed in pale blue pinstripes and is entirely proper, except for the pair of goggles perched on her head.

We join them just after the butler has handed Maude a note, and while Polly is in the middle of an inappropriate story.

POLLY

. . . . and when they carried that gentleman out on a stretcher, I said, "I never thought I'd say this, but I should've chosen the elephant!"

[Callista snickers, wanting to laugh fully but not quite daring while under Maude's eagle eye.]

MAUDE

Please stay on the topic at hand, Polina. We Ladies of the Society of Benevolent Goings-On have not had occasion to meet for thirteen long weeks. We need to assess the result of our efforts and move on.

POLLY

That *was* the result of my efforts.

MAUDE

Hortense?

HORTENSE

It was very boring in my area; I almost died of it.

[She touches her thin lips to her teacup and pulls it away again. Impossible to tell if any sustenance has escaped into her mouth.]

You and Callista went to the States—tell us of that.

POLLY

Yes, tell!

CALLISTA

Yes indeed, tell! Maude and I split up immediately on arrival in New Amsterdam. The only thing of importance is that I met a woman on the boat home who might be a good addition to the Society.

[Young Callista fidgets with her jacket, quite nervous. It is the first time she has put anyone forward for possible inclusion, and she does not know how Maude, in particular, will take it. Why, nearly half-a-year ago Polly put up a charwoman to join them. Maude won't let her live it down.]

Tell us what happened in the Wild West, Maude! Did you succeed in meeting any famous outlaws?

HORTENSE

Did you return by aeroblimp, as you swore to do?

POLLY

[Gleefully provoking. She still hasn't forgiven Maude over the charwoman incident. The charwoman maybe wasn't *perfectly* suitable, but she was a dear friend and deserved a chance.]

I wager she failed miserably, or she'd already be bragging about it. Let me guess; your temper got the best of you and ruined everything.

MAUDE

How dare—[collects herself with an effort; the brown velvet panels strain mightily at her sides.]

You will all have to wait for my account, as Callista's adventure is jostling for prominence. I understand from the butler that this woman from the boat has just arrived, and we must with haste decide whether or not to induct her.

Callista, as it is under your wish that we try this . . . Miss Cassowary-Jones, I suggest you tell us about her, and do try not to stumble over your words this time.

CALLISTA

[Stumbles] Well, I met her on board the *USS Truth And Freedom*, playing shuttlecocks with a crew of cigar-smoking sailors—

HORTENSE

Cigars!

POLLY

Shuttlecocks . . . .

CALLISTA

I don't know games. Perhaps it was horseshoes, or bingo, or cricket, but I definitely remember the cigars, because she was shearing off the end with a spring-loaded snipper she wore on one of her three belts. And strapped to her shoulder was a flask full of martini, or perhaps straight gin, and the sailors all called her Fred—

MAUDE

Fred?!

[Hortense notices the interrobang in Maude's voice and wonders at it. Perhaps Maude has taken a secret lover, also named Fred. Hortense wonders frequently who is loving whom in secret.]

MAUDE, cont.

That is, the type of inebriation is of really no importance, Callista. Can you not stay on topic? I am not convinced this Miss Cassowary-Jones is suitable.

HORTENSE

Mon dieu, she doesn't sound it. She sounds worse than the charwoman.

MAUDE

The Society has everything to lose by inducting someone unsuitable into its midst. We need to know her habits, her skills, her upbringing—

POLLY

Her taste in gin.

MAUDE

—to decide.

CALLISTA

Well. Well. Well—[determined to get the worst out, now that she's fully committed to this course]—she is American.

HORTENSE

I declare!

CALLISTA

She has a laugh that might be mistaken for the mating call of a crow.

POLLY

Saucy.

CALLISTA

And she has exceptionally good—

FRED

[Bursts through the french doors, hat flying.] I just can't set still waitin for all y'all to pronounce judgement.

CALLISTA

—hearing.

FRED

Pleased to meetcha.

[And now enters the fifth member of this story—Frederika Cassowary-Jones, a brash American with a decided western-American accent. FRED is in trousers and boots, and covered in hanging inventions, gears, etc. Something on her belt is leaking oil onto Maude's carpet, although that is not pertinent to the story unfolding here.]

CALLISTA

Oh dear. Miss Frederika, this is Polly, Hortense, and Maude, who can be frightening.

FRED

[Though American, Fred knows her manners. To each in turn she introduces herself, attempting to shake hands. Maude and Hortense are having none of it, Polly is happy to oblige.] Fred. Fred. Call me Fred.

[To Maude] Shore is a fine place, ma'am. Bigger'n Old Ethel's Dance Emporium, and that's a place kin hold forty-eight dancin girls doin a clockwise kick line.

[She demonstrates, next to the spinet. It is not immediately clear why a girl on trial would do high kicks for those about to decide her fate, so we must ascribe it to Nerves.]

MAUDE

Young woman, this boisterous display is most unseemly.

CALLISTA

And I asked you so nicely to wait in the hall, with the cucumber sandwiches.

HORTENSE

Just look at those trousers. And that hat!

POLLY

Wouldn't I like to trim *her* hat.

FRED

[She is not really abashed, so I leave it to yourself to imagine how her voice sounds: apologetic words but a lack of commitment to them down in her chest, where it counts.]

Goldarnit, I can't do nothin right. Look. Little 'Lista here said you needed help with your little Ladies' Society. Well, I'd been itchin to make my mark here in this foggy country a yours. So I shouldered up my guns, my flying goggles, and my A-1 Ace Super Steamy Blaster and here I am.

HORTENSE

Pistols. How . . . *Américain.*

POLLY

We're glad to meet you, Miss Frederika. Forgive the rude surprise of our more sheltered members.

[You see, Polly can say sentences without innuendo when she feels like it—she just doesn't often feel like it. What's life without double entendres? Boring, that's what, and Polly didn't work mumbledy-mumble years doing mumble on trains and mumble for the Prime Minister's wife just to be *bored* the rest of her days.]

FRED

[To Polly] Just Fred will do. I'm not fancy.

[To Maude] Fine place, I said. [Loudly] You ain't deaf, are you? You look familiar. I met a deaf woman once in a mine. I mean, she weren't deaf when we went in, but after she tried to cart off my gold and I had to fancy-shoot the hat off her monkey in a closed space, she lost her hearing.

POLLY

Is "hat off her monkey" a euphemism?

FRED

You'll pardon me if I don't rightly know that word. It was a small monkey, with a very red hat.

MAUDE

[She is struggling now to keep the famous temper in check, and Polly, who currently designs clothes for a living, notices the telltale signs of tiny threads bursting up and down the brown velvet vest.]

Young woman, this is a *Ladies'* Society. Forgive me if I don't think you're quite suitable to our goals. All opposed to Miss Cassowary-Jones' inclusion? Aye!

[There is silence from the others, and no hands are raised. Hortense is mulling over the etiquette of immediately rejecting someone you've only just met, and Polly quite likes Fred. Maude lowers her hand with bad grace.]

Well, it's tied for now. Carry on and say why you think you would fit in with our plans.

FRED
Hell, I know I ain't a lady like you, Miss Maude. I ain't stupid, just Texan.

Little 'Lista here told me about this here Ladies' Society after she saw me rope a man who threatened a girly on the boat. Trussed him up like a hog and dropped him into the Atlantic. I reckon if she invited me here that you've got a need for more of that sort of man-subduing thing.

Maybe when you do your charitable works you go into piss-poor dens of squalor where the brutes would soon grab a lady as see her, is that it? Or maybe you need a strong arm to carry you out if you faint when visiting the prisons? Well, the answer to that's me, cause I ain't afeared of anything but one, and that one thing's why I'm over here takin a rest cure. But you ain't likely to encounter *ghosts* among the poor, are you?

So that's what I reckon. You fine ladies need a bodyguard, one you can trust. Tell me that's it. Cause I know you ain't invited me in for my ability to pour tea with a pinky crooked up.

[A lovely beat of silence as Fred stares from one to the other. Finally Callista breaks the moment with a decision. The quaver is gone from her voice; she feels how it is to assert herself (it feels fine, so fine.)]

CALLISTA

What would you do if a hydro-mechanical squid hauled itself on land, squeezing the mayor's daughter in one rubberized tentacle and a nice new gaslight in another?

FRED

Shoot it, I reckon.

CALLISTA

Polly here mixed a chemical solution that melted squid, and only squid, into a compostable slurry that enriched the harbor and freed the young lady.

POLLY

[Purrs.] She was delightfully *grateful*.

CALLISTA

And what if you were taking the air with your parasol and nice new boots when you saw a train about to smack a small child? Could you run faster than the steam engine, grab the wee thing, haul yourself one-handed up on the cars and out of the way? Hortense did that.

[Callista is always particularly proud of Hortense's feats; for it seems to her that Hortense has had more to overcome than the rest of them.]

FRED

Pardon me if I don't rightly understand how a bitty thing like you could do that.

POLLY

Show her, Hortense.

[Polly is also rather proud of Hortense, as she has frequently helped her in the clothing and padding department.]

HORTENSE

[Hortense lifts her skirt slightly to reveal a trim, but very metal, ankle.] I am, how you say, *automaton*. You will tell anyone?

FRED

No?

HORTENSE

You tell, I kill.

[It is this sort of commitment to the cause that makes Maude proud of her.]

FRED

Definitely no.

CALLISTA

This is the Ladies' Society of Benevolent Goings-On, Fred. It is our mission to save the world from evil, whether our foes be mad professors with mechanical jaguars, armies of grandma zombies with knitting needle brain-chopsticks, or anything in between.

FRED

This'll take some gettin' used to, ma'am.

[Despite the proof of Hortense's ankle, Fred wonders if Callista has gone off the deep end. This crew of fine ladies go up against brain-chopstick-zombies, whatever those were? Impossible. She'd studied them all and not a one carried any of the fine A-1 Ace products that saved her life on a daily basis. Unless it was that good-looking Polly lady—she might be able to store an A-1 Ace Mini Gatling Gun in that crevasse in her bodice.]

CALLISTA

That's not all. We go off on exploratory works too. For example, when Maude and I went to the States, I was going to meet up with some women who knew the First Lady, and Maude had heard rumblings about a great uprising in America. She went to interview outlaws to see if the rumors were true.

FRED

My respect then, ma'am.

[Fred is willing to give credit where due, even in the personage of a brown velvet behemoth that represents the Society—and here Fred means society at large, not the Ladies' Society—trying to keep Fred in check. Fred does not wish to be kept in check.]

You must be braver than you look to meet some of them fellers in person.

POLLY

They wouldn't be in person, exactly. Maude here is our connection to the spirit world. Our medium.

FRED

[Shudders, all her tin doodads banging together.] Dealing with ghosts? There's only one thing that I'm afraid of, and that's—

[she looks dead at Maude.]

Aw, hell.

HORTENSE

What is it?

FRED

[She's alert now, pacing the room, hands going slowly but inexorably to holsters.] I know from where I know ya.

MAUDE

I vote to remove this deranged woman immediately. Immediately!

POLLY

You know her?

FRED

Yes, ma'am, she's the one who loosed all those ghou—all those ghoul—I feel sick.

CALLISTA

Maude! You didn't tell me you were planning to release ghouls!

MAUDE

I *wasn't* planning on it! And anyway, they weren't ghouls, they were ordinary ghosts . . . of outlaws . . . . *Hundreds* of them . . . .

FRED

On your feet, ma'am! I demand satisfaction for my psychological distress!

[Suddenly Fred and Maude are squaring off, the cowboy vs. Lady Establishment. Fred yanks out her A-1 Ace Super Steamy Blaster. Points it. Maude fumbles frantically in her skirt pockets, pulls out a crystal ball. Points it.]

Do you know what it's like to see an army of the undead coming after you?

MAUDE

I do now.

FRED

Especially when it's folks you know.

POLLY

Oh no, Fred—your friends and family?

FRED

No, folks I shot. Why'd you do it, ma'am? I saw you on Tombstone Hill, talking quietly to yerself, holding that ball. Thought you were loco. But then you started hopping up and down and whooping and carrying on and yer face got all red—

HORTENSE

Oh, Maude.

MAUDE

I don't have to answer to you, you . . . *woodsman.*

FRED

—and then they all rose up and started pouring after you, down into the city. Made Ole' Bill Willard fall flat dead at the sight of his mother tearin after him with a ghostly saucepan. She always was a harridan.

CALLISTA

You were just supposed to talk to them, not enrage them.

MAUDE

How was I to know they wouldn't act like gentleman?

HORTENSE

Oh, Maude.

MAUDE

One of them called me a battleship. And another one said . . . something a lady doesn't repeat, but it involved a description of where he'd put my ankles. You think I should just lie down and take that?

FRED

Them funnin' ya doesn't explain why you had to rile 'em up in return. They tore through the streets like a green dust-storm. The sheriff was too skeered to come out for days.

MAUDE

[She is out of words to explain how it is when you're having a perfectly nice conversation with Wild Larry Lawless, and asking him about his time in the afterlife, and maybe his time before, and okay maybe there's some flirting because after all it isn't that often that a woman meets a man who isn't afraid of her for talking to ghosts, and then that horrid Six-Shooter Sam comes up and says those crude comments, and she expects Larry will defend her so for once she won't have to punch out every guy that insults her (and then pretend that a man did it to save her reputation), but no. No, he just drifts over to his buddy and starts in too, and when she gets red-faced (and she can't help that) they all start needling her, and then all she can think to do is sic her old pal the Green Ghoullass on them and boy, does that get them going. That gets them running pell-mell and then they're gone, all gone from the hill, and she's alone, and it doesn't taste like victory.

She's out of those words, so she rounds on Fred.]

You know, I heard of you while I was there. A wild woman they couldn't do a thing with. A girl with no more manners than a . . . a *warthog*, they said, a girl who shoots first and asks questions later—

[Fred shoots Maude's crystal ball with her A-1 Ace Super Steamy Blaster. The boiling water makes the glass too hot to hold and Maude drops it to the carpet, squealing at her blistered fingers.]

MAUDE
Get her! Get her! All you ghosts, after that cowboy there!

FRED
Son of a half-broken, poo-slinging, fleabag mule—

[Fred hides from the imagined onslaught of spirits, behind chairs, under Polly's dress, still swearing. Maude dives for the ball, trying to pick it up with her skirts. This goes on until Callista says:]

CALLISTA
Stop it, stop it, stop it!

[She lowers her goggles onto her eyes and fastens her gaze on Maude, then Fred.]

Freeze, you two. Freeze!

[They do, unwillingly.]

FRED

What the—?

MAUDE

This is against our charter, Callista. I will have you fined!

HORTENSE

[Explains to Fred.] With the goggles, Callista is, how you say, *kinetique*? She rearranges your electricity.

CALLISTA

[Sinks to Maude's vacated chair, dizzy.] Bah, this gives me the vapours. If I release you will you two just shut up for a minute?

FRED

Where are the ghosts? I mean, yes, ma'am.

MAUDE

Fine.

CALLISTA

[Takes off the goggles, and Fred and Maude can move again.]

Now look, Maude. Fred would be the perfect fifth to our Society. She's quick on the draw, she's not afraid of anything—

FRED

Ghosts, ma'am.

CALLISTA

—and she's got legends building about her already. You heard the one about the girl who roped a whale and brought down Perilous Pirate Pete? The one about the girl who shot a star from the sky and used it to power a hydro-generator that saved Nevada? That's Fred.

MAUDE

That's you? I heard about that from one of the ghosts. [Wild Larry, of course—she had thought it a good sign that he was in awe of such an amazing woman.]

FRED

Shucks, weren't nothing. So, uh. Y'all want me then, huh?

CALLISTA

I'm not finished with you, *Miss* Frederika. If you want to join us, you have to be prepared to fit into society and keep your skills under wraps. This isn't the Wild West. I myself keep up a full-time life as an art student.

POLLY

And to support my expensive chemistry lab, I have a very fashionable salon. Not the sort where men come and jaw about their latest love poems.

[God forbid, is all we get from her thoughts here.]

A salon for women only, where we design and sew very expensive and adorable items.

HORTENSE

Unmentionables.

FRED

Art student, seamstress owner-lady. And you, Miss Hortense?

HORTENSE

I am married to a lord.

FRED
But you're an automatic whatsit. How does that work?

HORTENSE
Unmentionable.

MAUDE
And I am a wealthy maiden aunt with a strong interest in organizing garden shows. If you think you can possibly become one of us, you'd have to become . . . a *lady*.

FRED
[Swallows] I ain't never done that, but I reckon I could learn.

HORTENSE
If an automaton with a heart of gears can mimic a lady, so can you. I will teach you, but you will have to promise no more cigars. The smoke makes my grommets smell.

CALLISTA
I'll take you to student parties to practice proper mingling.

POLLY
And I'll get you out of those pants.

CALLISTA
All in favor of our new member, Miss Frederika Cassowary-Jones, say Aye.

CALLISTA, POLLY, HORTENSE
Aye! [They look expectantly at Maude.]

MAUDE
[Maude closes her eyes. This is the last moment when she's still fully in charge, for once Fred comes on, Maude will never be 100% the

boss again. But who is she kidding? Her last moment was before Fred burst through that door, or maybe her doom was sealed back when she invited Callista to join the group nine months ago. Callista is the leader of the future, anyone with half an eye can see that, and the only question is how long until Callista realizes it herself.]

Oh all right, aye.

FRED
[Miss Frederika Cassowary-Jones, for lack of a better way to express her feelings, tosses her hat in the air.] Yahoo!

[And here we leave the five women, each wondering what, exactly, they have gotten themselves into by this bargain. Fred in particular is wondering how one is supposed to be a lady when one encounters hydro-mechanical squids, French automata, and Old West ghosts. But these are tales for another time; suffice it to say we shall all meet again, and until we do, we toss our metaphorical cowboy hat with joyous abandon.]

INFLECTION

Beth was breaking down book boxes in the backroom on the day he left. She ran her boxcutter down taped seams, split the tape with slashing strokes that ran into the cardboard, ran through the corrugation, frayed bits of brown into fringe.

She had thought she would not see him again. Thought he would return to his home a zillion miles away and never say good-bye. Leave her to her own decisions.

But there he stood at the door, the metal door that never locked properly, the one that had to be yanked into submission.

"This is it," he said, and, "It is it."

It aggravated her that even here at the end he couldn't fill in his pronouns. His language didn't, and so he wasn't used to it; he was used to a verbal sea of its and hims modified by gesture, scent, touch. "I am he," he had said when they met, and upon the word "he" had touched his shoulder with one brittle, blue-tinged hand. That meant his name.

Hand, Beth thought. *Him*. And she ripped the knife through the lines between the flaps, sharp and fast straight into the box. What right had he to possess something that looked like a *hand*, to identify with *he*? Alien should mean alien. Incongruous.

Incompatible.

He moved into the narrow workspace between the piles of empty boxes and the rack of returns of picture books that hadn't sold. The normal scent of him was sharp and alcoholic, like licorice, like anisette. "I'm going back there," he said, and lifted his sharp chin in a way that meant *home*.

Beth said nothing, but unhooked her knife from the box and ran it through another seam. When she compressed the box, a cardboard flap fell out of the bottom, dumping out a book that she had missed while receiving. A Hemingway collection. She turned it over in her hands.

"I just don't think there should be a record," he said, looking down at her. "That I was here."

"I see."

"And it can't possibly turn out. You know. Like it ought." A flex of his double jointed elbow, the released scent of sulphur—inflections that signified *normal*.

"Normal, no," she said. Of course it couldn't be. "And that's bad?"

"It's up to you, of course. But think of the difficulties it will have. Neither one thing or another. You see that, don't you?"

Beth had told him her name but he never used it. His name for her was *you*, with a light touch on her chin. He did it now as he spoke, and the anisette of him curled along her skin. She did not know how he would describe her when he returned home, how he would represent *she* when she was not around to have her jawline stroked.

Silent now, his brittle hands touched her hair, her neck, her jaw again. Without the spoken pronoun what did the touch on her chin mean to him? Half a language was an echo, perhaps, a whisper, voices dying in the distance.

"I could come with you," Beth said suddenly. It had been lurking in the back of her mind for three weeks now, but she hadn't dared to say it, only express it in hand and eye and tongue. A zillion miles away. Away from everybody. The decision would be easy then, when she was fast in his arms, in flight from this life.

"It wouldn't work. Not among them," he said, and *them* was inflected with reverence, subordinance, personal shame. His hands left her face.

There seemed nothing else to say, so she held out the Hemingway collection so her hands had something to do. The cover art showed white hills in a brown landscape. Hills like white elephants, she thought, and suddenly held it out to him. "You'd better take it," she said. "I've already reported it missing, and you'll need something to read."

"Long journey," he agreed, and touched her chin, whispering, "You." Then his oddly-jointed frame was by the door again, leaning out, ready to be gone. Out of her life, out of her atmosphere. "No record, right?"

Beth crushed the box she held against her rounded belly, in a way that might have said, *I hate you for leaving*, if they spoke the same kind of language, if her physicality meant something to him. "No record," she said.

He was gone before her words faded.

She tossed the flattened box on the pile. She was down to the smallest boxes now. Too small for books; they had shipped side-lines—*Baby Tooth Keepsake Tins*, this one read. She turned the tiny thing over in her hand, seeking the small seams. A few inches here, and there, the boxcutter destroying that box as easily as the big ones.

Another cut, and it would be flat once more.

SILVERFIN HARBOR

I used to think there were only two ways off this island.

Ferry or sea-plane, and it was the ferry that mattered to me. The white ferry punctuated my days: taking the five-thirty across the sound to New Detroit, catching the four-thirty home. On the mainland, it was all 16:37s and 06:18s—the sky train, the subway. Company lunches, lab meetings, beautician's appointments. Closing time.

But now it's seven-thirty in the morning and all the ferries are gone. We're down to boats leaving now; the private ones, the charters. The air is thick, hot, heavy; the trees on Curie Island dotted with fire. Shouts. Crashes. It's the eruption they predicted. It'll render the entire Northwest Province uninhabitable. New Detroit, the islands—everything west of the Hindenburg Ranges, really.

My balcony railing is warm, as if by summer sun. My white bag—insulated—at my feet.

The boats are jetting past, one by one, swerving each other in wide swings. Heading for the ocean. The humans—those that aren't locals—are swarming off the island. But a silverfin pod is swimming into the harbor, towards the southern cove; cross-current to the flight. They are so hard to see—I rip off my gas mask, holding my breath and blinking against the stinging air.

My wallet vibrates—it is Crestien. "You're still there, aren't you?"

"Yes." The silverfin pod is leaping—I can't count them at this distance. It might be four.

"We're heading across the ocean to New Bangkok. Come with us, Lei. You could still be valuable to the company."

A quarter of the way around the world. "The eruption won't last forever," I say. "A few weeks for the air to clear. A few years for the temperatures to rise."

"Or it might not be inhabitable for ten, twenty years. Come now while you have connections. The lab has connections. It could be better for all of us."

"I'm a local," I say. "Don't come get me."

But that's the wrong thing. That edges Crestien's voice with panic. "We're coming, Lei. I'll come save you. Just sit tight."

But I am a local. I am.

I told *her* I was, and she didn't know that I wasn't tall enough, not scientific enough, not *island* enough.

I'm Lei. I'm a local, I said. She was so beautiful that first time. I can no longer see her face. I can't ever see faces—they fade the instant they turn away.

In my mind, Sully is more beautiful than she could have been. When all I have left are dry facts (she was there, she existed), I have to fill in the gaps. Concretely piece her together in my mind, and I know I will get her wrong.

She seemed short, so she must have been my height. I am used to looking at the tall locals. I can't label the color of her eyes, so they must have been dark. I only notice eyes I don't like.

I couldn't sketch it. Couldn't pick it out. But I loved the line of her jaw, the plane from cheek to jaw, the sharp drop to her neck.

I stared at it so often I should've memorized it.

But all I have left is her name—she no longer wears that face. If I had to recreate the world, from ferry drivers to fishermen, lab directors to locals, they would all wear a face made of nothing.

My Sully might as well have never existed at all.

When was the start of it all? The sharp line of her jaw, her glossy eyes, the silverfins? No, earlier that day. On the mainland, in New Detroit. In conference at my work at the lab. This was the gestalt of our story. My success.

"So you need my money." The blonde woman was from a rival body-modification lab, but now we had her in the conference room.

Crestien, Dr. Keith, and I, all hoping to turn her into an ally.

"No, *you* need this project," I said. "We're not talking about some idealistic scientific vision here. It's our lives we're fighting for. Our lives here on this planet. The lives of our children, grandchildren, great-grandchildren." The life of our company. "You've heard the stories of home. Smog, smoke, cement. A cancerous planet that our ancestors destroyed."

"The last mod you introduced" —and she smiled, thin and red— "rather a flop, wouldn't you say?"

Crestien's face, pink. I choked back a dirty look. The blonde was only trying to play it cool, trying to get a bigger percentage of the assets this project was going to recoup. I knew her type. "This is our home now."

Dr. Keith, nodding. I had been worried about this part of the speech. Not only was the project his baby, he was the only local in the room. The only true descendant of the first, idealistic colonists. They had dreamed of a new world, responsible, scientific—they were now huddled together on Curie Island. I didn't want him to be reminded of what we were doing to the land.

The woman's face glowed, making calculations in her head. I knew her sort; they saw this planet as theirs. They made no distinction between themselves (already raping, polluting—making half-assed eco-gestures that didn't cost them anything) and the original colonists. Mainlanders refused to know that there were other ways to live.

"This planet can be everything we want," I said. "But there's a reason the native life has these adaptive measures, the transformation cycles. The next eruption could come at any time."

"Oh, it'll die back down," she said. "It always does."

"Sometimes," I said patiently. "But it will erupt eventually, or another one will. The planet is ringed with volcanoes. And each one could be one that wipes out a city—or one that wipes out a world. The eruptions are inevitable here, but we owe it to ourselves to last it out—not through forcing bunkers on the earth, modding the air, polluting it as we once did. But through adapting to this planet, living as the locals and animals do.

"But change is scary. It has to trickle down into the public consciousness. We start with the risktakers, the X-gamers. The edge. The long-term goal? Not just a mod, but a true change to our germline. Enhanced humanity—the best parts of humans and silverfins. The best parts of the old planet and the new."

A breath before the finish.

"And it all starts with a subculture," I said. "It all starts with a mod."

The blonde was on the edge of her seat, eyes alight. A rousing speech about adaptation, and she was thinking of the mods she could sell; the subcultures she could spawn. Cash was in her eyes.

I leaned down to her. Woman to woman. "Are you with us?"

That night we went out to celebrate. I only stayed for one drink, but it was Friday, and the others were ramping up when I left. Dr. Keith was doing an interpretive dance about getting funding; I had a pretty good guess that he'd miss the last night ferry and have to wait for the four-thirty morning. I even convinced Crestien that he didn't need to walk me to the docks.

The six-thirty was early into dock and I got on it, swiping my wallet at the gate. It's called a round trip fare—you only pay to go to the islands, never to leave them. Other commuters streamed in behind me, true locals mixed with people like me. Not my usual four-thirty crowd, but I knew most of them by sight.

There were vacationing mainlanders, from New Detroit, with packs and folded sleeping cocoons. *Explorers*, the locals called them derisively. I wasn't ever sure what the locals called intruders like me. I'd lived twelve years on the island—but the locals had lived there eight and ten generations.

We moved in slow grace past the other mountains, islands. I knotted my hair back so I could stand on the upper deck and watch the mountains move. It was orderly at that moment, the ferry slipping around its familiar route, three sailboats to the west, one to the north, scooting out of our way. The water was flat and blue until we crossed it. Against the vastness a single gull dropped down beside us, pacing the ship. A single flight path, white and comprehensible.

The gull sunk to the water, wheeling.

Two explorers hung on the railing, watching the mainland recede. Something about the woman's back told me she was beautiful.

She had slung her pack to the deck and stood with one foot on it. Her friend had a certain grace, too—a comfort in his skin. He draped himself on the railing in the way teenage boys do.

The wind whipped away most of her voice; only the high notes came to me. "Not fair," whipped back. "Stoned." "Cash."

The kid straightened, leaned over her. Tall. An ex-pat local? Surely not. He didn't look too bright; he wore those drapey textured silks the fleshie subculture wore.

His arm pumping over his head. Her voice higher, indistinguishable from the wind. She thrust a closed fist at him—something, nothing. Her loose dark hair obscured her face. The tautness of her shoulders a cry.

He turned from her and she whirled around towards me—

I was staring. I tried to find focus at the front of the ferry—a bird, a ship. A patch of seaweed floating, brown and red.

A speedboat moving, a white triangle trailing a white triangle. A silverfin pod leaping out in the distance—too far away for the ferry to have to stop for them. Someone shouted "Silverfins!" and then I was surrounded, jostled by a large group of explorers, wallets held high to capture the distant acrobatics.

When I finally extricated myself, she was gone.

When we docked, I saw her again. Alone. She wavered on the ramp. A foot off, a foot back, then she looked behind her at the ferry—looked straight at me—and for an instant our eyes met. She turned away very deliberately and strode off the ferry, into the milling mass of explorers exclaiming over the quaint dock, the clever recycling centers, the cute boats.

I descended and started to climb the road to home. But instead I stopped and stood at the harbor rail, watching the mainlanders watch us. The ferry's thrum filled the low end of the air. White spume milled around its tail.

"Does it always rock like that?" She slung her pack to the ground, rested her forearms next to me on the recycled harbor railing. A sleepy smile. "I'm Sully, you should know."

God, I liked the idea that I should know. "I'm Lei. I'm a local."

"Yeah. I saw you on the ferry." She raised lazy eyebrows at me.

"And I saw you with someone." That flesh freak. I scanned her bare arms, looking for the bubbling skin of fleshie mods. But she looked clean. She may have smoked up with them, but she wasn't a flesh freak.

"Davey-boy took off. Thought I'd hang out here for the night. Maybe the silverfins will come back."

I looked sideways at her. "You like watching them, don't you?"

"Totally, yeah. They're so . . . alive."

"Come with me," I said. I settled the shoulder strap of my work bag back in place. "I know where they went." She fell in beside me as I led her south, down the frontage road, past the dock, past the bars.

"Something only the locals know, I take it."

"That's right," I said. I saw her eyes flick to the right, saw her tall friend disappearing into one of the subculture bars.

"I hate people who waste all their time, don't you?" she said. "Life should be *lived*."

She clearly meant her stoned friend, but I agreed with the sentiment. "Exactly," I said. "People who ruin their future for extra fun in the present. I'm with you on that."

Sully looked at everything as we walked—the grass, the sea, the birds—and I watched her. Once she threw her head back and breathed deeply through her nose, like an animal tasting the wind. We reached the fork in the road and turned east, down that rocky gray path to the cove.

I hoped the pod would be there—if not, what else could I show her? But there they were, playing in the cove: butting each other, tackling, rolling. The smallest one was leaping, great arcs that smacked into the water and sprayed the others. Inquisitive, it came up to us. I stuck my hand out over the water and it swam over and batted my fingers with its nose.

"See?" I said. "Just as promised."

She sat down on the rock, peeled off her sandals and let her feet dangle in the water. The silverfins were so close, bobbing up and down, their dark eyes looking sideways at the water, at the sky.

"They're so happy, so free," she said.

They were just animals, of course. The locals' studies never showed that they had anything approaching human intelligence. But the moment was right; I didn't dare intrude on her fancies with facts. "They're very charming," I said.

Sully put a hand out and the smallest silverfin rested its snout on her bare thigh. "You can see the intelligence in their eyes." She ran a finger along the ridge of its headbone and it bobbed its nose up to meet it. In that moment everything was still, Sully's finger extended, the silverfin taut in the water. Sully's breath caught, her eyes were warm and reverent. I had thought her intriguing before, but that moment I fell for her, irrevocably.

Then another silverfin tackled the smallest one, soaking Sully with seawater and ending the moment. The pair rolled over one another, smacking down and spraying droplets.

Sully laughed and stood. Her hair was tousling in the evening breeze. "Wouldn't it be gorgeous to swim with them?"

"Someday we will," I said. There was a burst of happiness in that moment—a sense of rightness. A beautiful girl, here in my cove, dreaming. I, telling her of the future—the world's future—I was helping to shape. "Someday we'll overcome our limitations—that's when we'll really connect with this planet."

"To change . . . ."

"Not just to change; to be *more*." My enthusiasm from the day's successes carried me closer to her. She was still watching them swim, slick and lithe. "The native silverfin is key—their unique growth cycle. They start as a crawling tadpole, but that form's expendable. Then they metamorphose to their marine form, gills and lungs, flukes and tail. They take on the survival skills they need for this planet. They can swim deep, live on through volcanic activity. To live here long-term—I mean, for millennia—we need to adapt; we need to be more like the silverfin." My left hand on the jutting rock behind her and then I could point past her with my right.

But her hips were turned out to sea, and hearing about the biology of silverfins wasn't a bit like swimming with them.

The sun was setting behind us. Its last rays hit that sharp plane of her cheek; beneath it her neck was dusk. Her warmth contrasted the curling air from the sea.

"Someday we'll be more." Those shadowed, glossy eyes turned to me; her warmth seemed to trap the words in my throat.

"You're right about that," she said, and then before I could do it, she kissed me.

A long lazy weekend then, the first of many. She made herself at home, one of those sleek women who can be comfortable anywhere, claim any territory. She padded around my house in my slippers, claimed my favorite teacup for her own. I watched her cradle it in slim fingers, touch it to white teeth, and didn't regret it. Davey-boy probably spent the whole weekend passed out on a couch in the bar, stoned to the gills. I never asked.

She went to the mainland with me early Monday morning. We stood on the upper deck and I leaned into her, testing to see how familiarity would suit us. She wrapped her arm around my waist. Warm girl, surrounding sea.

Sunrise on the harbor.

In the narrow stretch, the volcano cast a straight shadow. The bulge of its building dome was not reflected in the water. The light twisted, the water was vertically striped—orange blue orange blue orange. A dock on Curie Island was silhouetted against the orange water, a person sailing towards it. The black boat was dim against the blue water, bold against the orange.

We cut through the colors, bound for the mainland.

Despite catching the sunrise ferry, I was later into the office than I'd planned. I slipped into the conference room, unloaded my white work bag to my seat. Crestien set a coffee next to my elbow. I didn't have to taste it to know it had exactly one spoonful of honey. "Miss the ferry?" he said.

"I didn't *miss* it. It just stopped for forty minutes to let a silverfin pod go by."

"You should move to the mainland. I'll find you a little place near the lab."

"Little is right. Do you know how much apartments cost this close in?" As usual, I tried deflecting, but even a glimmer of encouragement was too much for Crestien.

His face expanded, blond head bobbing. "Oh, Lei, the company has connections. We can find you a good place. A balcony like you have now. I'd be glad to—"

"No."

He reddened. He did that so frequently around me that it lost meaning. I rubbed at my scalp, tried to figure out what to say to maintain my boundaries and not be rude—but he busied himself with his work. Dr. Keith and his lab techs came in. The pink on Crestien's face faded out to the tips of his ears and vanished.

I didn't want to be that close to work. Besides the lack of privacy, I saw it as failure. A failure to connect with the locals, with my island. To give up and take an anonymous apartment, where the mass of people overwhelm your connections, swallow the land and you. Their density makes them your daily interaction. Not mountains and flat water but landlords and traffic jams and refuse.

"It's progressing," Dr. Keith was saying.

"We need to move on to the next stage," said Crestien. He was all business now, the driven lab director determined to turn his company around. "It's time to get specimens."

Dr. Keith shook his head. "I need more time."

"I've seen the monkey-silverfins," said Crestien. "They look great."

"There's still tests I want to run. Something's being lost in translation."

"What?"

"I don't know," said Dr. Keith. "I don't have data on it. It's something I sense . . . ."

"Do you have the human sequencing modeled?"

"Yes. But—"

"I have complete confidence in you, Dr. Keith," Crestien said. "Your work always comes out spectacularly. Mod after mod an unqualified success."

Dr. Keith reddened at the praise, tried to press on.

Crestien didn't blink. "Except financially, of course."

Dr. Keith dropped his hands to the table.

"Money is everything, especially when you don't have any," said Crestien. "I don't need to remind any of you how important this project is to the lab's continuing to survive and thrive in a cutthroat world." He turned to one of the lab techs. "Time to round up some subjects. Lei's got the work-up on how little we can get away with paying them."

The mainlanders left the room.

"I'm too knowledgeable," said Dr. Keith. "They're using it against me. It's not right."

"What part's bothering you?"

"Oh, the capuchins," he said. "I can't identify it. Something's being lost. Ricky, he used to play this clever game with his food. He'd juggle oranges until I'd throw him another. He frequently made it to four. I kept tossing them in until he'd drop one—that was game over. But now . . . ."

"He looks healthy," I said. "I saw him splashing when you gave the funding tour."

"Yes, I know." He shook his head. "But the feedback—his responses, his eyes—it's like he doesn't understand me anymore. I can't put my finger on it. He's not the same."

I rubbed Dr. Keith's shoulder. "Cheer up," I said. "At least there's funding."

"I should go back to the island," he said. "Back to our labs in the center. Dr. Ina and I have our differences, but . . . that's where all the important work is occurring. Germ-line work, a true metamorphosis for humanity—it all comes from the scientists on the island."

"You're very important to this lab," I murmured. It was true, but my thoughts were already turning homeward, towards Sully and the island.

"I only want to be important to the world."

Despite Crestien's insistence on pushing forward, it was another two months before the trials advanced. One of the capuchin-silverfins went belly-up, and Dr. Keith stubbornly took his time over the body, ignoring Crestien's threats.

Sully came and went with me on the ferry, or I went and she stayed, and then I had someone to come home to. I liked the latter better, and not just for the welcome home. When she went into town with me she sometimes met me at the ferry smelling of fleshie smoke. Or, almost worse—soap and spearmint.

Lately I was more and more at work. There was a ton of paperwork to be filed with the insurance companies at this stage. I loved to find her using my house when I came home late, cooking or exercising or just lounging on something warm, waiting.

She was doing push ups on my kitchen floor one evening and it reminded me. "I don't know what you do," I said.

"You know very well," she said.

"I have a fantasy about it." I squatted beside her, put extra weight on her butt with my hand.

Sully grunted. "Yeah?"

"You're a porter on the mountain train. You carry bags for old ladies. Send people on one-way journeys through the Hindenburg ranges. Far-off cities."

"Your fantasy life." Push. "Needs work."

"Then you're a lab spy. A con artist. A rich woman's runaway mistress."

She collapsed under my hand, rolled, grinned up at me. My hand traveled with her across the side seam of her undershirt, under and onto the warm skin of her belly. She stroked my fingers through the ribbing of her shirt. "I wish. That'd be brilliant. Flat broke and need a job, more like."

"Then why the push ups?"

She shook her head up at me and her dark hair spilled across the cork floor. "Don't you like surviving?"

I ran both hands up under her shirt, pushing it back over her breasts, trapping her neck with the white. Her body was unmodded, perfect and clean. "If that's what this is," I said. "I'm all for it."

That's how it was: wonderful until suddenly it wasn't. A stupid fight. I didn't understand how it escalated so quickly.

I climbed the hill from the ferry and there—she was sprawled on my couch with Smash and Davey-boy, an entangled pile of naked animal limbs. They weren't fucking; I wasn't so stupid as to think that. They were stoned, the hookah on the floor beside them in a pile of Davey-boy's silks. They'd gathered soft things, textured things—the woven dishtowel, my beaded sweater, my felt coat. Smash was spooning Sully's linen pillow. Davey-boy's thigh was wrapped in my silk scarf.

I felt hot, invaded. Alien and alone in my own house. "Out. Out!"

Davey-boy stirred. "But your couch is all soft and nubbly."

"Nubbly," said Smash. "That's brilliant."

"Silk," said Davey-boy. "Soft. Warm." The words slurred from loose lips.

I ripped the scarf from Davey-boy, exposing a modded thigh, bubbling in gooseflesh. "Out. Leave us alone."

I stayed there, feeling stupid and very clothed, till they left. Sully was crouched, glaring. She swung off the couch and stumbled into the kitchen.

I followed her naked form, the silk scarf trailing from my hand. "I don't want them coming here."

Push ups. Sullen. "I need a job."

I knelt and stroked her bare back. "You're welcome to continue staying here."

"But not my friends."

"I don't love your friends, silly. I love you."

"There's always waitressing." Push. "The smoke bar." Push. "I can get my old job back if I crawl."

"Don't be silly. I make plenty at the lab. The silverfin project's going to pay off big. Waitressing is a waste of your time."

She struggled to her feet, her muscles over-relaxed from the drug. "I'm tired of your stupid silverfin project. Stop telling me how to spend my time."

"Then you figure it out. What do you want to be doing? You could train for something, study something. The island has the best education on the planet. This is an opportunity I'm giving you—you should take it."

Sully stumbled from the kitchen. "I need my family."

The words twisted in me. Came out new and ragged. "Strung out fucking *fleshies*."

She turned on me, her face lax and her eyelids low. "Cunt."

If she had had to pay for the ferry, she might have come back to me. I don't think she had any cash left at all.

But the ferry to the mainland is always free.

Leaving me didn't cost her anything.

Twenty lonely ferry rides, and then one that was more horribly isolating still. My house, my bed had been desolate for two weeks now. The new subjects were arriving that day to start the project and it always made me tense. And the volcano was bulging more than ever—the earthquakes had the mainlanders spooked. I couldn't get any peace from their chatter.

I tried to lose myself in the clumps of tall people. The locals were calm, Dr. Keith was calm. "Dr. Ina's germ-line work is progressing on the island base. They'll be ready for me to bring in my somatic work. We'll go underground. We'll survive. The locals can weather anything."

"Maybe not pyroclastic flow," joked one.

"We're hardly in danger of that in our location," said Dr. Keith sternly. "Eruptions, flood basalt . . . the skittish mainlanders will leave, New Detroit will fall. We'll reclaim this continent at last."

"Hurrah," said another, and that was echoed.

I looked up at the men and women around me, smiling and toasting the impending eruption. I tried to feel like I was included as a local, that I was one of them. But I wasn't sure I was supposed to.

Maybe they didn't know I was there.

From the ferry to the lab was much the same. New Detroit was tense; mainlanders walked with their shoulders hunched, starting at every tremor of sky rail or subway.

In this atmosphere, I didn't even notice that Crestien was wound tighter than usual.

"We've got the first test subjects downstairs," he said. "Modders, as usual." He was half-looking at me, like he didn't know what to say. But that was usual, so it didn't trip any circuits.

Not till I got down to the basement to sign off on their paperwork and I saw them.

All three of them; Davey-boy, Smash, Sully. And three more I didn't know; a girl in silks and two boys in clearsuits that displayed their blue skin fractals. I knew which lab sold that mod, but I didn't know which mainland subculture it signified.

Davey-boy and Smash were laughing and pushing. They stopped when they saw me. Smash, a little quicker, looked down at his wallet as if I might not sign off on transferring him the money. He was wrong there.

Sully was deliberately turned away, her hair covering her face. There was silence in the lab basement, but she wouldn't look at me.

Crestien. "Should I, um . . ."

"Talk to them," I said. And I pushed past the boys, grabbed Sully's arm. Pushed her toward the tanks. "What do you think you're doing? Selling us your body—it's not worth the money."

"I don't care about money."

My hands on her arms. "They're using you. You're disposable to them. Throwaway efforts till they can get it right."

"You don't get it."

"No, *you* don't. Science is about failures. Look at those blue boys talking to Crestien—how many failures do you think that lab had before they got it right? And that's just tattooing. Go home while you can. I'll give you money, if that's what you need. Just don't do this to me."

Dr. Keith interrupted us, laughing. "I know she's cute, but you can't have her. She's mine."

Sully chose that moment to break free. She headed to the group of specimens.

"You'll kill her."

"I won't kill her," he said. "I know that much." More seriously. "It is hard to be on the cutting edge, but this is a step towards evolution."

"You think this is really about evolution? This is about new mods, fancier mods. No germline changes. *Cash flow.* Crestien doesn't care about your ideals. None of the labs do. Why do you think we got the funding?"

Dr. Keith closed his eyes.

"You locals are so naïve," I said. "You think mainland culture is scientific."

"An economic society is a dead-end; it is not sustainable . . . ."

"That's all we've got, out here."

"But these compromises," he said. "They're worth it if we can learn to coexist on this world. Endure the eruptions. Our island lab—Dr Ina's been going the wrong direction with it, I thought." He rubbed at his forehead with long fingers. "I thought I could do more good here."

"I don't think I ever did."

Another two weeks came and went. I didn't take the ferry anywhere. I stayed on the island.

I stood on my balcony, watching the ferry dock. The harbor seemed so calm from this distance. Only up close was it a maze of ripples, clashing and breaking apart. I watched the harbor a lot, those days. I ignored my wallet when Crestien called.

I was on the balcony, and I saw her get off the ferry. Thought it was complete imagination, a hallucination brought on by the volcanic gases in the air, or more honestly, by my own desolate body.

Sully was gone; she wasn't going to come back to me and warm herself in my arms. We wouldn't fall together on my bed, my couch, my counter. I wouldn't bite her ear and she wouldn't laugh in mine.

There would be no Sully.

But it was Sully. She let herself in.

I turned when I heard her footfall in the bedroom doorway. I reached for her like an idiot, dropped my arms when she didn't move.

"Black," she said. Her voice had a new register. Lower, with an echoing timbre. "Spots. My eyes—dancing." She wavered where she stood, her face tired, out-of-focus. "Waving like water."

"Fuck." I crossed to the door. Grabbed her arms, shook her to me. "What did they do?"

Her arms under my hands were hard and her face in the light was mottled green, shiny patches discoloring her skin. I shook her, wanting the changes to be impermanent, a cloak I could free her from if I shook hard enough.

In that instant her eyes cleared. Cleared, hardened—did she see how I wanted to free her? Her hands went to my shoulders and she threw me back. "Let me go." Her new voice made her words ring. "I just came to say good-bye for awhile. The four of us go into the tanks tomorrow to start our cocoons."

"Four of you? There were six."

"Rachel gave up on day one. Dr. Keith brought out the needle and she went home. Didn't take a single dose. Poser."

"That's one," I said. "Davey-boy? Smash?"

"They're fine, we're all fine." Her hand touched her forehead, a bulge at her neck. "All fine."

"Tell me who died."

Silence. "One of the hopheads," she said finally. "His legs started fusing before his gills formed. He couldn't cocoon."

"Oh, Sully . . . ."

"Dr. Keith knows why," she said. "He fixed it. We're not having problems."

"Just look at you. You have problems you can't see."

"You don't understand anything," she said. "I'm moving forward. We'll be part of the planet. Free to swim wherever we want to go. We'll *live*."

"You fucking idiot. This planet is killing you."

"No one's killing me. I want this." She coughed, bending double. "Breathe."

"Sully!"

A stiff hand out, a push at my chest. "Don't you. Woman. Don't."

"Why did you come if you won't let me help you? What is this? Vengeance?"

Her eyes glazed, and she bent. "You can't follow me."

"Sully." I reached again to encircle her. But she ran, stumbling, losing herself in the darkness.

I ran to the ferry and watched for her, but I never saw how she left the island.

I tried to put her from my mind, but I failed. Finally one night I left my balcony and I took the last-but-two ferry to New Detroit. It would leave me one hour before the last ferry home.

My keycode still opened the door to the lab. Crestien had been too hopeful that I'd return.

There were ten glass tanks in the lab basement, five to a side. Black except where the fluorescent light picked out forms. The first two on the left were the failed dog-silverfins; they floated on their side, panting thick hard bellies and trailing mucous and slime.

On the right, the capuchin-silverfins. One tank had three; little lithe forms, still awake and swirling at this hour. The next tank was an older version—"Ricky," the one who had stopped understanding Dr. Keith's games. He was discolored white and green and one eye was scabbed over, but he swam around as lithely as any of the younger specimens.

I swung my flashlight on the other tanks.

Glass. Black.

Cocoons.

Displays on the outside of the tank labeled their experiment number, their specimen ID, their vitals. Their stats. And the coldest—a name on each, in quotation marks. "Davey-boy," this one said. The next: "Smash." "Rachel"—an empty tank. "Sully."

She was the last tank on the left.

I don't know if it was better knowing which one she was or not. She was maybe four feet from me, behind glass, in water, encased in mud. She seemed less irrevocably gone than that day she'd stood in my kitchen, choked with anger. Here I could imagine her, had to imagine her, soft and forgiving. When someone dies in the middle of an argument, it leaves the burden of forgiveness on the living.

That was the night that I stole Rachel's needles. They had been prepared, and flash-preserved, and I put them in my white insulated bag. There were a hundred special directions I didn't know, that I had no experience in. There was the sequencing that went right in the vertebrae, to tell the dorsal fin where to grow.

A hundred things like that.

But I took them with me.

The ripples of my memory collide, break apart. It must be the heat and the pounding of rock in water. My memories of Sully are whipped away and I am stuck in the present without her. I'm back on my balcony watching humans flee an eruption. The other islands are obscured now, by smoke and smog and fire.

Crestien stands at the door to my bedroom. I don't care to be surprised that he's used the company's emergency key. "The sea-plane," he says. "It's docked."

I don't move from the balcony.

"It'll be swarmed by the mob of swimmers—are you coming?"

"Yes, of course," I say. "Yes, yes," and I flap my arm behind me. "Take my suitcase, will you?" The suitcase is heavy with work clothes, patent leather heels. Things I will need if and only if I leave with him.

I can't see him, but I know he nods, hefts it from the bed, stands there as long as he dares. Until he has the guts to say—"You have five minutes." He is always gutless and I hate him for it. Hate the way he looks at my back with weak blue eyes.

The only person I want to see is Sully, and she leaves me in darkness. If only I could see her, just once more. I swear this time I would observe every last inch of her, I would remember every pore, every lash, every cell.

I squat, grip the white bag at my feet. Check, reassure: It is there.

One more memory.

One last glimpse.

The volcano was going to erupt, they were sure of it. The lab was leaving. Where, I didn't know, but I could guarantee they wouldn't be transporting four half-assed silverfins across a continent in the middle of an eruption. Crestien had a private plane. It seated twelve.

The cocoons were horribly unwieldy. The lab doors, stairs—none of that was made for machines and sea creatures. How did they expect to transport them from the basement to the water? The promises of open sea were empty all along.

I could hardly face it, but I didn't leave it all to Dr. Keith. We worked so fast on them that night—Davey-boy, Smash, blue-veined Criker. Davey-boy the best looking, shiny and pewter-colored like a true silverfin. So fast I hardly had time to think, didn't have time to try to communicate to them, any of them, what we were doing. I wrapped my green-skinned Sully in cloth and chains and we took them to the sea.

"Jesus, Lei, we can't wait any longer!" Crestien is white and red; his nostrils are red and wet.

Was that five minutes already?

The black of his pupil is going to swallow those awful blue eyes. He is in hysteria and he needs to get to that plane. For one compressed moment it doesn't seem to matter what he has done to my Sully; he is ripping my heart out. My eyes squeeze shut behind my mask. He needs to get to that plane.

I slap him hard. He steps raggedly back. The taut lines of his cheeks collapse and he steps back again. Again, and his eyes water and he pulls up the gas mask and then he goes. Stumbling from my house, running across the harbor, his black pants in lengthening strides. A silhouette I can't see into. I turn away; pick up my bag and leave. I don't bother to lock my door.

There are boats jetting from the harbor—they are crammed with people; bodies slip and fall into the blackness. People are floating in the harbor, in orange life jackets and gas masks, paddling east under their own steam. I hurry south, down the frontage road, past the dock, past the bars. The roar pounds around me. I push my earplugs in.

Nearly everyone who wants to can get off the island. That is what is heartbreaking. It will not be this orderly back in New Detroit. Half these people will never make it any farther east than the Hindenburg ranges. Maybe a third. If I were them, I would take my boat and head west out to the ocean. Try to reach New Bangkok by fishing boat, as risky as that would be. There won't be anything left of the city once the rich pack up for the other side of the world. The temperature will drop and the mainlanders will starve in all that cement. They should fight now, while they can.

Down the road to the fork, pumice spitting past my head. I stop at the junction and brush cinders from my eyelashes, blinking. A local hurries past—looks at me, jerks his head to the west, towards their fort in the center of the island. It is an invitation and the offer makes something convulse inside my chest. I can't see past his gas mask and bike helmet, but I probably know him. He shifts his backpack on his shoulders, repositions a pan tied to the buckles at his waist. Turns off on the road he indicated, heading inland. There are tall black shapes stretched along the road: walkers, bikers.

I should follow them. But I turn east to the cove. Stumble down that worn gray path, hands balancing on rocks. The air is hot. I feel choked even with the gas mask. It reminds me of New Vegas, the choking stinking city I grew up in, a lifetime ago.

I skid the last few feet, my bag rocking my arm. The pod is there. They bob their noses up at me; Davey-boy, Criker, Smash.

A long snout of mottled green. Sully.

They bob, the water lapping hard and fast at the rocks. Davey-boy zips away from us, arcs out of the water, his hard form dark against the orange sky. Smashes down again, tail smacking the water. The wave soaks me to my ankles, wets my bag. The water is warm and thick with black grit and white ash.

Sully rides his wave, up and down. She is shiny. Her green nose is peeling. She seems to look at me sideways, across the thick water.

I stick my hand in the water. I think I can touch her, stroke her back; I think she will arch her body for me and shudder.

They all come jostling in.

Criker, Davey-boy, Sully, Smash. They all butt each other and roll over one another and bat at my hand with their noses. Smash waves those flippers with the dumb curling tips and Davey-boy body-tackles him. Water soaks me.

My foot slides under me and I sit down hard on the rock, catching myself. I almost lose the bag. My feet slide into the water. The silver-fins are close to me, all looking sideways at me, at the water, at the sky.

Criker flips his blue-traced tail at me.

Sully bats at my thigh with her nose.

I lean forward and she rests her whole snout on my leg. Through my gas mask I am staring into silverfin eyes and they are dark. Like Criker's, like Smash's, like the panting dog-silverfins; dark, shiny. Shallow.

I will remember.

Davey-boy slams into her, knocking her from my knee. They roll over one another, soaking me with gritty spray.

I stand.

My white bag is sodden, half-falling from the rocks. I kick at it as I climb back to the fork in the path, kick and kick again, until it falls into the sea.

I wonder how long it will take to walk to the center of the island. I may have put my hiking boots in my suitcase.

The edge of a splash hits the back of my legs. I turn my head, but they are gone, leaving the island, heading for the open sea. The rocks are hot beneath my hands, my shin. Everything is black water and raging orange sky.

Out in the harbor, one of them leaps up. It seems to hang in the air, curled. Still and black against the fiery sky.

I turn away before she falls.

As We Report
to Gabriel

FRED

E ight days ago there was only me and Ten Motes. The house was thick with quiet, rigorously anti-fairy, clean as my five polished pink toes. Aileen had everything under her thumb.

Then a golden shimmer of fairy dust settled on little Linnie, and *then* a golden mass appeared on the doorstep, disguised as a person. The world turned slick with upside-downs.

Oh, Gabriel, there's heaps of things you don't know from being stuck in iron.

Let's start when the children reported the fairy in the attic.

FRED, WITH SOME INPUT FROM LINNIE'S SHIMMER

"Jonah says there's a fairy in the attic."

"Linnie!" said Aileen. Her earring fell to the glass vanity top. "We *never* say things like that. Good people do not let fairies live with them." She scooped up the drop of diamond, fastened it in her ear. The trembling earring sparked gold on the mirror. "And you know the attic's off-limits."

Linnie watched the diamond glitter. "Can I have one to play fairies with?"

"That's enough talk of fairies from you," said her mother. "I have a function to go to. Be good." She nodded at the woman in the doorway as she left. "Miss Smith, run the magnets over her."

Miss Smith the one-legged governess took Linnie to the kitchen, pulled the magnetic wand from the cupboard. Linnie's shimmer fled, and I had to concentrate hard on holding my shape. I only had a hazy notion of what went on above me till the wand was put away and the shimmer of fairy dust settled over Linnie once again. "You're clean, I guess," said Miss Smith dolefully. "Talking about fairies is your father's bad blood coming out in you. I'll figure out exercises to correct that."

You catch more humans with glitter than smoke. Linnie was enough your child to know that. She dimpled. "Will you show me again how your flesh knee connects to your artificial leg? It's amazing."

"Of course it is," said Miss Smith. But she smiled in that smug Miss Smith way and talk of new exercises was dropped.

Once Linnie had satisified her curiosity about Miss Smith's leg, she trotted up the stairs to Jonah's room to see if he would show her his fairy now. Jonah's door was shut tight and Linnie pounded. "Let me in! I won't break anything this time." But the door refused to open. She howled. "I'll get Miss Smith!"

She didn't expect this to work, but the door flickered and dissolved. She had never seen it do that. She darted in before it could reform.

Jonah was not in his room. But his blimps were—they sailed a smooth follow-the-leader around Jonah's bed, slalomed the hanging lights, and vanished into the closet.

Linnie got down on her hands and knees and watched as a blue-trimmed blimp bounced behind Jonah's rainboots and disappeared into a narrow gap in the wall. When Linnie stuck her hand through the gap, she felt carpet on the other side.

But Linnie knew this trick now. She raised a fist at the wall and looked at it with that powerfully gloomy Miss Smith stare. The wall shimmered into stairs.

"Linnie!" Miss Smith's bassoon voice.

"I'm playing blimps with Jonah," Linnie called back.

"One-half hour," Miss Smith said. "Your reading lessons won't do themselves."

"Right ho," said Linnie.

She disappeared up her brand-new stairs.

Ten Motes on Aileen's Earring

I cluster on her diamonds where I won't be seen. There is very little of me and it is hard to think. I am supposed to gather her words, share them later with the rest of me.

"One fairy-basher," she says to a servant, a Miss Color-Name I have already forgotten. Her language is brutal and coarse as she tries to be like them.

There are women talking and she moves closer. There is one here who holds my love's old office, whose name I will remember when I'm complete. A hard woman, who smiles at my love and talks cruelly of drowning changelings when she is gone.

"Aileen," she says. "I haven't seen you since your concession speech, after all that . . . unpleasantness with your love life. How are the dear, dear changel . . . children?"

Miss Color-Name brings my love the fairy-basher, a blue drink with chunks of lime. I wish they weren't tasty. I haven't had anything to drink in 1872 days.

"They're doing well," my love says.

"I can't remember; are they in school now?"

"Group schools are so common, don't you think? Hard to get a real education with all those dim-witted children around."

The hard woman's lips tighten and another woman laughs a pistol shot laugh. They bare their teeth in that wicked human way and the fairy-basher is so close to my perch on the diamond earrings and oh do I want a drink.

I get distracted at this distance from my mass. Once I was hiding on a girl's golden dress and I forgot I was someone and I went home with her and through the wash.

I can sit half of me on my love's lip and taste, just taste, and then I'll go back to watching.

Come on, Aileen. You made me thirsty.

Drink.

FRED, PLUS LINNIE'S SHIMMER

"Where are the fairies?" said Linnie.

Jonah sat on the forbidden attic windowsill where anyone could see him, staring down at the front porch of the house. Worse, the window was open and the blimps bobbled out, circled the sycamore, and bobbled back. "It's one fairy," he said, "and it's hiding. How did you get up here? The door was locked."

"Made the wall open," said Linnie. "Can't you do that?"

"No," said Jonah.

"How'd you come up, then?"

"The fairy told me where to find the key. Duh." He twisted on the sill, fiddling with the remote to the blimps.

Linnie looked around, but there was no golden whirlwind in the attic like Jonah had described. "So where's the fairy?"

"Most of it's on the front porch, but I don't think it wants us to know that." He pulled up his jacket hood and kicked the wall. A blimp shied away. "Anyway, there's still a little bit up here. By the stuff Dad left."

Linnie ran to that corner. There was a shimmer around their father's iron trunk, flecks of gold and diamond.

"Fairies sure are dirty," said Jonah.

"They're beautiful."

"Look at that dust," said Jonah. "I didn't know he'd get on everything. I hate him."

Linnie laid her head on the roughened metal lid. How did fairies feel? The bits of fairy slipped around her hair and fingers, warmed her like a good-night kiss on her cheek. She lay there and looked at Jonah sneering on the windowsill through a halo of whirling gold. Fairy dust stuck to her eyelashes.

The whirling kept her from noticing Jonah's shuddering at first. His hand jerked and the blimp remote sailed through the open window. He reddened with spasms.

Linnie ran, grabbed the front pockets of his jacket. His body tilted backwards, and Linnie thought this might really be it, that he might fall out the window, and she might go with him. She braced her feet against the wall under the window, pushed backwards with all her might. Her body was a rigid arch, her hands tight on the ripping pockets.

Jonah spasmed again and fell on her. Linnie's butt and then head clunked hard against the floor and her brother was a dead weight on her shoulder. His translucent hair poked her cheek. She squirmed out from underneath. Usually she would roll him onto his back, unless she was really mad at him, but this time she just lay there panting.

"Stupid brother," she said. He probably couldn't hear her, not when he was separated from his body like that.

The fairy dust that had been around her dad's iron chest floated over as if to see the excitement. It hovered over Jonah, then settled around him in a shimmer, a golden cloak you could only see from the right angle.

If it was trying to protect Jonah, it was too late. Linnie had done that all on her own when the grownups couldn't.

"Stupid fairy," said Linnie.

Dust Escapes, Becomes Kayley

On the front porch of Elderwood Hall, a girl appeared, built from a wind of gold dust. It dropped into place for shoes, legs, body, and when the last bit of dust flicked into the last lock of gold hair, she shook herself and colorized.

She did not press her hand into the magnetized iron lock. She could not do that. So she sighed with impatience, tossed her hair, and knocked a lame old-fashioned knock. She hoped Miss Smith and Fred answered.

Fred

Cousin Kayley wasn't the real cousin Kayley, but of course you know that, Gabriel. The real cousin Kayley played flute and was moody and hated her Aunt Aileen who had caused all the whispers of immorality. This Kayley sparkled in a way that the other did not. It took me less than a second to know it was really part of us, but at least five minutes to realize Jonah must have opened your trunk.

I wondered what you told him to get him to open it. Did he think it would fix everything? Did he even remember you, his disappeared dad?

I got Miss Smith to send the maid to fetch the children. Jonah dragged his feet on the stairs. He hooked his arm around the stair railing and kicked the parquet floor. Linnie set both feet on every step.

"You remember the kids," said Miss Smith to Kayley. "Linnie is five now and Jonah's almost eight." Jonah stared at the floor. "Straighten up, Jonah," she said. "What's wrong with you?"

He kicked the floor. Linnie kicked the floor.

"He had an episode," Linnie whispered.

Miss Smith wobbled. "Nonsense. He hasn't had an episode since he was five."

"He hides it."

"This is horrible," Miss Smith said. "Jonah, is this true?"

He looked at Linnie, back at his feet. "No. I was just messing with her."

Linnie went white. She ran, her pink shoes slipping on stairs.

"What a thing to pretend, Jonah. Now everything's upset."

Miss Smith started to go after Linnie, but I kept her leg rooted. I knew Kayley must be here to work our charm on the little half-humans.

"Come on Jonah," Kayley said. "Let's go find Linnie."

TEN MOTES ON AILEEN'S LACE COLLAR

I'm on the collar of her dress. I laid myself in a pattern to hide. Sometimes patterns help me think. I think I have a hangover.

She is telling Kayley that she can stay while Kayley's parents are abroad. I can plainly report her words, but I have spent 1873 days at the post of my love, and I can say my love is suspicious.

"Don't try to go in the attic," she says. "Don't let the kids go up either, if they tell you they can. It's locked and only I have the key."

"Skeleton in the closet?" says Kayley.

"Don't be smart with me," says Aileen. "If Gabriel did get out, you'd be just the sort of naïve kid he'd be soft and charming to. Get what he wants and then destroy your life. You stay away from the attic."

"Gotcha," says Kayley. Her eyes are brown and wicked, but underneath she is gold and diamond. I envy her mass. I want to leave my lace collar and go be part of a larger self. But I am at the post of my love and I must stay.

My love stands after Kayley is gone, flipping a rag doll back and forth between her long fingers. There is not enough of me to intuit what that means. Even 1873 days is not long enough for ten motes to divine all her different stillnesses.

My love squeezes the doll's chest. Then she is heading toward the east wing. I think she is going to the attic and I am excited.

She is, she is.

My love slides her key into the lock and the door opens onto the stairs to the attic. I am to burst. I have not been here in 1873 days, when I was the first ten motes to find the tiniest gap in the iron and slither through one mote at a time, sent to head for the post of my love.

It has been a long time that I have been listening; long by myself. I saw when at last there was enough of me to make Fred, and then a shimmer to hover around the changelings, and then suddenly this morning there was the huge mass of Kayley. But they are confusingly big and I can't connect to them. So much of me is still bound in iron. Fred shares with the shimmer on the little girl, and I am jealous of even that contact. I hope there is some of me loose in the attic; I know I am more than Fred and Kayley and shimmer. If not here, then much of me is still hidden and I don't know where I am.

My love crosses in faltering steps to the iron trunk. I am so excited I can't maintain my pattern and I move within her lace, swirling with delight.

She sinks to her knees, her fingers touch the lock—then they press to her lips above me, and her lace collar shakes, so she is crying. Her arms fall to the trunk, her head on her arms. I am captured between her collar and the skin of her arms, but from skin I can slide out and away and settle on one silver strand of hair. I slide with the movement of her head.

There is dust in the attic, but it is plain ordinary dust like we hate to mingle with. I am the only golden motes around.

I need another drink.

FRED, PLUS JONAH'S SHIMMER

"Do you guys know what changelings are?" said Kayley.

Linnie was face-down on her bed. Jonah hung in the doorway to the bedroom, half in and half out.

"Come in closer, will ya?" said Kayley. "You know what the word means?"

"It's a swear," he said. He stepped in just enough to let the door swing shut and pulled his hood up, tight around his translucent hair.

"Sorta. Not really. It means someone with one human and one fairy parent."

Linnie, muffled by pillow. "I hate fairies."

"What's to hate about fairies?"

"I hate fairies too," said Jonah.

Cousin Kayley sunk to the floor and pulled her knees to her chest. "Can you guys keep a secret?"

"What?"

"I'm a changeling."

Linnie lifted her tear-stained face from the pillow.

"You are not." Jonah tugged his hood lower so he couldn't see Linnie. "Aunt Beth and Uncle Stuart are human."

"It's easy for fairies to look human," Kayley said. "There's so much mass to each fairy, they can totally be two humans. Or three. Fairies can hide what they are for years as long as no one suspects. But it's hard to hide forever. Like the girl who runs the shoe shop; she's one but she keeps it secret. Don't say anything cause if she gets thrown out of town there'll be no place to go for awesome sandals like these." She stretched out her foot to show Linnie.

"Nuh-uh," said Jonah.

"Uh-huh," said Kayley. "They're the awesomest shoes ever."

"No, I mean," said Jonah. He squished his face up. "Who else?"

"Oh," said Kayley. "Well, there was like this woman in town who used to be on the city council. She had a secret boyfriend who was fairy. He was her assistant, and he also used part of himself to run for office and be her political friend guy. Fairies are so super smart that dividing themselves makes them seem more normal and human. He had fairy friends who were passing and human friends that maybe suspected but everything was cool till some conservative dope found him dusting in the golden town hall dome with three other fairies."

"What's dusting?" said Linnie. She pulled stuck strands of hair from her cheek.

Kayley whispered. "The fairies spread out and mix their dust all up with other fairies. Humans think it's gross but they're jealous. The woman was so mad that she locked him up in her house and sealed off the room." She jumped up. "Hey, you kids ever slide down your stairs on a mattress?"

Linnie sat all the way up. "You can do that?"

"Duh. No," said Jonah.

Kayley was already stripping sheets from Linnie's bed. "Come on. Let's go play being otters."

FRED PLUS SHIMMERS

After Kayley pretended she was a changeling, the kids slowly opened up to her. I helped keep Miss Smith away from them. Encouraged her to sit down and put her half leg up, and rationalize that Cousin Kayley was earning her keep by babysitting. And because Kayley had all our fairy charisma, she worked her magic on the kids much more quickly than any real cousin Kayley ever could.

In a week, Kayley had Linnie and Jonah playing fairies behind the shed. The ground was clover and dirt and shaggy grass, and the leaves of the last lilies were yellowing. A good stomping ground.

"Because I'm a changeling, I can do some things real fairies do," Kayley told them. "If I concentrate, I can move my hand through my own body." She held out one arm and chopped it with the other hand. Her fingers passed right through.

"Not very useful," said Jonah. "Unless maybe you had a broken bone and you could fix it."

"Maybe," agreed Kayley. "At first I did it accidentally and it was frightening. But now it's wicked cool. So I can do that and be like a totally real fairy, but you guys will have to pretend stuff."

"Linnie can go through walls," said Jonah.

"Oh yeah?" said Kayley, playing it cool. "That's cool stuff. It's so stupid that boring humans can't do that."

Jonah plopped down on the shaggy grass and leaned against the shed. "Fairies can read your mind," he said. "I bet that's why people hate them."

"No, they can't," said Kayley. "First they have to settle their dust all over you so they can pick up your body's cues. Then they're smart, so they guess based on that. They're pretty good guessers. And kinda stuck-up, so they're sure they're right. But they can be dead wrong. Depends on how much mass they have concentrated. Fairies spread out."

"That's what Jonah does," said Linnie. "Spread out."

Jonah wrenched his jacket around him. "I do not."

"Oh yeah?" said Kayley. "That's an awesome trick. I bet your dad would like to see it."

Jonah looked at Kayley for a long minute, and the shimmer on him suddenly knew that he knew.

After all, Jonah was the one to open your trunk when some of our motes whispered to him. He watched the fairy dust spill out, he watched Kayley form, and he now knew—because Kayley had told him—the properties of fairies.

"Okay," he said finally. "Dad."

JUST FRED

It's a pain intuiting through shimmers in the garden with the rest of me back in the kitchen, propped up on a table. But a good pain, a challenge pain. The satisfaction in our art comes from mapping patterns, laying your motes along seemingly arbitrary intricacies until bang! the pattern is clear. Don't you think so?

Long, long ago we only knew to spread ourselves out. We drifted in coppery forests and golden meadows, dusting with each other.

Back so long I can hardly hold the memory, we started playing solid things. Lizards and butterflies—new ways to enjoy the sun. Later we played at humans, and our humans played at playlets, speeches, drama, artform piled on artform. Then it was fantastical creatures with mock civilizations, as we outdid each other in imagination. But then real humans changed all our old patterns. The humans poisoned our homes with heavy metals and interference and so we took their shapes, with cilia-thick lungs and hard hard skin. We lost much, but we gained new patterns to explore.

It will be impossible to ever know all the patterns, I think, or at least I will be so advanced by then that this particular puzzle will be gone from memory.

Dust loves playing at forms. It's hard to let that go.

Fred plus Shimmers

And in the end, did we really need Kayley's fairy charisma? Jonah remembered you, after all. And Linnie was ready all along. One part-of-a-fairy and two changelings went up the secret stairway in Jonah's closet to let the rest of their father out of his iron prison.

"I can't touch the trunk," said Kayley. "It's iron."

"I can," said Jonah. "But I already opened it—that's where you came from. There wasn't anything else in there."

Kayley grimaced. "I know, but then where's the rest of me? Let's just try it."

Jonah grabbed one corner and Linnie the other and together they opened the iron trunk. But it was dust-free. Jonah stuck his hand in and groped around the bottom, but there seemed to be no false drawers.

"Did you see where the rest of you was put?" said Jonah. "I don't know, feel it?"

"Nope. My part was locked away first. I can't think through iron."

"If you're in the house, you've gotta be here," said Jonah. "It's the only spot we're not allowed in. Maybe—can you tell if anything in the attic looks different?"

The attic was a jumble of junk, walls of brick and plaster, low raftered ceilings. Jonah's blimps lay in a deflated pile under the windowsill. It seemed a hopeless question, and yet . . . .

"Hang on," Kayley said. "I'm gonna shimmer myself. You cool with that?"

"We're cool," said Jonah.

Kayley rippled gold, then broke apart into a million motes that flew through the attic. Golden dust settled on everything.

Linnie coughed, inhaling dust. Then, eyes huge, put her hand over her mouth.

"It's okay," said Jonah. There was gold dust all over his eyebrows, nostrils, lips. "They've been doing this forever."

For a moment, the attic gleamed like a treasure chest. Then the wind started in reverse, and the dust flew back together and formed Kayley, on the other end of the attic. She didn't bother to colorize. "It's this brick wall," she said, smacking it. "It doesn't match my old memories." She shimmered through it, squealed, shimmered back. "There's the box! But I can't open it; it's all iron. Jonah, you opened the last one." She was blurry with excitement.

"I can't take my body through the wall," said Jonah.

"I can," said Linnie.

"But I can separate and go with her," added Jonah. He laid down on the floor, and this time he hardly shook at all as he detached part of himself from his body. "Ready," he said faintly.

Linnie glared at the brick. From her point of view the wall dissolved, but from Jonah's point of view Linnie dissolved and stepped right through the brick. "I'm in," she called, and the separated Jonah slid along after her.

All that was in the brick room was a metal box, no bigger than Jonah's blimps. Linnie tried to pick it off the floor, but it was enormously heavy. She bent to raise the lid.

Out in the attic, Aileen burst in, followed by Miss Smith and the maid. "Gabriel," she cried, pointing at Kayley. "I thought you were using her to let you out. But you're not Kayley at all. You're Gabriel."

"Like, duh," said Kayley.

Then Aileen saw Jonah's body, comatose on the floor. Her mouth opened and she fell beside Jonah, cradling his chest to hers.

Behind the brick wall, Linnie's fingers kept slipping off the hasp. "It won't let me touch it."

Jonah's voice, hovering above her. "It's cause there's fairy dust on your fingers. Get out, Dad."

The golden shimmer slipped away from her fingers and back through the brick wall so there was none of us to see the exact instant when we were freed. All of us in that little room must be, had to be, in that impenetrable iron box.

There was an instant when time hung in the air and all our motes seemed to whirl in place.

And then—

GABRIEL

Then the iron box opened and I poured forth.
I am rushing and wild.
I am free.
 —not in trunk
 —nor attic
 —nor jewel box
 —nor leg
I need a drink.
That goes double for me. Do you know how annoying?
 to be a leg.
Lame, you want lame? I was totally this girl—
And I in a trunk.
I've got you beat; ten motes in a diamond's eye
 —let me share when Miss Smith forgot and shaved me
 —show how Jonah tumbled down flat
 —let me say: my love
My love:
 —You are still my love.
My loves.
Let me say—

GABRIEL—

"I need a drink."

"Yes, sir," said the maid.

From the other corner there was a shriek as Miss Smith fell to the ground. "My leg! Where's my leg?"

I swear, the part of me that had been stomped around on as Fred was selfishly amused. I would almost have let her keep me 'til she got her sea-legs back, except I badly needed reintegration, particularly with independent Fred. Parts of me had gathered a lot of data in the 1879 days while the rest had gathered only the blackness of two iron trunks. I would stay overly dense for a few days while I sorted myself out.

"Gabriel!" It was my love. Jonah had slid back into his body at the same time I did and Aileen held him to her side, keeping one arm around him. "Gabriel, you give her old leg back this instant. What did you do with it?"

I hate these questions. "Don't remember." I sounded like my seven-and-a-half year old son. Aileen could always do that to me.

"Oh, my leg," said Miss Smith, clutching at her flesh knee.

"I'll buy you a new one," I said.

"With what money?" said Aileen. "I don't have the clout to hire you now, and you can't run for office again. Everyone knows what you are." Her lip trembled and I remembered resting on it, drinking fairy-basher. "Everyone knows what *we* were."

"I could reshape," I said awkwardly. "Be a stranger come to town."

She shook her head. "Things are stricter for newcomers. Magnetized locks and X-ray testing. There's no place for you here." Jonah shook his head 'yes', which I chose to interpret as he thought his mother was wrong. I hoped he wanted me to stay.

"Here's your drink," said the maid. It was blue with chunks of lime; either she remembered I like those damn things or she had an unexpected sense of humor. I took a long deep swallow, the first real drink in five years.

"How will I run after the kids?" moaned Miss Smith.

"I know where her leg is," said Linnie.

"You do?"

"It's behind the piano. I thought it was a spare."

"Run and get Miss Smith's leg, please," said Aileen to the maid. She wavered where she stood, clutching Jonah, and I thought she wanted to run to me and fall into my arms, but no matter how many motes I settled on her, I would never know for sure. My theory of myself is that I stay with the puzzles that intrigue me the longest. My love is veined with deep and hidden streams.

"How would we live?" she said.

"One theory," I said cautiously, "is that we could live here, and be in love."

"It's just not *done*," she said. "Fairy-human relationships aren't appropriate."

"Neither are changelings," said Jonah. He wiggled free from Aileen's arm, pulling his hood all the way off. His hair was iridescent like my own. "I want to go to school, Mom."

"I might lose my job again."

"If Jonah's going, I'm going," said Linnie. I looked down and found she was holding my hand. She smiled up at me, with dimples.

"You're both going to school, and I'm not going back in that trunk," I said. "I'll stay home and raise the children. Teach Jonah how to handle his splitting and Linnie—well, Linnie can go through walls, but it's not causing you problems, is it?"

"Nope."

"But who knows what talent they'll develop next." I pulled Linnie toward me, ruffling her hair. "Choose all or none."

"Well . . . ." said Aileen.

"It's just not the same," Miss Smith said. She stomped between us, wavering on the dumb metal leg. Her arms flailed.

I sighed. There are always sacrifices to living among humans. "Weekdays and alternate Saturdays only." I took a sip of my fairy-basher, then added: "And not till next Tuesday." Fred needed firm squashing.

"Oh, thank you. I'll be real careful with you."

I looked at my love with all my mass. The rise and fall of her cheeks had reshaped themselves in the last five years. Her hair was streaked with silver. I think I will color mine to match. "Stay with me, Aileen," I said softly.

Deep inside, ten motes whispered: my love, my love.

And then Aileen ran to me and threw herself into my arms.

AFTERWORD

ON THE EYEBALL FLOOR

This marked my first "pro" sale, to *Strange Horizons*, and is still one of my favorite stories. I am a fan of the Americana tall tales of the old west—some of which were true cowboy tales, like Paul Bunyan, some of which were probably invented by their creators—Pecos Bill—and some of which were intentionally written as an American invention—Carl Sandberg's *Rootabaga Tales*. I enjoyed weaving those tales into this futuristic wild west. I also have a short collection of my own alternate wild west flash stories that I plan to eventually compile.

What's interesting to me—and what marks a lot of my stories—is that the germ of a story often comes from a strange or funny place. But then when I work on the drafts of the story, issues that my subconscious has been chewing over come bubbling up. I have never gone into a piece saying "yo, this is going to be about important stuff"—and I'm not saying that some other writer couldn't work that way, but for me that would kill it. Still, it's true that things I was thinking about, that are important to me, come up over and over again and work their way into my stories. Like burrs.

The unusual genesis of *this* story is that I made a goal one year (pre-kids, obviously) to write at least 500 words every day. The 500 words could be about anything. Some of those story seeds became good stories—some didn't. This particular day found me half-asleep on the futon, determined to put a few sentences or two down before going to bed—and thinking that eyeballs really squicked me out.

ON GLICKER STREET: A SEASONAL QUARTET

When I attended the Clarion West Workshop in 2006, there was a street nearby that looked like the street described in the fourth section of the story. Like Frederick, I wrote down the words "On Glicker Street it is always fall", and then took that home after the workshop and let it sit for awhile. The link to the four seasons suggested to me a linked set of four flashes, one for each season.

SELLING HOME

Pre-kids, I worked in the summers as a face painter. (I still do some face painting, just more sporadically.) I was down at the Blues Fest in Portland one year, 4th of July, getting ready to start the evening's work. I stood under the Hawthorne Bridge and looked up at the throngs of people hanging off the bridge, finding early spots for the night's fireworks, and listening to the blues and jazz. I imagined that the bridges kept going, one stacked on top of the next, the people and cars crowding them higher and higher.

So that was the seed—and you can see traces of it in the girls hanging around in bikinis (there were probably girls doing just that on the boats down on the river), and in the mention of the festivals higher up on the bridge.

Again, a seed has to be mashed with more things, more interesting things, and I always find out what the story really wants to be about once I start drafting and re-drafting. I became interested in the idea of Penny having to make the hard choice of what would be best for the family, and realizing that the best available solution might not involve keeping the family unit intact.

LEFT HAND

This was written off of a prompt from Vylar Kaftan, in the online writers' group Codex. The prompt was to write about a strange rivalry between a human and a machine. That led to the rivalry between the two hands here. It was recently published in a beautiful hardback book, *Gigantic Worlds*, with 50 other flash stories from people such as Ted Chiang and Charles Yu. I have since made one change to it from that volume, which is, I read it out loud at a library event and it suddenly dawned on me that you drum your fingers from pinky to index, not from index to pinky. At least, I do.

REHYDRATION

The seed for this poem is one of my most unusual ones. In this case, I saw someone on the internet trying, vaguely and ineffectively, to recall the movie *Children of the Corn*. Since I've never seen *Children of the Corn*, their stream-of-consciousness about kids and cornfields inspired this alternate explanation, instead.

RECALCULATING

This story first appeared at the late lamented *Brain Harvest*. This is one of my most reprinted stories—out of ten places I've sent it, it's appeared at six of them. I am only slowly getting used to my own GPS—and I haven't updated it for five years, so it gets very confused whenever I try to go to a new development. There are times when I find myself wandering around in Portland suburbs trying to find a face painting client or a friend's house, and then I start to think this story was prophetic.

THE BITRUNNERS

"We went to the moon to have fun, but the moon turned out to completely suck." That's the first line of M.T. Anderson's amazing book *Feed*. I stumbled across that first line long before I actually read the book, and it inspired the tone and cant of The Bitrunners. I then proceeeded to forget all about the inspiration, until my friend Alex Renwick lent me *Feed* and I remembered.

I love writing in invented slang, and although sometimes I try to practice moderation, this time I let it all go. This story was easy to write and hard to edit—I ended up with several times this amount of material as the narrator talked himself in circles, trying to inch closer to a story he didn't want to tell. Rich Horton picked it up for his *Year's Best Online SF* that year.

STANDARD COMFORT MEASURES IN EARTHLING PREGNANCIES

Yes, I wrote this story while pregnant. I was miserably morning sick with my second child, and I was standing in the kitchen in the middle of the night, looking down at a sheet helpfully titled "Standard Comfort Measures in Pregnancy." It listed many unhelpful things. *You can eat these 5 things*! Those 5 things are making me sick. *You cannot eat these 3 things*! Those 3 things actually sound good. *You probably have a headache*! You may not take anything that will help. Etc. It was all too short a jump to this story.

SUPER-BABY-MOMS GROUP SAVES THE DAY!

Shortly after the birth of that second child, I was part of a very *awesome* writer-moms support group with some other authors who had also recently had babies. My friend Alex Shvartsman had just asked me to send him something for his latest UFO volume of funny SFF stories, and it occurred to me that my super helpful writer-moms email group might be easily morphed into a slightly less-helpful, more entertaining one.

THAT SERIOUSLY OBNOXIOUS TIME I WAS STUCK AT WITCH RIMELDA'S ONE HUNDREDTH BIRTHDAY PARTY

When my (wonderful, marvelous) editor at Tor asked me for a story set in the world of *Seriously Wicked*, I immediately knew I wanted to write a prequel so I wouldn't spoil anything from the book. But what about? *Seriously Wicked* has a bunch of throw-away lines that Cam tosses off about her time living with a wicked witch. For example, "Like once I refused to hold the neighbor's cat so she could permanently mute its meow, and she turned me into fifteen hundred worms and made me compost the garden." I looked at a few of those, and then I remembered one anecdote I'd had to cut, about a disastrous pool party.

As a writer, this story is interesting to me because it really has two protagonists—Pink is the one who grows and changes the most, but Cam is telling the story (and is our regular heroine of the *Seriously Wicked* series) so she needed to be active in the story and grow and change as well.

SEE DANGEROUS EARTH-POSSIBLES!

I write a lot about families and the relationships within them. I also write about the effects of violence. This section of the book is where these two things combine. Which doesn't mean there aren't moments of humor in this section. One of the things I loved about the Kazuhiko Nakamura cover art for this collection is that it manages to be both dark and funny at the same time.

Back to this particular story: I was thrilled to sell "See DANGEROUS EARTH-POSSIBLES!" to the special *Women Destroy SF!* issue of *Lightspeed*. That is an incredible, definitive volume and I am proud to be part of it.

TURNING THE APPLES

I took a Clarion West One-Day Workshop with Ellen Klages back in 2008. She did an exercise where she gave us story prompts—I think they were pictures cut from magazines? At any rate, mine had a cell phone, or maybe a boy holding a cell phone on it, and I started writing down the voice of this boy who desperately needed to hawk these phones. I wrote a page or two there, then came home and finished it very quickly.

FACTS OF BONE

The genesis for "Facts of Bone" was an article about a rare and horrible genetic disorder called fibrodysplasia ossificans progressiva. I adapted it for this story set in a future on a distant planet (partly by making it adult onset, partly by speeding up the transformation of flesh into bone), and wrote about a family trying to cope with their own disorder. There are genetic variances that run in my own family—though nothing quite so chilling—and it creates a small group of people with knowledge about dealing with a unique situation. Additionally, I write a lot about sibling relationships, and there's a similar theme in my novel *Copperhead*, with two sisters struggling to define their relationship, and determine how much they are and are not allowed to do for each other.

WENDY WITH A COMET IN THE TAIL OF THE Y

I think those videos are ubiquitous now—the ones where someone takes a picture of themselves every day for a year, for example, and then you see a whole year go by in a minute. When I first started working on this story I was drawing from memory from an art exhibit I saw in Kansas City, a long time ago—I can't remember if it was at the Kemper or the Nelson. (The Nelson has the Calder sculpture, though, which is also in this story.) This was my attempt to translate the feeling of those videos into a story. One of the early titles was "The Ice Age of Vera," but it was helpfully pointed out to me that since the story is in first person, we never do learn Vera's name. So . . . maybe not as clear as it could be.

MISS VIOLET MAY FROM THE TWELVE THOUSAND LAKES

This is one of the alternate wild west flash stories mentioned above. The others so far are "Zebedee the Giant Man", "Iron Jo Jill", and "Z-Boy Blues." You can find Zebedee podcast at toastedcake.com as episode #92. Matt Haynes and I recorded all four stories as a give-away for The Pulp Stage's Indiegogo campaign last year, so it's possible they may pop up again as a reward or giveaway.

OLD DEAD FUTURES

This story was first called "The Mother and the Owl," which is a terrible title. I was trying to evoke the hard choice in Frank Stockton's "The Lady Or the Tiger?", but that's really no excuse. This story ran on Tor.com and was beautifully illustrated by Wesley Allsbrook.

A MILLION LITTLE PAPER AIRPLANE STORIES

This was a piece commissioned by Tor.com—they sent the same prompt of a lovely picture by Victor Mosquera to me, Max Gladstone, Beth Bernobich, and J.A. Souders. You can find all four pieces on Tor.com. I toyed with the idea of making this the title of the book, as it seems like a great title for a collection. But as the poem is partly about the inability to capture Story, to pin it down, I thought maybe not.

TEN

Yes, this is a story about Pong.

THE GOD-DEATH OF HALLA

This was my first sale to *Beneath Ceaseless Skies*, which kicked off a happy side-effect of not just publishing there, but regularly narrating for them. The seed for this was a dream: I dreamed the scene we never see in the story, when Gooseberry is forced to kill Halla's mother at the ring on the hill. That scene stayed in the story in the first draft, as a sort of a prologue, and then got cut. Another seed for this is my love of secondary world fantasy with interesting magic systems and gods. I still think this would be an interesting world to write a novel in, but I'm not sure what the overall story arc would be. Maybe someday I'll figure it out.

ONE EAR BACK

This is a retelling of the old Icelandic folk tale, "Kisa the Cat." I read a lot of fairy tales growing up, and this one stuck with me due to the odd nature of Kisa's curse. A good deed that had never been done before—what things would you do, in trying to break it? I thought you might be able to get a farce out of that, but when I started to write it, it was not a farce. And yes, we had a beloved little gray cat for many years—she has since passed away—and she would definitely do the one ear back thing.

GOLDEN APPLES

This is another story that came from a prompt from Vylar Kaftan on Codex—this time, to write about a race with a deadline and high stakes. Which made me think of Atalanta's race in Greek mythology, where her suitor throws golden apples her way to distract her from winning.

TINY ATROCITIES

I hate those moments when you suddenly remember something awful you did once. I tried to exorcise that feeling by giving those moments to a wicked witch. It didn't help.

MOON AT THE STARRY DINER

This story was written during week four of the Clarion West workshop. I remember having a long talk with Nalo Hopkinson, our teacher that week, about putting squids on mantelpieces. (Referencing the famous statement from Chekhov that if you introduce a gun in act 1 of your play, you'd better fire it by the end.) In this case, Jem and Moon walked into a diner with a squid and cowboy etc, and then I was stuck. I walked around the block several times (probably walking down Glicker street as well) when I realized that since I'd introduced a squid and a cowboy, they were going to have to have a standoff.

A couple years after this was published, Portland actor friends Matt Haynes and Brian Allard were putting on a show with their new company, The Pulp Stage. Brian wrote to see if I had any ten-minute plays for them. I didn't, but I thought perhaps I could adapt this story. I adapted it in a sort of Book-It style (Jem both spoke her lines as well as narrating some of the action), and it was performed in the first fringe festival show The Pulp Stage did.

HARD CHOICES

I love flash and I love seeing what you can do with the form. In this case, I wanted to see if I could effectively do a Choose Your Own Adventure as flash. "Hard Choices" first ran at *Brain Harvest*, and later Kaolin Fire turned it into a flash game at GUD magazine, which was fun.

HOW FREDERIKA CASSOWARY-JONES JOINED THE LADIES' SOCIETY OF BENEVOLENT GOINGS-ON

Shortly after The Pulp Stage accepted "Moon at the Starry Diner," I started experimenting with more play-like things. I have a theatre background as an actor, but unless you count my junior high opus, *Who Stole the Cookies from the Cookie Jar?* (it is every bit as amazing as it sounds), I hadn't really written any plays. So I wrote Frederika—and ended up writing it with not just dialogue, but with a large number of thoughts written in, as you see here. There is actually some precedent for this—some scripts have rather a lot of the playwright's notes to the actors—but when I finally submitted it to

The Pulp Stage, I did take everything out except the dialogue. The Pulp Stage has run this rather frequently, and I also included it in the epic room party that C. S. E. Cooney and I put on at the 2011 World Fantasy Con in San Diego. If I am remembering correctly, the cast was Cooney as Polly, me as Hortense, Meghan Sinoff as Callista, Liz Argall as Fred, and M. K. Hobson as Maude. It was a blast.

INFLECTION

Hemingway is not actually my favorite, but I do find the iceberg-like structure of "Hills Like White Elephants" interesting. I enjoyed finding another linguistic reason for our characters to communicate chiefly in elliptical pronouns.

SILVERFIN HARBOR

This story was written during week five of the Clarion West Workshop (and I got incredibly useful feedback on it from our teacher that week, Ellen Datlow, as well as from the class.)

I took a weekend off halfway through the workshop—my husband picked me up and we took a short drive up to the San Juan Islands, which we had never seen. I was at a bit of a crossroads prior to the workshop—wondering if I could really switch out of theatre and into writing. And then I discovered that if you are a writer, you can do that anywhere. I sat and sketched the harbor with words—filled pages with nothing but observations of the ferries and dock and harbor. One of the pages mentioned a woman standing at the balcony—and when I got back to the workshop on Sunday night, that inspired Lei, standing at the balcony while the volcano erupts around her.

Also, the original title for this was "Black Water Cocoon." Then it was pointed out to me that I had used the word "black" approximately 100x in the story. It became "Silverfin Harbor"—and then it was first printed in *The End of an Aeon*, which has Canadian roots, so it momentarily became "Silverfin Harbour."

AS WE REPORT TO GABRIEL

I remember I started and stopped this story a couple times, trying to figure out how to make it work. In the very first draft, none of the sections had headers ("Fred", "Ten Motes", etc)—thankfully I decided that headers were an excellent addition to make before anybody saw it for critique. I also remember when writing the first draft that I didn't know who or what Fred was disguised as yet, and cackling when I discovered it. *Ironskin* readers will note some of the world-building precursors in this story.

I have always loved writing at the border of science fiction and fantasy, I love unique structures, and I love stories about family. I love stories with rhythm and poetry. *Love, my love, you are still my love . . . .*

And perhaps most of all, I love stories where things work out reasonably all right in the end.

January 2016
Portland, OR

PUBLICATION NOTES

"On the Eyeball Floor" originally appeared in *Strange Horizons*, 2 June 2008 | "On Glicker Street: A Seasonal Quartet" originally appeared in *Escape Clause*, ed. Clélie Rich, October 2009 | "Selling Home" originally appeared in *Bull Spec* #6, Autumn 2011 | "Left Hand" originally appeared in *Gigantic Worlds*, September 2015 | "Rehydration" originally appeared in *Strange Horizons*, 9 Apr 2007 | "Recalculating" originally appeared in *Brain Harvest*, 20 June 2010 | "The Bitrunners" originally appeared in *Helix #9*, Summer 2008 | "Standard Comfort Measures in Earthling Pregnancies" originally appeared in *Worlds of Wonder* #3, 2016 | "Super Baby-Moms Group Saves the Day!" originally appeared in *UFO 3*, ed. Alex Shvartsman, October 2014 | "That Seriously Obnoxious Time I Was Stuck at Witch Rimelda's One Hundredth Birthday Party" originally appeared in *Tor.com*, 26 August 2015 | "See DANGEROUS EARTH- POSSIBLES!" originally appeared in *Lightspeed, Women Destroy SF!* issue, June 2014 | "Turning the Apples" originally appeared in *Strange Horizons*, 30 March 2009 | "Facts of Bone" originally appeared in *GUD Magazine* #3, Autumn 2008 | "Wendy with a Comet in the Tail of the Y" appears here for the first time | "Miss Violet May from the Twelve Thousand Lakes" originally appeared in *Daily SF*, 25 February 2014 | "Old Dead Futures" originally appeared in *Tor.com*, 17 July 2013 | "A Million Little Paper Airplane Stories" originally appeared in *Tor.com*, 9 October 2013 | "Ten" originally appeared in *Escape Artists* special "Tricks or Treats," October 2010 | "The God-Death of Halla" originally appeared in *Beneath Ceaseless Skies* #5, 4 December 2008 | "One Ear Back" originally appeared in *Beneath Ceaseless Skies* #97, 14 June 2012 | "Golden Apples" originally appeared in *Scheherezade's Bequest* #16, Fall 2012 | "tiny atrocities" originally appeared in *Abyss & Apex*, October 2012 | "Moon at the Starry Diner" originally appeared in *Heliotrope Magazine* #3, November 2007 | "Hard Choices" originally appeared in *Brain Harvest*, 7 June 2009 | "How Frederika Cassowary-Jones Joined the Ladies' Aid Society of Benevolent Goings-On" originally appeared in *Gears and Levers 2*, ed. Phyllis Irene Radford, January 2013 | "Inflection" originally appeared in *Daily SF*, 12 December 2011 | "Silverfin Harbor" originally appeared in *End of an Aeon*, ed. Bridget and Marti McKenna, Fairwood Press, July 2011 | "As We Report to Gabriel" originally appeared in *Fantasy Magazine*, 3 January 2011.

About the Author

Tina Connolly is the author of the Ironskin trilogy from Tor Books, and the Seriously Wicked series from Tor Teen. Her novels have been finalists for the Nebula and the Norton. Her stories have appeared in *Women Destroy SF, Lightspeed, Tor.com, Analog, Strange Horizons, Beneath Ceaseless Skies*, and many more. Her narrations have appeared all over, including *Podcastle, Pseudopod, Beneath Ceaseless Skies*, John Joseph Adams' The End is Nigh series, and more. She is one of the current co-hosts of *Escape Pod*, and runs the Parsec-winning flash fiction podcast *Toasted Cake*. She grew up in Lawrence, Kansas, but now lives with her family in Portland, Oregon, in an old house on a hill that came with a dragon in the basement and blackberry vines in the attic. Her website is tinaconnolly.com.

OTHER TITLES FROM FAIRWOOD PRESS

Joel-Brock the Brave & the Valorous Smalls
by Michael Bishop
trade paper & ltd hardcover: $16.99/$35
ISBN: 978-1-933846-53-8
ISBN: 978-1-933846-59-0

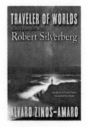

Traveler of Worlds: with Robert Silverberg
by Alvaro Zinos-Amaro
trade paper: $16.99
ISBN: 978-1-933846-63-7

Amaryllis
by Carrie Vaughn
trade paper: $17.99
ISBN: 978-1-933846-62-0

Seven Wonders of a Once and Future World
by Caroline M. Yoachim
trade paper: $17.99
ISBN: 978-1-933846-55-2

The Ultra Big Sleep
by Patrick Swenson
hard cover / trade: $27.99 / 17.99
ISBN: 978-1-933846-60-6
ISBN: 978-1-933846-61-3

The Specific Gravity of Grief
by Jay Lake
trade paper: $8.99
ISBN: 978-1-933846-57-6

Cracking the Sky
by Brenda Cooper
trade paper: $17.99
ISBN: 978-1-933846-50-7

The Child Goddess
by Louise Marley
trade paper: $16.99
ISBN: 978-1-933846-52-1

www.fairwoodpress.com
21528 104th Street Court East;
Bonney Lake, WA   98391

CPSIA information can be obtained
at www.ICGtesting.com
Printed in the USA
LVOW07s2005201117

557089LV00001B/78/P